# ALSO BY MAGGIE MCPHEE

Autumn In The Desert Series

*Death In Autumn*, prequel novella

*Renaissance*, Book 1

*Second Chances*, Book 2

*Never Too Late*, Book 3

# AT LAST

## AUTUMN IN THE DESERT, BOOK 4

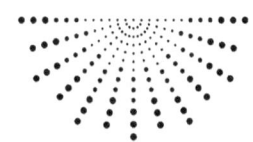

MAGGIE MCPHEE

Cover by: Zoran Petrovic, Fiverr.com name, visual arts

Map of Palm Lakes by: Maria Gandolfo, Fiverr.com name, Renflowergrapx

Copyright © 2018 Maggie & Nigel Percy

ISBN: 978-1-946014-29-0 (Ebook version)

ISBN: 978-1-946014-30-6 (Paperback version)

Sixth Sense Books

150 Buck Run E

Dahlonega, GA 30533

Email address: authormaggiemcphee@gmail.com

*In Memory of Mrs. Sophie Rogers,*
*my seventh grade English teacher, who encouraged me to write*

# CONTENTS

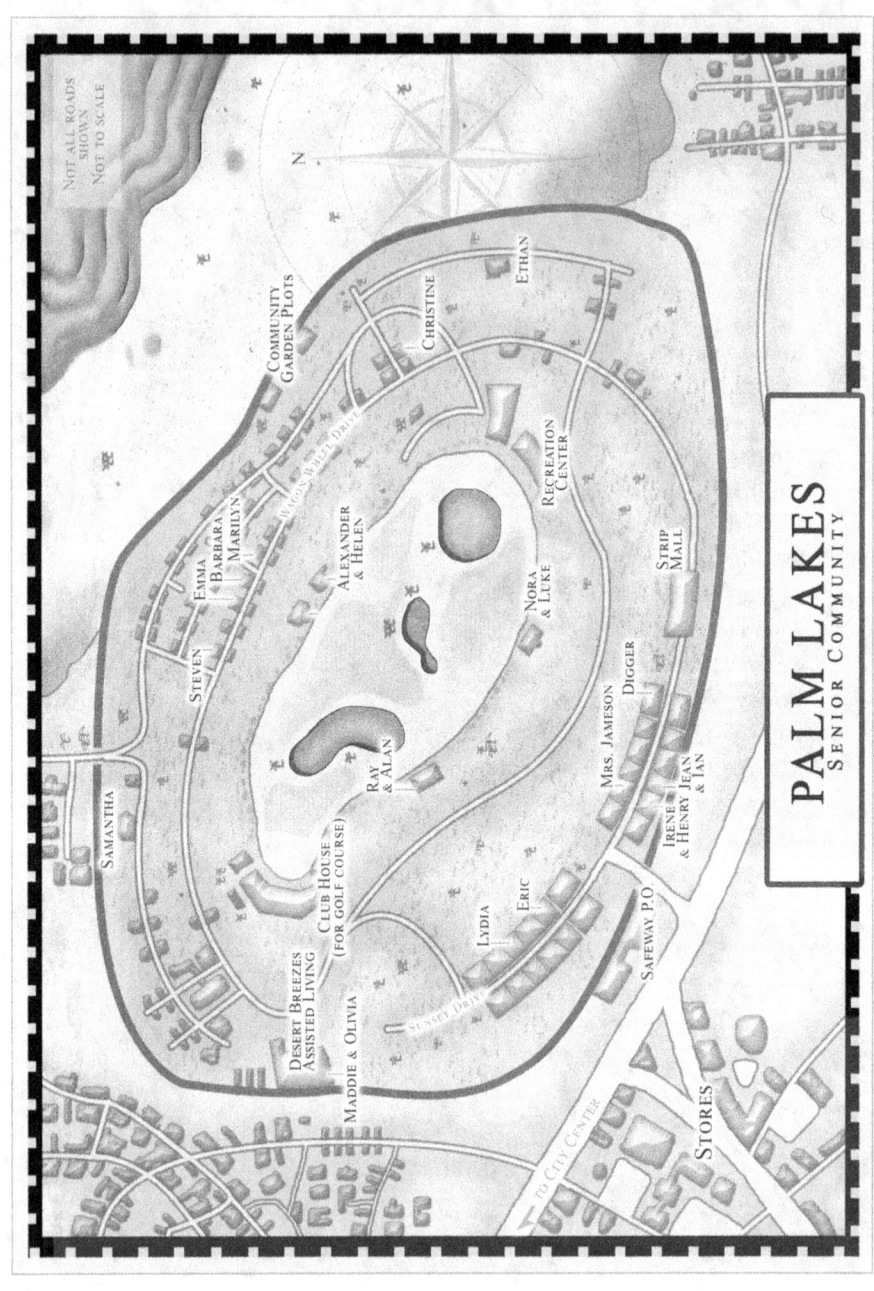

NOT ALL ROADS SHOWN
NOT TO SCALE

N

COMMUNITY GARDEN PLOTS

CHRISTINE

ETHAN

EMMA

BARBARA

MARILYN

W. GOS. SLHIT. DRIVE

ALEXANDER & HELEN

RECREATION CENTER

STEVEN

NORA & LUKE

STRIP MALL

SAMANTHA

RAY & ALAN

DIGGER

MRS. JAMESON

IRENE & HENRY JEAN & IAN

CLUB HOUSE
(FOR GOLF COURSE)

ERIC

LYDIA

SAFEWAY P.O.

DESERT BREEZES
ASSISTED LIVING

MADDIE & OLIVIA

SUNSET DRIVE

TO CITY CENTER

STORES

STORES

PALM LAKES
SENIOR COMMUNITY

# CHARACTERS

**Residents Of Palm Lakes**
Maddie O'Neill, widow
Samantha Taylor, the O'Neills' daughter, and her husband Arthur
Alexander & Helen Stirling
Mary Beth Costello, an illegal resident of Palm Lakes
Ethan Westerfield, widower and volunteer with The Helpers
Barbara Blackstone and her husband Ben and their dog, Jack
Eric Johnson and Lydia Stern
Ian and Jean Clarke
Bernie, a neighbor who is a widower
Christine Sommers
Steven Cooper, widower
Marilyn Jones and her dog Tammi
Olivia Deschamps, widow

**Wagon Wheel Drive residents (single family homes)**
Barbara and Ben Blackstone, & their dog Jack
Emma Lightman and Julio Rodriguez
Marilyn Jones and her dog Tammi
Steven Cooper, widower of Tanya

**Sunset Drive residents (condos)**
Lydia Stern
Eric Johnson
Irene & Henry Dubois
Jean & Ian Clarke

**Living along the golf course**
Alexander & Helen Stirling

**Living at Desert Breezes Assisted Living**
Olivia Deschamps
Maddie O'Neill
Sophie Aldridge
Nick Dwyer

**Nonresidents**
Jack Temple, landscaper
Ted, ex-husband of Marilyn

# ACKNOWLEDGMENTS

The writing of a novel is not a solo mission. There are many people who played a vital role in inspiring me, giving me experiences to draw on for themes and plots, encouraging me to press on until I completed the book and offering help and support in sharing the series with other readers. A heartfelt thanks to you all.

I could never have completed this project without the constant help of my husband and alpha reader, Nigel. This series isn't his kind of story, but he enthusiastically plunged into the job of editing and making suggestions for improvement. Any remaining errors are mine.

I am grateful to my advance readers for taking time out of their busy holiday season to read and review my book before it launched two days after Christmas. Special thanks go out to Jody and Denise, who alerted me to some typos in the manuscript. And last, but not least, I am very appreciative of my readers. I hope my series inspires you to have hope, to take chances and never to give up on life.

# SUNDAY, JUNE 23, 1996

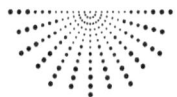

SOPHIE, 4:00AM

She was suffocating under the pressure of tons of earth. She struggled to scream, but no matter how hard she pushed, no sound escaped her mouth. There was no before and no after, just an endless now where she was trapped in powerlessness and confusion. The sheer terror of passing infinity in such a fashion finally propelled her out of the nightmare—that's what it was, though it had seemed so real—into a dark stillness. She gulped air frantically, gasping and choking at the same time.

It took her a few minutes to shed the terror of the dream, it was so vivid. When her heartbeat slowed to normal, her senses informed her that she wasn't buried underground. She was in bed. It was dark, but she could see faint light under a door on the far side of the room. Where was she? Her mind felt numb, her throat dry and scratchy as if she had screamed her head off, though she had no recollection of doing so. The terror crept back as she tried to move her limbs. Her body was unresponsive. Tears dampened her cheeks, but she couldn't raise an arm to wipe them. She could feel her fingers and toes, but they ignored her commands. This was almost as bad as the dream. What was wrong with her?

After a few ragged coughs, she tried to speak the question, but instead of words, all that came out of her mouth was a ragged grunt. That's when she remembered. She was in the assisted living section of Desert Breezes in Palm Lakes Senior Community, where she'd been moved after a stroke. The stroke had robbed her of speech and all but the smallest movement.

She could see from the empty bed next to hers that she didn't have a roommate, and for some reason, that realization fanned the flame of fear into a genuine blaze. Was she just reacting to the residue of the bad dream? Her mind wasn't working clearly. And her memory offered few facts to anchor her.

She couldn't shrug off the feeling of danger. The large red numbers on the bedside clock said 4:03. It would be hours before someone came to get her out of bed, since she couldn't do it herself. Her mind was muddled, but not so much she couldn't have expressed herself, if only she still had a voice. But the stroke had robbed her of that. And her hands were so weak, she couldn't hold a pen and write. She was isolated and powerless. A feeling of despair overwhelmed her.

Why was she so frightened? Then she heard the soft click of the door opening, and it all came rushing back as a shadow filled the backlit doorway. Running was impossible. Screaming was not an option. She wasn't strong enough to throw things or resist. Even if she could call for help, it wouldn't matter. The person charged with caring for her had just entered her room with evil intent. Hot tears flowed down her face. A prayer formed in her mind. "Please help me. Someone, please help me." But no one answered. No one ever answered.

# 2

# TUESDAY, JULY 2, 1996

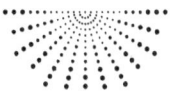

OLIVIA, 9:15AM

Olivia trudged down the carpeted hall after leaving the Desert Breezes dining room. Cooking for one didn't appeal to her, but she did enjoy a good meal. If only the dining room served something resembling fine cuisine. It was passable, but only just.

The rich maroon carpet slid by as she passed decorative alcoves that held shelves with vases of artificial flowers or niches with Native American figurines marking the divisions between apartments. Though the food wasn't anything to brag about, Desert Breezes catered to well-to-do seniors who no longer wanted the burden of a house and property, and it had the decor to prove it. The face it presented was upscale and luxurious; the reality of living here was something else, at least to her. She recalled her daughters oohing and ahhing over how nice it was when they took the tour before she sold her home. Their forced brightness hadn't fooled her then, and occasionally she wished they could be stuck here and see how they liked it, but what was the use of being negative? Deep down, she knew they were doing their best. She just had to cope. Hadn't she recovered from a broken hip, even come out of the disaster more fit and healthy? She wasn't going down without a fight.

As she unlocked her apartment door with the key on the neon pink, springy band around her wrist, she decided a cup of tea was just the thing to soothe her mind. Maddie hadn't been at breakfast again, and she was worried about her. That anxiety added to the weight of having learned that her friend Sophie was in the hospital after suffering another stroke several days ago. Olivia almost felt like she was living in a glorified nursing home. Yes, she needed a cup of tea.

She crossed the tiny tiled foyer and stepped into her kitchenette, which had a half-wall open to the living room that stretched to the sliding glass door and balcony that overlooked the golf course and purple mountains. The apartments on this side of the building had views that were almost as nice as those from her golf course home.

The small dining area opposite the kitchen held a table and four chairs that had occupied the breakfast nook in her previous home. The set was large for the cramped space, but then, all her furniture seemed oversized for this living space, a depressing reminder of how her life had shrunk.

Olivia filled the kettle and put it on to heat, then selected a mug from the cabinet, one that she'd gotten as a present from her youngest daughter years ago. She chose to think of it as a symbol of her daughter's love, though none of her three girls were much in evidence these days. Or so it seemed to her.

A brisk knock on the door shook her out of her moody reverie. She opened the door to Helen Stirling and a young woman. Helen's companion looked to be in her early 40s, with lush dark hair and stunning green eyes. Helen was older by two decades, but was still lithe and youthful, her strawberry blonde hair and smooth skin enough to inspire envy in anyone.

"Come in, Helen, it's nice to see you. How's my Spot doing?"

Helen flashed a warm smile. "She's a little rascal. Always has to be the center of attention. Smart as a whip. They say you shouldn't have a dog that's smarter than you are. I'm afraid I'm in that position." Helen turned and pointed to her companion. "My friend Mary Beth told me she was coming over to see Maddie today, and I wanted to introduce her to you." Helen grinned through the formal introduction. "Olivia, may I present my friend Mary Beth Costello? Mary Beth, this is Olivia Deschamps, who used to live next door to me."

Buzzing with curiosity, Olivia waved them in rather than shaking hands in the doorway. "How about a nice cup of tea?"

Helen grinned. "That would be lovely, if it's not too much trouble. It's already blisteringly hot outside; maybe that's why it seems so nippy in the air conditioning."

Her guests seated themselves on the sofa while Olivia added more water to the kettle and grabbed two additional mugs. She placed a variety of tea bags on a saucer and then loaded the tray with mugs, spoons, a sugar bowl and cream pitcher. The water came to a boil, and she smiled as she poured it into an old teapot that had been in her family for a hundred years.

As she turned around to take the tray into the living room, she nearly bumped into Mary Beth, who reached out. "Here, I'll take that over. It looks heavy."

Olivia nodded in gratitude and sat in a wing chair, glad to let Mary Beth play 'mother.' The younger woman doctored the tea according to each person's preference and passed mugs around.

The twinkle in Helen's eyes hinted a revelation was on the way. "Mary Beth and I are great friends. We met when I bought the condo next door to her mother's before I married Alexander. We used to gossip over a glass or two of wine in the evenings. I was the one who introduced her to Maddie. Maddie's taught her how to make jewelry, and she's selling her pieces at some of the gift shops in the resorts around here. Her work is gorgeous." Mary Beth listened to this with a shy smile, obviously embarrassed at the praise. "She's engaged to a man she met while doing jewelry at Maddie's. Isn't that romantic? Anyway, they're getting married next month and want to buy a house so they can start fresh. And guess whose house they are going to look at?"

Olivia had followed the circuitous path of the story, always one step behind. Then it hit her. She looked hard at Mary Beth. "My old place?"

Mary Beth grinned. "Yes. I stayed at Helen's casita for a couple months while they were in France, and I noticed the houses in the immediate area. I love the view across the golf course, and I was quite spoiled by the luxury. Then after Ethan proposed, we decided we needed a new place to begin our marriage." She paused as if looking for the right words. "He's a widower, you see, and I couldn't bring myself to live in the house he'd shared with his late wife. Maybe I'm being silly, but I want a place that is all ours. It was only after our realtor called and told us about a home she thought we'd like that I realized it was the house next door to Helen's. Can you imagine? I might be able to live next door to Helen again. We have an appointment to check it out this week, and I mentioned it to Helen. That's why she was eager to have me meet you." Enthusiasm fairly sparked off her.

Olivia sighed, remembering. "Well, it's a good old house. It had gotten too big for me, all by myself. My kids wouldn't hear of me staying there after I fell and broke my hip. Helen and her handsome husband were the ones to find me, because Spot—Spot was my dog before she was Helen's— was barking up a storm, because she knew I needed help, lying on the floor like that. So I put it on the market. Can't say I'm happy I did, but I guess it was time." She didn't mean to complain, but it was hard thinking about the contrast between her large golf course home and this cramped apartment.

Mary Beth's eyes shone with compassion. "I sympathize, Olivia. Maddie and I have been friends for a good while now, and she's heartbroken about having to leave her place. In fact, I was staying with her before I stayed at Helen's. It's a long story, but after my Mom died, I had to sell her place, because I'm too young to own it according to the covenants, but I'd made friends and had a job nearby, so I ended up staying here and there with friends in Palm Lakes so I could have time to figure things out. Then Ethan proposed, and I get to stay. I love Palm Lakes."

Olivia wondered how it felt to be the youngest resident of Palm Lakes Senior Community, but then again, everyone looked like a baby to her anymore. Even Helen. She wasn't sure how she felt about Mary Beth buying her house. Helen meant well, but Olivia still hated to be reminded that she'd been forced out of her home. She drank some tea to mask her confusion.

Apparently unaware of Olivia's torment, Helen pressed on in a voice filled with pleasure. "I'm selfishly hoping she and Ethan buy your house. They're wonderful people, and they'll take good care of it. And I'll get to be her neighbor again. She's quit her job at Palo Verde Landscaping in anticipation of her marriage, so I've told her she has to join our yoga group when she becomes an official resident next month." Helen smiled warmly at Mary Beth. If Helen liked Mary Beth, she must be a good person. Since someone was going to buy her house, it might as well be someone Helen liked.

"I hope you like my house, Mary Beth. It would be good to know someone will love it as much as I did. There are a lot of memories there for me." It seemed like all the good things in her life were in the past.

They sipped tea in silence for some minutes. Then a serious look crossed Helen's face. "Mary Beth and I are going to visit Maddie today. It's not her jewelry day, but with Maddie's health so precarious, we both like to visit her as often as we can."

Olivia nodded in agreement. "One thing I hate about living here. They're dropping like flies around me. It was bad enough in the neighborhood, but here, it seems someone dies or gets a death sentence just about every week. Maddie is brave, facing lung cancer with only weeks or months to live. I can't imagine how it feels, slowly losing your ability to breathe. It must be terrifying. And she never smoked a day in her life." She shook her head, still unable to process the incredibility of it. "I just found out that another friend of mine who lives here, Sophie, had a second stroke a few days ago and is back in the hospital. She used to live on this hall, but she had a stroke and they moved her to the assisted living wing. Lost her speech and most of her ability to move. I need to go to the hospital to visit her soon. She's got no one, and she hates hospitals, or so she used to say when she could still talk. She didn't seem to like this place much, either. As much as I gripe, this section is rather nice. But there's something creepy about the assisted living wing." She shuddered to think she might end up there like Sophie. Almost anything would be preferable.

They finished their tea, blanketed by a fog of depression. Helen stood up and began to load the tray. "Would you like to come with us to see Maddie?"

This was a godsend. She knew Maddie needed company, but it wasn't always easy to spend time alone with her now that the cancer was like an elephant in the room. Even without being terminally ill, Maddie was eccentric and sometimes difficult to talk to. But that seemed to be the kind of person Olivia befriended. "Sure, I was going to visit today. I was a little worried when she wasn't at breakfast."

They got up, and Helen carried the tray to the counter in the kitchenette. Then they trooped down the hall to Maddie's apartment and Mary Beth knocked on the door. "It's Mary Beth, Maddie."

"Come in, the door's unlocked," said Maddie in a muffled voice. Olivia was relieved. At least she hadn't died in the night. Horrible that such things were common here.

As they stepped into the apartment, Maddie was struggling to push herself to her feet, body bent and short dirty blonde hair disheveled, like she'd forgotten to brush it this morning. Her pale blue eyes widened to see three people enter her apartment, and a smile cracked her wrinkled face. "Can I get you all some coffee?"

Helen stepped up and gave Maddie a gentle hug, mindful of the pain her osteoporosis caused. "We just had tea at Olivia's on our way here. Nothing else for me."

"Me, neither," said Mary Beth, dropping to the couch and crossing her legs, rubbing her bare thighs. "It's cold in here, especially compared to outside."

Maddie frowned at her. "It's cold anywhere, compared to outside. It's like hell out there."

Olivia sat down next to Mary Beth and chuckled. "Life in the desert. It's hell sometimes."

Helen sat on the chair opposite the couch, and Maddie fell back into her recliner.

"So how do I rate such a crowd of visitors?" asked Maddie.

"I was going to come down today, because I didn't see you at breakfast," explained Olivia.

"I overslept. Been doing that a lot lately."

Helen smiled encouragingly. "You deserve to sleep in. Did you get breakfast?"

Maddie shook her head. "I had a cup of coffee, but I'm not hungry yet. I'll get something later."

"I've quit my job at Palo Verde, and that means I'll be able to come over more often, if you like," said Mary Beth. "We can still do jewelry on

Saturdays, but I was hoping you wouldn't mind if I came over more often than that. I promise to bring you some lasagna."

A big smile graced Maddie's worn face. "That would be nice. I love your cooking."

Helen chimed in. "She cooked a great Italian meal after we returned from our trip. I thought Alexander and I were gourmet cooks, but she's amazing."

Mary Beth shrugged her shoulders. "My Mom taught me to cook. She loved making traditional Italian dishes. I guess I got the genes for it."

Olivia listened to the exchange with interest. "I'm jealous. My daughters sometimes bring me food, but mostly I eat in the dining room. I can't make myself cook for just me. The kitchen is so tiny, and all my equipment got given away, and I don't have a dishwasher. It's too much like hard work."

"I agree," said Maddie. "I've lost weight since I moved here. I just don't eat as much."

Olivia saw flashes in the other ladies' eyes that said they wondered if the cancer was the cause of her weight loss. Maybe it was. "I've lost weight since I moved here, too. I still eat junk food, but not nearly as much as I used to. And I just don't feel like cooking. Plus the dining room doesn't have the greatest food."

"You can say that again," grumbled Maddie.

Mary Beth cocked her head to the side and looked at Olivia. "I'll have to bring you some lasagna, if you like Italian food. It's pretty easy to make up a large batch of spaghetti sauce, lasagna or ravioli."

Olivia's mouth began to water in anticipation. "I love Italian food, but I wouldn't want you to trouble yourself."

"I know, but I like to cook. Now that I'm going to have my own place with a spacious kitchen, it will be a pleasure. Besides, I need something to do with my time now that I've become a woman of leisure." Mary Beth's green eyes twinkled.

Gratified more than she could say, Olivia smiled at Mary Beth. "You're an angel. I'd love it, but only if it's no trouble."

That settled, Helen turned to Maddie. "How's Samantha doing? Since Samantha left Palo Verde Landscaping, Mary Beth doesn't see her often, which is sad. They liked working together, and they are of an age." She threw a smile at Mary Beth.

Maddie seemed to consider how to answer. "She may be my only daughter, but she doesn't tell me everything. I know she likes her new job with Jack at his landscaping company. He's fine looking. Tall, dark and handsome like a cowboy. Sometimes I wonder…" It looked like Maddie was deciding whether to say more. "He brings Beau to see me. I miss Beau like you miss Spot, Olivia."

Olivia wondered what Maddie was withholding, but didn't want to press her for more. "Such a shame we had to give up our pets to live here. I could have kept Spot, but without a yard, it would have been a real challenge. And Beau was too big, wasn't he? I haven't met him or this Jack fellow yet, but I'd like to."

"I can have him and Samantha knock on your door next time they visit."

"That would be nice."

The rest of the visit passed quickly, and Olivia returned to her apartment after bidding Helen and Mary Beth goodbye and getting further assurance from Mary Beth that she'd bring her some food. She felt a little guilty allowing someone she barely knew to make food for her, but living here was just so lonely, and Mary Beth's offer had seemed genuine.

Strange, but when she was alone in her house on the golf course, she was less lonely than now. Maybe it was partly because at home, she was surrounded by objects that warmed her heart with pleasant memories. She felt like she was living in a hotel room now, as if one morning, she'd have to check out and leave. Which of course was too close to the truth for comfort.

She went over to the small table where she had the schedule of the mini-bus that ferried residents around town. She could catch the 2:00 bus and visit Sophie in the hospital. She hadn't seen her in a while and felt bad that she hadn't even heard of her second stroke until now. Sophie literally had no one, and Olivia felt obliged to show support.

* * *

## STEVEN, 10:00AM

Steven sat on the couch, staring at nothing. It was quiet except for the occasional rumble of the air conditioning unit as it fired up. He could tell it was going to be another scorcher from how often the unit cycled and cringed at the thought of the electric bill. The curtains were closed, cloaking the living room in semidarkness. He preferred the shadows. They kept him from seeing Tanya all around him in the garish decor. His home resembled an upscale bordello, but he had always allowed Tanya to do whatever she wished with the house. Besides, it was easier to give in than to fight; she had no concept of discussion or debate. Probably came from having such a bastard for a father.

He really ought to redecorate so he wouldn't constantly be reminded of Tanya, but the divorce had cost him his meager savings and then some. That's how he justified not making any changes. Maybe he was punishing himself. He'd longed to escape their marriage for years, and when he finally found the strength, look what it led to. Some part of him felt as if he'd killed her himself.

His coffee had gone cold, but he was too listless to get up and refresh it. Why couldn't he break out of this funk? Tanya was his *ex*-wife, and she'd died months ago. For years, she'd done nothing but drink to excess and cut him into little pieces with her sharp tongue. Divorcing her had lifted a weight off his shoulders, but not long after that, Owen Schmidt had killed her.

Steven had been certain she was having an affair with the neighbor down the road, especially after how she'd acted at Barbara's Christmas party, but frankly, he'd been relieved. She'd been focused on someone else, and it had given him a measure of peace. Her affairs always had, which is why he'd never called her on them. And it gave him a chance to divorce her. He'd even begun to nurture thoughts of beginning again. Or at least just having peace and quiet in his life. Was that too much to ask?

The doorbell rang, shattering the silence. He forced himself to rise and shuffled to the door. Barbara Blackstone, wife of his golfing buddy Ben and neighbor a few houses down, greeted him with a kind smile. He let her in, but didn't offer to get her coffee. Everything seemed too hard to do these days, and she was very understanding.

She sat on the couch and he occupied the chair adjacent to it. He didn't make it any easier for her. He knew why she was here, and although some part of him appreciated the compassion, another part of him just wanted to be left alone. She didn't comment on the darkness.

"I came by to see how you're doing and invite you to have dinner with us tonight. Ben is grilling steaks, and I know how you love them. It will do you good to get out of the house."

He sighed. "I know you mean to help, but I'm not fit for company. I haven't even been able to work up to playing golf."

She reached over and gently patted his hand. "I know it's hard, but you need to get out now and then."

"OK, but I don't have much of an appetite." That was an understatement. He'd lost a lot of weight in the past months. He'd never been a jock, but now he was a spindly old guy. "I don't have the energy to cook, either. I know I should eat more." It was the most he was willing to admit.

"Then it's settled. The other thing I wanted to say was that Ben and I are concerned about you. You're our friend. I know it was hard on you about Tanya, and we think maybe you should get some help so that you can get past it."

"I don't want to pay to get shrunk. The divorce took my savings." He felt his mouth twist into a sardonic smile. At least he wasn't paying alimony anymore.

"If not that, how about a group that supports victims and their families? I have a friend who told me about this group that meets once a week at the Rec Center. She said it really helped her. Would you be willing to check it out?"

He hated to be negative, especially when it was so obvious he wasn't functioning well. "Yeah, I guess so."

"Good. When you come over tonight, I'll have the details written down for you. Will you go once and let me know how you like it? I don't want to recommend things if they aren't good, but my friend said it was worthwhile. Have you heard from your children lately?"

He shrugged. "They aren't that close to me. They call maybe once every month or two. It's my fault. I spent all my time working. And Tanya was a rotten mother. Too self-absorbed. Too whatever. Needless to say, she didn't fit in at all with the wives of my colleagues at work. The kids were eager to grow up and leave. I think she embarrassed them. Fact is, she embarrassed me, especially since we retired."

Barbara shook her head. "It must have been hard for her, comparing herself to the privileged wives of attorneys."

He was grateful for a chance to stop wallowing in self-pity. "They didn't dress like her, talk like her, act like her. To them, she was trailer trash, and I suppose they were right. She came from nothing. We both did, really. We shared a dream and the determination to make a better life together, and my becoming a lawyer seemed the best path. She worked hard to put me through law school; we didn't have enough for both of us to go to college, and in any case, she never liked school. Maybe I shouldn't have tried to drag her along with me. Or maybe I should have tried to get her to adapt. Or perhaps I should have insisted we both go to school, because that was what caused the gap between us. She stayed the same; I changed. At the time, it didn't seem so important. We were in love and naive. I wasn't embarrassed about her accent or manner of dress, though maybe I should have been. I only felt embarrassed when she took to the bottle. By then, there was nothing I could do, so I just stayed out of her way as much as possible. Our kids were ashamed of her, because they grew up with advantages, and she seemed like a hillbilly to them, right down to the accent. They never got to know her courage and ambition, the things that had drawn me to her in the first place. She was always stronger than I was, and I admired that. But she'd become an alcoholic by the time they were old enough to notice anything."

Barbara listened, her hands folded in her lap. She was the antithesis of Tanya. Empathetic, understanding, understatedly elegant, quiet. But there was steel in her. That was one thing the two women had in common, he observed silently.

Steven rubbed his face, trying to focus. "I'm rambling. Comes from being alone so much and running all kinds of scenarios through my head. What if I hadn't divorced her? Would she still be dead? Maybe not. But she'd still be an alcoholic. You'd think I'd be celebrating now that I'm rid of her. But somehow I feel responsible. Maybe I should have forced her into rehab before she wrecked the car. She would have hated me even more, but maybe she could have gotten off the booze. There just aren't any answers. I'm sorry I keep boring you with this."

Barbara's eyes narrowed. "You aren't responsible for what happened to Tanya. She chose to drink. She went with Owen. She was an adult. And fiercely independent from what I saw. She didn't want anyone telling her what to do. You know all that, but perhaps joining this group will give you a chance to see that what you are feeling is natural, that it can pass. It's time for you to rejoin the living." Barbara rose, then waved when he stood reflexively. "I'll show myself out. Come over around 4:30. We'll have a drink before dinner, or if you don't feel like alcohol, some iced tea."

He watched her graceful exit and slumped back into the chair. Maybe a hot cup of coffee would be good. He shook himself and stood, then carried his half-full mug of tepid coffee back into the kitchen. He was secretly glad for Barbara's invitations. He wasn't sure how he'd have made it this far if she and Ben hadn't been so persistent about helping him.

* * *

HELEN, 10:45AM

Helen trudged into her husband's office, Spot trailing behind her. Alexander sat at the desk, his back to her, working on his manuscript on the computer. The click of Spot's nails on the tile got his attention, and he turned to look at Helen. She practically melted under his loving emerald gaze.

He rose from his chair and put his arms around her as if she'd been gone for days, not hours. His hands caressed her face and back, then he gave her bottom a squeeze, making her laugh.

"I didn't mean to interrupt your work. I just wanted to let you know I'm back."

He ceased his caresses and looked into her eyes. "How's Maddie? And did Olivia take the news well?"

Helen sighed. "It's so hard to be with Maddie and pretend everything is OK. She is short of breath, weaker, but still feisty. It was easier visiting her with Mary Beth and Olivia. I guess we all feel awkward with death in the room. But I don't want Maddie to feel deserted. Something tells me she needs us, even though she'd never say."

He leaned down and kissed the top of her head. "You're doing a wonderful thing. I know it's hard. But I'm sure she appreciates it. How about a cup of tea or coffee? I need a break. You can tell me all about the visit."

Helen relaxed. Talking with him would help her decompress. "Thanks. Let's do that."

Minutes later, they sat side by side on the couch, her dog at her feet, cups of coffee on the table in front of them. Helen reveled in the warm comfort of Alexander's body close to hers. She couldn't get over how much her life had changed. Was it just last year her abusive husband Lou had died and she'd been thrown into chaos trying to adjust in so many ways? It hardly seemed possible. She reached over and stroked his thigh, then squeezed it. "I am the luckiest woman in the world."

"Of course you are," he teased, then leaned over to kiss her. "Now tell me what's going on at Desert Breezes."

She told herself he was only trying to help her feel better by talking about it, yet his gemstone eyes blazed with sincerity. He was so unlike Lou that it often felt like she was living in a fairy tale. "Olivia was OK with Mary Beth wanting to look at her house, but maybe she was sad, too. I had hoped she would be glad that someone nice was interested, but having to think about it must make her unhappy. Her apartment is lovely, but it's way smaller than her house, and she misses Spot. She's very brave and doesn't complain much." Helen continued to stroke his thigh absentmindedly. "Mary Beth is such a dear. She offered to bring Olivia food when she cooks for Maddie. She has such a generous heart. Olivia perked up at the offer. She says the food isn't very good in the dining room, and she can't bear to cook just for herself." She paused and lay her hand on Alexander's cheek. "I hope we don't end up living somewhere like that. I mean, it looks so nice on the outside, but it sounds dreadful."

"If you don't want to, we won't. I prefer to live on our own if at all possible. We need to stay healthy and fit so we can be independent for the rest of our lives. It's not an easy task."

Helen shook her head. "But it's worth it." Then she resolved to bring up a sore subject. "All the excitement about the weddings, and poor

Maddie, and Mary Beth maybe buying the house next door has totally distracted me from what we discovered on our trip to France. But it's creeping back into my mind and plaguing me. It even kept me awake last night. I want answers, but I don't see how I'll ever get them. And now I feel guilty, but I'm not sure it's warranted." She sighed in exasperation. "What do you think we should do?" Alexander gave her a look she'd learned to read. He wasn't going to solve this for her. "I know, I probably will never find out, and I need to just get on with life. But it's hard."

He took her hand and kissed it. "We know more than we did before, but I think you're going to have to be satisfied with what we learned. You'll never get complete closure. It's obvious that the diamonds you found in Lou's safe deposit box were contraband of some kind from the war. People aren't eager to talk about such things, even if they know all the details."

"I don't think the French boy was lying…listen to me calling him a boy. But he was as young as my own kids." He had the look of Lou. The resemblance was so striking, she knew he was Lou's love child. How could Lou have deserted him?

Alexander pulled her back to present time. "We were lucky to track him down. If he hadn't stayed in his mother's old neighborhood, we couldn't have located him. I didn't really expect much, but frankly, we got more than I would have thought, and that only because we traveled to France and sought him out."

"You're right. It must have been so hard on her, a single Mom. Lou was a jerk."

"I'd say that's an understatement. We were lucky the boy heard what he did and was willing to share it with us, especially since all the major players are dead."

Helen heaved a sigh. "I guess so. It's a case of be afraid what you ask for. He was so young when he overheard the argument. Can we be sure he remembered correctly?"

"The details make more sense to us than him, probably, since we found the diamonds and his mother's letters in Lou's safe deposit box."

"He was sure his Mom and uncle were in the Resistance during the war, though they didn't like to talk about it. They were barely adults at the time. I can only imagine what they went through. I keep trying to piece things together, but it's like a puzzle with too many pieces missing. What do you think happened?"

Alexander rolled his eyes. "You've only asked me that same question a hundred times. I'll say what I always say. You know Lou was in France in WWII. Looks like Lou took advantage of the girl. Seems somehow the point of intersection between them was a Nazi officer on the run in the chaos as the war ended. It would appear that although he was captured, he was subsequently released thanks to using the diamonds as a bribe. You can't be sure that Lou then absconded with all the diamonds, but I have to admit that what the boy overheard in the fight between his mother and uncle sounded like an ongoing tirade about Lou's betrayal and seemed to imply more than Lou fathering the boy. I believe Lou always thought about himself first, and he didn't share the diamonds, and he didn't want any further contact. It doesn't look like he ever replied to her letters. That he kept the letters seems to indicate he did have some feelings for her, just not enough to do the right thing. It probably came down to him not wanting to share the diamonds. Yet, he didn't use them, or who knows, maybe he did. We don't know how many there were to begin with."

Helen felt tears come to her eyes. "He left that poor girl on her own, pregnant with his child amid the ruins of a war. And he took the Nazi diamonds that were probably stolen from people who were killed in the Holocaust, and he arranged to let the Nazi go. I feel they're tainted. And if that woman or her brother were still alive, I'd feel we had to share them, but since they were stolen, that seems weird. Of course it's hopeless trying to find the original owners." She sighed in despair.

"We don't know for sure that Lou took all the diamonds, but it does appear that they felt betrayed in more ways than one, based on the ferocity of the argument. What do you feel is the right thing to do? You could give half the diamonds to that young man, but it won't change the past. Who knows if he'd want to have anything to do with them? You told him about Lou, but he seemed uninterested. Maybe he was just hurting. Are you intending to stay in touch with him?"

It was too much for Helen. She'd been so thrilled to find the diamonds, but the pain Lou's past caused was a large price to pay. "I don't feel he wants to ever hear from us again."

"I have to agree with you. I think he wants to forget."

17

Alexander seemed to find it easy to look at things rationally, but her emotions were all over the place. She felt she ought to do the right thing, but she had no idea what that was. There was no one to give the diamonds back to. "Sometimes I wish I'd never found them. It seemed like a treasure hunt with a fairy tale ending, but it's turned into a depressing muddle. I don't want to profit from Nazi diamonds, but I can't figure out what to do. Sometimes I think we should donate them to charity. I don't know what to do."

"They're yours to dispose of as you choose. I want you to feel good again. I agree that you need to resolve this. It's eating away at you."

His concern warmed her. She knew he wouldn't be upset if she gave the diamonds away, but she needed to hear him say it. "So you really don't care what I do? Even if I give them away?"

"Not a bit. But you need to be aware that our plan to move to the Virgin Islands may become a little more challenging if you do that. We're not hurting for funds, but living there is more expensive than here, and when I said we could move and afford a nice place there, I was counting the diamonds as part of our wealth. But what's important to me is that you feel good and do what feels right to you. We can figure a way to move without the diamonds. It might mean we need to take out a mortgage."

Helen didn't like the idea of debt, so the choice wasn't obvious to her. "I need to think on it some more. Thanks for being so kind about it. Lou would have…"

"Lou was an asshole," he interjected. "You're right that the diamonds are toxic for many reasons. They might be Nazi booty. They were certainly stolen. And Lou kept them hidden all these years. They may be the main reason he never acknowledged or helped his French son. They have a lot of negativity associated with them. Either you should give them to charity or we should convert them to cash and put it in the bank. I know it's kind of counterintuitive, but that way, they aren't a constant reminder of Lou and his transgressions."

"You're right. I'll decide one way or the other soon."

He pulled her into a hug. "Whatever you do is fine with me."

Helen was no closer to knowing what to do, but it felt good to be so loved.

18

* * *

MARY BETH, 12:05PM

From her vantage point just inside the entrance, Mary Beth spotted Helen and her friends at a table on the far side of the Jade Dragon restaurant. "They're over there, waiting for me. Thanks," she nodded to the woman who seated diners and began to wind her way around tables. She waved to Helen, who beamed at her.

The restaurant was packed, and a dull roar of conversations surrounded her as she picked her way across the bridge over the koi-filled stream that ran through the dining area. The scent of fried foods and Oriental spices made her realize how hungry she was, but as she neared the table where Helen sat, she was strangely overcome with nerves, as if she were going to a job interview. Which was silly. She was usually unafraid of judgment and tended to meet the world head on. But this was her first real social event since Ethan had proposed to her, and it was weird being a legitimate resident of Palm Lakes—well, nearly legitimate—after flying under the radar for so long.

As she approached the table, Helen pointed at the empty chair next to hers, and Mary Beth sat down gratefully and scanned the faces of the other women. On the other side of Helen, a youthful-looking brown-eyed woman with short auburn hair reached across Helen to shake Mary Beth's hand. "Hi, I'm Barbara. Helen used to live next door to me. All of us girls are in yoga class together. We hope you'll join us." She had a firm grip and welcoming eyes, and Mary Beth immediately felt more at home.

To Mary Beth's left, a stunning, quiet woman with sapphire eyes and straight black hair beamed at Mary Beth. "I'm Emma. I bought Helen's old house."

Mary Beth gasped. "You're Julio's..." she paused, struggling to find the right word. "...friend." That hadn't gone well at all. She hadn't meant to blurt out that she realized Emma was Julio's lover she'd heard so much gossip about. "I just quit working at Palo Verde Landscaping. I used to work with Julio. It's so nice to finally meet you." At least she hadn't said, 'I've heard so much about you.' She reached to shake hands, hoping the gesture would put the smile back on Emma's face.

19

Emma grinned. "I'm getting used to it."

The 'it' could mean anything, but probably referred to people discovering she was living with a Hispanic landscaper 15 years her junior. Of course, it helped that she didn't look a day over 45, if that. No wonder Julio had fallen for her, even to the point of proposing marriage.

The remaining two women, who'd been in a conversation the whole time Mary Beth was putting her foot in her mouth, stopped talking and looked her way. The shorter, earth-mother type with thick, dark hair hanging to her shoulders stood and reached across the table. "I'm Lydia. I hear you're getting married soon. Emma and I are, too. We thought it would be fun to share our wedding plans."

That sounded good to Mary Beth, who stood up to meet her halfway over the expanse of the table. She wasn't feeling confident about the wedding, because she had no family, and Ethan's son William was dead set against their marriage. She wasn't giving Ethan up, but she worried that the event might resemble a funeral. "I haven't made any plans to speak of, but I'd love to hear what you all are doing."

Lydia's friend reached over to shake hands. "I'm Jean. My husband Ian and I rent Helen's condo, the one she bought after selling her house. I understand she was your next-door neighbor for a while. It's all rather convoluted, when you try to explain it." Jean had blue eyes, short ash blonde hair and a pleasant smile. "Isn't it funny how people are brought together here? If you tried to write a book, no one would believe it."

Mary Beth murmured her agreement. Relieved to have met everyone and trying to remember names, she sat down again as the server arrived to take orders. Everyone was a regular, so it didn't take long. Mary Beth took a sip of ice water, hoping these women would accept her into their little group. It had been so long since she had more than one or two friends.

Barbara took charge of the conversation. "I think it would be great if you engaged ladies shared your wedding plans with us."

Emma paused, looking shy. Mary Beth didn't want to be the first to speak. Lydia laughed. "I'll go first. Eric and I thought August would be good for the wedding. Neither of us have any family to invite. You guys are my main friends. Eric might want to invite someone from the Posse, but basically, we thought we'd do a civil ceremony."

Mary Beth envied her a little, because family didn't guarantee an event would be more fun. She looked at Emma, who was still very withdrawn. Sympathizing with her reticence, Mary Beth charged ahead. "Well, Ethan and I were thinking August as well. I have no one to invite, except Helen, and maybe Maddie, if…" She didn't want to talk about Maddie's cancer and put a damper on everything. "I have almost no one to invite, and Ethan only has his son and daughter and their families. I'm not sure they'll be coming. The only thing we've decided is to marry on a Sunday, to give his kids a chance to travel on Saturday and not use as many vacation days." She wondered if she should express any reservations. What the hell. She'd already told Helen. "Ethan's son is opposed to the marriage, and if he comes, I'm concerned it will be unpleasant, especially since I have no family to balance the situation."

Emma's eyes widened. "I don't have anyone to invite to our wedding either, but Julio has a large family. And they'll all be coming. They're nice to me now, but it will be a bit strange having no one to invite. Other than you ladies." Her hands were clasped in her lap, and she looked down as if considering something. "Julio and I have been thinking about getting married in my back yard. We both love the outdoors so much. But beyond that, we haven't made plans."

Lydia added, "What a great place for a wedding! Your labyrinth has such lovely and peaceful energy, and your yard is beautiful. Eric and I have done so little to our tiny back yards, neither would be suitable." She grimaced.

Emma looked up. "We could have a joint ceremony in my yard." She turned to Mary Beth. "It would be fun to get married the same day."

Jean put her hand on Lydia's arm and grinned. "That would be perfect, wouldn't it, Lyd?"

"If you're serious, I'm in," said Lydia.

Mary Beth had to close her mouth and swallow. Helen had told her she'd be welcomed, but this was a shock.

"Of course, I'm serious," said Emma. "What about you, Mary Beth? Will you make it a triple wedding?"

"I would love to do that. I don't think Ethan would mind me speaking for him."

Barbara clapped her hands together. "It's settled, then. I want to host the wedding breakfast or reception after the ceremony. I'm next door to Emma's, so it will be convenient."

Helen tucked her strawberry blonde hair behind her ear. "Will you be able to do that with Amelia here?"

"Amelia is arriving soon for the rest of the summer, and it will be a bit wild with the grandchildren, but this will be easier to do than my normal August party. Or certainly no more work. I love to entertain, and I would like to be able to contribute something for my friends' special day." She turned to Mary Beth. "You know, Lydia and Jean there, along with Ian, restored my health with their magical healing abilities. Without their help, I'm not sure what would have happened to me."

"We were happy to do what we could," Jean said with a dismissive wave. "You don't owe us anything."

"We'll agree to disagree," said Barbara firmly. "Now all you girls need to do is pick a date."

After a bit of back and forth, the first Sunday in August was chosen, assuming the prospective bridegrooms agreed. Two servers arrived with platters of food, and conversation ceased as everyone dug in. At the end of the meal, they said goodbye after extracting a promise from Mary Beth to join the yoga class. Mary Beth had never done yoga, but if that was how they bonded, she was up for it. After all, she was younger than all of them, so how hard could it be?

After lunch, she pulled into Ethan's garage, glad to escape the heat of the car. The A/C didn't do much even at full blast in July, at least not in the few minutes it took to drive home from the restaurant. The monsoon humidity had her shirt sticking to her back already. The clouds were building into monstrous thunderheads, so it might rain later. Well, they needed it. She dismissed further thought of rain, because so often in the low desert, it didn't materialize.

Ethan sat on the couch with the newspaper, reading glasses perched on the end of his nose. His gray eyes lit up when he saw her. "I missed you. Did you have a nice time?" He knew she'd been concerned about her reception by the other ladies, the age difference being the main issue.

"It went well, just like you predicted." She held her hand up and gave him a sharp look. "No, don't say 'I told you so,' because that would be rubbing it in. They were all as nice as Helen promised, and I have a proposition for you." A wide smile said he was misunderstanding her. "I mean a suggestion the other ladies came up with for our wedding." His leer morphed into a warm grin as she pressed on. "Emma, the one who is living with Julio from Palo Verde, has a really nice yard from the sound of it, and she offered to have an outdoor triple wedding in her back yard. Then Barbara—I think she's the ringleader—offered to do a wedding breakfast afterwards, and she lives right next door." That had surprised Ethan. His jaw was practically on the floor. "What do you think? I was feeling it could soften any negativity from William, because there would be other people present. Oh, and is Sunday, August 4th OK?"

Ethan appeared to be bowled over, but finally found his voice. "That would be perfect for us. I was worried about you not having guests and William being snotty and ruining it. Having all those other people would probably guarantee he'd behave. At least in front of them."

Mary Beth snorted. "That's good enough for me. Let Winnie and her kids stay here, and make William and his family get a motel, if they come. There isn't room for everyone here, and I don't want to be around him too much."

Ethan's smile revealed even, white teeth. "That works for me."

"Before I can quit for the day, I need to go to Catherine's and do some more to get it ready for sale." She grinned at what she had said. "Listen to me—she left her condo to me in her will, and I still think of it as hers. Anyway, I have a few things to do over there. You don't need to come with me. I'll be back later for dinner. Or would you like to eat at my place?"

"Doesn't matter to me, but my kitchen is bigger than yours… Catherine's." He smiled agreeably.

"OK. We'll eat dinner here, but we go back to my place after. I'm going to feel a lot better when we move into the new house."

"You sound sure that we'll get that one next to Helen."

"I'll know when I see it. You loved the views from Helen's place, too, and I know you aren't friends with them, but she has been my best friend since I got here, her and Samantha and Maddie, but Helen most of all. I'd love to live next door to her again."

"Suits me. As long as you like what you see inside. When are we checking it out?"

"Tomorrow, I think. Well, I'll be back soon." She kissed him quickly and headed back out to the car.

As she pulled into the driveway at Catherine's—now her—condo, she spotted Julio across the street at Irene and Henry's place. She walked across the street through the haze of heat and stood patiently next to Julio, who was bent over a sage bush, digging around to find the dripper at its base. When he stood back up and saw her, he jumped in surprise. But then he flashed his 1000 watt smile. He was such a looker, with his long, wavy black hair and dark eyes. "Mary Beth, nice to see you."

He held out his hand to shake hers, a habit she had grown used to while working at Palo Verde Landscaping. It seemed all the Hispanic men were hand shakers. "Where's Emma? We just had lunch a while ago. Are you yard-watching for Irene and Henry?"

"Yes, they are Canadian snow birds, and they will be back later in the fall. Emma works with me on these jobs. She does the inside while I do the outside; she got here a few minutes ago. You can go in the front door if you want to see her."

"I don't want to interrupt what you're doing, but I will go in and thank her again. She told you she invited us all to get married the same day in her back yard?" *Shit*. She should have said 'your' back yard. She wondered if Julio was sensitive about things like that.

Apparently not, because he was still smiling warmly. "Yes, she told me. I think it will be very good. She has no one to invite, and my family is big. This will be much better for her."

"And for me," said Mary Beth. "I'm in the same situation."

"Her friends have been very kind to me. It will be a good day for us all." He pushed the brim of his straw hat back and wiped his forehead.

"I won't keep her long," promised Mary Beth as he went back to work.

Mary Beth found Emma in the bathroom, flushing the toilet and running water in the sink.

"Oh, you scared me!" she gasped when she turned and saw Mary Beth in the doorway.

"Sorry, I saw you were here. I own the condo across the street. This actually used to be my Mom's place. Isn't that a coincidence? In fact, that means Jean and Ian live next door in Helen's old condo, doesn't it? Listen to me babbling on. I wanted to thank you again for your generous offer of having the wedding at your place. It will be such a help to me. I can't tell you how I was dreading it, but now, it will be fun."

Emma surprised her by reaching over and touching her arm. "We all have our private challenges. Marriage is a big step."

"My first ended in divorce, and that's how I landed here. The age difference between me and Ethan has his son angry."

"Yes, that is to be expected. Julio's family were very unpleasant to me at first because I'm so much older than he."

"And it's changed?"

Emma beamed at her. "I finally won them over by ignoring the negativity. I can't promise it would work for you, but don't let yourself be dragged into any fight. Ethan obviously has chosen you, and that's that. Either his son will accommodate or not. At least he doesn't live nearby, right?"

"No, we won't be seeing him more than once a year, if that."

"That should make it easier. In any case, I'm glad we're having a joint ceremony. And it's terrific that Barbara is doing the reception. We're going to pitch in for supplies and all. I need to talk to Lydia, but would you like to contribute?"

"Absolutely."

Emma reached into a pocket and pulled out a business card. "Just call this number, and you'll get me. It's our business number. I'll talk with Lydia and should have a list by sometime tomorrow. Give me a ring and I'll share what we've come up with, and you can offer suggestions. I don't know what Barbara will want to serve, but there are a lot of catering places. We'll have to kind of guess at the budget, but we don't want her to absorb it all."

"Of course. Whatever you decide, I'll chip in."

"That's great," said Emma.

"Well, I'll let you get back to work. When I call, I'll give you my phone number."

Emma nodded. "See you in yoga class. It's the intermediate level that starts in a couple weeks. Let me know if you need help figuring out which one. I forget the exact starting date."

"OK." Mary Beth left the house, noticed Julio was at the side of the house checking the irrigation timer, and swam through the oppressive heat to the condo she couldn't stop calling Catherine's. She imagined her feet were leaving impressions in the asphalt, it was so hot.

Inside, she spent an hour completing the inventory of things to sell in the estate sale. It always made her sad to be here, because the place felt so empty without Catherine's joyful voice. Catherine had been like a mother to her, and it had been such a blow losing her so soon after losing her own mother. And a shock to discover Catherine had left everything to Mary Beth. At least the jars with $100,000 in cash were now safely stashed at Ethan's house. Which reminded her, they needed to funnel that money into a bank account soon. Catherine's bequest had allowed Mary Beth to insist that she and Ethan start their marriage at a new place. The alternative of living in his home had been a sticking point with Mary Beth, because she couldn't bear the thought of stepping into his late wife's shoes. She went back to work filled with gratitude for Catherine's generosity, marveling at the kindness of her new friends.

* * *

MARILYN, 2:30PM

The movers had finished unloading and left an hour ago, and Marilyn had been unpacking boxes ever since. At least they were kind enough to place the furniture where she asked, and she had marked the boxes as to what room they belonged in, so it had gone relatively smoothly.

She paused briefly to get a glass of ice water and gulped it down at the kitchen sink while sweat trickled down her back. She had the air conditioning on, but even set at 85 degrees, it felt horribly hot. The weather report had said it was 114 outside, and in fact, when she stepped inside after being out with the moving truck, it felt heavenly, but after an hour of hauling things out of boxes and putting them in cabinets and drawers, she was overheated and exhausted and tempted to set the thermostat to 70 degrees. She resisted the temptation. It was a dry heat, after all, she consoled herself, snorting at the saying she had already heard at least three times since arriving in Arizona. Maybe they'd get rain this afternoon. The clouds were darkening, but so far, not a drop had fallen.

She put her glass down on the counter, remarking to herself yet again at how unusually clean the house was. It was as if an obsessive house cleaner had lived here, but the realtor had said it was a single guy. Who knew a guy could be so particular? Even the baseboards gleamed. She imagined if she put on a white glove and did a test, it would be spotless at the end. Oh well, it was nice not to have to scrub in order to feel the place was habitable. She thought back to a few crummy apartments from her youth and marveled at how far she'd come.

Tammi had been released from her crate by the sliding glass door once the movers left, and she was lying in a corner of the great room on her dog bed, a quizzical look on her black face with the white stripe down the center. The trek across country from Virginia was a 2400 mile journey, and Marilyn had never been a long-distance driver, and doing it with a 90-pound Akita had its ups and downs. She'd needed to arrive before the moving van, and she'd succeeded, but she was desperately tired from driving so many hours a day. Tammi seemed to have enjoyed all the new sights and sounds, but expressed some uneasiness about what was coming next. Marilyn could relate to that. If only this move would be the solution to her problems.

"Do you need a drink, sweetie?" she asked Tammi, who cocked her head to the side in response. Tammi's food and water dishes lay in the corner of the kitchen on a cute mat with a pawprint pattern. "I'm not really hungry yet, but I got really thirsty." Tammi wagged her curly tail tentatively. The black-and-white pattern of Tammi's fur made her a flashy girl, and her intelligent brown eyes were almost human. Marilyn didn't know what she'd do without her.

"I think I'll quit for today, except to unpack the things we brought in the car. I might even order a pizza. What do think about that?" Tammi knew what the word pizza meant, and she wagged her tail in enthusiastic agreement.

Marilyn brushed her short gray hair back and headed to the master bedroom, which was as spic and span as the rest of the rooms. She wondered what had happened to the previous owner. The price certainly had been right—below market value, in fact, and she liked the neighborhood. All she knew is that he had died and there was a rush to sell his place.

In the bedroom, she emptied her suitcase, putting some clothes in her dresser and hanging a few in the spacious, walk-in closet. It felt good to begin to settle in and mark the place as her own. With two additional bedrooms, she had plenty of space to expand. She wondered if one room should be a guest bedroom and the other, a hobby room. Not that she expected to have any guests. She had no living relatives and few friends, certainly none who were likely to travel this far to see her. She refused to dwell on the sadness that realization stirred up.

She put the empty suitcase into the closet of the guest bedroom, as she felt she wouldn't be needing it soon. She got her pistol out of her purse and put it on the bedside table. It was a Smith and Wesson Ladysmith .38 revolver with Pachmayr grips, and she slept with it under her pillow, at least ever since she left Ted.

She looked out the bedroom window and was reminded that her first order of business was to figure out a fence for the back yard. She couldn't have Tammi running loose, and the dog needed space to exercise. The covenants were terribly strict, so she couldn't have a chain link fence, but surely there would be some affordable type. The buyout package from her job had been generous—in fact, that was what had provided the final impetus for her escape from Ted—so she could probably get the fence installed right away.

Over the next few days, the TV and phone would be hooked up, and she'd be set. She felt a little nervous not having a phone, but it had been impossible to guarantee when she'd arrive, and the phone company couldn't get out today on such late notice. One day wouldn't hurt. She hoped.

She almost couldn't believe she was really here. Was it only two months ago that she'd seen an article in the Sunday paper about the Palm Lakes Senior Community in the Arizona desert? For some reason, it had captivated her, the desert so filled with sunshine and blue skies, the antithesis of Virginia climate most of the year. The green of the golf course and the sparkling lakes surrounded by palm trees spelled paradise to her.

She'd said nothing to Ted at the time. She hadn't been sharing her thoughts with Ted for years, and communication had worsened after her return from the hospital. He wasn't ready to retire, anyway. His life was the police force. She believed it gave him justification for throwing his weight around. Too bad he apparently didn't get enough of that at work.

She'd grown weary of his fits of temper and physical violence. Early in their marriage, he just threw things, but when he saw she wasn't going to walk out on him, he started hitting her. One time, then two times. Never where anyone could see. She had no family and few friends, certainly none she'd talk to about Ted. He was a respected police officer. Who would believe her? He'd said as much a million times.

She'd told him she'd leave him if he ever put her in the hospital. And then, one day, he did. Rehab took a long time, and she could finally drive again, so the Sunday she saw the Palm Lakes article was the day she decided that's where she was going to live. She hadn't told him about the buyout option at her job, which made the purchase of the house via long distance simple, thanks to having kept her finances separate from his. That particular bone of contention saved her; thank heaven she'd held out about it. It was mind-boggling how fast everything had come together.

Why the desert? For sure, being thousands of miles from Ted was attractive, especially considering his reaction to her leaving. One night while he was out with the boys, she had moved out of their home without warning into a small apartment nearby, and she notified him by mail that she was divorcing him. He started stalking her as she prepared for her move, even made threats. Finally, she got a restraining order, but fat lot of good that did. It made her wish she'd simply hit the road and gone to AZ, but she'd wanted to get the divorce in VA and tie up loose ends.

That's when she began to sleep with the pistol under her pillow. She was a crack shot, thanks to a gun course and lots of time at the range, but then, so was Ted. It was a hobby they had both enjoyed when they first knew each other, but at some point, she became convinced he'd end up killing her one day, or her, him, and she didn't want to hang around to see which it would be.

She wasn't getting alimony or any kind of support from Ted. Maybe he wouldn't be able to find her. Perhaps if he abused his police powers, he could trace her. She didn't have the knowhow to get a new identity, and she had to get an Arizona driver's license sooner or later. Maybe if she waited a few months, he wouldn't find her. She'd used her maiden name to buy the house, and Jones was a pretty common name, and she'd never mentioned anything about Arizona to him. She hoped that by removing herself from his life, the whole situation would depressurize, and she could get on with living. She hated to wish he'd find someone else to abuse, but she had to admit she wished his attention would turn elsewhere.

Lingering in Virginia had given her one priceless reward. Tammi, whom she had adopted from an Akita rescue shortly after she left Ted, had turned out to be a wonderful companion, and between Tammi and the gun, she didn't think Ted would be able to sneak up on her.

The ringing of the doorbell and Tammi's single deep bark jerked Marilyn out of her reverie. Who could that be? She cautiously approached the front door and peered through the peephole. A woman with short auburn hair and lively brown eyes stood at the door. Marilyn released the breath she'd been holding. Still, she was slow to unlock the door and left the screen door locked, just in case.

"Hi, I'm Barbara. I live next door." The woman pointed to her left. "I won't keep you for long. I know you must be busy, but I wanted to offer to help you get settled in if I can. I understand you're alone here?"

A little shaken by the personal question, Marilyn hesitated. "Yes, it's just me and Tammi." She pointed at the Akita, who had appeared like a ghost beside her, intently watching the woman for threatening behavior.

"Oh, heavens, what a beautiful dog! We have a Jack Russell. He's kind of hyperactive. Tammi is beautiful and so well-behaved. I won't ask to come in, as I know you are busy unpacking, but how about coming over to our place for dinner tonight? My husband is grilling steaks, and he's good at it. Then you don't have to cook or order pizza and eat alone."

The idea was appealing, as Marilyn was exhausted. "That's awfully nice of you, but I'd hate to leave Tammi here by herself. She's so new to the house."

"If you think she'd get along with Jack, you can bring her."

"I haven't had her that long, but she doesn't seem inclined to make friends with other dogs. I suppose I can crate her. I wouldn't want to leave her for hours, though. She hates being cooped up, and we were in the car for days getting here. I need to get a fence put up."

"I can recommend just the company to do that. Come on over for dinner, and we'll be happy to answer any questions you have about Palm Lakes and make suggestions for any services you want to discover. And of course, the amenities for residents. You're going to love it here."

Barbara's enthusiasm was contagious. "I admit I was thinking of ordering Domino's; it would be nice to get to know more about my new home."

A strange look flitted across Barbara's face. What was that about? But Barbara composed herself so quickly, Marilyn thought she must have imagined it. "We're happy to help you any way we can."

"What time shall I come, and what can I bring?"

"Is 5:00 too early?"

"No. I'm probably going to fall into bed early tonight. It's been a hard week."

"Just bring yourself and your appetite."

"Sounds good. Thanks for the invitation."

Barbara smiled and left, and Marilyn hoped that she'd made the right choice.

* * *

BARBARA, 6:00PM

"Ben, could you pass the salad?" Barbara telegraphed her husband in the silent language learned over years of a happy marriage that things weren't going that well, and she needed his help. She saw him register her concern at how reticent their guests were. Maybe it had been a mistake to invite both Marilyn and Steven without letting them know about the other guest. But everyone was new to Marilyn, and Steven needed to get out of his gloomy house.

Her ploy hadn't succeeded famously, and she was chagrined. Marilyn seemed reluctant to give many details about her life before moving here, and Steven appeared to be absorbed in his own grim musings. The atmosphere was stilted, and she needed to do something to change it.

"Marilyn, your dog is very pretty," ventured Barbara.

A genuine smile illuminated Marilyn's face. "I haven't had her long. She's barely full grown, but weighs 90 pounds. I've taken her to one obedience class, but she clearly needs ongoing education." She snickered to herself.

"Jack could use some training, but we've never gotten around to it," noted Ben.

31

"Small dogs aren't as dangerous or obnoxious when untrained as big dogs are. Akitas have a reputation, and I don't want to take chances with her. I never let her run off leash, and no matter what it takes, I'm going to have her obedient." She paused and took a forkful of roast potatoes into her mouth and sighed. "These are delicious. You'll have to give me your recipe. I've never had potatoes so crispy on the outside and creamy on the inside."

Barbara was warmed by the compliment. She was proud of her cooking skills. That was one reason she loved to share them. "I'll copy it and bring it over tomorrow."

Jack had parked next to Marilyn's chair, instinctively aware that she was a dog person. Marilyn cast him a glance now and then, and finally asked Barbara, "Is it OK to give him something?"

"We don't feed him at the table. He'd soon take over the entire house if we did. But after we clear the table, you can give him the leftovers if you like. He seems to have bonded with you."

"Dogs and I always get along. Not so much humans." She left that statement hanging in the air, an obvious hint about her past, but Barbara let it slide.

"Marilyn, would you consider joining our little group for yoga? You don't have to have experience. It's just a nice way to socialize."

Marilyn's face lit up, and she said, "That sounds nice. I'd love to. I know there are a lot of clubs here. Do you know of one for dog obedience training?"

"I don't know, but I can find out. I'll give you the Rec Center number in case I come up blank." Barbara was pleased that Marilyn was diving into life in Palm Lakes and surprised that she had acquiesced so easily to the yoga suggestion. Maybe their friendship would grow, giving her a chance to share about Owen's house without looking like a gossip. Marilyn was going to find out sooner or later, and it should be from a friend.

Now she needed to wrestle Steven out of his funky mood. As if he'd telepathically heard her, Ben said, "Steven, it's time you and I went golfing. I've missed that. What do you say to tomorrow? I can easily get us a tee time since it's the height of summer."

A spark of interest stirred in Steven's brown eyes. "Sure, Ben. I've missed it, too." He said no more, but Barbara felt relief that Steven had decided to get into a more normal routine. She needed to remember to give him the referral to the support group before he left. She hated to pressure him, but she knew it would help if he'd go.

Steven had cast a few furtive glances at Marilyn during dinner, but had yet to address her beyond his first 'hello.' Barbara hoped the looks signaled some sort of interest in something outside of his own grief. She had a terrible tendency to matchmake, and when she'd seen Marilyn, she decided maybe it was just what Steven needed to draw him out of his shell. Marilyn was shy, but not depressed. Or didn't seem to be. Only time would tell.

Marilyn appeared to remember something and put her fork down. "You said you could recommend someone to give me an estimate on a fence."

"Oh, yes. You can do two kinds here, or rather three. One is a block wall six feet high. You can see that my other next door neighbor has one of them. You can do a simple wrought iron fence. That is less expensive. Then, there is an intermediate option, which is a low block wall topped by wrought iron, again six feet tall in total. I'll give you Julio's number. He lives next door with Emma. They're engaged to be married. He does excellent work."

Marilyn seemed to take the news in stride, but then she couldn't know that Julio was much younger than Emma and had met her while doing a landscaping job for her. She'd find out eventually, because Emma was part of the yoga group.

"I'm so glad I asked you. You have a wealth of information. I don't think I want a block wall, though it would be very secure. I might just do a plain wrought iron fence."

Relieved at Marilyn's preference, Barbara nodded. "That would be less expensive and it gives a more open feeling to your yard. Not everyone is the same, but some find the walls claustrophobic."

"I think I would," said Marilyn. "One of the things I like most about living here is the big sky. Where I come from, trees block out so much, or buildings. When I stand in my back yard, I can see Four Peaks in the far distance, to the east. It's my only view of the mountains, and I wouldn't want to lose it." She went back to cleaning her plate.

Dessert passed without a hitch, and Marilyn and Steven left at the same time, going in opposite directions down the sidewalk in the still sweltering heat, Steven with a slip of paper on which was written the support group details, and Marilyn with Julio's business card.

"I think that went well," said Barbara.

"Woman, you are always matchmaking." Ben grinned at her, a glint in his blue eyes.

"Well, it worked for Helen, didn't it?"

"Yes, it did. I'm not arguing, just observing."

Barbara grunted and then laughed. "You know me so well. I think we need to shake Steven out of his depression. I don't care if it goes beyond that. I don't know enough about Marilyn to be sure she's right for him anyway. I wish I could find an easy way to tell her about her house. The longer we wait, the more chance there is that someone else will tell her, and I'd hate her to get turned off to Palm Lakes."

Ben snorted. "I don't see how you can tell her in a subtle way that a serial killer owned the house before her and stored trophies of his kills in the master bedroom closet. Or that he killed Steven's wife, or rather, ex-wife."

She sighed. "You're right. There's no easy way, but I'm going to have to find one. And soon."

He pulled her into his arms, and her worries immediately drained away. "It will all work out." His assurances were based on nothing, but as usual, made her feel better.

# 3
# WEDNESDAY, JULY 17, 1996

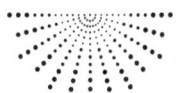

OLIVIA, 10:15AM

O livia sat opposite Maddie, enjoying a cup of coffee and a good chin wag. Maddie was looking good, all things considered. For selfish reasons, she wanted Maddie to keep looking good, to somehow beat this cancer thing. Maddie's question about Sophie intruded into her swirling thoughts.

She put her mug down on the table beside her and shook her head, "No, I haven't had much of a chance to visit Sophie since her last stroke. I went to the hospital a few times, and she was fast asleep every time. I'm not sure if that's good or bad. I'm going to go back again soon. Surely they'll be releasing her before long. This bus tour I went on last weekend sidetracked me." She heaved a sigh, wondering if she should share the nightmare it had been.

Maddie beat her to it. "I never went on a bus trip before. Stanley and I used to travel by car now and then, but we never went with groups. Stanley was way too private for that. And too much of a control freak. He always wanted to plan his own itinerary. I wish my health had lasted long enough so that I could have tried one. How did it go?"

"I wish I could say it was great, but it was a disaster of the first order. Well, I shouldn't be so negative. How can you complain when you get to visit the Grand Canyon? It is the most awe-inspiring place I have ever been and a delight to see. Of course, it was crowded beyond belief because summer is the high season. I fancy I heard at least a dozen foreign languages being spoken as we walked along the rim."

Maddie sighed. "I love the Grand Canyon. Haven't been there in years. So what went wrong?"

"The weather was perfect. Warm and sunny with fluffy white clouds in a perfect blue sky. The monsoon rains passed us by. Our tour guide was remarkably well-informed about plants, animals and geology, as well as history. He had a great sense of humor, and he was kind on the eyes, too. It was my traveling partner who was the problem."

"Did she snore?" Maddie asked, then snorted, setting off a coughing fit. "Are you OK?"

"Give me a minute. I shouldn't laugh like that." Maddie finally got her breath back after several ragged inhales.

At least Maddie was laughing. That lifted Olivia's spirits. "Julia lives on the second floor here. I met her in the dining room one day when you weren't there, and we had a meal together. She seemed friendly and nice. I went on a walk with her early in the morning a couple times. She used a walker, but seemed game to get some exercise. I like walking. Now that I've lost the extra weight, I feel good and have more energy. I thought when she suggested making a trip together that it might be fun. I haven't been on a trip for ages."

Maddie sighed, a dreamy look in her eyes. "Was this your first time on one of those bus tours? I know it must have taken hours to get to the Grand Canyon."

"Yes, it was, and you're right. It took about five hours, but these modern tour buses are nothing like old-time buses. The seats were very comfortable, and they had a clean bathroom. The trouble began when we boarded the bus. Of course, we intended to sit together and chat or read our books. I was taken aback when she announced that she had to have the window seat. She acted like it was a foregone conclusion that she should get it without asking my preference."

Maddie's mouth hung open in a big O.

"I told her as nicely as I could that I like looking out the window, too, and that maybe we could take turns, like one person got the window on the way up, and one on the way back. She frowned at my suggestion and said something like, 'I get carsick if I can't see out the window.' I confess that made me feel guilty for speaking up. I didn't want her to be ill. So I gave her the window seat. Little did I know that was just the beginning."

By now, Maddie had clamped her jaw shut, but was shaking her head, an anticipatory gleam in her pale blue eyes.

"When we got to the hotel, there was only one bellboy, and he quickly disappeared helping someone, and we'd brought our suitcases plus her walker, and her suitcase didn't have wheels. There was no way we were going to schlep all that stuff around ourselves. I was content to wait, just glad to be able to stretch my legs after sitting for hours, but she started complaining loudly enough for everyone to hear that the service was bad.

"I got embarrassed and tried to calm her down, saying a whole busload of people would tax any hotel's staff. But she wouldn't listen. Finally, a bellboy came and loaded our stuff onto a cart, and I discovered that Julia doesn't really need a walker. I'd never seen her navigate without one. She was just as nimble as I am, maybe moreso. I couldn't keep my jaw from dropping, but I didn't say anything. I wondered why she affected a handicap when she doesn't have one, but, as it turned out, that was the least of my worries."

Olivia paused to sip some coffee. Storytelling dried her mouth out. "We got into our room, and things went from bad to worse. It was spacious and clean with two queen size beds. She immediately explained why she had to have the bed nearest the window, though her reasoning made no sense to me. I gave in on that. Then we were unpacking and she groused that there weren't enough hangers. I told her to hang more than one thing per hanger, and she looked at me like I'd grown a second head. She handed me four hangers, but I saw that she had five. I asked her why she kept the extra one, and all she said was, 'because I need it,' as if her needing it meant she was entitled to have it. I admit I did say hang more than one item per hanger, so maybe she assumed I didn't care. That's what we both had to do in the end. I just felt pushed around by that point.

"Then she went into the bathroom and peered at the bathtub and made some disparaging comment about using it. I told her they clean everything between guests, but she let me know her real problem was using it after *me*, as if I had some communicable disease. I was speechless. She washed her hands, then wiped them on a towel and hung it on the rack to dry. Later, after I did the same, she came into the bathroom and wrenched my towel off the rack, saying she didn't want my towel to touch hers. She hung it over the shower curtain rod. I started to fume, because no one had ever been so rude to me."

Maddie, who was usually quite voluble in expressing her opinions about everything, was speechless. A pained look on her wrinkled face proved she was sympathetic, so Olivia continued. "It went downhill after that. She bitched about the food in the dining room. I thought the food was excellent and the selection wonderful. They had this meal called a Navajo taco. It was huge. The fry bread—I've never had anything like it—was topped with beef taco filling, chopped tomatoes, shredded lettuce and grated cheese. I swear it was enough for three people. Julia complained that the server had an accent. You know, they have this program where the servers are from other countries, and their name tags show what country they're from. I thought it was fun. They spoke good English, but she evidently has a thing about foreigners. I tried to ignore her, but her litany of complaints gave me a stomach ache.

"She wouldn't go into the shop on our walk later on when I wanted to get an ice cream cone, so I went in alone. And she has a crazy rule about going to bed at 8:30pm, and I told her I wasn't there to sleep. I wanted to have some fun. So I went down to the bar alone. Imagine me, going to a bar alone at my age! I did meet up with some people from the tour, so it wasn't bad. Julia was in bed with one of those eye masks on when I returned. I had to turn on a light, because she'd left all the lights off, and I can't find my way around a room, even with the glow from the TV, which she'd left on. She gave me a hard time about interrupting her sleep, but I'm sure she was awake when I got back. Why wouldn't she be? She insisted on leaving the TV on for background noise all night. It was shock after shock for the entire weekend. I was exhausted when we returned and never wanted to see her again. Can you imagine she asked if I'd like to go on a trip again with her? I couldn't figure out if she was joking, or if she really thought she'd been good company. I'd be happy never to see her again, but I'm sure we'll run into each other."

"Whatever you do, don't go on a trip with her again."

"I'm not that stupid, or that nice. She was a royal pain in the ass. Sorry for being crude."

Maddie cackled. "Don't need to watch your language around me. I think you're a saint for not giving her a massive put down."

"What good would that do? I have to live here and so does she. I don't want to start a war. But I'm not going to spend time with her at all from now on. I won't even eat with her. I have to admit, though, that I find myself scanning the dining room, worrying about fending her off, as if I'm the one who's done something wrong. I take a book to read, most meals, to avoid company. I don't know why I should feel guilty that I don't want to see her, but..."

Maddie shook her head sympathetically. After a few quiet moments, she cocked her head. "What if you and I eat dinner together in our apartments instead of in the dining room?" Maddie's voice quivered as if she were afraid of rejection. "Mary Beth and Samantha bring me food. Mary Beth brings you some. I don't know about you, but I don't eat big portions anymore. They have readymade meals in Safeway, like roasted whole chickens with all the trimmings. I'm not too keen on frozen dinners, but they have those, too. We could eat dinner at my place one night and at yours the next." A wistful look filled Maddie's pale blue eyes.

Olivia was sure Maddie was lonely, too. "Why not? We can stretch those kinds of meals and get some variety. Plus, that way, you can have a beer and I can have a glass of wine if we like."

Maddie's smile revealed crooked, coffee-stained teeth. "I only eat two meals a day as a rule. Breakfast and dinner."

"Let's give it a try. My place or yours tonight?"

"I have some great stew that Samantha made. Do you like beef stew?"

"Love it," said Olivia.

"Call me later this afternoon to give me time to reheat it." Maddie's relaxed face radiated satisfaction. Olivia hoped she hadn't gotten herself into another pickle, but she knew Maddie pretty well, and although she was outspoken and eccentric, she wasn't selfish like Julia.

"Now I'm kind of glad I had such a bad experience. I never have liked the food in the dining room. And since you aren't eating there often, and Sophie had her stroke, Julia was the only one I knew. I'll be pleased to cut back on dining there. It's lonely eating like that, nearly as bad as eating alone in my room." Olivia hated to admit how lonely she was.

"You aren't the only one who feels that way." They finished their coffee in companionable silence before Maddie spoke again. "What do you think is going on with Sophie? She's been in the hospital a long time. That's not usually a good sign."

"One of the nurses told me that she had another small stroke after she got there, and they wanted to make sure she was stabilized before sending her back, but I can tell they don't feel she's doing well. She hates hospitals, and I wonder if the stress of being there is hindering her recovery. I feel bad I've only been to visit her a few times, and she wasn't awake, and there's no one else I know of who visits, so she must feel deserted. I'm going to go again soon. I wish there were some way to be sure to catch her awake."

"It's not much fun having to stare death in the face."

Olivia didn't know how to answer that. Poor Maddie was staring death in the face daily. "I think you're very brave."

Maddie grunted. "It's not courage when you don't have a choice."

"You have a choice how you deal with what's been given you. Julia complains about everything, even imaginary things. I heard more complaints from her in one day than I've ever heard from you. I can't imagine her handling a serious illness with grace."

Maddie smiled awkwardly, apparently unaccustomed to compliments. Olivia lifted her coffee cup. "Here's to some great beef stew tonight."

They clinked their mugs together and quietly sipped coffee, lost in their own thoughts.

* * *

BARBARA, 10:45AM

"Amelia, are you almost ready to go?" Barbara checked that she had her wallet in her purse. She was a little nervous about taking her daughter to see Jean and Ian for a consultation. Even though she truly believed they had healed her of a brain tumor, it seemed unlikely they could pull off another miracle. She'd met with such skepticism the few times she'd tried to share her story with other friends that she'd quit sharing it, and that made her feel guilty. She was so grateful to Jean, Ian and Lydia, and she had hoped to refer business to them, but the whole concept of energy healing was just too unconventional for Palm Lakes.

Amelia shuffled into the living room as if exhausted from dragging a big weight around. It hurt Barbara to watch her. But what hurt most was the aura of defeat and sadness wrapped around her daughter. Her long, dark hair was dull, as were her blue eyes, muted by pain. She was too thin in her beige cotton shorts and sleeveless top. Barbara had to overcome the desire to hug her. Amelia didn't like being fussed over.

"Are you sure you're up for this?" asked Barbara, peering closely at her. Last thing she wanted to do was force Amelia.

"Sure, Mom. It beats getting poked and prodded by doctors. But don't get your hopes up." The air of powerlessness was contagious.

Barbara's heart sank. "They were able to help me. I don't know if they can help you, but it won't hurt and it won't be hard. Thanks for humoring me." She could tell Amelia was placating her as payment for all she was doing. Barbara pushed her concerns aside and put on a confident air. "Let's look on it as an adventure."

At the Sixth Sense Consulting office, Lydia greeted them and led them to Jean's treatment room. After an extensive questionnaire, Jean put her pen down and looked at them with a warm smile. "We can't make any promises about results, Amelia. As your mother knows. But I would like to suggest a treatment with Ian and me. If you like it, we'd want to repeat it, but we'll see how it goes rather than make assumptions. There are a few dietary changes I would like to suggest. They are based on scientific studies and anecdotal evidence, and they won't cost you anything and have no negative side effects."

Amelia looked at Barbara, and then back at Jean. Barbara was feeling the stirring of hope in her heart. At least Jean had some ideas they could pursue. Barbara waited for Amelia to respond. She didn't want to push her, but she wanted to try anything that might help.

Finally, Amelia sighed. "I'm afraid to get my hopes up. But I'll do whatever you say, if I can." She swept her hair back from her face and her smile came out more like a grimace on her pale face. "I'm desperate. As you can see."

Barbara reached over and held Amelia's hand. It felt cold to the touch.

Jean bit her lower lip as she peered at Amelia. "Studies have shown that MS-like symptoms can be associated with certain foods. So I'd like to suggest you remove those for at least a month and see what happens. You said you drink a lot of diet soda and use sugar substitutes. Also caffeine. I want you to quit drinking any sodas, diet or not, and eliminate sugar substitutes completely from your diet. No more caffeine. Not even regular tea. I want you to drink pure water, not tap water. Barbara, do you have an R/O system?"

"Yes, we wouldn't be without it."

"I want you to drink at least 55 ounces of water a day. Keep a chart if you have to. Get your Mom to help you. And I recommend that you get a copy of the book *Your Body's Many Cries For Water*. It isn't the smoothest read, but it is very convincing about dehydration causing all kinds of symptoms that appear to be diseases, but are just signs that your body needs water. Here's what it looks like." She pushed a worn paperback across her desktop, and Amelia and Barbara leaned forward to look at it. It wasn't a thick book.

"I'll be glad to read it," said Barbara. "Amelia is so tired these days. Maybe I could summarize it for her."

"That would do fine," said Jean. "Now I'll get Ian, and we'll do a treatment on you." Jean stood up and left the room, giving them a window to converse.

"Is this OK with you?" Barbara asked.

"Mom, this is much easier than anything anyone has asked me to do, and like I said, I'm desperate enough to try." Her blue eyes were hooded with pain.

"Thanks for doing this. I don't want you to do it just for me. If you find you can't handle it, we can quit. I just thought maybe for a month, to see if it helps."

"I'm good with it."

Jean and Ian came in, and Ian shook hands and in his delightful British accent explained how the treatment would go. Amelia looked mesmerized by his voice, which had to be a good thing. He suggested that during the treatment, Barbara wait in the reception area, and when Amelia nodded her agreement, Barbara took herself out and sat down with a magazine, hoping that Amelia would have the same miraculous results she'd had. But how many miracles could one person expect?

The minutes dragged on like she was in a time warp, but finally, Amelia appeared in the reception area. She looked different. The cloud was gone from her eyes. "Amelia, how did it go?"

Jean stood behind her with a bottle of water. "Amelia, you'll need to get started with your fluids. Go home and rest. Lie down and just relax. Call me if you have any questions at all. We'll see you next week."

Amelia nodded sleepily, but she looked better. When they got in the car, Barbara couldn't wait any longer. After turning on the A/C and opening the windows to release some of the stifling heat, she turned to Amelia. "So, how do you feel?"

"I'm almost afraid to say, but the pain is gone, and I don't know, I don't feel as down. I'm not sure. But I do feel better."

Heaving a sigh of relief, Barbara started the car and headed home. "I want you to lie down when we get home. I'll take care of the kids."

"Oh, Mom, they're used to me by now. They won't be too much trouble. They can play a game or watch TV."

"Remember the girl I told you about? Becky? The granddaughter of my friends Ray and Alan? She's coming over after lunch to play. She's a sweet kid, and she doesn't have other kids to play with here, so it will be a treat. I have a movie I rented for them. I think they'll get along."

"I'm sure they will." Amelia closed her eyes. There was a peacefulness about her that made Barbara smile. Maybe, just maybe, this would work out.

* * *

HELEN, 11:15AM

Helen sat at the desk in her 'office,' the guest bedroom in her golf-course mansion. She'd finally finished writing her novel. Well, in her heart she knew she could go on improving it forever, but she was ready to say it was done. But now that she'd completed it, she was strangely reluctant to tell Alexander. He was a published author who made lots of money as a food and travel writer. He was working on his latest project on French cuisine and the lifestyle and history of Provence. He was so successful, and she was such a novice. She was afraid he'd hate what she wrote, and she couldn't bear the thought of his judgment. Worse yet, she knew if he hated her novel, he'd pretend that he liked it. What she really wanted was for him to truly like it. But it wasn't even the kind of story he read, so what could she expect?

Her desk sat at the window with a view across the lakes on the golf course to the purple mountains beyond. Alexander's office looked out on the street, as he'd playfully pointed out to her. He said it was just as well, that looking at this view would be too distracting to him, but she found it soothing and inspiring.

She drank in the view for a minute to calm her nerves, then squared her shoulders and strode down the hallway to Alexander's office, where he sat staring at his computer, his back to her. Their Siamese cat Fido was wrapped around the back of the computer. Fido's head came up, blue eyes glaring at her, but Alexander hadn't heard. "Hi," she said shyly.

He turned around and rose from his seat, ever the gentleman. His emerald eyes twinkled in welcome, and he opened his arms. "So, you've finally come out of your cocoon."

She rushed to his arms and reveled in being wrapped up tight. He smelled delicious, and his warmth stirred thoughts of his clever hands and how they could entice ecstasy from her body. She shook off the pleasant distraction and looked up into his eyes. "I finished my book."

His assessing look turned warm. "Is that so? Shall we celebrate this milestone?"

Helen's insecurities took over her voice. "I only said I finished it. I didn't say it was good."

His frown spoke volumes. He was always reminding her that she needed to stop judging herself. The habit had been ingrained by her abusive late husband, but she knew he wasn't going to speak until she changed her viewpoint, so she softened her attitude. "OK, I didn't mean it was bad, but I have no way of knowing if it's good, do I? And I never gave serious thought to what came after I finished. It's like I can't believe I got this far. I'm exhausted."

He squeezed her playfully. "Next, we get you a professional editor and an agent and a publisher. Mine doesn't publish fiction, so we'll have to research a bit. But don't worry. It's all part of the process. And you need to grow a thick skin, because no matter how good it is, it may take time to find the right publisher. They don't take your book because it's good. They take it because it fills some niche they have that needs filling, one they think will make them money. Rejection does not mean your book is unworthy of publication. You'll need to be in it for the long haul."

She felt herself retreating into her shell like a scared turtle in spite of his confidence. He'd described the process to her before, and she'd heard about it in the writing class she took, but somehow, she'd managed to convince herself that getting the book written was the hard part. Now it seemed she had another mountain to climb. *Quit borrowing trouble.* "I am happy about finishing the book."

He flashed even, white teeth in a warm smile. "Then let's be wild and have a glass of wine to celebrate, even though it's early in the day."

She chuckled and followed him into the kitchen as he reached into the wine cooler and pulled out a bottle of Sauvignon Blanc. "This will do nicely. Grab a couple glasses." He opened the bottle and filled the glasses. "Let's go out into the living room and have a toast."

His enthusiasm encouraged her, and she began to feel that she might have what it took to keep working towards her goal of being a published author. As they sat on the couch, she found the nerve to ask him. "Will you read my book? I know it's not your kind of story, but…"

He reached over and kissed her on the lips. "Of course I will. And I promise to tell you the truth about how I like it, but you're right, it isn't my usual kind of book, so I'm not really your audience. But I won't read it until the editor is done with it, and that will probably take months."

Her jaw hit the floor. "That long?"

"We need to find a good one, and they tend to be busy. But you're not in a hurry, and having it edited properly will make it more likely to get a contract."

"That makes sense."

"Meanwhile, you can began on the sequel."

"Sequel?" she squeaked. She'd barely thought beyond finishing this one. She moodily sipped her wine.

"Well, you want to write more than one book, don't you?"

"I guess so. But I hadn't planned on making this a series." Her mind cast about for ways to continue to the story, but she came up blank. Maybe she was lacking in creativity. "This story was based on my life experience, and I'm not sure how I can expand it into a series." He seemed to think she was as prolific with ideas as he was.

"You'll figure something out. Or maybe you can start something totally new." He gulped the last of his wine and started to rise. She could tell he was ready to go back to work. She wished she could be as focused as he was.

She reached over and touched his wrist. "Before you go, I want to say that I've decided that I'd like to convert the diamonds to cash and keep the money." He sat back down and stared at her.

"Are you sure?"

"Yes. There's no one to give them to, at least, not anyone whom I feel they truly belong to. I don't like looking at them anymore. I don't like thinking what they represent. But I'd like to use the money to give us the life we want together."

"As long as you're sure…"

"I am."

"Great. We'll take care of that and set a date to go to St. Croix. It's hurricane season, but we can keep an eye on the weather. Are you game for it?"

She felt herself relax. "I can't wait."

He stood and pulled her to her feet and hugged her again. "Congratulations, my little author." He turned and went back down the hall to his office.

She finished her wine, then glanced at the wall clock and decided to ring Mary Beth and share her news. She was pleased when her friend answered. "I'm so glad you're home. I wanted to share my good news."

Mary Beth laughed richly. "I have news for you, too. I'm glad you called. You go first."

"I finished my novel." Helen felt silly bragging about it, but Mary Beth wouldn't think she was stuck up.

"Congratulations, girl! We ought to celebrate. Let me take you out to lunch to celebrate. Any time you'd like. My treat."

"I wasn't trying to wangle an invitation, but it would be nice to have lunch together."

"We can celebrate both our news. Ethan and I have put an offer on Olivia's house. We might be neighbors before you know it."

"I'm so happy for you, Mary Beth. And for me. I will be glad to have you living next door. I haven't made any friends in this neighborhood yet. You're still planning to join our little yoga group?"

"Sure, why not? I'm not that fitness-oriented, but it should be fun. I'm looking forward to making some new friends."

"Do you think you'll get in the house before the wedding?"

"Probably not, but soon after, I hope. I am nearly ready to put Catherine's condo on the market, and Ethan and I will put his house up soon, too. There is just so much going on."

"How about the wedding plans?"

"Now that Emma has offered her back yard for the ceremony, it should go smoothly. I'm so relieved to have others present. I have no family, and Ethan's son is a real piece of work. But he will probably behave himself in a crowd of strangers…I hope."

"I sympathize, Mary Beth. My kids were pretty awful about my marrying Alexander. I still have no idea why. There was no inheritance that was being postponed for them. For a while there, I faced working at Wal-Mart until I dropped, just to pay my bills. Sometimes I wonder what it is about kids today. Oh, I didn't mean to include you in that. I forget how young you are sometimes."

Mary Beth laughed heartily. "No problem. My Mom was very traditional. I don't understand most people my age, either. How's Friday for lunch? Can I tear you away from your movie star husband?"

Helen chuckled. "He won't mind. He's pretty immersed in his latest book. He's glad that I have girlfriends and things to do."

"Italian or Chinese for lunch?"

"Chinese. No one can compete with your Italian cooking."

"Sounds good. I'll make a reservation for noon on Friday. I'll pick you up a bit before noon?"

"I'll be ready."

They hung up, and Helen wandered into the kitchen. She decided she'd make lunch today. She didn't feel quite ready to plunge into the next part of her writing journey. Maybe a chicken salad with a Thai peanut dressing on a bed of lettuce with a glass of white wine would appeal to Alexander.

Humming to herself, she began to gather the ingredients together on the counter.

* * *

SAMANTHA, 2:30PM

Samantha put the finishing touches on the Hatfields' landscape design and stared at it, envisioning how it would look after three years, after most of the plants had matured. She didn't believe in overplanting a yard just to make it look more full. That added to the maintenance costs and ended up making the yard look like a jungle, not to mention driving up the price tag. She was careful to explain to her clients that they needed to be patient and allow the yard to mature before judging it. Fortunately, that was easier now that her clients were not all retired. She hadn't heard the joke about not buying green bananas even once since starting to work at Temple Landscaping.

She checked her watch and decided to clean her desk and head home. Her 'office' was a small room with a battered metal desk and old office chair and nothing else. The worst part of it was her back was to the door, and she had trouble concentrating because of that. There was no way she could rearrange the furniture to allow her to face the door, so she just put up with it. Her boss Jack didn't have a much bigger office, though he did have a nice bookshelf, a second chair for visitors and wall space for a few pictures. Well, she didn't spend a lot of time here anyway.

She hadn't stood or turned to face the door, but the silence had softened, and she knew someone was standing in the doorway. Her heart began to race, a blood vessel in her neck tapping a drumbeat. She swiveled her chair slowly, not wanting to show her alarm. Jack's tall frame filled the doorway, making the room shrink even more.

"Hi," she said lamely.

His crooked grin answered her, mischief in his dark eyes. She caught a whiff of aftershave over a hint of male sweat, a surprisingly pleasant combination on him.

"I was just getting ready to leave," she managed to blurt.

48

"I'm glad I caught you." A twinkling in his eyes said he wanted to do more than catch her.

She sighed. "Please don't make it hard on me."

He raised one eyebrow, giving his chiseled face a sardonic look. "Why not? You make it hard on me."

She wasn't going to grace that comment with a response.

He folded his arms across his broad chest. "You know, I could bring Beau to visit your Mom during the week some night. I don't have to wait for the weekend. Don't you go over after work sometimes?"

She swallowed and nodded. "Yes, I go over most nights for a little while, or at least call her. But there's no way she won't suspect something if you do that. No boss would do that for an employee. I think she's already suspicious, although she hasn't said anything. Arthur hardly ever comes with me, but you can't assume that. If he saw you there on a weeknight, he'd explode."

"I want to see you more often. During working hours, we have too much work to do. I want to be able to spend time outside of work with you."

She wanted that, too, but even if they did nothing wrong, meeting him without telling her husband was stupid. "I know I told you I was planning to divorce Arthur, but that right now wasn't the time, with Mom dying of cancer. I know it's hard to wait. It is for me, too. I just want to do this the right way. I want to be able to get to know you, even to date, before we jump into something bigger. I've been worrying about your offer to put me up when I leave Arthur. I can't accept. I have to live on my own somehow. It would mess up the divorce if I went to you when I leave him. I haven't figured out where I'll go, but I can't live with you until after the divorce is finalized. And the more I think about it, the more I want us to have a chance to get to know one another more before either of us commits to anything long term."

His eyes darkened as he scowled. "You aren't changing your mind about us, are you?"

"No, of course, not." She drew in a ragged breath. "I just don't want to rush into anything. It wouldn't be good for either of us."

"I know we haven't had the luxury of dating. But working with you,

49

taking the class with you, seeing you with your Mom is enough for me. We belong together."

Not 'I love you,' but not too bad. Samantha believed her feelings for Jack were more than an infatuation or a distraction from her flagging marriage, but she wanted to be sure. She wanted a real, lasting love and partnership this time, and she wasn't going to settle for less. "I'm not disagreeing. I don't mean to sound like I'm backpedaling. I'm not." She began to wring her hands. She couldn't get enough air. "I need to go."

Instead of stepping back, Jack stepped into the office, eating up all the remaining space. He leaned down and kissed her on the cheek, setting her heart aflutter. Then he trailed his finger down the side of her face and kissed her gently on the lips. Before she could react, he was gone. It wasn't much as kisses went, but she got the message. It was a claiming kind of kiss, like a husband does to a wife in public, even though there were no spectators. She was strangely reassured by his territorial behavior. She couldn't recall Arthur ever kissing her in public. He didn't even like to hold hands. Not that she wanted anyone to see Jack kiss her. That could be disastrous. But her office was out of the way. He must have made sure no one was nearby. She hoped he had.

Samantha gathered her belongings and left for home. At least the long drive gave her lots of time to think. Too bad she couldn't find the answers she sought, regardless of how much thinking she did.

* * *

STEVEN, 2:55PM

She sat on the opposite side of the circle of chairs from Steven, her blue eyes cast down, her hands knit together nervously. People continued to filter in to the small room, but no one was conversing. Everyone seemed shy and withdrawn. He was struggling to overcome his shock at seeing his new neighbor at the first meeting of the support group. What kind of trauma was Marilyn recovering from? She'd seemed reserved at dinner with Barbara and Ben, but he would never have guessed she had a secret history like him. At just that moment, she looked up, straight into his eyes, as if she were aware of his attention. A fleeting smile crossed her face, then she cast her eyes back down, obviously as uncomfortable as he was to be here.

Steven wondered for a second if Barbara was matchmaking, but no, it couldn't be that. Why would she think two wounded people belonged together? Besides, Marilyn didn't seem damaged. At dinner the other night, she'd finally displayed a warm sense of humor once her guard was down, and she was obviously intelligent. She appeared fit and moved with a quiet grace. Her hair was gray, and she had some lines on her face, but there was an elegance about her that lent her an ageless quality. If he'd been in the market, he wouldn't have minded dating her.

He couldn't stop himself from comparing her to Tanya. Tanya militantly bleached her hair her whole life. She'd fought getting old with a boob job, a facelift and just about every expensive anti-aging cream on the market. She'd dressed like a hooker, always in those ridiculous spiked heels and low-cut blouses, probably to convince herself she still had it. She'd needed constant reinforcement from men about her desirability. With chagrin, he acknowledged that his refusal to pay her the attention she demanded was one reason she took to having affairs. And that had led to her murder.

He wondered. What was he going to reveal here today? He couldn't bear the thought of being the one to tell Marilyn she was living in a house once owned by a serial killer. Someone would tell her. Someday. But it didn't have to be him. He had no designs on her, but that would surely kill any chance he had with her if he bore the bad news. Not that she'd be interested in him.

A woman marched into the room and sat in the chair which occupied the center of the circle. She looked to be about 45 and wore a navy blue pants suit with a white silk blouse. The only spot of color in her ensemble was a red handkerchief peeking out of her jacket pocket. Wire-rimmed glasses and minimal makeup contributed to the no-nonsense air she radiated. Her dark hair was tamed in a tight bun at the base of her neck, and her only jewelry was a gold pendant with a shape he couldn't decipher and an expensive-looking gold wristwatch, which she glanced at. She clapped her hands together. "Can everyone please take a seat?"

Quickly, the few standing attendees grabbed seats. "My name is Mary Jennings," she began, "and for the next several weeks, I'll be facilitating this group session. Each of you has had a trauma in your life that you want to heal. This is a safe place where you can be totally honest, tell as little or as much of what's going on as you wish, and get unconditional support. I only have one ground rule. This is a place of non-judgment and safety. If you feel judgmental towards anyone, keep it to yourself. We will only speak with support and compassion. Nothing said in this room gets repeated outside of it. Can we all agree to that?" She looked around sternly and got affirmative nods and murmurs. "Shall we start? Please tell us your first name and a little bit about why you are here." She pointed at Steven like he was a student in her class, and she wanted him to give the answer. Suddenly, he felt like he was on the spot. He hadn't even rehearsed what he was going to say, in part, because he didn't really want to be here. He had imagined coming one time, just so he could tell Barbara he gave it a whirl. Well, now he was stuck. He had to tell his story.

He remained seated and mentally squirmed. He didn't want to be horrible about Tanya, but he still felt anger towards her. How much should he share? All eyes were looking at him, and he imagined they were relieved that he was going first.

He cleared his throat. "My name is Steven. Around last Thanksgiving, I decided to divorce my wife. We'd been married since we were very young, and we have a couple kids, but they're adults. We'd grown apart over the years, and she took to drinking and having affairs. We fought a lot. We no longer had anything in common. She began an affair with a man who lived in Palm Lakes, and I got fed up and demanded a divorce." He glanced up and saw all eyes riveted on him. He dragged in a breath. "That's not why I'm here. She didn't fight the divorce, other than to try and take me to the cleaners." There were a few muted chuckles and murmurs of support. "I got her set up in a condo here in Palm Lakes, and she began to see her lover on the quiet to avoid losing her alimony payments. It all sounds so sordid and commonplace until I get to the part where it turned out her lover was a serial killer who had murdered at least 18 women in the Southwest over the past 10 to 15 years. Probably more, but those were the ones they managed to prove after he was shot by a Posse guy in the middle of murdering my wife—my ex-wife."

Mouths hung open and some eyes were filled with sympathy. Other people had the look of vultures who wanted to hear all the gory details.

But the only reaction he wanted to see was Marilyn's. Shock filled her face, her jaw slightly open and eyes wide but brimming with compassion. Why it mattered to him what she thought, he didn't know. He was just so tired of being a loser.

Sweat had begun to trickle down his back in spite of the chill air, and he rubbed his thighs tensely, unsure how much to reveal. He wasn't comfortable talking about feelings. He coughed and then continued. "I didn't love her anymore. Her verbal abusiveness and drinking were out of control. But if I hadn't divorced her just then, she might still be alive. I know it isn't my fault she was murdered; even though at times I hated her, I never wished her dead. Especially not at the hands of that maniac. But I feel somehow responsible for her death, and I'm angry with her for putting me in this position. I can't seem to dig myself out of the hole I'm in."

He shut down. This was the first time he'd shared his feelings in public, and he was wrung out with the effort. He nodded to Mary. "That's all I want to say."

An elderly woman raised her hand tentatively. Mary pointed to her, and the wrinkled woman spoke in a clear voice. "Young man, I'm so sorry about what happened, but you really need to stop feeling responsible. It isn't your fault."

Murmurs of agreement swelled through the group. Mary chimed in. "Steven, thank you for sharing your story with us. We know how hard that was." She glanced at the elderly woman, then back at Steven. "I think Steven knows what you said is right, don't you, Steven? But knowing it in your head is not the same as feeling it in your heart. Survivor's guilt is bad enough, but Steven has other feelings he's trying to resolve. Steven, we're here for you if we can help." Everyone nodded and affirmed what Mary said.

They proceeded in clockwise fashion around the circle, but having laid himself open so completely, Steven didn't even hear what others were saying until it came to Marilyn's turn. Then he snapped out of his funk.

"My name is Marilyn. I recently moved to Palm Lakes from Virginia." She dropped her eyes to the floor and paused, as if trying to gather her thoughts or her courage. "I came here to escape an abusive relationship. I don't want my ex to know where I am. He's very scary. He used to beat me up regularly, but I left after he put me in the hospital. He stalked me and threatened me when I left him, and he abused his power as a cop. I had to get away, and I did my best to just disappear, but who knows whether he'll find me? I just want to start a new life. But I'm not sure I will ever feel safe, and that's why I'm here. My neighbor suggested that I get some support so I wouldn't feel so all alone. I think that's the hard part. I don't have family or friends to turn to, and I want a support network and to build a new life. That's all."

Steven was gobsmacked. Marilyn looked so normal, for lack of a better term. She'd endured much more than he had, yet she somehow managed to pick up and move across country, get and train a dog and begin a new life. His admiration for her soared. But somewhere in there, he felt like a loser for being mired in self-pity for months over Tanya's murder.

He looked in her eyes as she continued to share her story, but hardly heard the words. She was truly amazing. He was suddenly aware that she was a very attractive woman. He hadn't responded to a woman that way in years. Maybe he was coming back to life, too. He smiled to himself and sat back in his chair, glad he had attended.

The session continued after a couple people offered Marilyn advice, comments and support, and the rest of the circle told their stories. At 3:45, everyone had finished sharing, and Mary called an end to the session and asked that they meet again next week, after thanking them and reminding them of the confidential nature of what they'd shared. Steven hadn't planned to come a second time, but now that Marilyn was there and asked for support from the group, he had a motive to come back. He liked her and wanted to get to know her better. He also felt the urge to protect her. He hadn't been able to keep Tanya safe, but maybe he could help Marilyn.

As the crowd moved slowly towards the doors, Steven tried to catch up with Marilyn. Just outside in the hall, he pulled up beside her. Then he wasn't sure what to say. He didn't want to appear to be accosting her. She'd just gotten out of an abusive relationship, for God's sake. Tongue-tied, he walked beside her out into the sweltering heat of the parking lot. She smiled shyly at him. "I didn't know you'd be here."

He shrugged his shoulders. "I almost didn't come, but I promised Barbara I'd give it a shot."

"When I told her a little about my history, she insisted I come, too. I don't know how much it can help, but I do need to create a support network, and this seemed as good a start as any." Her sparkly blue eyes showed no fear, but he now knew she buried it deep.

Without even thinking, he blurted out, "The coffee shop here makes a decent cup of coffee. Want to get one?"

Her apologetic smile felled him. "If you don't mind, I feel all talked out for today. Maybe next time?"

"Sure, sure," he blathered. *What an idiot I am!* "I didn't mean to impose." He turned to head towards where he'd parked, but she put a restraining hand on his arm.

"I only meant that I don't feel like I'm good company right now. This is the first time I ever told anyone about my past. I just want to go home and rest a bit."

He sighed. "I know what you mean. I never said it out loud myself. I've been stewing for months, getting nowhere. It feels good to put it out there, but it's also enervating."

"Exactly. See you next week in the session? Maybe we can go for coffee after."

He grinned hopefully. "Absolutely."

* * *

MARY BETH, 6:50PM

Mary Beth could hear Ethan in the kitchen loading the dishwasher. She loved how he pitched in around the house. Her ex had never lifted a finger in the kitchen even though they both worked. On one memorable occasion, he pointed to the busy highway outside their tiny apartment and said, "When you see an iceberg driving down Rt 143, that's when I'll do women's work." Maybe Ethan had learned skills since he'd been a widower for years, but she was pretty sure it was more than that. He was just a better man than her stupid ex. She was lucky to have him.

Mary Beth glanced around Ethan's living room at the evidence of her only reservation about their relationship. The framed photos of Ethan and his family still cluttered every flat surface. She hadn't broached the topic of how it made her feel out of place, surrounded by all these memories that she had no part in. She didn't want him to feel he had to throw out his past. But she sure wished there weren't so many pictures. Maybe when they moved, she could ask him to keep them in a guest room or something.

Being so picky made her feel like a bitch. Sighing with frustration, she walked into the kitchen, where Ethan was bent over the dishwasher with a large pot in his hand. She stroked his back, and he stood up fast, startled. He must not have heard her come in. Maybe she should suggest he get his hearing checked.

He turned loving gray eyes on her. "That was some meal. I'm going to have to watch what I eat." He patted his paunch and grimaced. "My metabolism isn't like it used to be."

"That makes two of us," said Mary Beth, wrapping her arms around him. "I love you just the way you are."

He grinned at that, and she was grateful that his self-doubt seemed to be diminishing.

"I was going to go see Maddie and Olivia and ask if they're coming to the wedding. Mostly, I just want to say hi to Maddie. She's fading a bit." She bit her lip at the thought of losing yet another maternal figure in her life.

Ethan hugged her tightly. "I'm so sorry you're going through this again. I know Maddie has been special to you. Give her my best. I'm not her favorite person, so I'll stay home."

Mary Beth play punched him on the upper arm. "She's just ornery. She appreciated all you did for her when you were with The Helpers. She'd have been lost otherwise."

"Still, she couldn't bring herself to say thanks and most of the time was prickly with me. I know she meant no harm, but I think you'll have a nicer visit without me there. She doesn't approve of the age difference between us."

"Well, she isn't the one marrying you. I am. And I'm not worried. She'll have to get used to it." Not that Maddie was going to be around long enough to get used to anything. Mary Beth felt her eyes filling. "I won't be long."

Ethan released her and kissed her on the cheek. "When you get back, we'll have a nice glass of chianti to finish off that bottle."

"Sounds like a plan." She gathered her purse and keys and drove to Desert Breezes. The sun was low on the horizon and the heat a smothering blanket as she got out of her car. The visitor parking lot was largely empty at this time of day, and she hoped that Samantha would be there, as she often came by to spend time with her mother after dinner. Arthur and Maddie didn't get on well, and he rarely came, so she might get a chance to visit with her friend. She hadn't seen a lot of Samantha since she'd left Palo Verde Landscaping, where they'd both worked.

After signing in at the desk, Mary Beth waited for the elevator. It was a slow one and always taxed her nerves. No one was in sight. The hallway was deathly quiet. When she knocked on Maddie's door, she heard a muffled, "Come in." Maddie didn't leave the door locked except at night so she didn't have to expend energy answering it.

As she stepped into the apartment, she saw that Olivia and Maddie were seated at the small dining table playing Yahtzee. It warmed her heart that Olivia had taken Maddie under her wing. Maddie was so eccentric, she had trouble making and keeping friends.

She stepped up behind Maddie's seat. "Who's winning?"

Olivia threw three 5s, then on her next throw, a fourth 5, and on her final toss with the remaining die, another 5. Both ladies whooped in joy. It obviously wasn't a competition. "Yahtzee," said Olivia.

"Well done," said Maddie. That's your second one this game. You're on a roll."

"I'm winning," Olivia grinned sheepishly. "If only I had this kind of luck with the lottery."

Maddie snorted, then got into a coughing fit. Tethered to her oxygen tank, she seemed to be getting enough oxygen, but Mary Beth was concerned about the shortness of breath. She patted Maddie gently on the back. "Take it easy there. We don't want to have to call the paramedics."

"Then don't make me laugh again," ordered Maddie. "Have a seat. Pour yourself a glass of wine or have a beer while we finish this game. We're nearly done. We play after dinner. I reheated some of Samantha's beef stew. It was my night to cook." She cackled at the joke and then started hacking again, and Mary Beth stroked her back until she got her breath.

Mary Beth popped open a beer as much to placate Maddie as for thirst and sat in one of the two other chairs at the dinette table. The game was quickly ended, with Olivia the winner by over 100 points, but Maddie didn't seem to care.

Mary Beth was glad she had the company. "I wanted to see you, but also to ask both of you if you're coming to my wedding on Sunday the 4th of August."

"I'd be pleased to attend," said Olivia.

"I would, too, but I'm not getting around well these days. I huff and puff just walking from here to the bathroom, and I'm attached to that oxygen tank. I think it's best if I stay home." Maddie seemed genuinely disappointed.

"I understand. It's bound to be quite hot, and that might be too much for you, but I'll send you a plate from the reception via Olivia, or Samantha, if she's planning to see you after. Barbara's hosting the reception at her house. Helen says she really knows how to put on a spread."

Maddie nodded, "She always invited me and Stanley to her parties, but we never went. He was such a picky eater and didn't like to socialize. But I heard from Helen that she always had great food. I'm sure it will be very nice."

Mary Beth warmed to the subject. "I'm excited about being able to get married in Emma's yard. They say it's beautiful, and that way, I don't have to worry about William making a scene. At least I hope not."

Olivia huffed. "We won't allow that. You just point me at him if he needs a talking to. He has no right to ruin your wedding."

Mary Beth smiled at the support. "I don't think it will be necessary, but he's all yours if he acts up."

Maddie clucked her tongue. "Kids these days…"

They dissolved into laughter, interrupted by a knock on the door. "That must be Samantha," said Maddie. "Come in," she yelled.

Samantha entered, her greenish blue eyes taking in the scene. "Looks like a party. Why wasn't I invited?"

"We just finished our Yahtzee game after our meal of your stew. We're alternately hosting dinner."

Olivia stood. "I ought to be going. It was a great meal. Thanks, Maddie. Thanks for making the stew, Samantha. I have a book calling me. I'll see you tomorrow, Maddie. You take care."

Maddie regarded Olivia with watery blue eyes. "I'll do that." Olivia departed. "Have a drink, Samantha."

Samantha seemed distracted, but she took a beer out of the fridge and popped the top. She and Mary Beth hovered while Maddie drew herself up and shuffled over to her recliner. Thank heaven the oxygen line was long enough to let her go anywhere in the room without dragging the tank around. "Samantha, bring me my beer if you don't mind." Samantha retrieved Maddie's beer from the table.

Mary Beth decided to fill Samantha in. "I was telling them about the wedding. Olivia's coming, but Maddie can't. Will you be able to come, Samantha? Arthur is welcome, too, if he wants."

"I'm planning on attending, but I don't know about Arthur. Can I let you know later?"

"Hell, yeah. No problem."

The visit continued for another 30 minutes, mostly with details of the upcoming wedding, but also with a promise from Mary Beth that she'd bring more food and was planning to do jewelry this Saturday with Maddie, which seemed to lift Maddie's spirits. She couldn't help noticing that Samantha seemed off in another world the whole time.

When they left together, Mary Beth could contain herself no longer. "Come over to my condo. I have a bottle of wine there. We can chat for a few minutes if you like."

The elevator opened to the lobby floor. Samantha sighed. "I do need someone to talk to. But I can't stay long. Arthur knows I won't stay here past a certain time, and I don't want him wondering where I've gone."

"Surely you have a right to spend time with me if you wish?" Mary Beth was indignant that Arthur was being a pain.

"It isn't that. It's just that he'd wonder if that's where I really was, and even if you alibied me, he might not believe it." They walked out to where Samantha had parked her red Temple Landscaping pickup. "I really ought to go home."

Mary Beth wasn't about to let that happen. "We can just sit and talk in your car if you like."

Samantha's eyes were brimming with tears. "That would be nice." She got into the driver's side, and Mary Beth hopped into the passenger seat, ignoring how the plastic burned her bare legs.

"So what's going on that has you so upset?"

Samantha seemed to consider her answer. "I can't make it much longer with Arthur. He's been getting more and more difficult since I took the job with Jack, even though he pushed me to. Even though nothing has happened between me and Jack. I feel like I'm walking on eggshells all the time. Arthur finds fault in everything I do. I know it's been hard with Mom having lung cancer. They don't get along, and I spend a lot of time with her after work. But he seems to resent the time I spend at the job I like and with Mom. Not that he ever says as much." She put her hands on the steering wheel and clenched it. "Jack wants me to leave Arthur and come live with him. That's unrealistic and stupid, but I'd love to." She shook her head and banged the steering wheel with a fist. "Why do things have to be so complicated?"

Listening to her, Mary Beth had a brainstorm. "Look, I don't know when you plan to split, but Ethan and I are putting in a bid on a house. It's next door to Helen, and it's big. If you leave Arthur, you can either stay at Catherine's condo or with us in the new house. You won't be any trouble. I am selling the condo, but until I get it on the market, you can use it."

Samantha sighed with relief. "I can't tell you how much that takes off me. I can't afford a hotel, and I basically don't have anyone to turn to. If I stayed in Palm Lakes, it would also keep things looking good. I want to have a chance to get to know Jack after I leave Arthur. He doesn't seem to need that, but I do. I don't want to jump from the frying pan into the fire. It's so complicated with Jack. He's my boss. If things go wrong, I don't have a job."

"You could easily get your job back at Palo Verde," suggested Mary Beth.

"Maybe, but once my Mom goes, I won't have any ties to the area. I didn't mean that how it sounded. You're here, and you're the closest thing I have to a sister. But you're the only one. And if things don't work out with Jack, where would I work and live? Besides, I don't want to chance seeing Arthur all the time, but I have nothing closer to town. It's beginning to creep me out. It seems like such a risk I'm taking, and there are no guarantees it will work out."

Mary Beth wasn't sure what to say. "I haven't had much to do with

Jack, but what I've seen and heard makes me think he's OK. And you have a place with me for as long as you need it."

"You don't think Ethan would mind having me there? You guys are just getting married. You'd probably like some privacy."

"We'll be fine. He knows you are my only same-age friend here, and I know he'll support my offer. You'll be working five days a week anyhow, and hopefully spending some evenings and weekends with Jack and Maddie. You just need an official place to live, right?"

Light seemed to dawn in Samantha's eyes. "Yes, that's true. I wouldn't have to be underfoot a lot. Thanks for the offer. I accept. I've been holding off making plans because I had no idea where I'd go."

"Now you know. You want a glass of wine?"

"Nah. I better head home. Tomorrow's a work day. I'm pretty beat."

"OK, but remember I'm here for anything. I'm not working anymore, so I have time on my hands."

"Must be nice being a lady of leisure."

"I could get used to it." Mary Beth let herself out the passenger door and slammed it shut. "See you later, for sure at the wedding, right?"

"I wouldn't miss it for the world." Samantha beamed at her, looking and sounding much lighter, and waved goodbye as she drove away.

# 4
# SUNDAY, AUGUST 4, 1996

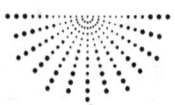

JACK, 10:45AM

*J*ack wiped the sweat from his brow as he bent down to pick up the tennis ball he'd been throwing for Beau, the yellow Lab he'd acquired from Sam's mother. The dog focused all his attention on Jack, or rather, on the ball in Jack's hand, seemingly oblivious to the humidity of the monsoon weather.

"One more throw, fella? I don't want to give you heat stroke. I think you'd keep chasing it as long as I kept throwing it." A vigorous body wag indicated an affirmative. Jack drew his hand back, faked a throw that failed to distract Beau, then tossed the ball to the far end of the yard, where it bounced several times before Beau caught up and snagged it. Fairly bursting with joy, Beau trotted back to Jack, then placed the ball at his feet.

Jack leaned down to pick up the ball and stroked Beau's head. "You're a good man, Beau. That's all for now. Get a drink." Beau went over to the dish that sat in the shade of the patio and lapped up some water, splashing more on the concrete than he swallowed. Then he watched in rapture as water dripping off his muzzle created ripples in the surface of the remaining water. He plunged his muzzle in to chase them and began the process again. His engagement with the process was so complete, Jack didn't have the heart to stop him. At least the mess was outdoors and would dry up fast. Must be a Labrador trait being so fond of water.

Jack reached for the glass of ice water on the nearby table and chugged it down. Funny how even humidity of 28% felt positively drenching at 105 degrees. The monsoon was the only time Jack broke a sweat without exercising. He couldn't imagine living back East or in the South. Sam came from Maryland, and she told him summer was pretty awful there, with your clothes plastered to your body a lot of the time. Thank heaven it was rarely like that here.

Thinking of Sam triggered the frustration he'd been burying. It was so irritating to wait on the sidelines while she sorted out her life. He understood she was under a lot of stress with her mother dying of cancer and having to get her Mom's house sold. She'd had to learn a whole new routine at his landscaping company but had picked it up like a champ. She made work look easy, but then told him it was hard to do what was needed to get out of her unhappy marriage. Was there a chance she wasn't really serious about him? He didn't like to dwell on that thought.

He set the empty glass down on the table, then slumped into a nearby chair. Beau came over and set his massive head in Jack's lap, and Jack petted him and watched as Beau's eyes shut in ecstasy at the attention. "It doesn't take much to please you, does it, big fella? Do you think Sam will like living here?" He stared out across the yard, assessing it from Sam's point of view. His subdivision of one-acre lots was old, the plantings well established and the covenants forbidding further subdivision. A massive palo verde tree graced his back yard, not even threatening to touch the walls that marked the border of his property, unlike similar trees in newer communities that had to be pruned back constantly. A hummingbird feeder hung from its branches like the one that hung above him on the patio.

"Our yard is much nicer than hers, isn't it, Beau? Not that I've seen Sam's. But I know her yard is way smaller, and the plants are not full grown. I've done a nice job of landscaping mine. Do you think she'll like it?" He didn't wait for an answer, but took his glass and went back inside, pausing for Beau to come through the doorway before shutting the sliding glass door and locking it.

This was the part he wasn't sure she'd like. The property was big and well-landscaped, but the house was old. A typical rancher, it didn't have any frills or fancy decor. It was clean and neat, but when he regarded it critically, he had to admit it was obvious a bachelor lived here. There were no soft touches. Just venetian blinds on the windows and functional furniture that was verging on scruffy. The harder he looked, the more concerned he became. He had never seen Sam's house, for obvious reasons, but it had to be at least fifteen years younger than his. On the outside, his house looked more than respectable, with its white stucco walls and red tile roof in good repair, even if the look was far from unique. No, it was the inside that needed help, but Jack didn't have the funds to change anything, even if he knew what to do.

As he walked from room to room trying to convince himself Sam would be happy giving up her Palm Lakes home to live with him, Beau followed, toenails clicking on the saltillo tile floor. The kitchen was spacious, thanks to the home being old, and the dining room flowed from the kitchen in an open plan that gave a sense of space. The living room, what they might call a great room now, was also spacious, not dwarfed by the large television that represented one of Jack's few splurges. The leather furniture was in decent shape, but the room had no color, and the few pictures hanging on the wall were just prints he'd picked up somewhere.

He trailed down the narrow hallway, looking into the bedrooms one by one. There were three, along with two baths. The larger bath adjoined the master bedroom, and the other was between the remaining two bedrooms. One bedroom was his exercise room. He wondered if Sam would want the space for something else. The third bedroom, set up as a guest bedroom, didn't get much use, as he had few visitors. The master bedroom was spacious enough for his king bed. Still, no curtains or fancy shades covered the windows, and there were no decorations. A bookshelf held lots of books on one wall, and an old oak dresser with a mirror covered the other. He perused the book titles as he ran a finger along the spines. Some thrillers, mysteries, lots of botanical guides and textbooks from college, a handful of books on how to run a small business.

He looked around the bedroom, imagining Sam in the bed amidst a tangle of sheets, her hair spread across the pillow and a sated look on her face. That was the future he wanted to focus on.

Galvanized to do something to prepare for Sam's eventual arrival, Jack rearranged his dresser to free up half the drawers. He carried the extra clothes he couldn't fit into his drawers into the walk-in closet. He was sure this wasn't as big as they made them now, but he'd installed lots of shelving, and he'd never filled it, so clearing out half of it was pretty easy. The whole time he worked, Beau watched him with interest.

When he finished, he was sweating again. He wished Sam was here. Sam was at a wedding which was taking place in a friend's back yard today. He'd been invited, but he didn't like the idea of putting Sam on the spot, even if her friends knew about him. He knew Mary Beth did. And what if Arthur changed his mind at the last minute and showed up? What would Jack have done then? It just wasn't worth it. But it underlined the annoying truth that he was the 'other man' at this point, and he didn't like it.

Well, at least he was ready for her to move in, if that ever happened. He looked at Beau, who continued to stare at him. "Do you think she'll like living here with us?" Beau cocked his head, but said nothing. "I know she saw it when she brought you over here, but I could tell she wasn't looking much. She was so nervous, I bet she doesn't remember anything about the place. She couldn't wait to leave. Probably thought I was going to jump her." He grinned—the thought had crossed his mind at the time—then sighed, signaling for Beau to follow him back down the hall.

He knew what was bugging him. He wanted to be Sam's man, publicly and privately, and he was tired of waiting. The months since she had accepted his job offer felt like years. It wasn't enough that he saw her every weekday, that they worked together. He wanted to accompany her to social occasions and watch her interact with her friends. He wanted to be able to reach out and touch her whenever he felt like it, wherever they were.

It was in that instant that he knew what he would do. Sam's Mom was lonely, and she wasn't going to the wedding, and she loved it when he brought Beau over for a visit. Arthur never went to visit Maddie alone, so it would be safe to go today. And maybe, if he got lucky, Sam would show up after the wedding.

"What do you say we go see Maddie?" Beau didn't respond. "Want to go for a ride?" That got him going. Beau jumped up, wagged his tail and barked several times, heading for the door to the garage. "OK, give me a minute and we'll go." He was pretty sure Beau knew where they were going.

He took a quick shower and changed into better clothes and headed out. He stopped by his business on the way and put together a makeshift bouquet of flowers from the containers on the front porch of the office building. It looked homemade enough that Maddie probably would not rant about it. She didn't like store-bought flowers. Said they were a waste of money. But what woman didn't like flowers? The drive to Palm Lakes went swiftly, with him thinking of Sam the whole way, and how and when they would begin their life together.

The woman at the desk at Desert Breezes knew Jack by now and signed him in after reaching over to pet Beau, who had become a welcome visitor due to his winning personality.

When Jack knocked on Maddie's door, a tremulous voice asked who it was. "It's me. Jack Temple. I brought Beau for a visit."

"Oh, come in."

As soon as he entered and slipped Beau off the leash, the dog scrambled over to Maddie and threw himself on the floor at her feet, presenting his belly for a rub. Maddie couldn't reach over that far, so Beau got up and accepted a pat on the head. "Oh, I'm so glad to see you. Both of you. Samantha had to go to the wedding, and I wanted to, but it's just too much trouble dragging this tank around, and she was worried about the heat."

Maddie seemed put out at being left out of the wedding, so Jack held out the flowers, and after a brief scowl, she smiled. "Why don't you put them in some water? I don't have a vase, but maybe a tall glass or something."

"No problem, I'll find something for them." He couldn't find anything suitable in the cupboards, but then decided the empty wine bottle on the counter would work. By the time he had rearranged the flowers and filled the bottle with water, he had a satisfactory little bouquet, which he placed on the small dining table. "How's this?" he asked as he centered it on the table.

"That'll do." Maddie gave him a rare smile. "What are you doing here? You didn't have to come all that way for me."

"Why the heck not? You're worth it, aren't you?"

She cackled at his flirting. Then she coughed for a minute, and he was worried she'd hurt herself. "Are you OK?"

"No, I'm dying," she replied. It chilled him how calmly she said it. He had no idea how to respond. "Sorry I said that. It always upsets people when I say it out loud. I guess we're all headed the same place. I just know I'm getting there sooner rather than later." She sounded resigned, but he didn't miss the sadness underneath the bravado.

"I knew you'd be alone, and you might need some cheering up, or at least some company, and Beau here is really good at that."

She laughed, then pointed at the refrigerator. "Help yourself to a beer. It's past 11am, so it's OK. Get me one while you're at it."

He obliged and brought them each back a cold Bud. He sat down, wondering for the first time what they'd talk about. He'd never been here alone before. It was easier letting Sam guide the conversation in topics that her mother found calming. "Is there anything on TV today?"

"This time of year, nothing that I'm interested in except old movies. But before you distract me, I have a question for you."

Maddie's tone brought him up short. He felt an inquisition coming on. "What's that?"

"You know what I'm going to ask. What are you planning to do with my daughter?"

Maddie was no slouch in the brains department. "You mean are my intentions honorable?"

That won him another cackling followed by a hacking cough as Maddie struggled to get her breath. "That's about it."

"Well, since you asked, I'll tell you. But I hope you'll keep it to yourself. I want to marry her. But it isn't all that easy to proceed, given she's already married."

"To that zero?" Maddie wasn't easy on her son-in-law.

"I've never met the guy, but I get the impression Sam isn't happy. She doesn't like hurting people, and also, she doesn't want to be far from you. I totally understand that, but it has me hovering around her, waiting for things to get resolved."

"And that isn't easy for you?"

"No. I prefer action. Waiting is hard, not knowing what will happen."

Maddie gave him a penetrating stare, and he tried not to wilt under it.

67

"I love her." It had been hard to say out loud to someone other than Sam. But it needed saying.

"That's what I was waiting to hear. If you love her, she's worth waiting for. I'm not long for this world, and once I'm gone, she'll have no reason to stay in Palm Lakes. My house will sell either way. I never liked Arthur. I think he married her as a trophy wife. Isn't that what they call it when an old guy marries a younger woman just to make himself feel he's still young?"

Jack nodded. It matched his assessment, and he'd never even met the guy.

"I'm not saying he's a bad person. But he's wrong for my daughter. I wish she'd get herself shucked of him and start over. I was no kind of example for her, staying with her father all those years, but it's a different world now, and Samantha is far more competent than I ever was, in so many ways. She should be happy. But all she does is work and take care of people." Maddie struggled to get her breath. "I need to stop talking. Let's see if we can find a movie worth watching."

Jack grinned at her and held up his beer in salute. "Whatever you choose is fine with me and Beau."

* * *

MARY BETH, 11:50AM

"It's hot as hell," Mary Beth muttered as she stepped off Emma's patio into the bright sunlight.

"You got that right," commented Ethan, his gray eyes twinkling at her language.

"Sorry, I couldn't help myself. I'm already melting." She fanned her face in a futile gesture. "I'll need to stay in the shade as much as possible. I'm already wilted."

"You look great to me." Ethan put his arm around her shoulders. "Nervous?"

Thank heaven his eyes shone with confidence. "Hell, no. I'm ready and eager. But I'm staying in the shade until the ceremony. I can mingle at the reception."

"I'll get you a cold drink." Ethan departed without waiting for an answer. They were already like an old married couple who read each other's minds.

Mary Beth went back to the patio and eased herself into a chair, careful not to muss her dress. She rarely wore fancy clothes, and it was annoying and exciting at the same time to be so dolled up. She was getting married! She thought the off-white silk dress went well with the black onyx necklace and earrings she'd made for the occasion. If only Mom could see her now. She distracted herself from the wave of sadness that filled her eyes with tears by studying the people milling about Emma's yard as she fingered the beads in her necklace.

Most prominent from her viewpoint were Lydia and Eric, one of the other two couples getting married, who stood at the center of the labyrinth. Lydia gazed up at Eric, whose hands were on her shoulders, her eyes shining with love. Mary Beth couldn't see his face, but his posture showed that his attention was riveted on Lydia.

Lydia caressed Eric with her eyes, those brown lights that could see invisible energies around people. Lydia called the energy around people an aura, and described it as having many colors. Mary Beth was still trying to process the revelation that Lydia could look at a person's aura and know so much about their health, emotions and even if they were evil. It was almost incredible, but then she'd asked for a reading after Lydia had shared her secret the other day. Everything Lydia saw was dead on. Not that Mary Beth had much in the way of secrets, and Lydia could have pumped Helen for facts, but, no, Helen could keep confidences. And hadn't Lydia told her she'd known Owen Schmidt was a killer just by seeing the black that permeated his aura? Her psychic awareness had prompted greater vigilance on Eric's part, leading to Owen's death during his attack on his lover, Tanya. Mary Beth shuddered at the thought of having that much sensitivity to what was going on with others. She'd always had a tendency not to notice things, which had its down side but seemed preferable to seeing too much.

She reflected that these people were going to make very interesting friends. Lydia was a psychically gifted woman married to a retired cop. Julio and Emma were a reverse May-December romance that was probably still shocking those who met them. The opposite age difference between

69

her and Ethan had prompted a negative reaction from his son, and no doubt would do the same with some people here in Palm Lakes.

The brides weren't your stereotypical grandmas. Funny how that led to the realization that none of the brides even had children. How strange was that? And neither Eric nor Julio, either.

Which reminded Mary Beth to glance in William's direction. Ethan's son stood stiffly with his wife by the citrus tree, looking like he was marking time until he could leave. And the ceremony hadn't even started.

A cold glass of water appeared in front of her. "Thanks. I need that." She smiled at Ethan and gulped a few mouthfuls, grateful for how it chilled her insides going down.

"Doesn't Emma look beautiful?" Mary Beth nodded to the left, where the ceremony was going to take place. The officiant was engaged in conversation with Emma, who was draped in an amazing royal blue dress that clung in all the right places. It was sexy but very classy. Made Mary Beth feel plain in spite of her finery, but she stomped the envy before it could grow. Ethan loved her just as she was, including the few extra pounds she couldn't seem to shed.

Her bridegroom rubbed her back and leaned down to kiss her cheek, apparently divining her thoughts. "I think you're the most beautiful woman here." His voice was so sincere, she teared up as she reached to stroke his chin. Obviously, today was going to be a day of waterworks.

At just that moment, Julio's dark eyes met hers from his place beside Emma, and his mouth split into a huge grin, showing even, white teeth in a caramel face. She couldn't help but grin back at her former boss, marveling yet again that he'd renounced his bachelor lifestyle for Emma. Seeing them together had convinced her what they had was real.

A petulant voice pierced her joyful mood. "When are they going to get this show on the road? Not all of us are desert rats. We're frying here!"

Mary Beth turned toward William while glancing at Ethan to make sure his son's outburst wasn't upsetting him.

"Why don't you go inside and get a cold drink, boy? It won't be long." Ethan's dismissal of his son's petulance gave her hope, though she hated to see the sparks of anger fly between them.

Surprisingly, William huffed off without commenting, followed meekly by his wife, who had seemed out of her depth this whole visit. Maybe she wanted to be cordial, but felt a need not to counter her husband's behavior out of loyalty.

A few minutes later, Emma called everyone over for the ceremony, and the couples assembled around the officiant. The sun beat down heartlessly, and Mary Beth felt sweat trickling down from her armpits, but she pulled her focus back to what was happening and managed to say "I do" while gazing into Ethan's gray eyes. He had to be melting, too, but all his attention was on her, as if he was trying to telegraph his love to her. She swallowed as tears filled her eyes and smiled at him, so grateful for his devotion. Then, almost anticlimactically, the ceremony was over, and everyone trooped next door through the heat to Barbara's cool and welcoming house for the reception.

Barbara and Ben called the group together and proposed a champagne toast to the newlyweds, and William was mercifully quiet and left soon after. Mary Beth took a deep breath and released it in gratitude as she watched him and his family go out Barbara's door.

She jumped when Lydia's warm voice spoke from behind her, "You'll feel much better now."

"You don't have to be psychic to know that," joked Mary Beth, turning to smile at her.

"He's a dickhead," offered Eric, who stood towering like a Viking behind his new wife, who elbowed him. "Well, he is. I don't have special vision, and even I could see that."

Mary Beth giggled. "I won't argue with either of you."

The whole crowd drifted over to the counter, which was heavily laden with delicious-looking food. Guess she wasn't going to lose weight this week. But at least she'd kicked the cigarette habit without gaining a ton.

She put their empty champagne glasses by the sink and began to fill a plate with food, since everyone was waiting for the newlyweds to eat first. Ethan piled his plate high and grabbed two bottles of beer from a cooler at the end of the counter, and they headed over to a love seat in the spacious great room.

They sat down, and Ethan popped the tops on both bottles and handed her one. Then he raised his bottle, "To my lovely wife. And to many happy years together."

She raised her bottle, clinking it with his. "I second that emotion."

They drank to the toast and dived into the food. She was really and truly married and going to live in Palm Lakes legitimately. It was almost too much to believe her dreams had come true.

\* \* \*

MADDIE, 2:30PM

Horses thundered across the screen as the Western raced towards its predictable conclusion. Maddie loved old Westerns, especially those with John Wayne. She stole a glance at Jack, who sat on the couch with Beau at his feet. His revelation had shaken her, but she wasn't sure why. She'd suspected something was going on between him and Samantha. Perhaps it was the depth of affection he conveyed that shook her. No one had ever loved her like that. His natural desire to act was being held in check by his consideration for Samantha. He wasn't whining or blaming her. She'd never known a man she could admire, at least not one she knew personally.

Jack was engrossed in the movie, his sharp features focused on the screen, unaware of her scrutiny. He wasn't exactly handsome. What word should she use? Virile? Masculine? He wasn't a pretty boy, but he sure looked good in a rough-hewn way. Coal-dark eyes, shiny black hair that hung between his shoulders. She'd never liked long hair on a man, but on him it looked good. Not for the first time she reckoned he'd look good in a Western.

She tore her eyes away and stared at the screen. She'd seen it so many times, she had all the dialogue memorized, but she still enjoyed watching it. It was such a pleasure having company. She wondered if he'd come more often if Samantha left Arthur sooner rather than later.

Samantha would come by after the wedding; she was sure of that. Jack obviously hoped to catch Samantha—it didn't appear to be a planned visit, though, which made her curious. She wasn't sure how to handle Samantha about this recent development. Samantha was stubborn, and if Maddie pushed her to leave Arthur, it might delay things. On the other hand, if she knew Maddie approved of Jack, maybe she'd overcome her reluctance to put the divorce behind her.

She wasn't used to thinking about things like this. She tended to stay out of Samantha's life, but this time, maybe her daughter needed her Mom to help her make the right choice. She wasn't sure her opinion counted with Samantha, but one thing Maddie was sure of: she didn't want to be the reason Samantha lingered in a bad marriage. That meant she needed to come up with a strategy. What else did she have to spend time on, anyway?

\* \* \*

SAMANTHA, 2:50 PM

Samantha knocked on the door and announced herself, suddenly feeling quite tired from all the excitement of the day. Well, she didn't have much more to do before she could put her feet up. She was so engrossed with that thought and with putting the plate of food from the reception in Mom's refrigerator, that she didn't notice Jack and Beau until she almost reached the sitting area.

Shock ran through her, followed by a stab of fear. Why was he here? He'd never come alone before. Had he told Mom about them? She did her best to recover and smiled. "What a nice surprise to see you and Beau, Jack. Mom, how are you doing today?"

Mom looked at her and shrugged one shoulder expressively, but said nothing. She looked good, though, her wrinkled face flushed as if with enjoyment. A wine bottle on the dining table held a bouquet. Jack must have brought the flowers. She wondered if Mom had criticized him for it.

"Why don't you join us and have a beer?" Mom asked.

Samantha nodded and got a Bud out of the refrigerator. She walked over to the couch and sank down next to Jack, close but not touching. She hadn't missed his admiring glance; he seemed impressed with her wedding outfit. Good. She never got to wear nice clothes around him, and it pleased her that he seemed impressed by the aqua and white cotton sundress. It wasn't expensive, but she thought it was feminine and the sea foam green turquoise necklace her mother had made a few years ago complimented it. She'd gone to a lot of trouble to braid her hair in an 'up' do, and she smiled to herself in satisfaction as she tapped the top of the can a few times and popped it open. "I didn't drink much at the reception, so I'll allow myself one beer. It's murderously hot outside, and yesterday's thunderstorm made it steamy. But I'm glad it didn't rain today. That would have been worse."

Maddie switched off the TV. The sudden silence was deafening. "How did the wedding go? I'll be asking Olivia her impressions later, but I'd like to hear what you thought."

Samantha had been storing up images to share, aware that Mom was sad about not attending. "The weather was pretty brutal. The humidity is high, and people were sweating in their finery. I heard Ethan's son complaining. I think all of us were eager to get into the air conditioning after the ceremony.

"Mary Beth and Ethan looked great. She had a lovely cream silk dress and a necklace and earrings of carved black onyx that she'd made; you would have loved it, Mom. Ethan was wearing a jacket, but not a suit, and he shed the jacket right after the ceremony. You would have loved his bolo tie, shaped like a roadrunner with bits of turquoise and coral for the plumage; it was really classy.

" Lydia and Eric—I hadn't met them before—were dressed in Arizona formal. She had on a long dress and peasant style blouse with the most gorgeous squash blossom necklace. Must be worth a fortune. Eric had on black jeans, a Western shirt and sharp-looking boots—Tony Lama, I'm thinking.

"Speaking of boots, Julio had on snakeskin boots and was also in black jeans with a really nice white silk dress shirt and bolo tie with a hunk of turquoise as big as his thumb. Emma wasn't dressed in her usual shapeless outfit. You don't know her well, but she always wears loose clothes that hide her figure. She had on a royal blue dress that was tailored beautifully and brought out the color of her eyes. She's a stunner when she wants to be. Julio couldn't keep his eyes off her. I swear he really loves her. Who would have guessed he could be monogamous?"

Maddie stared off into space, her eyes unfocused, as if she were imagining what Samantha described.

"How was the reception?" Jack asked. Samantha turned his way and smiled.

"You should have come. It was terrific. The food was amazing, and they had so much of it, they tried to get everyone to take some home. I gave in and have some nibbles for later and brought a plate for Mom. I couldn't do a dinner after that. Arthur will just have to get by on snacks." She flinched inwardly at saying Arthur's name in front of Jack.

He chose that moment to rise. "I ought to head home now. It's been a nice visit, Maddie. Thanks for the beer and the movie." He went over and leaned down to give her a hug, then gave her a kiss on the cheek.

Mom's eyes lit up at that. She reached over and petted Beau, who was crowding on her other side. "Thanks for the flowers and for coming to see me." That must have been hard for her to say. Mom never liked getting flowers. But no, she seemed to genuinely appreciate the gesture. Would wonders never cease?

Jack pinned Samantha with dark eyes as he walked past. "See you tomorrow, Sam." He didn't touch her, but he wouldn't do that in front of Mom, would he? It was lucky his back was to Mom, because his look was possessive and smoldering. She wondered if Mom knew what was going on. She walked Jack and Beau to the door and returned to the dining table and sniffed the flowers. "They smell good. I didn't think you liked getting flowers."

Mom grunted. "It was so kind of him to come by like he did, I wasn't going to hurt his feelings. Besides, he said they came from the containers at his office, so it's not like he spent money. He said he knows I wouldn't put up with store-bought flowers. And he's right. That boy is smart. And he's nice, too."

Samantha wasn't sure what to say. It sounded like a leading comment. "Yes, it was very thoughtful of him."

"So who all was at the wedding?" Mom changed the subject so fast, Samantha was left speechless for a second. "Oh, not many people. Julio's family was there, at least the adults—his brothers and their wives. Emma doesn't have anyone. Mary Beth had no one except Olivia. Lydia had her business partners Jean and Ian, I think his name was. What a gorgeous accent he has! Eric had an old friend from the Posse named Nick. Ethan's son and daughter both came with their children. His son William was standoffish, but I'd been warned he was against the marriage, so I just avoided him. Barbara, who hosted the reception, was there with Ben. Marilyn—the woman who bought Owen Schmidt's house, Steven Cooper.

Oh, and Helen and Alexander, of course. I think that was it. I wish you could have gone, but I think the heat would have been too much for you."

Mom smiled weakly. "I don't stand the heat that well anymore. You're probably right." It was definitely a red letter day. Mom rarely told Samantha she was right.

She glanced down at the table to the necklaces spread out on the work cloth. "These are turning out really nice. I'm glad you decided to use turquoise. There's something special about it. And these are a totally different shade of turquoise than this one," she said as she fingered the beads around her neck.

"I was just glad I had enough to make them all the same. There's still the earrings to do, and I have only finished four of the necklaces, but I think I'll manage to complete them." Samantha shivered at the the reminder.

"They're going to be special. Thanks for making them. I know they will be treasured. I'm certainly going to treasure mine." Samantha reached over and stroked one of the completed necklaces.

"You must be tired. You didn't need to come over."

"I thought you'd been alone all day, and I wanted to tell you about the wedding. I know Olivia and Helen and Mary Beth will all be sharing with you. It was a lovely event. But you're right, I'm tired. What do you have planned for later?"

"It's movie night, and Olivia is coming over for dinner and we're going to the movie. I don't know what it is, but it's good to get out, and I can manage going downstairs, even if I can't go much farther." Regret and resentment colored her words.

Samantha decided to exit before it got more awkward, before Mom asked about Jack. "I'll go then. I'll call tomorrow or maybe come over on the way home from work."

"You don't need to do that every day."

"I want to, Mom. Let me at least do that."

Mom looked at her with glistening eyes and nodded mutely. Samantha gave her a kiss and girded her loins for going back to Arthur and giving yet another account of the wedding.

\* \* \*

## NICK, 5:00PM

Nick sat in his recliner, still dressed in his wedding finery. It was kind of fun to dress up now and then. His dress boots rarely got any wear these days. And since he didn't go to church, this was the first time since his wife's funeral in January that he'd worn a jacket. Not that he wore it for long. Still, with the heat and humidity, he'd probably have to get the jacket dry cleaned.

His big hand was gripping a glass of ice with two fingers of bourbon. He hadn't drunk at the wedding. He wasn't big on booze these days. But the event had shaken him more than he had anticipated. Seeing those three couples, including his good friend Eric, getting married and looking so happy cut him deeply. He thought he was over the loss of his wife, but seeing three couples in love reminded him how alone he was.

His son hadn't spoken to him often since his wife's funeral, and even then, he was close-mouthed. He'd never approved of their moving to Arizona, and he never let an opportunity pass to tell his Dad how he felt it was selfish. For whatever reason, he'd aimed most of his venom at Nick. They'd never gotten along well, and when his wife died, that seemed to sever the last link between them. He had no clue what to do about it.

This was his first weekend at Desert Breezes since moving out of his house, and already he wondered if he'd made a mistake. Sure, it was a relief not to have a big house and yard to look after, but he felt more like he was waiting to die than he ever felt before. Maybe it was just the new surroundings. He should try to be patient and give it time.

At 84, time was in short supply, and he wanted to make the most of it. But he couldn't generate a lot of enthusiasm. He found eating in the dining room less than exciting, but he wasn't any kind of cook, so who was he to complain? And already, the widows were circling him like vultures around a fresh meal. In his old house, he felt more insulated from their attentions. He knew bachelors were in short supply, but it never ceased to amaze him how predatory the widows—and even a few married women—were. He suspected he'd be eating in his room or ordering out a lot.

Now that his house was on the market and he was moved in to Desert Breezes, he needed to do something with his time. His horse Rudi was a fine young quarter horse, and it would take time to bring him up to snuff, so that would be at the top of his list. A sunrise ride was just the thing, as it beat the heat and started the day right. And he'd always meant to join the silversmithing club, so he'd do that soon. He couldn't stand the thought of being cooped up in a small apartment all the time. Maybe he'd check out the movie downstairs tonight, even if it meant braving the vultures.

His thoughts drifted back to the wedding. It was beautifully done, even though the weather was horrible. Eric looked as happy as he'd ever seen his old partner from the Posse.

What Eric had suffered after nearly being killed by Owen Schmidt had driven Nick from the Posse. Lydia had kept her head and called the police, but Nick had arrived first, because he was closer. He rendered assistance until the police and ambulance arrived, but it had shaken him badly. Nick had been a police chief in a small New York town, but he'd never run into such a bloody situation as when he arrived at Tanya Cooper's condo to find Owen shot dead, Tanya dead with her throat cut and Eric bleeding from a bad knife wound, Lydia desperately trying to stop the bleeding. So much blood, so much death. How could such a thing happen in Palm Lakes? His shoes and the knees of his pants had been so bloody, he'd thrown them out. He wished he could erase the images from his mind as easily, but they stained his dreams.

He took a sip of bourbon and pushed the bloody images aside. Eric was recovering nicely after a bout of serious post traumatic stress, and it looked like he was enjoying life without the Posse. If Eric could do it, so could he.

At least he wouldn't need to worry about dinner tonight. He'd had plenty to eat at the reception, and they had pressed him with some leftovers that he could reheat in the microwave.

* * *

OLIVIA, 5:30PM

Olivia knocked on Maddie's door, then pushed it open without waiting for a response. She lay the dish of warmed lasagna on the counter and greeted Maddie, who was looking bright. It was easier to bring dinner to Maddie than to drag her down the hall. She'd been dreading tonight, because she knew Maddie was sad about not going to the wedding, but maybe it would be OK. "Did Samantha come by after the wedding? She told me she was going to."

Maddie nodded enthusiastically, though she didn't try to rise from her recliner. "Yes, she told me all about it, but I want to hear your impressions, too. I got a surprise visit from Jack and Beau, and we watched a movie and had a beer together."

Olivia considered the tone of Maddie's voice. Maddie was fairly bursting with something. "Has he ever come by alone before?"

"No, this was the first time. He brought those flowers, too." Maddie pointed to the bottle on the dining table that held a small bouquet of flowers.

"That was considerate of him." Olivia was certain there was more to tell.

Maddie huffed. "Yes, he is a good boy, but I think he wanted to see me without Samantha." She paused as if unsure what to say.

"So what happened, if you don't mind me asking? You've got me really curious." Olivia smiled to encourage Maddie.

"The long and the short of it is he's in love with Samantha. He calls her Sam, which I've never liked, but I can't make myself take him to task for it. I think he's a private person, and telling me was hard for him, but I asked him outright what his intentions were, and he answered me straight, which I admire." Maddie swept her hand through her short, dirty blonde hair. "It's no secret that I never liked Arthur. He's a big nothing in my book. I think Jack truly cares for her, and I need to think what to do." Maddie's breath ran out and she waved a hand as a sign to wait.

"What do you think you can do? Do you know how far it's gone?"

Maddie chuckled. "Obviously not as far as he wants. He's a typical male that way. I'd bet she's holding him off until I die. I don't want to keep them apart, and I don't want to feel I need to die so she can get on with her life. I'd like to see my daughter happy before I go." She frowned as her eyes filled with tears.

Olivia scarcely knew what to say, so she covered her confusion by getting plates and silverware out of the cabinets. It was so uncomfortable when Maddie talked about dying. She hated the thought of losing her friend. "Maddie, why don't you just tell her what you told me? She probably thinks it would stress you out for her to leave Arthur now. Maybe she thinks you'd frown on a divorce."

"You're right about that. And she's probably worried about being far away from me. I have no idea what she'd do if she left Arthur. I can't offer her a place to stay. Maybe Mary Beth would. It would be a mess if she moved in with Jack before the divorce, but you know young people these days." She shook her head.

"I vote for you telling her what you told me. She'll do what she wants, but you should tell her what you want. It might not have occurred to her that you would support her divorce. You told me you stayed in a bad marriage, and maybe she feels you would judge her."

"That's true. I need to get my courage up, so I can tell her what I think. She might be surprised."

"Now that we've settled that, how about we have a relaxed dinner and then go to the movie downstairs? I made us small portions, because I know they brought you treats from the wedding, and I stuffed myself."

Maddie nodded in agreement, and Olivia began to serve the lasagna.

"Would you like something to drink?" asked Maddie.

"No, I drank enough at the wedding. I'm pretty full, too, so you're going to have to eat most of the lasagna."

Maddie grinned. "I'm not a big eater anymore, but I'll do my best. So what can you tell me about the wedding?"

Olivia racked her brain to find a variation on what Samantha had probably related to her. "Well, I'm sure you know by now that the heat was awful and the ceremony beautiful and the reception loaded with yummy food. I didn't know most of the attendees. There were women from a yoga group they all go to, and there were neighbors. The other two brides were Lydia and Emma, the one who bought Helen's old house. Lydia's business partners Ian and Jean were there. His British accent is to die for. I could have listened to him recite from the phone book. Then there was another man…" She hesitated, not wanting to share everything, as it seemed so strange. "He was a good friend of Eric's from the Posse. You remember Eric Johnson, who shot and killed Owen Schmidt while he was attacking Tanya Cooper, your old neighbor?"

Maddie shuddered visibly. "That story gives me the creeps. Owen Schmidt was always a quiet man, but we had no idea there was anything wrong with him. To think he killed all those women, and he lived on our street! What is the world coming to?"

"This man Nick was on the posse with Eric. I had a long chat with him." She paused, thinking about how natural it felt to talk to him, a total stranger. "He looks to be about my age, probably past 80, and he's a big man. Not fat, mind you, but big and solid. He's tanned like he spends a lot of time in the sun, and his eyes are the most brilliant blue." She was getting into dangerous territory. She didn't want to share with Maddie how affected she was by those eyes. "He looked big and able to handle himself, but he told me he quit the Posse after that murder. He was apparently the first responder on the scene. He didn't go into gory detail, but you could see in his eyes how affected he was by what he saw."

Maddie was scrutinizing her with pale blue eyes. "You found him attractive," she accused.

"I suppose in a way I did. He sort of reminds me of John Wayne. He towered over me, must be over six feet tall, and spare with words, but he seemed to be the kind of man who says what he means, if you catch my drift." Maddie cackled, and that made Olivia smile. "It isn't often you meet a decent single man our age in Palm Lakes."

"That's a fact," agreed Maddie. "Is he a bachelor or a widower?"

"I don't know. We didn't talk about personal stuff. But you'd think if he had a wife, she'd have been with him."

"I guess we'll never know." Maddie was proven wrong, at least a little, when they went to the movie room after dinner.

Maddie had shuffled her walker with the small oxygen tank in the basket up next to an aisle seat, and Olivia sat beside her. The room was buzzing with conversation, and the smell of fresh popped corn filled the air. A sign announced that the movie would be "The Big Country," and although John Wayne wasn't in it, Maddie was looking excited.

People were filing in, many with walkers, finding seats and speaking to friends, when Olivia felt a presence and turned to her left. Towering over her was Nick Dwyer, the man she'd met at the wedding. He pointed to the seat. "Is this seat taken?"

She gave him a wordless 'no' by nodding, unable to think. He sat down and looked past her at Maddie. She shook herself and said, "Maddie, I'd like you to meet Nick Dwyer. He was at the wedding today." Maddie leaned forward to see Nick, and he extended his big hand to her. Shaking it, Maddie smiled foolishly and finally said, "Nice to meet you. Olivia told me all about the wedding. I couldn't make it. Too many things to drag around these days."

He bobbed his head seriously. "I'm sorry you couldn't come."

The film started, and it was so long, people were eager to leave as soon as the credits started. Nick rose and bowed to them. "I'll be leaving, then. Maybe I'll see you ladies later on." He turned and stalked out of the room.

Maddie turned to Olivia. "You weren't kidding, were you?"

Olivia sniffed. "I don't exaggerate."

"I should hope not." Maddie grinned. "So why did he sit next to you?"

"I'm sure I don't know, and it isn't likely he'll tell me."

Maddie laughed out loud. "I think the story is far from over. You have to promise to tell me everything."

Olivia just smiled, halfway hoping Maddie was right.

## 5

# SATURDAY, AUGUST 17, 1996

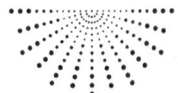

OLIVIA, 10:10AM

*O*livia bent down to pet her beloved Spot, who was still a
hyperactive ball of fluffy butterscotch fur. "She hasn't changed a
bit. Thanks for bringing her for a visit."

Helen grinned. "Spot loves to ride in the car, and she loves seeing you.
It's my pleasure to bring her over."

"She seems to remember me."

Helen harrumphed. "Really, Olivia. How could she forget you? You
were her family for years."

Olivia reveled in the silky feel of Spot's fur as she stroked her. Bright
button eyes regarded her with dark intelligence and love. A pang of
loneliness hit her. "I do miss her a lot. However, you've made it possible
for me to still be a part of her life, and I appreciate that. Maddie feels the
same about Jack bringing Beau to visit."

"Maddie loves that dog. I can remember Stanley used to walk him
around the neighborhood. He was too much for Maddie to handle—the
dog, not the man." Olivia chuckled as Helen continued. "When I'd go

across the street to visit, Beau was always on guard duty, especially after Stanley died. He seemed to know Maddie hated being alone."

Who doesn't hate being alone, thought Olivia, but kept it to herself. Her thoughts turned to Maddie. "Speaking of Maddie, she's fading. It's like a slow downhill slide, a little bit each day. I don't know how to help her. I'm afraid she'll end up in the assisted living wing."

Helen gazed at her, blue eyes searching. Olivia's tone must have revealed her worries. "I know it's hard to give up independence, and I wouldn't want to," said Helen, "but considering Maddie's condition, might that be a reasonable choice? She'll need more care than Samantha can provide, working full time. Or do you have other concerns?" A flash of something flitted through Helen's eyes. "Is this about your friend Sophie?"

Olivia heaved a sigh. "Yes. It's Sophie. You know she had a couple strokes and has been back and forth from the hospital? She only recently returned to Desert Breezes after the last stroke, about a week ago." She paused, wondering if she'd sound crazy. She bought time by hauling Spot onto her lap and snuggling her. "It's been a busy summer for me. I didn't go to see her in the hospital as often as I had intended to, and when I went, she was always asleep. They had her sedated, supposedly because she was agitated. It bothered me that she was drugged, but what can you do? Just after the wedding, she was awake when I visited. It really affected me." She put Spot back on the floor and looked into Helen's blue eyes. "The strokes have made it very hard for her to move, and she's lost her speech for the most part. She can make noises, but that's about it. They aren't predicting she'll recover. In fact, my impression is that they're surprised she's still with us."

"Oh, I'm so sorry," Helen whispered with feeling.

Olivia nodded. "It's hard to see people fall apart, but that's not really my main concern, strange as it sounds. I'm worried something bad may be going on in the assisted living wing."

"What kind of bad?"

Olivia gathered her courage to express the insane conclusion she'd reached purely on an intuitive hunch. "It's hard to put it into words; it's more how I felt. She was awake that last time in the hospital, and she seemed alert. I was doing all the talking, of course, telling her about the wedding, patting her hand, trying to cheer her up. I recalled she'd once told me she hates hospitals, and she'd already spent weeks there. So I reassured her that she'd soon be coming back to Desert Breezes, thinking that was a cheerful thought. And oh, my, was I mistaken! She couldn't articulate, of course, but her eyes popped wide open in what I'd swear was pure terror, and she became very upset and struggled to speak, but only grunts came out. I tried to calm her, but I ended up having to ask the nurse for help, and they sedated her."

Helen's brow furrowed as she contemplated Olivia's words. "Why do you think she reacted that way?"

"My question exactly. I'm sure she understood me, so why that reaction? Why would coming back here scare the hell out of her?"

Helen shook her head. "I don't know her, but I trust you know her well enough to recognize something is off. But what could cause such a negative response?"

"The only thing that occurred to me is that there could be some kind of elder abuse going on there. But that's a serious charge." Olivia sighed again. "All I have to go on is the look on her face. It haunts me. I know something is wrong, but what can I do?"

They sat in silence for a couple minutes, nursing cups of coffee. Finally, Helen spoke. "You have to do what you feel is best. Can you speak to the nurse in that wing, or are you afraid she's the problem?"

"I just don't know. Last I heard, Sophie has no roommate, so that can't be the problem. There are attendants present day and night, and the nurse in charge is present in the daytime—I don't think she has daily interaction with the residents, but I could be wrong—and so there aren't many people it could be, if it is even true. It occurred to me that she might be losing it and hallucinating or thinking that her nightmares are real. How can I tell what shape her mind is in? All I know is that she is terrified, and to her it is real. I spoke to the nurse in the hospital, and she told me Sophie has been very agitated, which is why they medicate her. I have so little to go on."

"You need to catch her awake and ask her more."

Olivia was relieved Helen wasn't dismissing her concerns. "She's been back for several days. If I can question her, maybe I can get enough to figure this out." She wasn't certain she really wanted to know the truth, and she wasn't looking forward to stirring the pot.

Later that afternoon, Olivia stopped by Sophie's place and found her

85

napping again. She went to the room where the attendants gathered when they weren't working, hoping to get some intelligence on Sophie's condition. Two women in scrubs sat in comfortable armchairs. The younger one, plump with short bleached blonde hair, was flipping through a magazine and didn't even look up at Olivia. The second woman appeared to be in her thirties and had a no-nonsense air to match her sensible but ugly shoes and a severe nun-like haircut. Staring at a clipboard, she was marking items with a pen. She paused on hearing Olivia enter and peered at her through wire-rimmed glasses. "Can I help you?" she said in a voice that betrayed she resented the interruption.

"Yes, I'm a friend of Sophie Aldridge. She's asleep every time I come to visit."

"That's because she's on sedatives." The woman bent her head to her clipboard and continued to mark the page.

"Is that normal for someone in her condition?"

The attendant pinned her with a cold stare. "Are you family?"

"No, I'm her friend. We were neighbors before her stroke." Olivia summoned all her courage. "I'm the only one she has, and it concerns me that she's always asleep."

"I'm not at liberty to discuss her condition or treatment except with family. You can take this up with the nurse in charge if you like. She may make an exception. I cannot." The woman's tart voice indicated she considered the conversation over.

The younger woman looked up from her magazine, eyes sympathetic, but said nothing.

"Thank you," said Olivia with as much courtesy as she could muster. This hadn't reassured her in any way. She'd have to go to the nurse in charge, whoever that was.

\* \* \*

HELEN, 12:30PM

Helen pulled her car into the garage and got out, barely noticing the stifling heat. She plodded into the house, feeling like she was walking in Jupiter's gravity. Or whichever planet it was that made you weigh more.

Never mind. She dropped her purse on the table where she always left it and went back to change into more comfortable clothes, which at this time of year meant none at all, though she wasn't willing to turn nudist yet. After slipping into a loose sleeveless top and shorts, she padded barefoot into the kitchen, pulled a bottle of wine out of the wine cooler and poured herself a glass. She couldn't remember the last time she'd been so down.

The chilled white wine was going down nicely—and fast—when strong arms slipped around her middle, pulling her back against Alexander's firm and fragrant body. She managed not to spill a drop, put her glass on the counter and turned to bury her face in his chest, drawing a ragged breath.

"I wondered why you didn't come to see me. What's wrong?"

Tears filled her eyes and she bit her tongue, willing them back. "I've had a bad day. I'm sorry. It's beastly hot out, Olivia has me worried and Sally…don't even ask."

"Here, I'll pour myself a glass and we'll hash it all out."

Something inside Helen unwound at his kindness, and she let out a big sigh. The overwhelm passed, but irritation and worry lingered. She allowed Alexander to lead her to the couch and sat close, with her thigh touching his for comfort.

He looked intently at her. "Tell me every little detail."

She took a moment to admire his swept-back silver hair and his casual but expensive outfit. He rarely wore shorts, no matter how hot it was. Black, crisply pleated linen trousers and a white polo top accentuated his extravagant good looks. Sandals of butter-soft leather graced his feet.

She stared at his feet for a moment, gathering the events of the morning into some kind of order. Taking a deep breath, Helen reviewed her day as if screening a videotape. "Well, I was doing OK when I dropped Spot back after seeing Olivia, but the longer I thought about what she'd told me, the more concerned I became. But it might be nothing."

"You don't sound like you think it's nothing."

"I wish I did. Olivia has a friend—her name is Sophie—who had to move to the assisted living wing at Desert Breezes due to a stroke and shortly after suffered more strokes that robbed her of speech and most movement. But awful as that is, that isn't the problem. Olivia is convinced elder abuse is going on in that wing, and she's determined to sleuth it out and save Sophie, so determined that I'm worried for her."

She looked into his emerald green eyes and saw a reflection of her concern.

"How did she get caught up in such a thing?"

"Sophie has no one else, so Olivia was trying to be supportive. Every time she went to the hospital, Sophie was sleeping because they had her sedated. At the hospital, she caught Sophie awake and had a conversation with her, a one-sided conversation to be sure. When she told Sophie she'd soon be back at Desert Breezes, Sophie looked terrified. Olivia says it makes no sense, because Sophie once told her she hates the hospital worse than anything."

"That's all?"

"Well, Sophie can't speak, but Olivia is convinced it's real. Now that Sophie's back, she's determined to get to the bottom of this."

Alexander ran a hand over his chin, and she could hear the gentle rasp of stubble. A stab of love shot through her. He always took her seriously. And she was still awed by his good looks.

"Olivia's a smart cookie. But what can she do?"

"I'm concerned that if she pokes around and someone is doing wrong, she could be at risk. At the very least, she's likely to be treated badly for even asking."

"She should go to the authorities."

"But what authorities? And tell them what? That Sophie looked scared? No one will credit her but the guilty party."

He nodded. "You're right. I think you should advise her not to make a move without telling you, so that someone always knows where she is and what she is doing."

"I'll call and suggest that. I don't know if she'll do it."

"Speaking of calls, Mary Beth phoned while you were out."

"What about?"

His grin meant good news. "She was excited to announce their bid on Olivia's house was accepted. They will be moving in the end of this month if all goes well."

Joy filled Helen, dispelling some of the lingering gloom. "Oh, that's great news!"

He flashed his movie star smile. "I knew that would cheer you up. What's more, she said if we go to St. Croix in September, they'll watch

Spot. She can even go stay with them, since it's her old house. Fido can stay here. He'd probably enjoy a break from all of us."

Helen chuckled. "That would be perfect. And we can maybe get Julio and Emma to watch the yard and house, depending on how long we'll be gone."

"I don't expect it will take longer than two weeks to do what we need to do."

"Well, then maybe we don't need yard watching. That reminds me of my biggest annoyance. Sally." She sighed deeply. Her youngest daughter seemed to be an endless fount of challenges since she'd moved to the area the previous year, pregnant, alone and jobless.

Alexander took her hand. "I know Sally was always your favorite, and it's been disappointing these past months for you, but Eric is lucky she turned down his marriage proposal. He's much better off with Lydia."

She rolled her eyes. "He'd be better off with almost anyone else. I hate to say that about my own daughter, but she's manipulative, self-centered and irresponsible. I don't say that lightly. I don't know why I was shocked today to see she has a new boyfriend. This one is a black musician, unemployed, of course. He has that strange hairdo."

"Dreadlocks?"

"That's it. He looked pleasant but out of it. He and Sally were watching TV while Camille lay in her crib crying. They gave me some lame excuse. The poor child needed her diaper changed, so I did it. They have so few clothes for her, almost nothing that I haven't bought. It makes me mad. It feels like Sally doesn't really want to admit she has a child."

"I assume that means you gave her money," he said pointedly.

She pushed aside a defensive tightening. "Yes, I did, and I told her to spend it all on clothes and toys for Camille. I wonder if maybe she does what she does to get me to pay for the child's needs."

"She's making a good salary in her job, if what she's told you is true. She should have enough to provide for the child. Maybe it would be wiser if you just bought what you think Camille needs yourself. That way you can be sure the money is all going to Camille."

Chagrined, Helen agreed. "You're right. From now on I will. I'm afraid she's spending money on drugs. Anyway, when I told her we might be away in September, she got upset and said they'd been thinking of going

89

on a trip and wanted to leave Camille with us." Alexander's raised eyebrows said it all. "Don't worry, I told her we weren't changing our plans on her account, but I said I'm open to doing it another time if she gives us enough notice. She can only take so much time off from her job, so it won't get out of control." She put her empty wine glass on the coffee table. "I worry about Camille's future. Sally isn't a good mother, but I don't really want to raise her child. I don't know how Ray and Alan do it. Taking on Becky was a big deal. I'm not sure I could."

"We'll do what we have to do, but let's hope Sally doesn't go off the rails. I'm still honeymooning. I'm not ready for children quite yet." His laughing eyes defused her irritation and worry.

"I love you so much."

He drew her into a big hug. "And I love you."

\* \* \*

BARBARA, 2:15PM

Marilyn sat across from Barbara, nibbling on a freshly made oatmeal raisin cookie. "Mmm, these are delicious and still warm," she murmured and raised the glass of iced tea to her lips. "I haven't baked in ages. This may drive me to."

Barbara grinned, pleased to have a guest so obviously enjoy herself. "How's Tammi?"

"She loves the new fence and the dog door. But she hates the heat, so she only spends time outside on the patio in the mornings. I've been thinking of getting one of those misters put in. They're divine."

"We love ours, but they do get clogged from the salts in the water. Still, it's a godsend on a hot day."

Marilyn reached down to pet Jack, who lay asleep on her sandaled feet. "It's quiet. Where are Amelia and the girls?"

"She took them to the zoo. I can hardly believe it. Hauling them around in the heat wouldn't be my idea of an outing." Then Barbara laughed out loud. "I can't help it. She's so much better, I can hardly believe it."

"I'm so happy for you." Marilyn hesitated. "Does that mean you can stay in Palm Lakes?"

"Yes, we had a family summit yesterday, and Amelia assured us she will be OK. I keep shaking myself, waiting to wake up to the old reality, but it appears her symptoms are in remission."

"That's a blessing," said Marilyn.

"No, it's a miracle. Jean and Ian have given me another miracle. Ben and I were seriously looking at selling out and moving near Amelia. Now we won't have to."

"I'm selfishly grateful. I like having you as a neighbor."

Barbara debated bring up the subject of Owen Schmidt and revealing Marilyn was living in his house. That had been the driving reason behind inviting Marilyn over—she wanted to get it over with, but the woman's demeanor seemed a bit subdued today. Maybe another time. She was afraid to wait much longer. Sooner or later, Marilyn would find out, and she might feel betrayed that her friends had stayed silent. "Is everything OK?"

Marilyn looked up and her light blue eyes suddenly filled with tears. "Don't mind me. I'm being silly. I had a shock a couple days ago."

Alarm shot through Barbara, but she waited for Marilyn to continue.

"I got a package in the mail from my ex. I hadn't told him where I was living. He's still in Virginia. He knows where I am, or at least he thinks he knows."

"If you feel like talking, I'm happy to listen. Sharing a problem can sometimes ease the burden."

Marilyn nodded, eyes glistening. "That support group is great. I'm getting a fresh start thanks to it. When the package arrived, it dragged me back into the past. As I told you, my ex-husband was violent. That's what finally drove me away. I hoped he'd never find me. He isn't paying alimony, and I have a restraining order on him, but it was drawn up in Virginia. Now he's found me."

Her sigh touched Barbara's heart. "Was the package threatening?"

"No, just the opposite. That's the thing that bothers me. The box was full of crap, stuff you'd find in the back of a forgotten cabinet. Most of it belonged in the trash and wasn't even mine. There was no note. It creeped me out."

"Why do you suppose he sent it?"

"To scare me. Or at least I assume that was the point. And I am scared.

But maybe he isn't sure it's me. Jones is a common name. Maybe he hopes to get a response out of me, or perhaps he just wants to scare me. Or possibly it's a warning that he will be coming to get me. Like, 'you can run, but you can't hide' sort of thing."

"Are you sure it's from him?"

"Well, there was no return address, but it was mailed from Virginia. I'm sure it's him. It just feels like something he'd do."

Barbara wished she could help, but couldn't think how. "I hope you know we're here for you. Call us any time, day or night. If you get freaked out, come stay with us. I know Tammi is a good watchdog, but it's important to know you aren't alone in this."

Marilyn's sigh was one of relief. Her eyes were dry, and she smiled crookedly. "I'm so lucky to have such great neighbors." She sniffed, then added, "Steven has been very supportive, too. I believe he likes the therapy group as much as I do. But he's probably told you, since you recommended it."

Marilyn reached for her glass as Barbara speculated just how interested Steven was in supporting Marilyn. They were both such lovely people.

"I better get going," Marilyn said after draining her glass. "Thanks so much for everything." She stood and threw another smile at Barbara. This one lit her eyes.

It looked like today wouldn't be the day she told Marilyn about Owen. Barbara nibbled her lower lip while escorting her neighbor to the door, Jack prancing at her heels. She hated the thought of frightening Marilyn even more by sharing the gruesome facts about her house, but how long could she afford to wait?

* * *

SAMANTHA, 6:30PM

The phone rang, and Samantha debated ignoring it. Arthur never answered the phone when she was home, as if she were his secretary. Pushing annoyance aside, she strode into the kitchen and picked up the handset from the base.

"Hello," she said in a tone that betrayed her irritation.

"Samantha, I'm so glad to catch you at home. Didn't Arthur give you my message? I've been wanting to talk with you for days about the CSL tea."

Samantha slumped into a nearby chair. She was exhausted from bouncing between her job, her home and her mother, not to mention her relationship with Jack. "Yes, he did, Christine. I'm sorry. I'm running in circles and just haven't had a chance to call you." She knew it sounded lame, but it was true. She dreaded being sucked into the sorority-like event. Why had she ever allowed Christine to convince her to join CSL?

"I know how much you have on your plate, which is why I signed you up for one of the easiest jobs. We're having the tea at Loretta's house. She has a huge place on the golf course with a large room for all the tables. I think I told you how the tea works? It's our biggest charity event of the year, and we often make a few thousand dollars between the raffle tickets and the tea service. I signed you up to do the centerpieces for the five tables."

Christine's commandant tone made it clear Samantha had no choice. She groaned inwardly. She didn't fit in with any of the CSL activities and regretted joining, but didn't want to hurt Christine, who'd been so eager to sponsor her. "What do I need to do, and what's the deadline?" She hoped she didn't sound as disinterested as she felt.

"You have a $25 budget as a base. Use your imagination. The tables will have white linen tablecloths, and the tea will be a formal one, so nothing too casual. But nothing trite."

For $25? Samantha was going to have to kick in her own money. She wasn't crafty, didn't shop much and had no idea what to do. "Do you mean something like a bud vase with a single red rose?"

"That's the idea, only try to make it unique. Classy but not hackneyed. I'm sure you'll come up with something great."

*Easy for her to say.* "When do they need to be ready?"

"You have two weeks."

Sighing with relief, Samantha glanced at the clock. "I can do that. I'll check with you later to run ideas by you, but I need to run now. My Spanish class starts at 7, and I don't want to be late."

"You run along, then. We'll talk soon."

Samantha ended the call. The dishes were done, and Arthur was sitting in the great room watching TV. She stepped into the room and spoke to the back of his head. "I'm going to go to class now. I'll be back in a little over an hour. I won't be stopping by Mom's."

"Fine," he said tartly. She knew he wanted her to ask what was wrong, but if she gave in, that would be seen as devious when she finally asked for a divorce, so she pretended not to notice. It made her nerves feel like a guitar string being plucked. She needed to put all this behind her, but her head throbbed just thinking about it.

Tangentially, she wondered what Christine would think when she found out. She hadn't mustered the courage to tell her judgmental friend that she planned to divorce Arthur. They hadn't been friends for long, and Christine's obsession with enforcing the covenants as a member of the HOA had shown Samantha a dark side of her that she'd yet to process. Would she be as harsh towards a friend as she was toward strangers?

Still in the clothes she'd worn to work, Samantha drove to the Rec Center and hustled into the classroom. She took a seat beside Emma Lightman—no, it was Rodriguez now, since she'd married Julio, Samantha's former boss.

"Hi," said Emma softly, crystal blue eyes twinkling. Then her smile morphed to a frown. "You look tired."

"Thanks, I needed that."

Emma looked crestfallen. "I didn't mean…"

"Don't be silly. I was kidding. You're right. I'm tired. But I do enjoy this class. I hope I can learn enough to talk to our crews at work. I'm finding it hard to study." Samantha didn't want to tell the older woman she felt too old for school.

"Julio's family have offered to help me learn. Can you believe it? I think they were impressed I'm making the effort. I will feel more a part of the family if I'm fluent in Spanish. A number of the elders don't speak much English."

"I'll be grateful if I can make myself understood at all. How are they helping you?"

"It's kind of like immersion. They speak only Spanish around me, use simple words and speak slowly and try to get me to participate. It's kind of scary, but it seems to be helping me."

"Wow, that sounds intense." Samantha was impressed with Emma's commitment, but then, she'd plunged into the suggestions Samantha had given her for repairing her digestion some time back. And she'd seen great progress. There was steel in that woman.

The teacher called the class to order, and an hour later, Emma and Samantha were walking through the lobby on their way to their cars. Samantha came to a sudden decision. "I'm going to make a quick call before I head home."

Emma regarded her with curiosity, but didn't ask why she couldn't wait to use her home phone. "I'll see you next week."

Samantha nodded and went to the phone booth she'd come to think of as hers. She dialed Jack's number from memory.

"How was class?" he asked without preamble. His voice poured over her like a balm.

"OK. It's a little overwhelming. I've been out of school so long, I find it hard to apply myself, and I really don't have much time to study."

"It isn't your age. You are doing too much. And you're under a lot of stress."

"Thanks. Maybe that's it." She didn't know what to say that wouldn't make him feel worse about their situation. She probably shouldn't have called him, but the weekends were the worst. "Will you be coming to see Mom tomorrow? I'm sure Arthur isn't coming. He's barely speaking to me."

"You know I'll be there. I don't like having to wait all weekend to see you." There was a tinge of resentment in his voice, and she couldn't blame him, but she wasn't ready yet to tell Arthur she was leaving him. She had so much she wanted to say to Jack, but she was too fragile to attempt it and afraid that it would sound insincere even if she did, so she signed off and returned home, grateful Jack was willing to drive out to Palm Lakes tomorrow.

\* \* \*

STEVEN, 7:45PM

Twilight had begun to cloak the back yard in shadows. Steven sat on the patio, glass in hand, listening to the hummers sweeping in like miniature dive bombers to get their last drink of the day. Tempers were flaring and frantic noises accompanied the altercations between the showy males, like last call in a bar.

Steven sipped his iced tea, grateful for the chill as he swallowed it. It must be over 100 degrees still, and he knew from experience that in this sheltered alcove, it wouldn't drop below 90 tonight. So why was he sitting out here in the heat? He couldn't stand being surrounded by the garish decor inside. The animal print furnishings, the rivers of blood red, even the prints on the wall were pure Tanya. It was as if she'd just stepped out to pick up a bottle of vodka and would return momentarily. Her energy taunted him as much now as it ever did when she was alive.

He recalled his Thanksgiving visit to the rehab place, where she'd gone after her DUI. It had been heartless of him to break the news of the divorce to her that way. He'd known it then, but her behavior had driven him to act in ways that made him a different person, a meaner person. He had wanted to hurt her the way she'd been hurting him for years. Now he was ashamed of himself.

For the millionth time, he wondered if she'd still be alive if he hadn't divorced her. The group therapy sessions had convinced him he needed to get closure, but he didn't know how. Maybe he wasn't ready to forgive himself, as they had suggested. His sons had made little effort to stay in touch, confirming for him that others also held him responsible. Yet they'd never shown respect for their mother. She'd been an embarrassment to them for nearly as long as she had been to him.

The restlessness churned him inside and out, and he got up and paced the short patio as the light began to fade into darkness. Sometimes he felt like getting in the car and just driving away, but his resources these days were limited, so that would be stupid. Although it would give him a much needed change of scenery.

Why kid himself? It wasn't just Tanya. He was bewitched by Marilyn. Her quiet competence, strength and understated femininity were attractive, and he hadn't been drawn to a woman in years. After hearing about her ex, he found himself fantasizing about being her knight in shining armor. Maybe he was overcompensating for not being able to protect Tanya, but he'd lay odds every man in that group felt the same. There was something magnetic about her. Yet she remained aloof. They'd had coffee a few times, but her attitude prevented him from asking her to dinner. He couldn't bear rejection just now. Worse yet, he hadn't told her about Owen owning her house. Maybe he was the pussy Tanya had always accused him of being. He kept telling himself he'd talk to her about it, but she already had so much to worry about, he didn't want to contribute to her troubles. Plus, he didn't want to be the bearer of bad news. It certainly wouldn't make her like him. But what if she got mad when she found out? What if she blamed him for holding out on her? It seemed like a lose-lose situation to him.

Annoyed, he pitched the last of his iced tea into the yard and stepped back into the air conditioned living room. The contrast with the outdoor heat took his breath away.

It was time he shaped up. Literally. Daily workouts were what he needed. He'd gained weight back, only to become saggy and weak. If he wanted Marilyn to see him, he needed to look better. Having made that commitment, he felt content to drop onto the sofa and watch some TV. Tomorrow he'd get started on a fitness regime.

# 6

# THURSDAY, AUGUST 22, 1996

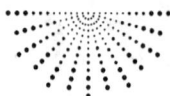

OLIVIA, 3:15PM

*O*livia fretted about how to dress for her appointment with Nurse Yakamura. She knew she was automatically at a disadvantage because she wasn't related to Sophie and had no medical standing. Furthermore, though it ticked her off, she knew her age was against her. She'd suffered plenty of medical condescension during her broken hip incident.

Staring in the bathroom mirror, she approved the look of the black slacks and red silk blouse, and she hoped her jeweled sandals would add casual elegance to the ensemble. The fifteen minutes she'd devoted to war paint had taken ten years off her age. Maybe she should do this every day, but then, she didn't usually have anyone to impress. Her thinning white hair was shiny snow white, not a hair out of place. She was startled to realize that she looked good, at least for her age. She couldn't remember how many years it had been since she'd looked in a mirror without cringing at how fat and old she'd become. The exercise and change of diet after her fall had trimmed her up dramatically, but for some reason, even buying a new wardrobe to replace loose clothes hadn't drummed that fact into her consciousness. Yes, by golly, she looked downright elegant. Maybe she could pull this off, after all.

Straightening her spine, she headed off to her appointment with the nurse in the assisted living wing. She was determined to help Sophie, though she was still clueless how to do so. She popped her head into Sophie's room on the way, but although her friend opened her eyes, she had a glazed look that smacked of drugs. Frustrated again at Sophie's quality of life, she strode purposefully down the hall to the nurse's office.

There was no receptionist. Nurse Yakamura sat behind a big desk, reading glasses perched on the end of her nose as she scanned some paperwork. Her coal black hair was coiled in a tight bun, and her mauve suit projected professionalism and style. She appeared to be maybe 45 years old.

Dark brown humorless eyes glanced up at Olivia. Nurse Yakamura pointed to a chair on the opposite side of the desk. "You must be Mrs. D. Please have a seat," she said without warmth.

Olivia nodded and seated herself in the hard wooden chair that was strong on function, not comfort. Maybe Nurse Y. didn't like visitors to linger.

Acting like she had no idea what Olivia had come for, Nurse Yakamura asked, "What can I do for you?" The question was coated in ice and conveyed that she was a very busy person who didn't suffer fools.

Olivia gulped, suddenly feeling insignificant. Nurse Yakamura's attitude challenged Olivia to plead her case convincingly, and she had so little to go on. "I've come to express my concern about Sophie Aldridge."

Cocking her eyebrows, the nurse replied sardonically, "One's condition is generally precarious after suffering more than one major stroke. Are you a relative?"

It hadn't taken long for her to ask. Olivia wondered if lying would get her anywhere. Probably not. They were using that excuse to brush her off. If she said yes, they'd probably ask for proof, like a power of attorney. Perhaps their records showed that Sophie had no next of kin, and this was an attempt to get Olivia to misrepresent herself. For all she knew, it could be a criminal offense to impersonate family in such a situation. Olivia felt sweat bloom in her armpits, and her fear was interrupted by the ridiculous thought that now she'd have to dry clean the blouse. "No, I'm her only friend, and I am very worried about her."

In Nurse Ratched style, Nurse Yakamura grabbed the pause to take back control. "I'm afraid privacy policy forbids us discussing the details of Mrs. Albright's case with anyone but family."

Anger smoldered in Olivia. "Aldridge. Her name is Sophie Aldridge. Can't you even recall her name? I know Sophie, and something is wrong. She couldn't tell me exactly what, but I know she was terrified about returning to Desert Breezes, and that only makes sense if something bad is going on here." Even to herself, her assertion sounded crazy. She knew she'd overstepped, had no evidence and her anger would work against her.

Sympathy and condescension oozed from Nurse Yakamura. "Mrs. D., it isn't uncommon for elderly patients to be agitated by the constricting results of a stroke. Your friend is sedated for her own good, and maybe she is experiencing some side effects from the sedation and having nightmares or even hallucinations. Our staff is limited. Honestly, the doctor didn't expect her to survive the last stroke. It was quite massive."

Olivia's stomach dropped. Though she'd expected as much, it still shocked her to hear Sophie was under a death sentence. Nurse Yakamura continued. "It's understandable you want what's best for your friend, and we are trying to provide her with the best care we can. I'm violating policy by assuring you there is nothing more we can do for her. It isn't likely she will recover. Seeing her like this has upset you. I urge you to see your doctor. Perhaps medication would help ease your agitation."

Olivia ignored the insulting redirection. She would get no help here. Nurse Yakamura had decided she was a senile old woman and a pain in the ass. Mouth clenched shut to prevent an acerbic reply, Olivia rose stiffly and nodded, then sped out of the office. She was so upset she didn't pause at Sophie's room.

When she got back to her apartment, she sank onto the couch and began to cry. She could see no way she could help Sophie, but she wasn't going to give up. Maybe she *was* a foolish old woman, but her intuition was screaming that something was rotten in assisted living.

\* \* \*

## SAMANTHA, 7:40PM

Samantha rinsed out the hummingbird feeder parts, which afforded her the opportunity of hiding her shock. The running water had hopefully masked her gasp.

"I know you heard me, Samantha. When are you going to tell me the truth about you and Jack? After I'm dead?" Her mother's voice cut her like a sharp knife. She hadn't heard this much strength in it for a long time.

A familiar knot clenched her stomach. She really didn't need this confrontation. She put the parts of the feeder on the counter and turned around, trying to frame an answer that gave nothing away. "Jack has been very kind, giving Beau a home. He respects and appreciates my work. There isn't anything else to tell." That was more true than she wanted it to be.

Mom grunted. "Well, if so, at least you have the good sense not to get involved with him before you leave Arthur. When do you plan to do that? Are you waiting for me to die?"

Samantha cringed at the harsh truth. It had become a linear project with a checklist that placed Mom's death before her divorce. But she wasn't doing it for nefarious or even selfish reasons. She sighed and trudged over to sit on the couch. Forcing herself to look Mom in the eye, she found she couldn't dissemble. "I never intended it that way. I just want to put you first."

Mom didn't look surprised. She shook her head and frowned more furrows into her face. "I've been waiting for you to tell me for weeks. Did you want me to die thinking you were going to stay trapped in that marriage?"

Samantha closed her open mouth. "You have so much going on now. I thought worrying about me would drag you down. And if I proceed with a divorce now, it will take some of my nonexistent free time, and I don't want to impact our time together. Plus, I was sure you wouldn't approve."

A smile creased Mom's face. "At last. I wish you had told me long ago. I had to wring the truth out of Jack."

Samantha shot to a standing position. "Jack told you? How could he?" Anger at his betrayal swept through her.

"Hold your horses. I said I wrung it out of him. That boy is no squealer, but he's no liar, either. He had no choice. And he pleased me by saying he loves you."

Samantha sank slowly back onto the couch, shocked by the revelation. "He didn't tell me he told you."

"That's because I made it clear I wanted to hear from you, but I got worried you weren't ever going to tell me." A frown reprimanded Samantha, but dissipated quickly.

"You stayed married to Dad all those years, and you weren't happy."

"Times have changed. Or maybe I can't bear to see you fritter your life away in an empty marriage when you could have so much more. It would do my heart good to see you start a new life before I go. I didn't have the courage, but I know you do."

One shock replaced another. Mom rarely complimented her. Samantha registered what this meant. As hard as divorcing Arthur would be, knowing Mom was behind her lifted a huge weight that made it seem easier. "You really don't mind?"

"I want you to be happy. You're my only child. I especially want you to have a happier life than mine. It would please me to see you start fresh with Jack."

Samantha felt physical relief as she lay down the burden of guilt over the divorce. "OK. I'll do it. I'll make sure I can still come by often to see you."

Mom jumped right in. "You can't live with Jack. You need somewhere neutral until you're divorced."

"Oh, Mom, I won't ask Arthur for alimony, so it really doesn't matter much, and I've looked into it. I can get a no fault divorce easily."

Mom narrowed her eyes. "You get half of everything. He'll have to mortgage the house if he wants to keep it—I know you don't plan to ask for it. You're too young to own it. He won't be happy to go into debt and lose your income, no matter how small it is. He might not even be able to maintain his current standard of living, so he won't be thanking you for not asking for alimony. In fact, since all he's got is his retirement, he might even be able to ask you for some. Don't give him cause to fight by flaunting Jack."

Silence fell as they both pondered options. Samantha hadn't given any thought to Arthur asking for alimony. That was downright weird, but who knew what he'd do when she asked for a divorce? Mom spoke first. "I've been thinking, and Mary Beth is your best bet. She is moving into a big new house next week, and she'll have lots of room. She'll let you stay with her."

"It's true she offered me a place, but she just got married, and moving is very chaotic. The last thing she needs is a roommate."

"Pish and tush. She owes me and others for putting a roof over her head. She'll welcome the chance to help you. Besides, she's your friend. You two are like sisters."

Samantha hadn't thought to look at it that way and said so.

Mom snorted. "I figured. Now go fill the hummingbird feeder and start planning how and when to tell Arthur. Don't put it off."

Samantha rose, put a hand on Mom's shoulder in gratitude, then completed her task in a daze. Now all she needed was to summon the courage to tell Arthur. Then she realized this meant she could call Jack on the way home and break the good news. A smile blossomed from deep inside her at the thought of finally taking action.

Mom had given her her blessing to follow her heart. This was as unexpected as snow here for Christmas, and every bit as delightful a surprise. She faced Mom, annoyed how hard it was for her to form the words. "I don't know how to thank you. This changes everything for me." Then she went over and gave her a hug. Mom smiled at her with eyes shining.

She left Desert Breezes primed for action and stopped by the Rec Center to call Jack. He answered the phone on the first ring. "Hi, it's me." Her heart thumped with the excitement of sharing her news. "I just visited Mom. She told me to ditch Arthur and marry you." She held her breath for his reaction.

"I told you she liked me," said Jack, a flicker of humor in his voice. "So are you going to take her advice?"

"I realized that she was the biggest obstacle to my taking action. She removed it when she said to leave Arthur. She even suggested I stay with Mary Beth, which I am going to do. I wanted to tell you right away. I feel like I've won the lottery. I'm going home now to think out the steps, but I had to tell you first. You still want me to?"

He snorted. "Seriously, you jest. You know I've been pacing like a caged lion waiting for you to leave him. Do it."

She sighed with relief. It was going to work out. "Thanks. I just needed to hear you say it before I do the deed."

"Consider it said."

She murmured words of agreement and hung up. Telling Arthur was going to be hard, but she also needed to tell Christine. She'd only hinted about her marriage difficulties, and with the CSL tea coming up in nine days, she needed to come clean with Christine to avoid having her call the house after she left, and she was planning to leave almost immediately after breaking the news to Arthur.

She was ashamed she hadn't done a damn thing for the CSL fund-raising tea. There were too many more important things going on, and she couldn't psych herself to focus on it. If she failed in her assignment, Christine would be upset for being let down, and Samantha didn't want to do that. Maybe if she told her friend about the coming separation, Christine could reassign the task to someone with less going on. Yes, it made sense to tell her now and tie up that loose end.

She dialed Christine's number from memory. "Hi, it's me. Samantha."

"Oh, hi, Samantha. Are you calling about the centerpieces for the tea?" Christine was all business. Samantha envied her for the tea being the most dramatic thing going on in her life.

"Yes and no. I've been really swamped, and I haven't had a chance to come up with any worthwhile ideas. The reason I'm calling is I have some news that might impact my ability to participate in the event." She cursed herself for not having come up with a good way to tell Christine. She wasn't good on her feet at all.

"What's going on?"

Samantha gathered her courage and plunged ahead. "Well, you know I said things weren't going that smoothly with me and Arthur? I'm asking him for a divorce."

Silence stretched to an uncomfortable point.

"Did you hear me?"

"Yes, I did. Why are you leaving Arthur? Has he done something terrible?"

Samantha had no intention of airing dirty laundry with Christine. She wasn't a gossip, but she was very judgmental, and Arthur was going to have to live in Palm Lakes. There was no use telling about his past indiscretion, as it didn't bear directly on her decision. She struggled to find something honest to say that wasn't too revealing. "Arthur and I have been drifting apart for years, and it just isn't working between us." It sounded thin even to her.

"Can't you get counseling or something?"

"Arthur doesn't believe in that. I've tried to muddle on through, and he seems content with what we have, but honestly, I'm not. It's like sleepwalking through life. I want more." Maybe that had been a mistake.

"Is there someone else?" Christine asked tartly.

"My choice is entirely due to the fact that our marriage is and has been empty for some time now. I am not sleeping around on him." No point in attracting judgment by telling her about Jack.

"Well, this is just awful. How could you do this to me?"

*What?* "Do what to you?" Samantha blurted in shock.

"You don't see how this affects me? I sponsored you in CSL, and this scandal will be all over Palm Lakes in no time. It will destroy the tea. And it makes me look like an idiot for bringing you into CSL."

Samantha didn't know what to say. It never entered her mind that Christine would feel this way.

"In the interest of the tea being a success, I think you should withdraw from CSL and give me back your CSL pin. I can just say you're moving away. You are leaving Palm Lakes, aren't you?"

She felt like she was being run out of town on a rail. "Eventually, I will. My Mom will be gone, and my job is across town, and Arthur will probably keep the house. So yes." *Was this even happening?* It was surreal.

"Fine. You can drop your pin by or mail it to me. Whatever you want. Maybe mailing it would be better. No need for drama."

*What drama? She was the one creating a drama.* Boy, she'd been wrong about Christine being her friend. Tears came to her eyes. She was being thrown out with the garbage. Well, at least this prepared her for the down side of this decision. Telling Arthur was going to be harder. "Fine, I'll mail the pin to you." Samantha hung up without waiting for a reply.

The silver lining was she didn't have to worry about the centerpieces for the tea. That gave her a measure of satisfaction. She wiped her eyes and went to the ladies room to splash water in her face. Looking in the mirror, she could see the traces of all the emotions of the day: surprise, joy, sadness at betrayal. She took a deep breath and forced herself to relax. It was going to be all right. The important things were working out.

She needed to try and sleep tonight and rehearse what she'd say to Arthur. No, first she needed to call Mary Beth. At least she was certain of the response she'd get there. She went back to the phone booth and dialed her friend. Two minutes later, she headed home, or what would soon be her ex-home, assured of a place to stay while she got the divorce.

# 7

# TUESDAY, SEPTEMBER 3, 1996

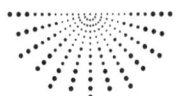

MARILYN, 5:40AM

*T*he clock said 5:40am when Marilyn turned over and checked it for what seemed like the hundredth time that night. Dawn was breaking, spilling weak light around the edges of the thick bedroom curtains, promising that once again, a seemingly endless night was over.

Reaching under her pillow, Marilyn withdrew the .38 revolver and placed it on the bedside table, reassured by its weight. Though having the gun close to hand was comforting, it had failed to drive off the fears that had plagued her all night, fear that she might have to face Ted, and fear of the outcome. If he never came, but she continued to be afraid, she would have allowed him to ruin her life. If he showed up and tried to hurt her, she'd lose no matter who won the fight. It seemed the only winning solution was if she could go back in time and erase Ted from her life. She rubbed her scratchy eyes and pushed herself to a sitting position, feeling as if she weighed a ton.

Ted's card lay on the nightstand, a freakish reminder that he hadn't moved on. A young woman danced through a meadow of wildflowers on the front of the card. Her black and white puppy, eerily like a young

Tammi, had a crude black bull's-eye drawn over it in Sharpie pen. She shuddered at the threat. Ted had found out about Tammi, not that Marilyn had gone to great pains to hide her. After all, Tammi was meant as a deterrent to Ted's violence.

She didn't have to look inside to recall the message scrawled in Ted's barely legible hand. "I know where you are" it warned in blood-red ink. *Nice touch, asshole.* No signature, no overt threat, no return address, though it was mailed in Virginia several days ago near where they had once lived.

She could report it and get another restraining order, or maybe even have him charged with harassment, but she knew any attention would only fuel his morbid fantasy of controlling her, of making her live in fear of his power. Ignoring him was the best choice.

A flicker of concern that he would kill Tammi flooded through her, but she told herself that was just his way of grabbing her attention. Then she decided that his mind was so convoluted she should not reject any idea out of hand. She'd never seen him harm an animal, but she needed to protect Tammi from him.

He knew how to find her. She picked up the card with two fingers as if it were a rotting fish, then consigned it to the trash can near the nightstand. "Take that, you bastard," she whispered angrily. She should have done that the minute she received it. No matter. She dropped back to sit on the bed, aching with sleepiness.

She needed to think, to formulate some defense. She absentmindedly rubbed her upper arms to chase away the goose pimples, then remembered how one summer, he'd blown up and punched both her upper arms repeatedly. The next day, they'd been horribly sore, black and blue. She covered them for work, but made no attempts to hide the injuries at home. He'd never referred to the bruising. By then, he'd found she wasn't leaving, so apologies were superfluous. Shuddering again, she sent gratitude to the Universe or whatever God was out there that she'd escaped his abuse. As bad is it was to have him taunting her with threats, at least it was from a distance. She could sense his frustration and even desperation from over two thousand miles away, but the distance helped. A little.

Tammi had come over from her bed in the corner the minute Marilyn sat up. Intelligent brown eyes radiated concern, and Tammi rested her huge head on Marilyn's knee. Petting Tammi soothed the tempest within her. There was no reason to assume Ted would invest in a flight or road trip of nearly 2500 miles. Sure, he was angry and mentally imbalanced, but he was also a cheapskate. Sending a card or box was one thing. A trip across country was unthinkable. Maybe.

She put her revolver in the nightstand's drawer and set out to face the day, which was as inviting as a trek across a desert. She felt so alone and exhausted. How could she concentrate on anything with this going on? Her one concession to her worries about Ted was locking the dog door at night. It was probably too small to grant anyone access, but she also wanted to keep Tammi from a nighttime encounter. She might be paranoid, but she wouldn't put it past Ted to poison a dog. She'd walk the perimeter of the yard every morning from now on and check for foreign objects.

Patrolling the fence in the early morning light calmed Marilyn. The birdsong wasn't nearly as raucous as back in Virginia, but mourning doves and quail were sounding off, and the occasional bark of a neighbor's dog pierced her thoughts. The air was noticeably cooler than it had been at dawn in August and July, but still warm enough to warrant wearing shorts. The humidity of the monsoon had fled, returning the desert to its normal dry heat.

The new fence with its wrought iron on top of stuccoed block was the best investment she'd made. Getting over it would be a challenge. She kept the gate locked, so that entry was denied any but the most highly motivated. Ted could still lob poisoned meat over the fence, but walking up to her back yard was risky. He certainly wouldn't attempt it in daylight, and nighttime around here was like a cemetery, so he'd stand out like a sore thumb. Perhaps if she reported seeing a prowler, the Posse would patrol her street more vigilantly. She balked at the idea of fibbing, but it really wasn't that far from the truth, and it would help her sleep better knowing the Posse was on the job.

As she continued the patrol, she noticed her shrubs and two citrus trees were lush and green. Apparently the irrigation system was functioning well. She hadn't gotten around to learning much about that. She made a mental note of asking Barbara about setting the timer. Surely the change of weather required a change of watering, but she was clueless about plants.

In fact, she vaguely remembered she needed to fertilize her citrus trees this time of year. Emma or Julio could tell her.

Glad to have mundane details to distract her, she finished the yard inspection, Tammi at her heels.

* * *

MARY BETH, 7:00AM

Mary Beth stepped into the kitchen, making noise so as not to startle Samantha, who stood at the sink peeling an orange, her back to the doorway.

Samantha turned as if startled. "Oh, hi. I didn't expect you'd be up so early. Did I wake you? I tried to be quiet." Samantha wore the worried look she'd had ever since moving in a little over a week ago. Dark circles smudged under her eyes, speaking of poor sleep, and Mary Beth was certain she'd lost weight. Not to mention a new wrinkle between her eyebrows from her perpetual frown.

"You didn't wake me," Mary Beth lied. No need to add to her worries. "The split floor plan helps a lot." She walked to the coffee pot, which was full of fresh brew. Pouring herself a cup, she sat at the breakfast bar. "You look stressed and tired."

"Yeah, well, I'm late again for work. Jack doesn't mind. He knows I'll get back on track, but it bothers me. I've got all this help, yet I'm floundering." She shoved an orange section into her mouth and chewed aggressively.

"No, you're not floundering. Divorce is a messy thing, no matter what the circumstances. You're too kind to Arthur, taking all the responsibility for the breakup. Trust me, he did more than his fair share."

Samantha frowned more, if that was even possible. "I shouldn't have told you he had an affair. That's ancient history and has no bearing on now. I guess I wanted to have one person not judge me."

"Ancient history? Surely, his affair was a precipitator of the divorce, no matter how long ago it was. How could you ever hope to trust him again? And who judged you? Your Mom has been great. Don't get me wrong, but it surprised the hell out of me how supportive she's been. She even pushed you into leaving him."

Samantha laughed, the frown draining from her face. She brought the remains of her orange to the counter and sat beside Mary Beth, still chuckling. "Yeah, who knew Mom would be an ally?" She munched on another orange segment while Mary Beth sipped her coffee, unsure what to say next.

Samantha paused, a piece of orange poised in the air before her mouth. "Christine was upset. She said something along the lines of I hadn't given any thought to the position I'd put her in with CSL and for the tea they were having, as word of my divorce would ruin the event. She threw me out of CSL and even asked for her stupid pin back."

"They have a pin?" Mary Beth tried to picture Samantha in some uptight sorority. "Do they have a secret handshake?" she quipped, then immediately regretted her lighthearted reply.

Samantha barked in laughter, then went quiet.

Anger welled up in Mary Beth. Her friend deserved more loyalty than that. "What exactly did she say?"

Samantha recounted the conversation with the former client she had befriended. Mary Beth struggled to overcome speechlessness. "What a fucking cow!" she blurted out.

The smile she had seen only rarely in recent days lit up Samantha's face. "Thanks for that. I realize she's embarrassed that she sponsored me. I also think she's annoyed that I wouldn't confide in her about why I'm leaving Arthur. I didn't want to make life in Palm Lakes harder for Arthur by airing dirty laundry. I never have trusted Christine the way I do you."

The confession warmed Mary Beth's heart. "You know you're like a sister to me. I'm glad I can be here for you. Like a good sister, I have to nudge you about healthy choices. You need to eat and sleep more. You need to set aside guilt. You're doing the right thing."

Samantha's wan smile said she wasn't there yet. "I still have to remove my things from our house. Arthur is looking into a mortgage so he can buy me out. I rented a storage unit near work, and I have my truck, and Arthur and I have agreed on how to divide things. I'm feeling nervous about retrieving my belongings. Obviously, I can't bring Jack to help load them, and I can't easily do it alone, and I don't want to ask Arthur. I'm afraid it might push him over the edge."

"Of course, Jack can't help. In fact, you should tell him to avoid Palm Lakes until the divorce is final, just to be safe."

Chagrin emanated from Samantha. "I know. It's good sense, but Mom loves Jack and looks forward to seeing him and Beau. I don't think Arthur's the violent or even jealous type, but…"

"Maybe Jack can come visit, but you need me or someone else there in case Arthur shows up at your Mom's place. He won't act out in front of anyone else. And Ethan and I will help you load and move your belongings to storage. Is there anything large? Ethan is OK on anything except really heavy stuff."

"The only furniture I'm taking is my childhood dresser, and it's small. I do have a lot of books and some clothes and a few other things, though."

"We can handle that. Get the small moving boxes from the U-Haul place. That will keep the weight down."

Samantha sighed. "I don't know what I would do without you." She reached up to wipe tears from her eyes.

Mary Beth reached over and gripped her shoulder. "What are friends for? I am indebted to so many people for putting a roof over my head before my marriage. It's my pleasure to help you."

"I'll try not to impose on your hospitality for too long."

"It takes what it takes. You're hardly ever here, anyway. You work and take care of Maddie. We hardly even notice you. You plan on staying here until the divorce is final."

Samantha nodded and stood up. "I need to get to work."

"This will be over before you know it." The words sounded hollow to Mary Beth, but what else could she say to her friend?

She watched Samantha gather her things and leave through the garage. Maybe she could crawl back into bed and snuggle up to her new husband. She needed some warmth and reassurance.

* * *

## STEVEN, 9:30AM

Steven sat on the couch, staring at the phone. He'd been doing that for thirty minutes while his coffee went cold. Each time he pumped up his courage and picked up the handset, it turned into a hundred-pound weight, and he set it down.

When was the last time he'd felt this fearful and uncertain? When he was sixteen and was working up the nerve to ask Janice what's-her-name for a date? The humiliation of her rejection, though it was decades old, washed over him. All he wanted now was for Marilyn to accept his dinner invitation with pleasure. He'd planned the menu, but hadn't bought anything yet, just in case.

A chilled white wine and some cheese and crackers to start would be nice. Or maybe that was too fancy? No, it was easy and yet special. Then he'd grill some juicy steaks and serve potatoes baked in the microwave, or started in the microwave and finished on the grill, along with a tossed salad. For dessert, something from the bakery at Safeway. They made some fancy single-serving desserts. Women liked chocolate, didn't they? He'd never asked Marilyn her preferences.

If he could work up the courage to call, he could run the menu by her. He reached for the phone again and imagined her rejecting him. No matter how casual and friendly he tried to make it sound, it was still a date, and she'd know it.

She hadn't given him a bit of encouragement, but she did seem to enjoy his company. They'd gone for coffee after the group session several times, and she seemed relaxed with him, even laughed at his lame jokes. Now that the support group was no longer meeting, if he wanted to see her, he had to make his own opportunities. And although the group sessions hadn't filled him with self-confidence, he was becoming aware that he was now open to possibilities in a way he hadn't been for years. He may not be brave, but he wanted to have Marilyn continue to be part of his life, and he wanted his life to continue to change.

He glanced around the living room, wincing at the garish decor. He wasn't eager to have her see it. She'd know instantly the kind of person Tanya was, or at least what she projected to others. It didn't seem to reflect well on his choice of partners, but there was nothing he could do. Maybe he could save up and redecorate. But enough of that. He was just making excuses. He needed to overcome his fear and damn well call her. Anything would be better than this not knowing.

Annoyed at his waffling and mentally hearing the strident voice of Tanya calling him a wimp spurred him to quickly dial Marilyn's number. As the phone began to ring, he wondered how many times to let it ring before hanging up, then realized she might have one of those message machines. His stomach dropped at the thought of leaving her a message. No, he'd just hang up on the fifth ring, or the sixth.

"Hello?" Marilyn's voice trembled, or seemed to.

"It's me. Steven."

Marilyn sighed, but it sounded like relief, not annoyance. "Hi, Steven. How are you?"

"Fine, thank you. I just called on the off chance that I could convince you to come over and take a gamble on my cooking tonight. They had rib eye steaks on sale—(lie), and I hate cooking for one—(truth). I was thinking a simple meal of steak, baked potato and a salad. What do you say?" He hadn't been able to keep the stiltedness out of his tone, but at least he'd done it. He cringed, waiting for the expected refusal.

"That would be nice. Tell me when. I'll bring a bottle of red wine. Can Tammi come? I hate to leave her alone."

He didn't care if she brought the Tasmanian devil, as long as she showed up. "Sure, bring her along." He decided not to ask about the rest of the menu and concluded by telling her to show up at 5pm.

After hanging up, he slouched on the sofa, immensely pleased with himself. The tension had drained from his muscles and he could finally breathe easily. Now all he had to do was find some ribeye steaks and make a great meal.

* * *

MADDIE, 10:45AM

Maddie stared at the small, gold-toned gift box that sat on her dining table. It was the last of the necklace and earring sets she'd made for her loved ones. She laid a proprietary hand on the square box and lifted the lid. The turquoise and silver necklace lay coiled on the soft bed of fluff, earrings in the center. A smile warmed Maddie from head to toe. They had turned out gorgeous. She couldn't articulate the joy she got from creating beautiful things; she simply felt lit from within when she regarded one of her creations.

This last set was Olivia's. She'd give it to her tonight before dinner and bingo. Everyone had been so appreciative of their gift. Barbara and Helen, always so sweet, bubbled over with gratitude. In her typical thoughtful way, Helen immediately put hers on to model for Maddie, and oh, the necklace was the perfect length and turquoise sure was her color.

Maybe their gratitude was tinged with sadness, knowing Maddie had probably made her last necklace. Samantha tried to hide it, but she'd gotten teary-eyed when accepting hers. Maddie had learned to live with the sadness, but in a strange way, it made her feel good not to be alone in her grief about life slipping away from her.

Thank God Samantha had made her move with Arthur. Now that Samantha was staying with Mary Beth, Maddie felt such relief. Arthur had never liked her, maybe because he knew she was wise to him. He didn't treat Samantha like he treasured her. Instead, he swanned about playing tennis and let her work full time. They didn't have a partnership. He had freedom, a young wife and a meal ticket. So what if he had a pension? It wouldn't have been enough to retire and live in Palm Lakes. Which stirred her concern that maybe Arthur would react strongly to the divorce. His way of life was threatened. He had never seemed to lean towards anger or violence; he'd never even raised his voice to her in spite of disliking her. Yet, there was a depth to his silence that hinted perhaps he buried his anger rather than flaunting it. She shook off her worries. Samantha would be out of Palm Lakes soon enough, and she could rest assured that Samantha would start life anew, the way Maddie had always dreamed she would. That was what mattered.

She felt a pang of guilt at the thought that she'd pushed Samantha so hard because of her own fractured marriage, but shoved it aside. She wasn't trying to live vicariously through her. She wanted Samantha to be happy, and Jack, well, he felt like the real McCoy. He answered straight, even when he didn't want to. He put Samantha's feelings first, though it obviously chafed his pride. She felt he really loved Samantha. Maybe her daughter would have what Maddie had never experienced. And if she could have a hand in that, what a great legacy.

She strained to push herself up from the dining table and shuffled to her recliner, panting with each step, eager to relax with some mindless entertainment. After getting seated and adjusting the oxygen tubing, she took time to recover and only then remembered she hadn't had anything to eat or drink since last night. She wasn't hungry, rarely was these days, but she could use a drink. But the kitchenette seemed miles away, so she ignored the thirst like she usually did when it was inconvenient and reached for the TV remote. Maybe there was an old movie on. She flipped through the channels, grateful for a chance to take her mind off the future.

* * *

STEVEN, 5:15PM

Steven glanced surreptitiously at Marilyn, who stood next to him on the patio, glass of chilled Chardonnay in hand, as he checked the temperature of the grill. He forced himself to sound more relaxed than he felt. "It's nearly there. You don't have to stay out in this heat. I won't be long, just want to put the steaks on."

She was staring at the raw steaks on the plate, but she seemed miles away. "Really, I don't mind," she said. "Back home, at this time of year I'd be pouring sweat—pardon how graphic I am. This is a dry heat," she said emphatically.

He chuckled at the well-worn joke. "It helps that the patio faces north. At least in summer. We should have a patio on the opposite side for winter, so you could catch the warmth."

She didn't reply, her gaze unfocused.

Was it being with him, or was something troubling her? Not really sure he wanted to know, he asked, "What's wrong?" He hoped her distress wasn't discomfort at being in his home.

She looked at him with focus for the first time since she'd arrived, pale blue eyes filled with trouble. "I'm having a bad day." She turned and walked to a chair, followed by her monstrous dog. Steven found the animal's silence and sharp intelligence a bit unnerving. Tammi was more like a person than a dog.

He waited for her to continue as he carefully arranged the steaks on the rack. He relaxed a fraction. Her distraction didn't seem to be about him. The soaked mesquite chips in the small aluminum pan below the steaks pumped out fragrant smoke that would add flavor to the meat. He hadn't done this in quite some time, and he hoped he hadn't lost his touch. He closed the top of the grill and took the empty plate over to the small table and sat down, wanting to help, but not sure he could.

Finally, Marilyn drained the rest of her wine and sighed. "I don't mean to complain, and I probably shouldn't involve you." She turned the empty glass in her hand, fingering the condensation. "Ted sent me a card. Not a nice card. I threw it out. It had a woman with a puppy that looked like Tammi on the front. He'd drawn a bull's-eye over the dog. Inside he wrote in red ink, 'I know where you are.' I got upset, but I'm doing better now."

"That bastard," muttered Steven, anger flaring. "He has no right. Can you report him? What can we do?" *Where had the 'we' come from?* Marilyn didn't seem to have noticed his word choice.

"He didn't sign it, but it was his handwriting. It isn't a real threat, and I've thought about it a lot, and I don't think he'd come all this way. He hates to spend money, and why come 2500 miles to stalk me?"

Steven didn't know Ted except by what Marilyn had shared, but the man was obviously violent. Now he appeared to be obsessed. He didn't want to scare her any more than she already was, and he had no idea how to assess the threat. Maybe she was right. Or maybe the guy had murder on his mind."You are good about locking up, even when you are home?" It seemed a lame comment, but he couldn't think of anything else to say. Who was he, Superman? He couldn't protect her from a rogue cop, even if he wanted to.

"Of course. And I don't go out after dark. Tammi is with me at home, plus I have a gun and know how to use it."

*A gun?* She thought it might come to that? Guns made him nervous, which only accentuated his feelings of inadequacy in dealing with a violent ex, but he had to offer something. "You can call me anytime, day or night. And I don't care if it's nothing. In fact, I'd prefer if it turned out to be nothing. I'm no Rambo, as you can plainly see." He gestured to his body and grinned, hoping to lighten the mood.

"Oh, Steven. That means a lot to me. Barbara has made the same offer. She even said Tammi and I could come stay with her if we needed to. You guys can be my neighborhood watch. Just call the Posse if you see anyone strange hanging around."

"You can count on me." Desperate to change the mood, he said, "How about we go inside? The steaks won't take long. The salad is ready. I want to transfer the potatoes from the microwave to the top rack of the grill." He stood, plate in hand, waiting for her, hoping they could transition to a lighter subject. He was in over his head completely. She needed more than an aging intellectual. She needed a retired SEAL or other macho superhero type.

Marilyn picked up her empty glass, and she and Tammi followed him into the kitchen. The air conditioning blasted him when they stepped inside. "I don't have the A/C on that low, but it sure feels cold after standing out there."

He did his chores and returned to the kitchen, where Marilyn stood listlessly. This was a downer. How could he inject some lightness into the evening? He grabbed the red wine she'd brought, noted it was a nice vintage, and opened it and poured them each a glass. "Let's try this wine. It looks fantastic." At this rate of drinking, he'd be blitzed by dessert, but what the heck? "Let's go sit for a while." He led the way into the living room.

Marilyn sat on the couch and Tammi lay down at her feet. Steven took a chair nearby, not wanting to crowd her. Desperate for something to say, he ventured, "You haven't commented on my decor."

Marilyn laughed out loud, and it sounded genuine. "You're such a hoot, Steven. Just what I need to cheer up."

"So that means you don't like my style?" he asked coyly.

"I never would have guessed. If you say you're going to slip into something comfortable, don't come out dressed like Donna Summer." Her face was split by a genuine smile.

He raised an eyebrow dramatically. "Donna Summer? My dear, it would have to be Diana Ross."

They both giggled. Glad the tension was gone, he added, "I do need to redecorate. I left that to Tanya, and this just isn't me."

"It's a relief to hear that."

The timer in the kitchen chimed, and Steven jumped up to check the steaks. A very leisurely hour later, they sat at the dining table finishing their crème brulée. The conversation had mercifully veered away from Ted to lighter topics. He'd enjoyed discovering their mutual interest in old movies and classic science fiction stories.

"This has been the best meal I've had in ages," sighed Marilyn, patting her stomach. "I'm not much of a cook."

"Tammi can have the steak trimmings now, or I'll give you a doggie bag."

Marilyn groaned at his humor. "That's thoughtful. Whatever is easiest. She'd be happy to have them now. She's been watching my every move. We don't have steak very often. In fact, I'm not sure I've ever had it since I got Tammi. That trick with the mesquite was something else! You're a real gourmet cook."

He preened at the compliment. Tanya had never complimented him about anything, at least not after their first year of marriage. "I've always enjoyed cooking, but when I was working, I was too busy. Once I retired, I started doing a little experimenting. Nothing fancy, but I cook a mean roast chicken."

"I'm sure you do. I find I'm uninspired to cook just for me. The move and everything…well, we're only now settling in, and then Ted resurfaced, and it threw me off. I'll have to make you dinner. I'm pretty good with a crock pot, but I've never made anything exotic. Ted was a meat and potatoes guy, and he didn't like trying new things. I've promised myself I'm going to branch out and get into ethnic food, but I haven't had the energy yet. Do you like Mexican? I thought I'd give that a try."

"I love Mexican. Just not too hot. I like spice, but not a 3-alarm fire. I was out in Monterey on travel some years back and went to a Thai restaurant on Cannery Row. The guy asked if I wanted my food a 'little bit hot.' His accent was pretty thick, and 'little' came out as 'leelel'. I stressed that I only wanted it a little bit hot. When I tasted my meal, it blew the top off my head. I couldn't eat it, it was so hot, but I didn't have the guts to complain. I couldn't be sure he'd understood me. I suspect he enjoyed playing tricks on the tourist."

Marilyn had a hand over her mouth as if trying not to laugh. "You're too nice."

"I've never been accused of that. I'm a lawyer, for God's sake."

They both laughed, and he stood to clear the table. She rose to help, and before long, the dishwasher was loaded and Tammi had scarfed down her treat and was staring at them, perhaps hoping for more.

"Where has the time gone? I had no idea it was this late," said Marilyn.

The clock on the stove said 11:06. Steven hadn't noticed the time passing. "I'll walk you home."

"Nonsense, I only live a couple houses down the street."

"I won't have you going out alone after dark. You said you don't do that." He looked at her pointedly.

"I have Tammi."

"I won't negotiate with you." This was one thing he felt competent to do, and he wasn't going to give in.

"OK, you can walk us home." She rolled her eyes in mock sarcasm, but smiled.

They stepped out into a warm night and a sky full of stars, a last quarter moon sending faint light across the landscape. He paused on the sidewalk and pointed. "You can see the Milky Way. It would be better if there was no moon."

Marilyn gasped. "It's so beautiful. I had no idea we could see it here."

"Only at certain times of year. One of the benefits of being at the edge of developed land. I doubt they see it in the city. You can't always see it here. Sometimes in summer we get awful inversions, and the smog gets trapped and muddies the sky."

They sauntered down the street, then turned up Marilyn's walk. Her whole body tensed up as they approached her front door. He wondered if it was about him or about Ted. He'd given a lot of thought to what he'd do if he ever reached this point with her, and he was still torn. He didn't want to push too hard, but the evening had awakened feelings he thought were long dead, and he wondered if she felt the same. Probably had Ted on her mind too much to think of romance.

They paused at the door as she fiddled nervously with her keys. Her hesitation made him decisive. He reached over and took them from her. "I'm going to sweep through the house—Tammi can help—then I'll check out back and let you get to bed. You'll sleep better if you feel safe."

"How could you tell I didn't like returning to an empty house after dark?"

"It was logical. You've had quite a scare. It will get easier." He resisted the urge to touch her then, though she looked fragile and in need of a hug. It would be ambiguous, and he wasn't sure he'd be content with just a friendly hug. The timing was off, curse Ted and his own indecisiveness.

Five minutes later, inspection completed, he shook her hand, patted Tammi gingerly on the head and came away with a whole hand, and smiled with more happiness than he felt and walked home. As he treaded down the concrete walk, he told himself next time. Next time, he promised himself, he'd kiss her. But somewhere deep inside, he wasn't sure he had the courage to face possible rejection. Maybe he was using Ted as a convenient excuse.

* * *

OLIVIA, 5:30PM

"Oh, my, Maddie, this is stunning! I do adore turquoise." Olivia held her necklace to the light, then put it on. It gave a splash of color to her white blouse. After struggling a bit with the clasp, she smoothed the necklace out and lifted the earrings out of the box. "Lucky for me I have pierced ears." She took off her simple gold hoops and put on the dangly turquoise earrings with french earwires. "I do like this style. So easy to put on."

Maddie regarded her with a pleased expression. "I'm glad you like it."

"Like it? That's a colossal understatement. It's a real privilege to have custom-made jewelry. I'll treasure this set." She put her other earrings in the gift box and laid it on the end table.

Maddie went to haul herself out of her recliner, but Olivia put a hand out. "You sit down. I can manage something as simple as spaghetti." She strode over to the small stove and saw that the water wasn't yet boiling, then returned to the living room. "Patience. Not ready yet. But the sauce looks and smells delicious."

Maddie nodded at the compliment. "I decided to simmer it. I don't usually get enough of a head start to do that, but they say it adds flavor."

"I'm sure it will be perfect. So, are you up for bingo tonight? We don't have to go."

Maddie started to answer, but fell into a coughing jag. Once she regained her breath, she said, "It's my only chance to get out, going to things downstairs. You know I can't ride in a car anymore. Hurts too much. I'd like to do things for as long as I can. I'm short of breath, but if I go slow, I'll be all right. How about a beer or glass of wine with dinner?"

"I'd just love a glass of wine. I'll serve us up, dear. Shall I get the drinks now or with dinner?"

Maddie answered forcefully, "I could use a beer now."

Olivia smiled and fetched a cold Bud for Maddie and a glass of red wine for herself. An hour later, after a filling meal of homemade spaghetti, they moseyed downstairs to the large room used for movies and bingo.

They were fifteen minutes early, but already a few people had claimed seats in the first row of tables, the best place for the hard of hearing, as they sat nearest the speakers. Maddie chose the end seat in the second row of tables, and Olivia sat next to her after helping Maddie stash her walker with oxygen tank out of the walkway.

Olivia watched people trickle in, mainly one at a time, but the occasional cluster of friends or married couple. Maddie dozed off, tired from the effort of trekking from her room, causing Olivia to question how many bingo nights she had left. She fingered her necklace, sad for the decline of a brave and generous spirit, but also sorry for herself. First Sophie, now Maddie. She had no other real friends here. If only she could find someone who'd be around for longer than a few months. Perhaps that was too much to hope for at her age.

"Is this seat taken?" a familiar deep voice asked. She looked up into Nick Dwyer's smiling blue eyes. He was big and solid as a mountain. Nearly took her breath away.

"Please join us," she said when she got her wits about her. Maddie continued to snore softly. Olivia shrugged her shoulders. "Maddie tires easily. The walk down at the end of a long day takes it out of her. I'll wake her when the game starts."

Nick settled into the seat next to Olivia, and she felt like a wall had been erected very close to her. He pointed to her necklace. "Nice turquoise."

Olivia grinned. "Maddie made it for me. She gave it to me tonight before we came down." She caressed the stones lovingly. "She's very talented."

"She certainly is." Nick hesitated, then said, "I've been thinking of joining the silversmithing club. It sounds like fun."

Olivia raised her eyebrows. Nick had hidden depths. "What else do you like to do?"

"I own a 3-yr-old quarter horse that I ride most mornings. I'm training him for a trail horse. Nothing fancy. At my age, you feel lucky if you can ride without falling off." He chuckled at his own joke.

"I love horses. I rode as a girl, but haven't in ages. And I probably would fall off. What color is your horse?"

"He's a buckskin gelding."

Olivia oohed appreciatively. "They're pretty."

"He's a looker, but he might object to being called pretty." He peered into her eyes. "You want to meet him? He's real friendly. I board him just a few miles from here."

Embarrassment swamped Olivia. She hadn't been fishing for an invitation. But she longed for a chance to see something outside of Desert Breezes. She'd sold her car when she put her house on the market at her daughters' insistence, and she regretted it every day. She was tethered to Desert Breezes and the few places the Desert Breezes bus went and wherever her daughters were willing to drive her on the few occasions they visited. "I'd love to meet him."

Nick pulled a pen out of his pocket and looked about for something to write on, then found a scrap of paper in his pocket. "What's your number? I'll call tomorrow and set something up."

She watched as he wrote the number down, feeling like a young girl setting up a first date with the captain of the football team. It gave her a flutter to think she'd been invited to meet Nick's horse. She wondered why he'd invited her. He didn't seem the gregarious type. He certainly had a lot of interests, and he was imposing physically. She wondered again how old he was.

Just then, a disembodied voice announced the start of the game.

Maddie stirred and pushed herself upright. "I must have drifted off for a minute."

Olivia patted her arm. "Nick's joined us."

When Nick leaned across Olivia to shake Maddie's hand, Olivia caught a whiff of aftershave and clean shirt. "Nice to see you again, Maddie."

Bingo began, and for the next hour they laughed and talked, and Maddie even won the final game and the biggest prize of the night, a box of chocolates. Everyone else got a small candy bar as a consolation prize.

Glowing with pleasure, Maddie chattered more than she had in weeks. Nick walked them to the elevator and rode up to their floor and escorted them to Maddie's place. Before Olivia had a chance to consider inviting him in for a beer—it wasn't her place, after all—he took his leave. "I'm just down the hall and around the corner." He strode down the hallway after a wave and a smile.

Maddie stood in the doorway looking bemused, but then recovered. She unlocked the door using the key on the neon green coiled plastic bracelet on her wrist. "Don't you dare leave, Olivia. You have some explaining to do." Maddie hung the key on the inside doorknob and closed the door.

Olivia had been hugging the pleasure of her conversation with Nick to herself, but she didn't mind sharing. It wasn't any big deal, anyway.

Maddie pulled a can of beer out of the tiny refrigerator and turned to Olivia. "Get yourself a drink and then come over and tell me what's going on with you and that gorgeous man."

Olivia resigned herself to sharing everything with Maddie. It was the least she could do to give her friend a vicarious thrill. They sat with their drinks in the living room. "He just appeared and asked to sit with us. I think he's trying to avoid predatory women."

Maddie snorted. "Don't make me laugh when I'm trying to drink. I'll get beer up my nose." She studied Olivia for a minute. "You may be right. But why you?"

"I honestly can't say. I don't push myself on him and have no designs of any kind. Maybe he senses that."

Maddie nodded, but looked unconvinced. "He's a big guy, like the Duke. Not handsome any more than the Duke was, but very attractive, if you know what I mean."

Olivia couldn't agree more. "He must be over six feet tall. And he's big, but not fat or soft. He told me he rides his horse every day."

Maddie's jaw dropped. "He has a horse? Oh, my God!" She shook her head, a dreamy look on her wrinkled face. "He really is like the Duke."

"He invited me out to meet his horse. He said he'd call me tomorrow about it."

"When did all this happen?"

"While you were sleeping, before bingo started."

"Next time, wake me up. I'm missing out on all the good stuff. Will you tell me how it goes?" Maddie asked wistfully.

Olivia purposely downgraded the invitation. "He might forget he offered, but if he remembers, I'll tell you all about it."

"What an adventure," sighed Maddie enviously.

"We'll see." It was all Olivia was willing to say. She knocked back the tiny bit of wine in her glass. "I'm heading home. I'll see you tomorrow."

The said their goodbyes, and Olivia locked the door as she left, so Maddie didn't have to get up. She hadn't told Maddie she had further plans for the evening. She was going to make a run over to the assisted living wing and see what was happening there. She'd been so frustrated by Nurse Yakamura's brushing her off. She needed evidence to support her claim, but since she wasn't sure what was going on, she didn't know how to get it. It wouldn't hurt to do some recon, as they said in the movies.

Back in her apartment, she changed into more casual clothes, what her daughters would call her grungies—sweat pants, cotton shirt, sneakers. She lovingly placed her new necklace and earrings in her jewelry box. It was barely 9pm, but late enough for her purposes. She would pretend to visit Sophie and get the lay of the land.

Energized by the adventure and feeling like a spy, she set out. The halls were empty. TVs blared behind several doors as she walked past, but most apartments were silent. Bedtime came early at Desert Breezes. She rounded the corner at the end of the hall after passing Maddie's place, where she could hear a Western movie playing. Everyone seemed to be deaf to some degree here, so no one complained about the noise. They just took out their hearing aids at night. Her hearing was still pretty good, knock wood.

As she marched down the next hall, she wondered which apartment was Nick's. The door to the assisted wing at the end of the hall was shut, but never locked, and she slipped through it, noticing as usual a faint scent of Pine-sol with a fainter underlying odor of urine. She wrinkled her nose in distaste as she approached the room where she'd first met the day attendants. That room was empty and felt as if no one had been there for a while.

She walked down the hallway, grimacing at its utilitarian gray vinyl tile and burgundy walls. No attempt had been made to make this wing look like anything but what it was: a nursing home or hospital environment. The contrast with the independent living area was a painful reminder of her possible future.

Because she wore sneakers, her steps carried her down the hall in silence. Everyone in this wing appeared to be in bed asleep. She saw no lights under doorways, heard no TVs blasting dialogue. The doors that were open in daytime were all shut, giving Olivia the creepy feeling of being all alone in a menacing environment. Where was the attendant? She'd yet to see anyone. She continued down the hallway towards Nurse Yakamura's office, the last room on the right, where light poured out the doorway.

She stepped into the office doorway and saw a pair of large, booted feet propped up on Nurse Y's desk. She bet that was something Nurse Y wouldn't like. She couldn't immediately see the face of the man because of the girlie magazine he was holding. She knew it was one of those by the picture on the front of a naked young woman with oversized breasts. The magazine lowered slowly to reveal a thirty-something man with long greasy dark hair, tanned skin and a body that looked like he'd played high school football, but had had no exercise since, the bearlike shape softened by many pitchers of beer. With his size and his close-set, nearly black eyes and face pitted with acne scars, he had a sinister air. She took a breath and forced herself not to step back. She shouldn't be afraid of him, but she was.

He hadn't risen from his chair, nor had he addressed her. There was an aura of carelessness in his posture, what some might call unprofessionalism, as if he were lounging at home rather than working. Indeed, his sneer seemed a territorial challenge that set her insides quivering. "What do you want?" he barked, his lips thin with disdain.

She drew herself up to her full height, which wasn't much. "I came to visit my friend Sophie Aldridge."

"She can't have visitors this late. Besides, she's on meds and sleeping. Come back during the day. I'm alone here and have to supervise everything. I can't be dealing with visitors." His voice dripped with dismissal.

He hadn't even stood up. He slouched back to his girlie magazine and ignored her, but she felt a challenge radiating off him, as if he would welcome a chance to establish his dominance. She didn't know why, but tangling with him felt dangerous. "Alright, then." She left with as much dignity as possible, annoyed at her retreat, but unable to see what else she could have done.

By the time she got back to her apartment, she was shivering in fear. She poured herself a medicinal tot of brandy and reviewed what she'd learned. An unpleasant, big man was alone on that hall at night. He didn't want anyone hanging around. Did it mean anything? Maybe not. Some people were just unpleasant. That didn't make him a criminal. However, she couldn't shake the creepy feeling he gave her. He hadn't actually threatened her, but he surely did frighten her. And he clearly didn't want anyone around.

She finished her drink. She needed to sleep on this to decide what her next step was. Really, she didn't have much more than she'd started with. Tomorrow, maybe she'd go see Nurse Yakamura again. Or maybe not.

# 8

# WEDNESDAY, SEPTEMBER 11, 1996

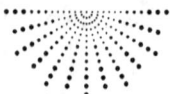

OLIVIA, 10:45AM

*O*livia hung up the phone and stared at it, stunned. She felt the bottom had dropped out of her universe. Shaky from Nurse Yakamura's revelation, she had a sudden need for something to steady her, to stop the sensation of spinning helplessly in a maelstrom, but she couldn't think of anything adequate to the task.

If only. If only she'd pressed the matter harder, the resolution would have been faster. She couldn't bear to think what the weeks of delay had meant to Sophie and that other poor woman. There might even be more victims. Nurse Yakamura was now on a crusade, however belatedly, and Olivia was certain that the awful man would end up in jail where he belonged. But how can you make restitution for what he'd done?

Olivia shakily poured herself a double brandy and wandered into the bathroom. She decided abruptly that a hot soak would soothe her ragged nerves. She filled the tub and added lavender bath salts, then stripped and threw her clothes on the floor and slipped into the steaming, scented water. The heat coaxed tension from her muscles, and the lavender fragrance relaxed her. Sipping the brandy, she tried to deal with the news rationally.

She recalled her latest visit to Nurse Yakamura several days ago vividly, as once again, her worries had been dismissed out of hand. Nurse Y. explained, as if to a child, how having only one attendant at night meant a strong man was the best choice, and what was Olivia doing visiting her friend so late at night, anyway? The nurse even made a snide comment about her active imagination, as if she were manufacturing drama out of loneliness or boredom.

Nurse Yakamura sounded like a totally different person today, so appreciative of Olivia's participation in apprehending a suspected rapist. Of course, it wasn't solely due to Olivia, as she explained. A family member of another disabled resident had raised the alarm, too, forcing Nurse Yakamura to do her job and interview everyone, including Sophie, while they weren't sedated. Nurse Yakamura didn't reveal how many victims were discovered, and Olivia didn't really want to know. It was enough to know her intuition had been correct.

She felt no thrill at having helped nab the sexual predator, no satisfaction at this final outcome.

Nurse Yakamura had asked to be called Trudy, as if they were now best friends or collaborators, but Olivia wasn't fooled by the change in attitude. Trudy had gotten her to promise not to talk with the media, not that she wanted to, but it was obvious the nurse's main concern was bad publicity. Olivia simmered with anger at the woman's lack of care for the residents who were her responsibility.

Olivia let out a huge sigh, then another. It was over, and nothing could be changed. At least she never gave up trying to help Sophie.

Sophie...she needed to visit Sophie. Sophie probably grasped what was going on, but Olivia doubted she was getting much support. She realized she was procrastinating about facing Sophie, because in spite of the outcome, she felt she had failed her friend. Hard as it would be, she needed to get over there and commiserate with her. Maybe they'd back off on the sedation now that the cause of Sophie's agitation had been removed.

Galvanized to take action, Olivia polished off the brandy and stepped out of the bath, noticing tangentially how easy it was compared to a year ago. She tossed the clothes she'd thrown on the floor into the laundry hamper and quickly dressed in casual wear for a trip to the assisted living wing.

Sophie was awake and alert when Olivia marched in and seated herself in the chair next to Sophie's bed. Sophie's dark eyes followed her every step and seemed unnaturally bright.

Olivia reached over for her friend's hand and squeezed it gently. "I'm so glad to see you awake, Sophie. I've come often, but you were always sleeping."

A shadow of a smile flitted across Sophie's face. She struggled as if wanting to speak, but only managed to grunt.

"Don't bother, dear. I know all about it. They caught that nasty man. He won't bother you ever again. He's in jail." Well, she hoped he was. Certainly, he was gone for good.

A tear slid down Sophie's cheek. Olivia hesitated. She wanted to tell her friend she'd gotten her message and tried to help, but it had taken so long to get results that she felt ashamed. It would sound like she was making excuses. They sat quietly for a few minutes. Finally, Olivia said, "I know you tried to tell me in the hospital that day. I'm sorry it took so long to get anything done." Sophie's tears continued, and Olivia was swamped with misery. "I'm so sorry." Olivia felt tears fill her own eyes and blinked them back. As she sank deeper into sadness, Olivia was jerked out of her self-blame by a single strong squeeze from Sophie's hand. Her eyes popped open in surprise to see a big smile on Sophie's tear-washed face.

"Thaaa oo."

Olivia hadn't seen Sophie show such strength and vocalization in many weeks. It must have taken a monumental effort. Sighing from the strain, Sophie closed her eyes and slipped into sleep. Olivia sat long enough to be sure she'd stay asleep, then extracted her hand from Sophie's surprisingly strong grip.

Back in her apartment, Olivia struggled to find something to occupy herself as remorseful thoughts ricocheted around inside her head. Glad for once that the dining room was open, she decided to get lunch, even though she wasn't really hungry.

* * *

NICK, 12:10PM

Nick had nearly polished off the roast beef sandwich he'd put together from ingredients on the deli table in the dining room. The bread was fresh whole grain, and the roast beef was rare and tender, thinly sliced just the way he liked. They probably didn't cook it here, but no matter. It was still tasty. If only they had the spicy English mustard he preferred. He could bring his own to lunch, but that seemed a little over the top.

As he swallowed his last bite, he saw Olivia Deschamps enter the dining room. She was dressed far more casually than usual in faded pink sweats, a white t-shirt and sneakers. She looked left and right, scanning the room with a hint of desperation in her eyes, or so it seemed. He wondered what was wrong.

Her eyes landed on him, and she moved as if a tractor beam was reeling her in to his table. She was neither the flighty nor the predatory type, so he wondered what had emboldened her to seek him out, or even if she'd been looking specifically for him. She had never approached him in the dining room. In fact, he rarely saw her there.

She barged up to his table for four and placed her hand on the empty chair opposite his. "May I?" she indicated with her other hand.

Curious, he nodded. "Sure. Would you like me to get you a sandwich or something to drink?"

She grimaced. "I'm not really hungry. I just needed to get out. I don't know what I'm doing." She seemed close to tears, and he hated dealing with a weeping woman. He'd dealt with many as a cop, both suspects and victims, but his personality wasn't suited to discussing feelings or offering insights that might alleviate emotional pain. He paused, hoping she'd reveal more without him pressing her. Silence often worked with suspects, so why not with other people?

She sniffed and swept her hand across her eyes. He reached reflexively into his pocket, trying to recall if his handkerchief was clean, but she seemed to divine his intention and waved him away. "I'll be all right."

"I don't often see you here," he said, reaching for a neutral subject.

"I avoid it as much as possible. I eat breakfast at my place, and Maddie and I alternate hosting dinner most nights."

"That sounds nice."

She had calmed slightly, but fiddled with the cloth napkin as if still agitated.

"You sure I can't get you a drink?" He preferred action to talk in situations like this.

"They don't have what I need." She pulled another face. "I'm not a big drinker, but not too long ago I had a double brandy. I'm just dealing with a shock. Though I really shouldn't be shocked."

She'd totally lost him. "Would you care to talk about it?" He half hoped she wouldn't, because being a confessor or counselor had never been his strong suit. "Better yet, why not come to my place? I'll fix you a drink. Unless you came to have lunch." He couldn't believe what had just come out of his mouth. He never invited anyone to his place. Well, it was too late to rescind the offer. He gazed at her steadily.

She stood up. "That's kind of you, but I'd hate to impose."

That was woman-speak for 'ask me again.' Even he knew that much. "'No imposition. A post-prandial drink suits me fine, and I don't like to drink alone." They stood and made their way down the hall to his apartment, which was only a few doors down the connecting hallway, the one that led to the assisted living wing. He saw Olivia glance at the door to that wing with a shiver.

Nick unlocked his apartment door and stepped aside to let Olivia enter. As he followed her, he scanned the room for signs of poor housekeeping. The staff cleaned weekly, but he was responsible for having things in their place. It didn't look too bad, at least, not to him.

He escorted her to the sofa. "Make yourself at home, Livvie. What can I get you? I have bourbon or bourbon." He grinned self-consciously. "I'm not much of a drinker, and I drank my last beer days ago."

He didn't know what prompted him to shorten her name, but she smiled warmly, so he hadn't offended her. "Bourbon is fine. Neat."

He poured them each two fingers of Jack Daniel's Black Label and joined her on the couch. "So do you want to tell me what's bothering you?"

She frowned and sipped her drink as if trying to decide whether to share. Finally, she put the glass on the coffee table and straightened her shoulders. "I may have mentioned my friend Sophie to you?"

"The one who had strokes and is in the nursing wing?"

"Yes. I'm upset about her. No, I'm mad at myself. I knew something bad was happening, but I was unable to help, and it went on for weeks and weeks." She put her hand to her eyes and let out a sob.

He put his arm around her shoulders to offer encouragement, but he was still in the dark about what the drama was.

She turned to him and buried her face in his chest, sobbing jaggedly. He just held her and patted her back tentatively.

In a few moments, she collected herself and pushed back, a horrified look on her face. "I'm so sorry. I don't know what came over me." She sniffed, and he extracted his handkerchief from a pocket and handed it to her. She dabbed her eyes delicately and wiped her nose and pocketed it. "I'll clean it and return it to you."

*Women.* They could be so fussy about things that didn't matter. Her dark eyes radiated pain, but the tears had stopped. She looked at him as if seeing him for the first time. "I've been keeping it to myself for so long. I told Helen, but it obviously made her and Alexander worry, so I quit sharing with her. I suppose I needed to tell someone."

"You haven't told me anything," he reminded her.

Wide-eyed, she laughed. "You're right. I'm sorry. Here I am falling apart. You must think I'm one of those hysterical females."

As a matter of fact, he thought no such thing in spite of her strange behavior. Hysteria, real hysteria, didn't seem to fit Livvie, but he kept the thought to himself. "If you want to tell me, I'm happy to listen." He just hoped it wasn't some girlie thing beyond his comprehension.

She drew in a breath, then reached for her liquid courage, as if holding onto something would steady her. "Well, as you know, some weeks back— too many—Sophie had a stroke and had to move to assisted living after returning from the hospital. Shortly after, she had another stroke, and it was a big one. They kept her in the hospital a long time." She paused long enough to sip more bourbon. "I visited her a number of times, but she was always sedated. They said she was highly agitated, and they didn't want her to hurt herself. I don't see how she could have. She couldn't speak and could hardly move. I can see how that would be frightening."

He nodded as he imagined himself confined to a bed, unable to speak. Life wouldn't be worth living.

"So one day, I lucked out and caught her awake. I talked with her, just trying to cheer her up. She'd once told me she hated hospitals, so I made a point of reassuring her that she'd soon be back at Desert Breezes. It didn't have the effect I'd intended. Sophie looked terrified and tried to say something, but she couldn't form words, and became more and more upset. I finally got the nurse, who sedated her."

Nick made a leap forward and didn't like where this was headed. Her eyes pleaded for understanding. "It was so little to go on, but I knew in my heart what it meant. I just had no idea who to turn to."

"So you thought something was going on in the assisted living wing that had Sophie afraid to go back?"

"Exactly. But I had no evidence, nor hope of getting any, since Sophie was always drugged. I wasted so much time second guessing what I'd seen and looking for more reasonable explanations for her reaction, not sure who to turn to. The staff here didn't want to talk to me, since I'm not Sophie's family, but she has no one else. The head nurse brushed me off twice. Acted like I was an attention-seeking, demented old woman."

"I'm guessing she changed her mind."

"Only because another patient's family member made the same complaint several days ago." Hew jaw was clenched in anger, and she shook her head, tears filling her eyes. "The night attendant was raping the disabled women." She knocked back the rest of the bourbon in one gulp.

"It's thanks to you he was caught."

"I should have forced that damn nurse to question Sophie. I was sure after I saw the guy that night that he was a predator."

Nick's stomach sank. "What do you mean 'that night'?"

"When I couldn't get them to listen to me, I went over one night about 9pm to check things out, and there was a lone attendant, a creepy guy who was very rude to me."

"Olivia, you put yourself in danger doing that!"

"What else was I supposed to do? Not that it helped. I visited the nurse again after that, and she still didn't pay any attention. If someone else hadn't complained, he'd still be raping women."

"If you hadn't gone to them, they probably would have dismissed the other person's concern. Having two different people complaining made it real."

Her eyes were riveted on him. "I never thought of that. Maybe you're right. I've been so upset since Nurse Yakamura—she wants me to call her Trudy now—called with the news. Only to get me to promise not to talk to the media, mind you. I keep thinking I could have stopped him sooner, but honestly, I can't think how, short of putting a bullet in him."

He raised one eyebrow at how feisty she was. If she was serious, he wouldn't want to be on her bad side.

Then she shrank into herself, suddenly looking old and defeated, but all he could think was how brave she'd been to take on the system all by herself. He picked up their glasses. "I think we both deserve another drink." She smiled weakly.

On his return, she was much recovered and accepted the drink shyly. "I'm sorry to have burdened you. Let's talk about something pleasant. How's Rudi doing?"

"He's coming along fine. I'm glad you came out to meet him. But you can't change the subject like that. I have something to say."

She glanced down at her drink as if expecting a lecture, and he was tempted to oblige her, but he decided to soften it. "Livvie, I'm not going to say I think you should go off investigating crimes on your own, but I'm bowled over at your courage. I saw a lot in the war and as a cop, and even on the Posse, but that was different. It takes a lot of moxie to do what you did, to stand up to the authorities and refuse to give up. I admire the hell out of you." She looked up, beaming at the compliment. "And if you ever go off alone like that again, I'll turn you over my knee." Her smile turned into a big O of surprise and maybe even speculation, then indignation. "What I mean is, you come to me. I'll be your backup. OK? No more lone heroics."

She stared, measuring his words or him. "It's a deal. But I think my sleuthing days are done."

They both laughed.

To keep things light, he regaled her with stories of his clumsy first efforts at the silversmith club and managed to keep things rolling for another ten minutes, then ran out of things to say. It was the most he'd talked to anyone in months, and instead of taxing him, it had energized him. He realized he enjoyed her company.

135

"I was thinking of taking a walk after sundown tonight. It's not so hot anymore, and it's fun to watch the wildlife. The bats swoop around the streetlights catching bugs, and sometimes I see coyotes and rabbits. You said you like to walk. How about going with me?"

He'd surprised her. Her mouth hung open for a few seconds, then she smiled. "I usually walk in the morning, but it would be more fun to have company. I'd love to join you. Shall I come by after the sun goes down?"

"I'll swing by your place, and I'll call first."

She rose. "Then I'll be going. Thanks for listening to my blubbering. You've given me a new perspective. I think I can move on."

He stood to walk her to the door. "And no more Lone Ranger. You've got me for backup. Right?"

"I promise." Her eyes twinkled as she went into the hall. "Thanks for listening. I feel a lot better now. See you later."

"Later." The door clicked shut. Ever since his wife died, he'd avoided becoming entangled in anyone's life, but he liked Livvie. She had hidden depths and wasn't giving up on life like so many did at their age. Maybe they'd become friends. Desert Breezes was looking better all the time.

* * *

BARBARA, 2:10PM

Barbara fidgeted as she sat on the couch in Marilyn's living room. She was suppressing the horrible memory of being told Owen Schmidt, the former owner of this house, was a serial killer and had also killed her cat, Fluffy. The fur from Fluffy's tail had been one of the grisly trophies found in a not-so-well-hidden compartment behind the wall of his bedroom closet. Somehow, she had to share this horrifying information with Marilyn, and her normal confidence had fled. This just wasn't the type of conversation she was used to having. For a fleeting moment, she entertained the idea of postponing the inevitable, but she rejected that easy out.

Tammi lay on the floor beside Marilyn, dark eyes riveted on Barbara. Worry cast a shadow across Marilyn's face. "Is everything all right? Why did you ask to see me privately?"

"This was not an appropriate topic for lunch with the girls, but it's time someone told you." Way past time.

Marilyn cocked her left eyebrow. "That sounds ominous."

Barbara tried not to sigh. "I'll let you decide for yourself. I didn't want to share this with you until I knew you better, but then this problem with Ted started, and it seemed to me you had enough to deal with. Yet if I wait much longer, you'll find out in a way that could be worse."

"Now you really have me worried."

Barbara shook her head, hating the hunted look in Marilyn's eyes. "This is just historical information. It has no bearing on your life. It shouldn't cause you trouble, but if you let it, it could disturb you."

Marilyn's right hand was balled in a tight fist, and she reached down to stroke Tammi, who was tensely watching both women.

"I'm messing this up. I'm sorry. I'll just say it. The reason you got such a great price on this house is the previous owner died suddenly." Barbara longed for something to drink, but pressed on. "His name was Owen Schmidt, and he was shot by Eric Johnson, Lydia's husband, while he was killing Tanya Cooper, Steven's ex-wife." She let it sink in.

Marilyn stared at her, blue eyes wide open and mouth an O of shock.

"It turns out that Owen was a serial killer. They know because they found trophies hidden in his bedroom closet and matched many of them to missing person reports. They think he may even have killed his mother when he was a teenager." Barbara, paused, gauging Marilyn's reaction. That was enough for now.

Marilyn's fist covered her mouth as if to stifle a scream. Her eyes were soaked with horror. Finally, her fist dropped to her lap. She seemed unable to speak.

"None of the women were killed here. The realtor would have been obliged to tell you if that was the case. Owen seemed like a normal guy. He did keep to himself, but that isn't a bad thing. We were all shocked to hear he was a serial killer. Mind you, he had complained about my pets running loose, but it was only after he died that we got confirmation that he had killed my cat. But that makes him sound like a maniac. The truth was, he seemed so normal."

Marilyn still hadn't recovered her voice. She'd curled her bare feet under her torso and wrapped her arms protectively around herself in an approximation of fetal position. This wasn't going well at all. Maybe she should have brought Ben, but no, having a man present might have made it worse.

Marilyn suddenly bolted to her feet, followed by Tammi. "This calls for a drink. Glass of wine?"

Barbara sighed in relief. "I thought you'd never ask."

Marilyn gave a grim, short laugh and strode into the kitchen, returning shortly with two glasses of white wine. Barbara gulped half the glass down gratefully, then regarded Marilyn with concern. "I know it sounds lame, but the history of the house doesn't have to affect you."

Marilyn didn't look convinced. "This is just what I needed."

"Yes, I'm so sorry to add to your problems. We thought it might be better if a friend told you."

"You're right. I know it was hard for you, too, and I do appreciate your telling me. I thought the place had a weird vibe. It was obsessively clean, but it didn't feel 'good' clean, if you know what I mean. I thought it was just me and my stuff."

That was the opening Barbara was waiting for. "This might sound foo-foo, but as you say, you can feel the energy of a place. I've been working with Jean and Ian as you know, and I got miraculous results. So did Amelia. They also do house clearings to make the energy healthy and harmonious and get rid of anything detrimental. I've been planning to get a house clearing now that Amelia and my grandchildren have gone home. It seems to me your place could use a good energy clearing, too."

Marilyn stared at her, wheels of thought turning behind her eyes. "I'm not into New Age stuff, but I trust your judgment. You're so practical, and I do like Jean and Lydia, even if I don't know Ian well. Why not? It can't hurt, and it might help."

Barbara's muscles relaxed, and she had another sip of wine. "If I know Lydia and Jean, you'll have a hard time paying them. They'll want to do it for free."

"Well, I don't expect them to work for free."

"Take it up with them, but do get them to do a clearing one way or another. And let me know how it goes."

Marilyn drank her wine, a thoughtful look in her blue eyes. "Maybe I can get them to ward the house against Ted." She laughed weakly.

They sipped wine for a while in silence, then Marilyn sat up straight, annoyance written all over her face. "Why didn't Steven or someone tell me about this before now?"

Barbara sighed. "We all talked about it. Right from the start, we wanted to tell you sooner rather than later, but just as we decided it was time, the crap hit the fan about Ted. None of us felt that hearing about Owen Schmidt was going to help you feel safer. " She chewed her lip. "I'm sorry, but we all felt we needed to wait a little bit longer, and a couple weeks turned into eight before we knew it. Steven was afraid to be the bearer of bad news. He felt it might go easier coming from a woman. I volunteered to be the one to tell you. I'm sorry if we waited too long. It wasn't on purpose."

Marilyn shook her head. "I'm the one who's sorry. What a horrible bit of news to have to hand someone. I was looking at it solely from my point of view. It's not something I'd rush to tell a new neighbor, either."

"Thanks for being understanding. It's been wearing us all down, trying to pick the right time." Barbara watched a shiver run through Marilyn. "It's really creepy information. I do believe getting a house clearing will help give you a fresh start. I'm not just saying that."

Marilyn smiled weakly. "I know. Thanks. I'll do it for sure. Now you can tell everyone the cat's out of the bag, and they don't have to tippy toe around the subject anymore. Though I don't really want to discuss it in detail with anyone."

"Don't worry. No one else wants to, either. Everyone was traumatized to some extent by what happened. It left poor Steven a shell of his former self. He was never extroverted or self-confident in social situations, but it seems Tanya's murder took the stuffing out of him. He seems to be recovering since going to the support group."

Marilyn covered her eyes. "Oh my God. The poor man. I wasn't thinking. Of course, he wouldn't want to talk about the guy who murdered his ex-wife. Thanks for helping me put it in perspective."

Barbara reached over and patted Marilyn's arm. "Eric and Lydia are recovering. Steven is doing better all the time. The neighbors are putting it behind them. It takes time. We'll all get past it eventually." They finished their wine in a thoughtful quiet.

* * *

## MADDIE, 5:30PM

Maddie watched the strange repeating pattern on the wall behind Olivia. It was like someone had drawn a geometric design on the white wall; worse yet, it wasn't quite stationary. Samantha had told her not to worry too much about the hallucinations, but Maddie knew it was a bad sign that their frequency was increasing. Sometimes she wondered if her mind would go before her body. The spaghetti she'd just finished sat in her stomach like a lump of wet concrete, even though she'd eaten very little. Stress had a way of doing this to her. The story of Olivia's friend Sophie was harrowing. She shook her head and closed her eyes, hoping the pattern on the wall would disappear.

"I wasn't sure if I should tell you, because I didn't want to upset you. It's all over now. But I thought it would be better for you to hear the whole story from me. These things take on a life of their own once they get public." Olivia frowned from her seat across the dining table. "Can I get you another beer?"

"Later. I'm not done this one yet. I still can't get over how you persevered in trying to help Sophie. Without you, that poor woman…" Words failed her. She blinked back hot tears. How could anyone be so evil?

"I wish I could have done more, faster. But I did my best. And it's over. I certainly hope that's my last detective job. Nick made me promise." Olivia clammed up. She maybe hadn't intended to talk about Nick.

"So what does our favorite cowboy have to do with this crime?" Maddie was determined to find out what was going on with Olivia and Nick. "You did say you'd share with me." No harm using a little guilt for leverage.

Olivia cast a sour look her way. "I know, but there isn't that much to share. I told you I got to meet his horse, Rudi. He's a beautiful big buckskin. And so well-mannered. Since that day, I hadn't seen him. Until today." Olivia squirmed in her seat, then rose to clear the table.

"You're trying to distract me. Sit down and tell me the rest."

Olivia put down the plates and sank to her chair, a blush rising up her face past the frown. "I ran into him earlier today, while I was still distressed by all this, and he could tell I was in a state. He invited me to his place for a drink."

Maddie went to respond but was overcome by a coughing fit. She struggled to relax and checked the oxygen line and finally got her breath back. "That sounds like progress."

Olivia glared at her. "Progress? You think I'm working my wiles on him?"

"No, but he seems to be an exceptional man, and some woman will snap him up. Why not you?"

"Oh, pshaw." Olivia waved at her dismissively. "Like what I need is to remarry. Leroy was a good husband compared to most, and I count myself lucky. Why take another chance?"

"You *are* lucky." Maddie felt a burn of envy. Her marriage had been a jail sentence. "It seems to me if you have one good marriage, you could have another." Maddie liked Olivia, and Nick seemed so nice. Maybe she was turning into a matchmaker in her final days. First, Samantha. Now, Olivia.

Olivia's silence seemed a good omen as she stood and began to stack plates and gather silverware. A small smile blossomed on her face, and her brown eyes sparkled. "Maybe you're right. I'm not looking to marry again, but Nick was awful kind to me. He even threatened to spank me if I ever did anything like that again."

"Really?" Maddie speculated about Nick's intentions, but said nothing.

"Well, it was just his way of telling me not to try and handle anything like that alone. He offered to help."

Maddie bit her tongue before repeating 'Really?'. This was progress, whether Olivia knew it or not. "Do you have plans to see him?"

Olivia paused as if trying to decide whether to be honest, then said, "He and I are going for a walk after sundown tonight. Don't you make more of it than it is."

This was getting interesting. "You have to tell me about it tomorrow. Promise." It was delightful to have something to think about besides her rapidly deteriorating health.

Olivia sighed. "You are making a big deal out of nothing. It's just a walk." She carted the dirty dishes over to the sink and began to wash them, then said dreamily in a low voice, "He calls me Livvie."

Maddie was right for sure. Nick was interested, but she wasn't going to push any more tonight. "Thanks for being there for me, Olivia. Sophie is lucky to have you as a friend, and so am I."

# 9

# MONDAY, OCTOBER 7, 1996

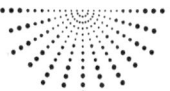

SAMANTHA, 9:45AM

"Samantha, you have a call on line 2," yelled Temple Landscaping's receptionist, Suzie.

Samantha glanced at the design she'd been working on and went out to the spare desk near the receptionist that had the phone all staff except Jack used, since he had one in his office.

Who could it be? She shuddered at the thought it might be Arthur, but surely he wouldn't call her at work? She regarded the phone with trepidation. "This is Samantha," she said after pushing the button for line 2. She hadn't been able to disguise the tremor in her voice.

"Hello, Ms. Taylor, this is Yolanda at Hummingbird Haven Hospice. It's about your mother."

An invisible fist clenched Samantha's stomach, threatening to disgorge the remains of her meager breakfast. "Is she..."

"No, I'm sorry to have frightened you. She's just very upset. I hate to call you at work, but she doesn't remember she asked to be in hospice. She's demanding to see you and is quite angry about being here." Yolanda paused. "She thinks you put her here against her will, and she won't listen

143

to us. This happens sometimes, and we've found the best solution is to have a family member come in and resolve it. Or try to."

Samantha's heart sank. How could Mom have forgotten it was her request? Well, she had been showing signs of dementia—the doctor told her that the hallucinations of patterns on the wall hinted at a specific type, not that it really mattered now. She sighed, "I'll be there in 40 minutes."

"Thanks, Ms. Taylor."

She put the phone down. She ought to tell Jack, but he was out on a job. She'd leave him a note in his office and explain when she got back. He was so flexible about her hours, she was beginning to burn with guilt. She knew he was only trying to help, but it made her feel too obliged to him.

During the drive to hospice, she wondered what she was walking into. Mom had quietly told her Friday evening—was it only three days ago?—that she was ready to go to hospice, that she couldn't do things on her own anymore, and she was adamant about not going to the assisted living wing, in spite of the rapist having been caught. Samantha was relieved, as Mom's condition had deteriorated terribly, and it was time. She had wondered when Mom brought up hospice if she remembered it was a one-way ticket, but wasn't stupid enough to ask. Mom was so easily put off about any decision. It had torn Samantha up when Mom asked if she could bring the small dresser from her bedroom with her. She hadn't seemed reassured when Samantha told her the room was already furnished. She knew Mom just wanted something of her own as an anchor, to give her courage on this last step in her journey. Surprisingly, Mom relented, and the move occurred on Sunday with no trouble. She should have known it was too easy. Mom awakened this morning with no memory of how she'd gotten to such a strange place.

When she finally parked at hospice, Samantha had talked herself into facing the music, whatever it was. Yolanda, a sweet and strangely jolly middle-aged woman given her occupation, was thrilled to see her. "Thank you so much for coming. Would you like me to go with you?"

"No, thank you, I can handle it." She hoped she was right. Samantha strode down the hall, crossed the central courtyard that gave the hospice its name, didn't linger to enjoy the many hummingbirds darting around the feeders in the garden that was open to the blue fall sky, and stopped at the doorway of her mother's room. Mom needed her to be calm and gentle, so she took a deep breath and prepared for some abuse, determined not to lose her temper.

Samantha crept slowly into the room, half hoping Mom was out like a light, but that would only delay the inevitable. She gazed with sadness at the withered body in the bed. The oxygen line was attached to Mom's face, and her eyes were partly shut. How could she look so much worse than she had yesterday? It was as if she had shriveled into a dried-out husk.

As Samantha sank into the chair beside the bed, Mom's eyes fluttered open. When she registered her daughter sitting there, her eyes widened and she gasped for breath. Samantha gently touched her mother's frail hand. When had she gotten so bony? Blue veins stood out like a road map of an unhappy life on the wrinkled skin.

"Why?" Mom rasped.

Samantha tried to smile and gently squeezed Mom's hand. "What's wrong, Mom? They called me at work to say you were very upset."

"Why did you put me here?" Mom's pale blue eyes filled with tears as her voice took on a sharp edge. "Why did you make me come here?" The accusation hung weakly in the air between them, but Mom's anger was real. How could she have forgotten? More importantly, how could she think that of Samantha?

"Mom, don't you remember on Friday, three days ago, you told me you were ready to move to hospice? You said you weren't up to being on your own, that it had gotten too hard." *Please remember.*

A look flashed across Mom's face, but vanished before it could take hold. "I don't want to be here. I want to go home now."

"But Mom, you're having trouble even getting to the toilet. That's why they put the portable commode by your bed here. And they help you use it. Remember? You need the help. This is so much better than you getting in trouble alone in your apartment in the middle of the night. Remember you asked not to go to the assisted living wing?"

Mom's blank look showed more resignation than comprehension. "I can't go back home?"

"You have the help you need here. The people are really nice, and they'll take you to the courtyard to see the hummingbirds any time you feel up to it. I'll come every day to visit, I promise."

145

A sigh slipped through Mom's lips. "I want to go home. Why did you make me come here?"

Samantha felt her eyes fill with tears. It was no use arguing. "Mom, I have to go back to work, but I'll come visit right after, OK? I'll stay as long as you want me to."

Mom nodded, but the acceptance was no victory for Samantha. Mom closed her eyes and Samantha wasn't sure if it was to dismiss her or just because she was worn out with fighting. She lingered after Mom slipped off to sleep, then patted her hand and went out to the reception area. Yolanda looked at her with compassion in her brown eyes. "They get that way sometimes. We don't like to overmedicate them. It's better to try and help them understand. Is she OK?"

Samantha nodded. "She's asleep now. She's convinced I made her come here against her will. I hope she remembers the truth soon. I have to return to work, but I'll be back later this afternoon."

"Thanks for coming. I'm sure she'll be better by then."

Samantha wished she could be that optimistic. It was bad enough watching her mother die by inches, but somehow she'd hoped Mom would be close to her through the end. Instead, she seemed to be reaching for an excuse to push her daughter away.

It was approaching lunch time when she pulled in to Temple Landscaping's parking lot. Jack's truck was there, so he would have gotten her message. She wasn't sure she could speak to him without breaking down, but she had to face him. She wasn't getting much work done these days, and he didn't deserve that. She leaned her head against the steering wheel, blinking back tears and trying to draw strength from deep inside, but her well of strength seemed to have dried up.

As she trudged into the building, some instinct said that she should turn around and go home, not that she had any home to go to. She had the feeling she was heading for an encounter that would not end well, though she didn't know why she should feel that way. Maybe stress was making her a defeatist.

She stood in the doorway of her office, looking at the half-done design, regarding it with a total lack of interest. It was going to be hard to concentrate enough to do it well. Making a quick choice, she turned and strode into Jack's office. He sat behind his battered desk going through papers of some kind. When he looked up, a smile flashed across his face, but just as quickly vanished.

She knew she must look haggard. "You got my message?"

He nodded once, concern radiating from his dark eyes. "Yes, how's your Mom?"

Samantha sighed and sank into the chair next to his desk. "Not good. She doesn't remember asking to go to hospice. She thinks I forced her. It's like the move to Desert Breezes all over again, only worse this time. She looked terrible. She didn't have enough energy to fight me for long, but I'm afraid she isn't going to remember, and she'll blame me and then die, alienated and mad." The words brought the fear out in the open, and she hung her head, fighting back tears.

"That's terrible. I'm sorry. Is there anything I can do?"

"You've already done too much, Jack. I haven't been working enough hours, and I took off this morning without even telling you."

Jack looked almost hurt, and her mind wasn't clear enough to understand why. She was the one who was hurting. His voice was gentle but firm. "You left me a note, and I told you we can pay you whatever hours you work, so just take it easy on yourself."

All the upset bubbled to the surface, and she hurled it at Jack, knowing it was wrong, but unable to contain herself. "I don't want to feel I owe you. I haven't decided what to do when the divorce is final, and it's like you're manipulating me into feeling I have to move in with you."

Jack's mouth hung open, but he recovered quickly. His dark eyes shone with anger. "I am not trying to manipulate you. I was trying to support you. I don't know what else I'm supposed to do. I sit here waiting for you to decide about our future, and it's driving me crazy. But I haven't done anything wrong." His lips thinned into a frown.

At some level, Samantha knew he was right, but she was so used to doing things herself, it felt like manipulation when Jack tried to help. She should just get up and go to her office and finish the design and try to collect herself, but her blood was humming with anger, and she had to vent or she'd explode. "I'm not sure this is working out. I need to feel I'm in charge of my life and have the right to choose whatever is best for me. I've been feeling pushed for months now, and I still don't know when the divorce will be final. I need time to get myself together. I can't do that worrying about how you're going to take every choice I make."

"Why don't you go home and rest?" His voice resonated with restrained anger.

"I'm thinking maybe I should just quit altogether."

Jack's eyes widened at that, but he didn't take the bait. Finally, she rose. "I'm going home. I have to visit Mom later. I don't even know if she'll remember I promised, but I have to do it, and I'm in no condition to work. If you have to let me go, I'll understand completely. I have become unreliable, and it's probably causing you a lot of trouble." She didn't wait for his reply, just marched to her office, grabbed her belongings and rushed to her truck. She'd never done anything as irresponsible as leaving a job half-done, and already she hated herself for doing it, but she couldn't make herself go back inside.

Of course, it wasn't her truck, so even if she were trying to escape, she'd still have to come back to return it. She banged her fist on the steering wheel and moaned. Everything was falling apart, and it was her fault. She had no money, no home, no husband and no future. Jack hadn't deserved her outburst, and she was afraid he'd take her up on her offer and let her go. She had become a liability to his business, and she still hadn't delivered on the promise of a relationship.

She headed out of the parking lot, a bleak future of loneliness and misunderstanding stretching ahead of her.

* * *

MARY BETH, 11:55 AM

Mary Beth was folding clothes in the laundry room when she heard Samantha's truck pull into the garage. Ethan had gone to run some errands, and Mary Beth had a gut feeling that might be good, because Samantha never came home at lunchtime. It took too big a chunk out of her day. This could only mean one thing—trouble.

Sighing, she opened the door to the garage and waited for Samantha, who hadn't noticed her standing there. As Samantha slammed the truck's door and turned to enter the house, Mary Beth saw swollen, red eyes and tear-stained cheeks. Water didn't last long in the desert, so Samantha must have been doing some serious crying.

Startled at seeing Mary Beth in the doorway, Samantha almost dropped her bag, her blue-green eyes popped in shock. "I didn't see you there."

"What's wrong?"

"Is it that obvious?"

"Come on, you know you can't hide anything from me. We're soul sisters. But if you must know, I'm smart enough to see the signs of trouble. You never come home at lunch. You've been crying." A sudden stab of fear shot through Mary Beth. "Is it your mother?"

"Yes and no. Let me come in, and I'll tell you." Samantha gently turned Mary Beth's shoulder, and they proceeded to the kitchen.

"Is Ethan home?" Samantha looked around anxiously.

"No, he's out for a while. He'll be back for lunch by 12:30."

Samantha dropped her bag on an empty chair and sank into another at the breakfast table that sat in a bay window looking across the golf course, but she didn't look at the scenery. She was staring blankly at her left thumbnail.

Mary Beth debated what to offer Samantha. She could stretch lunch three ways easily, but food wasn't what Samantha needed now. "Are you going back to work today? Because if you aren't, how about a cold beer or a glass of wine?"

For some reason, that caused Samantha to fall apart. She put her face in her hands and started blubbering. Mary Beth walked over and put an arm on her friend's shoulders, unsure how to help. Samantha never lost control like this.

"I'm so sorry. I'm such a mess." Samantha sat up straight and reached for a paper napkin to blow her nose. She wiped her eyes and regarded Mary Beth with mournful eyes. "I had a bad morning."

"That sounds like a bit of an understatement."

Samantha barked a short laugh. "I guess so. Hospice called me at work and demanded I come in, because Mom went off the rails. She forgot she chose to go to hospice and was saying I forced her to, and they wanted me to reason with her." Samantha rolled her eyes. "As if I could ever do that under the best of conditions. But Mom was really agitated, and they didn't want to have to sedate her."

Mary Beth knew from personal experience that Maddie could be contrary and vocal in her opinions, but this was too much. Poor Samantha. Poor Maddie. "How awful for you both." Somehow, she knew this wasn't all of it. "What happened when you went to see her?"

"She didn't remember she chose to go into hospice. I didn't fight with her, but it tore me up having her accuse me of being so mean. She did the same when she went to live at Desert Breezes, forgot it was her idea. I've done my best for her and always waited for her to make the decision of when to move, even though it was hard on me, but she forgets. It's like she doesn't trust me and assumes I have evil intent."

"You know your Mom. By tonight, she'll have forgotten the whole incident. She doesn't like unpleasantness."

"You're probably right. I'm going to see her later this afternoon, but I just don't have the energy right now. I sat with her until she fell asleep and drove back to work. I was in a state. It was like all Mom's anger and agitation transferred to me." She paused and stared into space.

Mary Beth stood up. "That does it. We both deserve a drink. Beer or wine?"

"Beer," whispered Samantha with no feeling.

Mary Beth popped the tops on two chilled bottles of Stella Artois and brought them back to the breakfast nook. She placed one in front of Samantha and took a long pull from hers. Then she looked Samantha in the eye. "So what happened that has you so broken up. It isn't just Maddie's craziness. You handle that fine."

Samantha's voice was a disconsolate whisper. "I think I just broke up with Jack. Or quit my job. Or both." Then she began to cry again, ignoring her beer.

"What? You're shittin' me!"

Samantha's crying went on for a minute longer, but it felt like hours. Finally, she grabbed another napkin out of the holder and blew her nose. "Jack was trying to be nice to me, but I can tell how frustrated he is. I'm not working reliable hours. I left this morning without permission because I couldn't reach him. He seemed angry when I got all upset. I don't blame him. It was unprofessional. But I'm so tired of being pulled in so many directions—Mom, Jack, Arthur, work, selling Mom's house, even Spanish class. I just cracked up. I told him I should quit and left. He didn't come after me or radio me. Why would he? That would make it a public spectacle."

Drama was the last thing she associated with Samantha. "So you snapped. You've been under a lot of stress. Give him some time to cool down. It will all work out."

Samantha's frown said she didn't agree. "Maybe this is my punishment for filing for divorce. Arthur's been really depressed, while at the same time arguing about every little detail as if delaying the divorce can make it go away." She reached for her beer and took a swig. "It's not that I regret leaving him, but I feel responsible for his misery. And I'm seeing a side of him I don't like, so it's weird. He's being petty. I know I have no right to complain, since I asked for the divorce, but I'm trying to be fair, and he's acting like I'm a bitch for wanting anything. It's obvious he'd love to see me walk away with only the clothes on my back. How can you claim to love someone and yet be so mean?"

"Don't ask me. My divorce was worse than yours, if you can believe it. He'd cheated on me and wanted a free pass, and when I wouldn't give it to him, it all blew up. The only people who win are the lawyers."

"That's for sure. And even though he's complaining about how well off I am, I can barely get by until it's over. I think that's one reason he's dragging his feet. And without my job, I can't do anything. I'll have to return my truck to Jack, and I'll have almost no money. Mom hasn't got any, either, until her house sells." She broke down again.

It was time to end this pity party. "Look, girl. You can stay here as long as you like, free room and board. We can afford it, and you're my best friend. You'll have plenty of money when your divorce is final; he has to buy out your half of the house. And last but not least, I'm sure you still have a job and a man. Shit happens at times like this. So what? You love each other. Call him tonight and talk it through. Or he'll call you."

Samantha smiled wanly. "I'd rather he called, but I owe him an apology. You're right. I'll call him at home so he can speak freely."

"Now that we've settled that, you can help me fix lunch. I seared some tuna steaks, and I'm making tuna salad from them. You can have it on bread or by itself. How does that sound?"

"Sure you have enough?"

"You know me. I always make more than enough. Come on and help me with the chopping."

The rest of the afternoon was quiet, with Samantha absent for a long visit with her mother. She returned looking slightly calmer than she had at noon. Just after 5pm, the phone rang while Mary Beth was debating whether to reheat leftover lasagna or make burgers and fries for dinner. Jack still hadn't called, and she hoped it was he. Ethan sat in the living room watching the news on TV. Samantha hadn't raced from her room to answer the phone, so Mary Beth picked it up on the kitchen handset.

"Hi, it's me," Helen's voice announced. Mary Beth looked up to see Samantha standing in the kitchen doorway and shook her head. Samantha turned and left, a dejected look on her face.

"Hi, Helen, I'm glad you called. I have some bad news. Maddie's in hospice and going downhill fast. I don't think she'll last until you return from your trip."

"Oh, no," said Helen. "I knew it was coming, but didn't like to think about it. Have you been to see her?"

"She just went in yesterday. I'm going tomorrow. She's been very disturbed since the move, and I wanted to give her a chance to settle in."

"Please give her our love and tell her I wish I could be there."

"I will," promised Mary Beth.

"I was calling to see how my furry children are doing."

"They're fine. Fido seems to be enjoying his solitude, and I've had Spot over to visit Olivia. Spot seems happy here, but she'll be glad to get back to her real home."

"Wonderful. We'll be back next Tuesday. You have my number here if you need me."

"We'll be dandy. Enjoy the rest of your vacation. I didn't mean to depress you, but thought you ought to know about Maddie."

"Thanks, Mary Beth. I'm glad you told me."

Mary Beth hung up. The sad news had kept her from pumping Helen for details of her trip, but she'd find out soon enough whether Helen and Alexander had decided St. Croix was where they wanted to live the rest of their lives. She was swamped by a sense of loss. Samantha would eventually move into the city, and if Helen and Alexander moved to St. Croix, it would be lonely for her. She wanted her friends to be happy, but why couldn't they be happy in Palm Lakes?

She shrugged off her sadness. She needed to stop thinking like the displaced, lone person she'd been since Mom died. She had Ethan now; she wouldn't be alone even if all her friends moved. She had a beautiful home and a man who loved her. The gloom evaporated, replaced by a feeling of warmth.

She hoped Samantha wouldn't wait too long to call Jack. It was strange he hadn't rung her, but maybe he wondered if she would even be home. She grabbed the handset and went back to Samantha's room. Her friend sat listlessly on the bed, a book in hand, obviously not reading it. "I've brought you the phone so you can have a private chat with Jack before dinner. Do you care whether we have burgers or lasagna?"

Samantha shook her head negatively.

"Call him now. You've given him enough time. You don't want him calling during dinner. I haven't told Ethan anything yet. I was going to let you say whatever you wanted, but he's going to notice at some point, and it would be better for you if you knew what was happening. I still think it's going to be all right."

Samantha took the handset and smiled. "Thanks. You're right. I'll call him in a minute, then come help with dinner."

"I don't need any help. I'd rather you got this resolved." With that, she marched back to the kitchen and got to work.

\* \* \*

MARILYN, 12:30PM

Marilyn addressed Jean across the table that was spread with a feast of Chinese dishes. "I really can tell a difference since you did the space clearing. I had no idea. Not to be offensive, but the whole idea sounded so woo-woo." Marilyn helped herself to more rice to dilute the fire of the kung pao chicken. She loved the Jade Dragon restaurant, and it was such a relief to have women friends to talk with. She wished they had told her sooner about Owen Schmidt, but now that the secret was out and dealt with, she felt a stronger bond with them. She'd even forgiven Steven for wimping out and not telling her. Well, mostly.

Jean laughed, startling Marilyn from her thoughts. "Don't worry. Ian and I are used to being called different, among other things."

Barbara paused while pouring herself some tea. "I went over to Marilyn's place after you did the space clearing, and it was like she had repainted or something. It was…sparkly. And my place feels much lighter. I'm so glad I had you do a clearing on our place, too."

Marilyn ate a few more bites, considering how much more of her drama to share, but they'd all been so kind, she blurted, "I just hope it keeps Ted away."

Lydia's dark brown eyes searched her, and Marilyn knew she was being read, as Lydia had told her she could see people's energy fields, and what she saw told her a lot about them. She was probably reading stress and fear in Marilyn, but it didn't take a psychic to see that. "That's your ex?" asked Lydia.

She hadn't told anyone but Barbara and Steven the details of the harassment. It hit her that she had little room to point a finger at them about not telling her about Owen Schmidt. It was time she shared her story. "Yeah, he's being a pain. Every now and then I get an unsigned threatening card or a box of trash. At first it terrified me, but I'm getting used to it. He'll quit eventually." She almost added, 'I hope,' but couldn't bear to reveal the level of stress his actions had engendered.

Lydia raised an eyebrow eloquently, but said nothing. Marilyn wasn't going to be able to hide anything from her.

In a soft voice, Emma asked, "What do you mean 'threatening'?"

"One card had a puppy that looked like Tammi with a bull's-eye drawn over it. It said, 'I know where you are.' That kind of nonsense. Nothing I can take action on. I had a restraining order in Virginia, but I didn't want to do anything like that here. He's unlikely to drive 2500 miles, isn't he?"

Worried faces stared back at her in silence. It made her more concerned to see their reaction. She wanted to think she could take Ted with a grain of salt. "Do you think I should do something?"

Lydia nodded slowly. "I can ask Eric if he has connections in Virginia. Maybe he could find out what your ex is doing. Cops do favors for retired brothers-in-arms."

"Julio knows how to shoot. I could ask him if he'd teach you." Emma's bloodthirsty suggestion was so out of character, it attracted everyone's attention, though Lydia didn't seem as surprised as the rest. Emma looked around at their stunned faces. "Well, she can't sit there waiting for him and do nothing. She needs to protect herself."

Marilyn figured there was a story there, because Emma was such a gentle, quiet person. "I have a gun and I'm a good shot. Ted knows it. I hope it doesn't come to that."

Emma smiled with satisfaction and went back to eating her mu shu pork.

Barbara added, "Please call me any time for help. And we have a spare bedroom you can use if you need a safe house."

Mary Beth offered, "Let me know if I can help. I currently have a boarder, but I could take in another. We have plenty of room. I can't take Tammi, though, because right now I have Spot while Helen and Alexander are away, but they'll be back soon."

Marilyn was overwhelmed by the support. "I didn't mean to make a big deal out of it. Ted's angry, but he'll get over it." She hoped no one except Lydia detected her uncertainty.

Conversation turned to lighter topics after that, and Marilyn returned home and took Tammi for a walk. When she got back, she called Lydia and accepted her offer of Eric's help. Lydia couldn't promise anything, but any news would be useful. Marilyn wished she could call her old friends in Virginia, but they'd all been cops and cops' wives. She didn't have any special friends she trusted.

Later, Steven called and chatted for a few minutes and invited her for barbecue. She accepted because she was alone and scared and he made her feel safer. But she hoped he didn't consider it a date. He'd never made a move on her, never even touched her, and that led her to believe that he had no interests beyond friendship grown from mutual tragedy.

She was pretty sure their relationship would never grow into anything more. Especially because he'd withheld the information about Owen. Maybe she was being harsh, but although she'd forgiven him, his actions seemed cowardly and selfish, no matter how Barbara had painted them. She grunted, annoyed at herself for being judgmental. No one was perfect, and Steven really did seem to care about her. She needed to count her blessings. He was nice, thoughtful, smart and kind. What more could she want in a man? He was everything Ted wasn't, but it didn't feel like enough. Sighing, she put those thoughts aside and decided to take Tammi for a long walk.

* * *

OLIVIA, 5:30PM

Olivia sank onto the sofa, tears filling her eyes. Seeing Maddie in hospice had cut a hole in her. Maddie was barely responsive, shriveled to a tiny husk of the vibrant, feisty woman she'd grown to love, like a cut flower that was drying up, ready to be discarded.

Maddie had held Olivia's hand like it was a lifeline, repeating in a hushed and bitter voice that Samantha had forced her to move there, and she wanted to go home, which Olivia took to mean Desert Breezes, though Maddie had never been happy there.

It broke Olivia's heart to be unable to help her friend. She was sure Maddie was confused, but what difference did it make? Her pain was all too real, even though Olivia was sure Samantha hadn't pressured Maddie.

Finally, Maddie had slipped into a deep sleep, reminding Olivia of her frequent visits to Sophie. That triggered another stab of loss. This morning, she'd gone to visit Sophie and found her room empty. Though the attendant tried to sound compassionate, she couldn't mask the apathy born of seeing death too often. No one had bothered to report Sophie's death to Olivia. Why would they? She wasn't family. She'd been expecting the bad news for a long time, but somehow, arriving at the vacant room stunned her. It was as if Sophie had never existed. There was no trace of her, no talk of personal effects. She even had trouble getting details about the funeral service. Well, there wasn't going to be one, just a quiet cremation and interment, as if Sophie was something they just wanted to forget. In spite of Olivia's campaign that uncovered the rapist, or maybe because of it, those in power had not softened their attitude about keeping things from her.

Why were remorse and regret her constant companions? She'd tried so hard for Sophie and Maddie, but somehow felt she'd failed. Maybe it was rooted in selfishness. She didn't want to end up like her friends, rejected, alone and confused.

Suddenly Nick came to mind. Lately, that happened a lot. She worried she was entering her second (or third) childhood, nominating him for the job of being her white knight who would fight dragons and rescue her from unspeakable reality. But how could even a white knight rescue her from death or old age?

She wiped her tears and shook her head. Her lower back was aching, and she shifted from her slouched position on the couch. She could and often did sit with one leg folded up under her, but her back protested, so she sat up straight and put her foot on the floor.

There was no point calling any of her daughters. They didn't know their mother's friends. She'd never even told them about the rapist who'd preyed on helpless women in the assisted living wing. They were so busy with their jobs, families and their own problems. She could tell they thought she had it made, not having to do housework, not even having to cook, having all that free time. How could she complain to them that she was bored, scared and lonely? They'd have no sympathy.

Her stomach rumbled, reminding her she hadn't eaten since the bagel at breakfast. The thought of cooking depressed her, and she'd emptied the tiny pantry of junk food, so that wasn't an option. Eating healthy was a pain sometimes. It was too late to go shopping for dinner items. It looked like she'd have to brave the dining room. She and Maddie had eaten the last of Mary Beth's lasagna Saturday night before Maddie had moved into Hummingbird Haven Hospice; a grim and funereal dinner that was. She wondered tangentially if Mary Beth would stop bringing her food now that Maddie wasn't at Desert Breezes. Well, it had been great while it lasted. Mary Beth had been more attentive than her own girls, but she owed Olivia nothing. She suppressed the unruly recurrent desire that her daughters were more like Mary Beth or Samantha. There was no point in comparing them, and it just dragged her down.

She might as well go to the dining room. It wasn't great, but it would fill her up. She wondered if Nick would be there. He hadn't invited her for a walk or to visit his horse since the last time, and for the hundredth time she wondered if she'd done something offensive or worse yet, if he found spending time with her a chore or boring or annoying. He seemed a very self-contained person. Maybe he wasn't plagued with the loneliness that ached through her. Once again, she longed for her golf course home. It had been too big, but there, she'd had Spot and her neighbors and felt like a contributing member of the community.

Sighing in resignation, she went to the bathroom and touched up her hair and checked her makeup. The mascara hadn't run, or at least, it didn't appear to have. Even with the magnifying makeup mirror and its powerful lights, she wasn't always sure she was seeing clearly. It would just have to be good enough. It didn't occur to her that she'd gone back to paying more attention to her appearance since meeting Nick.

She trudged her way to the dining room, which was surprisingly busy. Searching for an empty table, her glance paused on Nick, who sat alone at a two-seat table by the windows that overlooked the parking lot, the golf course and mountains to the east. Having the dining room on the second floor certainly improved the view, but Olivia wasn't looking at the mountains. She was debating whether to approach Nick, who hadn't yet seen her. He was busy cutting whatever mystery meat was on the menu tonight. Would he prefer to eat alone?

Just then, as if feeling her scrutiny, he looked up from his plate and locked onto her with brilliant blue eyes. A smile cracked his stern visage.

She moved in his direction as if drawn by a magnet, not really exercising any choice. He stood up as she approached and pointed to the empty chair. "Join me?" he asked rhetorically.

He didn't seem annoyed. She couldn't perceive any stiltedness or formality. "Thank you." She sat in the chair, collecting herself. The buzz of conversation continued around her as she searched for words. Her mind had suddenly gone blank, but she felt a great sense of peace, as if she were just where she needed to be.

Nick regarded her quizzically, causing her to recall the last time she'd cornered him here. It was almost like mind-reading. A sly look in his eyes seemed an observation about her coming here looking for him, and she had to admit he wasn't wrong if that was what he was speculating. Just being with him calmed the turmoil she'd been suffering. She ought to be embarrassed, but she wasn't. How strange. She'd think about it later.

"Can I fix you a plate?" He half raised from his seat.

She started from the warm, fuzzy feeling long enough to respond. "Oh, I can get it." She forced herself to rise, necessitating his standing. "Please keep eating. I'll be right back."

She wandered over to the buffet table and put a little of this and that on a plate, barely aware of her choices and suddenly not that hungry. When she returned to their table, he only half rose as she sat down. Good. She didn't want him acting so formal.

He said nothing as they ate their meal, and she found the silence soothing. When his plate was clean, he said, "Can I bring you some dessert?"

"Oh, no, thanks. This is enough for me."

He patted his nonexistent paunch. "I never could resist bread pudding, and I spotted some on the dessert table. I shouldn't, but I'm going to splurge. I'll just have to walk it off later tonight." He lumbered over to the dessert table and perused the choices and brought back two tiny dessert dishes piled with bread pudding. "I know you said you didn't want any, but with your girlish figure, you can get away with it. This is the best dessert they have, and it always goes fast."

It was a deceptively small serving, and the fragrance of cinnamon wafted across the table. Just this once wouldn't hurt. It didn't occur to her that she was feeling an appetite now. She reached for the dish and flashed him a smile of gratitude. "All right, but now I'll have to walk it off, too." She clamped her mouth shut in mortification and covered her gaff by taking the bread pudding and inhaling the spicy, rich fragrance. She hoped he didn't think she was fishing for another invitation to join him on his walk. Whatever had gotten into her? Embarrassed, she dug into the pudding, the flavors caressing her mouth and driving the worries away, a beautiful balance of subtle spices, the sweetness of raisins and sugar and the richness of butter and some kind of liquor. She'd never liked the food here before. Maybe it was the company that made it taste so good.

She watched as Nick slowly savored each bite. A sheepish look overcame him. "I have a real sweet tooth, but I try not to indulge too often."

"It is unusually good, isn't it? Thanks for bringing me some." They finished their dessert in companionable silence.

When they finished, she suddenly felt awkward and rose to go back to her room. He insisted on escorting her back. She almost invited him in for a drink, but didn't want to appear forward.

"Are you going to walk with me tonight? You need to burn those calories." His voice was laced with humor.

Hiding her surprise, she said, "I'd love to. When?"

"We're losing the light; might as well go right away."

It was almost like going on a date. She shivered in anticipation, hoping he hadn't noticed. "I need to get a jacket or something."

"I need one, too."

The temperature had dropped after the sun set, and Olivia was glad for the sweater she'd brought. He walked at a pace she could match. She'd noticed his thoughtfulness last time they'd walked and appreciated it. Before she knew it, they were standing on the golf course watching the mountains change color as the lingering pinks and finally the purples overshadowed them. The sprinklers came on, startling them both from the beautiful vista, and they turned to walk back home.

They were in the elevator before he said anything, and when he did, it wasn't what she would have expected. "You look like you had a bad day today. How about a drink at my place?"

Anything to allow her to postpone sitting in her empty apartment. "I'm sorry if I've been bad company."

"No. It's not that. I could tell you were not yourself. You don't have to talk about it."

They stepped out of the elevator and walked down the hallway to his room. She said nothing until he handed her a glass with two fingers of bourbon, shrugging in apology. "I still don't have anything else to offer you."

"This is fine, thanks."

He sat beside her and didn't prod her for information. She was grateful for that. More than anything, she just wanted to forget everything that had happened earlier today. "Thanks for being so kind. I really appreciate it."

He grinned and clinked glasses with her. "Would you like to watch some TV?"

Grateful that he wasn't trying to draw her into conversation, she nodded. She didn't care what they watched. She just wanted company.

Almost three hours later, she decided she had to return home. Two drinks had left her light-headed and sleepy. He walked her back to her door and before she could unlock it, he put his arms around her and pulled her into a hug. He was so big and solid, and his warmth wrapped around her, soothing her sadness and pain. She blinked back tears, unwilling to fall apart after being strong for so long.

He gently kissed the top of her head. "It will be OK." It was a silly thing to say, since he didn't have a clue what was bothering her, but somehow, it was just what she needed. "I'll call you tomorrow and see how you're doing."

Then, before she could think of a response, he turned and stalked back down the hall. It had been years since she'd been held by a man, at least one of her own age, and she felt bereft now that his warm strength was gone. Unwilling to try to parse out her feelings through the fuzziness, she went into her apartment, undressed without washing her face or brushing her teeth and collapsed gratefully into bed. She was asleep almost before she hit the pillow.

* * *

SAMANTHA, 9:15 PM

Grateful that Ethan and Mary Beth had gone to bed (she hoped they weren't hiding from her or escaping to their bedroom for the privacy she'd robbed them of by moving in), Samantha reached for the phone to dial Jack's number for the fifth time in four hours. Her nerves were frayed to the breaking point as she imagined him looking at Caller ID and putting the phone down in disgust. Nothing else seemed to explain his not answering. She hadn't been able to eat dinner, she was so worried, and it was obvious Ethan had noticed her distress, but he had said nothing. She paused, swamped by anxiety about the future.

Her day had gone downhill after the visit to hospice. She felt she was standing on a narrow ledge above a huge drop as the cliff face and path crumbled around her. Everything was spinning out of control. Mom was dying. Mom's house still hadn't sold, her savings were gone, and the bills and her divorce had forced her to start charging payments on her lone credit card, as Mom's expenses exceeded her meager income.

Why had Dad left Mom in such financial hardship? She'd been wondering ever since he'd dragged her aside for a private chat a couple

161

years ago to give her details of his finances. Time and time he'd shown her, and she'd never had the nerve to ask why there was so little money, no safety net. He hadn't been rich, but he'd been conservative and miserly enough that there should have been life insurance or some savings for Mom when he died. She wondered for the millionth time where the money had gone, but he'd taken the answers to his grave.

The money worries and Mom's imminent demise plagued her slightly less than the hurt inflicted by Mom's accusations this morning. It seemed like the ultimate rejection of all she'd done to help her fractious mother.

*Face it, girl. It's more that that. It's about Jack.* The phone seemed to weigh 200 pounds. She lay it down, grateful it was cordless and she could use it in the privacy of her bedroom. Surely by now, Mary Beth or Ethan were fed up with the drama she'd brought into their lives. She was falling apart over Jack more than anything else but didn't want to admit it.

She'd chosen to get divorced because it was the right thing, not because of Jack. She almost had herself convinced of that until this morning. She had been getting concessions he never offered other employees, but he seemed to have reached his limit when she offhandedly mentioned quitting. Whatever had prompted her to be so rash?

She'd expected to hear from him by now, but not only had he been silent, he wasn't answering his phone. And that made her question her choices for the past ten months. What would she have without Jack? No job. No home. No man. No family. No future.

At this point, she wasn't sure she still had a job, which was one reason she'd been phoning Jack. She'd never known him to be out of an evening, which was why she worried he was ignoring her calls. But there could be another logical explanation. She simply couldn't guess what that was. Driving over there would be worse, especially if he wasn't there or didn't want to see her, but she found herself having to resist a strong impulse to hop in the truck and see it all through to the end, no matter what that might be.

Just what she needed, to turn into some kind of stalker. She looked at the clock. 9:25 was late to be calling whether he was there or not. She tried not to call anyone between 9pm and 9am simply out of courtesy, but she honestly didn't know what to do tomorrow without talking to him.

She lay the handset on the bed and went into the bathroom to splash cold water on her aching eyes. Somewhat revived, she sat on the bed and tried to examine things from a more detached perspective.

The people at hospice said Mom's memory lapse and accusation weren't that unusual. It was a manifestation of Mom's fear of approaching death. She didn't mean to hurt her daughter. Maybe if the scene hadn't been repeated this afternoon, Samantha could have overlooked it, like she did with so many of Mom's outbursts. Mom had been withdrawn and resentful this time, though she accepted where she was. Samantha wasn't sure what she'd expected. Mom had never been effusive in her praise, nor had she been lavish in displays of affection, but the cold bitterness surprised Samantha. It even made her wish she didn't have to go back, but she was going to be there every day no matter what. Otherwise, how could she live with herself? She just had to keep telling herself not to take it personally.

Mary Beth was sympathetic and went over to visit Mom today, and her visit hadn't gone a lot better than Samantha's. She wondered if Mary Beth would ever go back. No, that was an unworthy thought. Mary Beth would go back, because like Samantha, she loved Mom.

One more try to reach Jack and then she'd give up for the night. It had been an hour since her last attempt. If he didn't answer this time, she'd try to get some sleep. His phone rang twice, and she imagined him annoyed at the intrusion and unplugging the phone. She almost disconnected, but his voice penetrated her grim fantasy.

"Sam?" He sounded surprised and strained.

"Yes. I'm sorry to bother you so late." She wasn't sure what to say next. Stupid, considering she'd had hours to prepare.

"I was out."

If he was, that was a relief. She didn't want to presume to ask where he'd been. What if he was fibbing? Her silence must have prodded him, because he added, "There was a fire at work. I just got back." The exhaustion that tinged his voice drew sympathy from her as she processed her shock.

"How bad was it?"

"It could have been worse. There's insurance that I hope will cover repairs, but we lost half the main building, and it will take time to replace. At least our stock is OK. None of the plants were harmed, and our building materials are fine. If I hadn't had Manuel as a resident watchman, we would have lost the whole building for sure. He caught the fire early and went to fight it by himself after calling 911. He's a hero as far as I'm concerned."

"Did he get hurt?"

"No, he's fine. He's actually rather proud of himself, strutting around telling anyone who will listen how he saved Temple Landscaping."

Samantha could visualize his grin. She'd only met Manuel once. He was an older Hispanic man who inhabited a worn single-wide trailer at the back of the growing yard and was paid to watch over the property, as midnight raids for landscaping materials were not unheard of. The fence around the property was more for show than anything else.

Samantha was ashamed. She'd been imagining everything was about her, and here Jack's business was endangered.

Before she could apologize, he spoke, "Look, the crews will complete the current job orders, but I'm shutting down for new work while we sort this out. I hope it won't take too long, as I don't have much put aside. Why don't you take a week or ten days off. Paid, of course."

And not see him for that long? What would she do with herself? And paid? But she ought to accept. She could focus on Mom and the divorce that way. She cringed at the thought. "OK. You sure I can't help with this?"

"Suzie will help file the insurance claim while I line up the repairs. How's your Mom? I'm sorry I didn't ask before."

As if he didn't have enough on his mind. She'd been so wrong about him. "Not much change. She's withdrawn and unhappy. She seems to be shrinking. It's hard to describe." She reached for the right words. "Like the life force is slowly draining from her, leaving an empty shell behind."

"Do you want me to come over?"

She longed to say yes, but knew better. "She isn't responding well to anyone. I'd rather you remember her as she was. She liked you, and I want to leave it at that."

"Whatever you say. Call me with any news." He didn't have to explain what he meant.

"I will."

## 10

# TUESDAY, OCTOBER 15, 1996

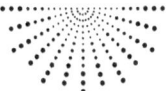

MARILYN, 10:15AM

*M*arilyn turned off the vacuum cleaner and listened; she thought she'd heard the phone. Then it rang again. She ran to the nearest phone, the one in the bedroom, and answered, out of breath from the mad dash.

"Hi, Marilyn, it's Lydia. I'm going to put Eric on. He has some news for you."

"Thanks, Lydia." Marilyn's stomach clenched. She wasn't sure what news could be good.

"I'm here if I can help in any way. Here's Eric."

Before Marilyn could thank her again, Lydia was replaced by Eric. "Hi, Marilyn. I don't have much. I was able to find out that Ted no longer is on the force. He was fired after he made a particularly violent arrest. This happened in late August. I couldn't get further details. I'm guessing he still has his pension, but it's unlikely he'll ever work in law enforcement of any type in the future with a black mark like that on his record."

"Oh," was all Marilyn could manage. Ted had always had a short fuse. Maybe when he couldn't take it out on her anymore, he snapped.

"I know that isn't much, but it might explain the harassment."

"Yes," she agreed. "I really appreciate your helping me."

"I don't know how you're set for money, but you could hire a PI to dig deeper. The advantage would be in confirming his financial and job situation and maybe even his intentions and state of mind. I know your main concern is if he'll stop at the nasty mail or show up in person. He probably got no severance package, but he might be able to borrow if he had good credit or equity in his house. I wish I had more, but that's all I got."

"How would I go about hiring a PI?"

"I can maybe help with that. I'll see if I can turn up a referral for you."

"Thanks, Eric. That sounds great."

After she hung up, she was so deflated, she didn't feel like finishing the vacuuming. This whole thing with Ted was wearing her down. Maybe he was crazy enough to charge a trip to Arizona on a credit card. Being a cop meant everything to him. He'd always had a volcanic personality, and now, he had little to live for. He must be burning up with rage. And he'd always taken his anger out on her.

Once again, she felt guilty for wishing he'd find someone else to bother. It literally hadn't occurred to her that he might turn this obsessive. Too late now. She had to deal with it. At least she had the money to do some investigating. Maybe it would buy her some peace of mind. But what if it did just the opposite? She sighed and sank into the couch. At least knowing would allow her to prepare.

Sensing Marilyn's mood, Tammi came over and put her big head in Marilyn's lap. It was just what Marilyn needed. "I love you so much," she said, hugging the furry body. Tammi didn't lick her; she was reserved with her kisses, which suited Marilyn perfectly. They sat like that for a few minutes.

Whatever happened, she had a good support system. She'd just have to take it one day at a time.

\* \* \*

## JACK, 10:45AM

Jack slammed the handset down on the old-style rotary phone in his office. "Damn." That wasn't strong enough to express his frustration. "Fuck," he muttered under his breath. Not that anyone would hear. Suzie was at the reception desk, and the other office staff were on furlough since the fire. Was it his anger burning him up, or was it already that hot? The A/C unit had been yet another casualty of the blaze.

He hadn't seen this coming, but he had to admit that every time he'd thought of the insurance since the fire, he'd gotten a twinge. Now he knew why. The agent had explained in painstaking detail that Jack was woefully underinsured and would be responsible for a hefty portion of the repair costs. In fact, most of them, since his deductible was so high. And he just didn't have the cash or credit.

He'd been telling himself he'd just get a little bit more ahead, then he could afford better coverage. His premiums were punitive as it was (what the hell was he paying for, anyway?), and with what he contributed for employee benefits and taxes, it left him little profit, and he'd been reinvesting that in improvements to the business.

Things had been looking up in the last year, and now this. How would he recover? Maybe instead of rebuilding, he could just tear down the damaged part of the building and patch up what was left. It would leave him with substantially less square footage, and even that much repair was going to cost more than he had, so he shrank from going that route.

He wished he could talk to Sam, but he didn't want to admit how this event had pushed his business back a few years. Would she be willing to join a struggling business? It could be years before Temple Landscaping recovered. His profit margin was that slim.

He didn't regret investing in his employees. They had better pay and benefits than anyone in the field, and he was repaid in loyalty and good performance that had helped build his company's reputation and attracted a high-end clientele.

He thought of Sam again. She'd be coming back to work soon, probably next week. There was no point lying to her, but…would she want to throw her lot in with his now? Maybe it was just as well her divorce was dragging on. She might have second thoughts, and it would be better that she back out now than later, after moving in with him.

He went back to shuffling the insurance papers. The sooner he got this behind him, the sooner he'd know just how bad it was.

\* \* \*

HELEN, 12:30PM

Helen frowned at her chicken salad sandwich. Alexander had made it just how she liked it, with bits of apple and toasted cashew, but she had no appetite.

"You're looking at it like it might bite you," he said cautiously.

She smiled weakly. "I know. I'm blue. Sorry to be a party pooper."

He put his half-eaten sandwich down and regraded her with emerald eyes. "Anyone would be. Maddie's in bad shape."

"At least I got to see her, although I don't think she was aware I was in the room. She kept moaning and calling for Martin."

"Who's Martin?"

"I ran into Samantha on the way out and she reminded me it's the name of her favorite saint. She used to have a big statue of him in her living room with a votive light in front of it. She must have been praying."

"Hmmm."

"They don't expect her to last another 24 hours. It's depressing me. She was so creative with her jewelry, as well as being the most generous person I've ever known. Her eccentricities were endearing."

He cocked his head at her. "I know you love Maddie, and I'm sad that you're losing her. But it isn't just Maddie. You're upset about the mail we came home to."

"That, too," she admitted. Helen had been shrinking inward since their return from the Virgin Islands, a defensive behavior she thought she'd outgrown after marrying Alexander. Apparently the traumatized victim of Lou's abuse lingered deep in her psyche, waiting for an excuse to appear. She struggled to sit up straight and rise above the mire of negativity that swamped her. "I expected rejection. You prepared me. It still hurts."

Alexander reached over and pushed her hair back from her face, then caressed her cheek. "I know. But it doesn't mean your book is bad. If it doesn't fit an agent's needs and experience, it doesn't matter how good it is. They will reject it. You need to toughen yourself, because it isn't about you. You'll find the right agent if you persist."

His reassurance restored her sagging spirits. "Thank you. I'm not giving up. It's just that there are too many downers right now."

He squeezed her hand. "You have a lot going on. How about our trip? That was wonderful, wasn't it? Isn't St. Croix everything we imagined? Blue skies, turquoise water, a rainbow of fish, excellent food, palm trees and deserted white sand beaches."

She cringed at his enthusiasm. He'd fallen in love with the island, and it was as he described, but some part of her was reluctant to commit to a move. She hadn't known how to share her reservations, and she still didn't.

"You don't feel the way I do," he stated with a certainty that made her withdraw more.

"Guilty as charged. I didn't know how to tell you. I'm not sure I will always feel this way. I hoped it would change. With Maddie and not being able to find an agent for my book, I'm not feeling that positive about anything." Her voice slid into silence.

"Don't you think I deserve to hear how you feel, even if you can't describe it perfectly? Don't you trust me?" The sharp edge in his voice triggered a fear cascade from her previous marriage. Suddenly, she wanted to run and hide in the bedroom closet. She didn't feel safe around angry men. She knew she was overreacting but was powerless to stop the adrenaline rush. She avoided looking at Alexander, afraid of seeing anger on his face, and tried to still her quivering body. Tears began to fill her eyes, and she cursed herself for being such a weakling. *Damn Lou to hell.* Even dead, he twisted her in knots. She started breathing deeply to ward off the looming panic attack. It wasn't fair. Alexander had a right to be upset at her for holding back. It implied mistrust, and nothing could be farther from the truth. Plus, in the end, her drama would make it all about her, as if she were his victim. She gathered her courage to mend things, but he spoke first.

"I'm sorry." He stood up and pulled her into a hug and rocked her, stroking her hair as if she were a small child. "I didn't mean to sound angry. I was disturbed you didn't tell me before now, but I know confrontation frightens you. I didn't mean to react that way."

As usual, his behavior trumped hers. "I'm the one who should apologize. You're so patient and understanding. I don't know what I did to deserve you."

He chuckled and hugged her more tightly. "You brought joy to my life for the first time in years. I can never do enough to express my gratitude." He kissed the top of her head. "Do you feel ready to tell me what bothered you about St. Croix? I'm surprised I didn't notice while we were there."

"I wanted to tell you, but I haven't been able to define it myself. Like I said, I hoped it was something that would pass. I loved the island. It was an incredible vacation. Maybe not quite Bora Bora." She paused and smiled dreamily, reminiscing about their honeymoon. "But to live there...I feel hesitant. It bothered me to see the poverty. People living in nothing more than shacks, then down the road, a huge mansion or five-star resort. And remember the taxi driver who drove us to our vacation rental, because the rental car place had shut down early? He wore a clean but threadbare white undershirt with holes in it from being washed so often. He regaled us with his philosophy of life. The love-hate relationship with tourists. But what I can't forget is his statement that 'a poor people is a happy people,' as if progress was bad."

"We have plenty of poverty here."

She sighed. "I know. It may be hypocritical, but I prefer not to have it right in my face. I felt guilty living so lavishly when around us people were ground down by poverty, despite what the cab driver said."

Alexander stared out the kitchen window at the golf course. "You don't feel that way here?"

"I haven't until now," she admitted. "It's as if living in Palm Lakes creates an illusion. I know people here have problems, but everyone has a nice house and car. On the island, big homes and poor ones mingle. It seems to highlight the gap between the haves and have nots. Some of the homes were 10,000 square foot mansions, and right down the road would be some ramshackle, falling-down hovel. I know I'm being foolish, and life is that way, but I can't help it."

He led her into the living room and sat down with her on the couch.

She was grateful to have this off her chest, but still afraid of shattering their dream, worried it would drive a wedge between them.

"I don't think you're foolish. You're compassionate and empathetic, and we have options. We can drop our plan to move. We're happy here. Or, we could live in one of the few retirement communities on St. Croix, so it would be more like Palm Lakes. They have that one community built around a golf course. I don't think it's age-restricted, but it's upscale. I know there isn't much choice, but it would be comparable. Or, you could channel your energy into helping the less fortunate. We can invest both time and money in helping the community."

She couldn't detect a preference in his voice, and yet surely he had one? It wasn't the first time he'd bowled her over with understanding. She doubted she'd ever get used to it, and that was for the best, because she wouldn't ever take him for granted that way. "Thank you so much. You're right. We don't have to decide now, and we do have choices. I was focusing too much on my discomfort. I don't want to abandon our dream. I just need time to reframe."

He pulled her into an embrace. "We have all the time in the world."

* * *

OLIVIA, 5:15 PM

The buzz of conversations and clinking of dishes and silverware registered on Olivia's senses as she pulled her focus away from the novel that lay open on the table. She stared at her plate of food with distaste. She'd been totally immersed in her story, and it was a bit of a shock to return to the banality of Desert Breeze's dining room. She really ought to eat before her meal got cold, but rubber chicken wasn't her thing. They billed it as chicken cordon bleu, but to Olivia, that stretched credulity.

She never would have guessed that moving to Desert Breezes would be better than going to a fat farm. She was in the best shape she'd been in for years between her frequent walking and the uninspired meals in the dining room. If she kept eating here, she'd be as thin as a stick before long. Well, as long as she avoided the bread pudding.

"Is this seat taken?" Nick's booming bass broke through her reverie.

She didn't try to hide her relief. "Of course not." She hadn't been aware until this minute that she'd hoped to see him here. How transparent was she, sitting here reading a book, ignoring her food? She felt her face flush with embarrassment and hoped he didn't notice.

He balanced his tray on the table's edge and unloaded his drink and dinner plate. "Back in a minute." He wove his way between tables and around someone's parked scooter to return the empty tray to a stack headed for the dishwasher.

Her eyes lingered on him as he strode back, unaware of her scrutiny. He was nodding to a few acquaintances and paused to exchange words with a couple she didn't know. My, but he was big. He wasn't quite what you'd call barrel-chested, but he was solid all over. His large hands—she'd noticed them before and wondered if they made silversmith work difficult —gripped the back of an empty chair as he leaned forward to converse with the husband of the couple. At least, she assumed they were married. She'd seen them once or twice at movie night and bingo.

Nick was dressed as usual in long pants, cowboy boots and a long-sleeved shirt. Sometimes he wore jeans, at least when he went riding. She'd never seen him in shorts or sandals like so many of the men here. Maybe he liked playing cowboy. It seemed to captivate many retirees, who loved to dress up in bolo ties and wear cowboy hats, but Nick had a horse, so he was entitled. Plus it suited him to a tee.

The chat ended and Nick paced back to the table, dodging a walker that was parked in the aisle.

"Sorry about that," he said as he took his seat. "Just saying hi to some friends. Do you know the Czerniks? They used to be neighbors of mine. They're one reason I moved to Desert Breezes. They convinced me I'd like it."

He didn't sound convinced to Olivia, but she didn't pause to wonder why. "No, I've seen them around, but I haven't met them yet."

"Maybe we can get them to go to dinner with us sometime."

"You mean a real dinner?" The question escaped her before she had a chance to think.

Nick choked on a laugh. "Yes, a real dinner. I know what you think of the food here."

Odd. He'd never invited her to a meal here or anywhere. She tingled with anticipation in spite of telling herself not to make too much of it. He seemed to assume they were friends, which was nice. His attention warmed her. They'd taken a few walks together and had a drink or two, but he'd never said or done anything to imply they were more than casual acquaintances. Was going out to dinner with friends significant? Oh dear, he was watching her think.

He misinterpreted her silence. "I see the wheels turning. Don't worry, the Czerniks are nice people. You'll love them. I know it's been hard on you about Sophie and Maddie. I thought it would be good to get out with folks."

Olivia felt tears fill her eyes. She hadn't wanted to plague him with her sadness. She nodded in gratitude.

"If you don't mind my asking, how's Maddie?"

Olivia shook her head. "Bad. She isn't really here anymore. She talks to someone named Martin, asking for help. She didn't even acknowledge me when I visited this morning; lucky for me the bus stops there. At least she didn't seem to be in pain."

"Who's Martin?"

"All I know is her husband was named Stanley, and it seemed they weren't happy together. I haven't seen her daughter to ask her, and no one at hospice had a clue."

He forked some mashed potatoes into his mouth, but his bright blue eyes never wavered from her. "I'm sorry, Livvie. It's hard watching someone die."

Her mind got caught on the diminutive he'd used. No one else had ever called her that. Then abruptly she realized he was talking about his wife, whom he'd never mentioned before. "Were you and your wife close?" *Whatever prompted such a nosy question?* "You don't have to answer me. That was presumptuous."

She covered her embarrassment by drinking her iced tea. When she put the glass down, he was still regarding her with a thoughtful expression. "Yes, we were. We had our ups and downs like most people, but it always felt to me like we were a team, not just two people on separate paths, if that makes any sense."

She smiled. "Oh, yes. How nice for you both."

He grinned sheepishly. "I was no bargain. Being a police chief, even in a small town, demands a lot of time. She got stuck raising Joe pretty much alone. I regret that now, because he and I have little in common. But she never complained, and I always felt we were a support for each other. We made decisions together, contrary to what Joe thinks."

What was that about? She didn't dare ask. She'd been too nosy as it was. "Children can be hard," said Olivia. "You can only do your best and trust it's good enough."

He shrugged as if annoyed. "How did we get on this topic?"

*He's uncomfortable talking about this.* "You were commiserating with me about Sophie and Maddie, which I appreciate. None of us gets out of this life alive, but you're right, losing two friends in such a short time has been hard for me. Makes me face my age. Listen to me. Harder for them than for me, but I feel utterly cast adrift. I miss them. Maddie and I both disliked the food here, even though we've paid for it, but neither of us felt like cooking for one. Mary Beth—the girl Maddie taught jewelry to; you were at her wedding—brought her food often, and so did her daughter, Samantha. Even my daughters occasionally bring some food. So we made a pact. We alternated hosting each other for dinner and shared food. When we didn't have food from the girls, we made our own, but at least it wasn't cooking for one or eating alone. That's over now, which is why you've seen me here lately. I'm feeling sorry for myself. Mary Beth still brings me something now and then, but I hate eating alone."

He had a sparkle in his eyes. "All I know how to make is reservations, but if you don't mind takeout and restaurant food, I'd be willing to join the dinner club."

*What?* Had he just said what she thought? What did it mean? Maybe he simply missed home cooking. "You don't have to offer to do that to cheer me up."

"Cheer you up? I want some real food. I know I said the dining room is fine, but that's compared to having pizza every night or sardines on crackers. You'd be doing me a favor."

Olivia put her fork down and extended her hand. "It's a deal, then."

He enveloped her hand in a warm, firm handshake. "Deal."

What was she getting into? Sharing meals with Nick was not the same as with Maddie, was it? But why shouldn't it be, just because he was a man? It was so comforting to have someone to eat with. They were adults;

they had a right to be friends. But what would people think if they found out? Especially her daughters? She pushed that worry aside. "Do they have bread pudding for dessert tonight?"

His smile revealed even, white teeth. She tangentially wondered if they were real; everything about him seemed so genuine. "Not tonight. I would have snagged us a couple."

"That's OK. I don't need the extra calories."

"You look like you could use a bit of fattening up to me." His eyes dropped to his plate as he scooped up some peas and devoured them.

It didn't sound like he was flirting. Instead, the thought behind his words wrapped her in a cocoon of acceptance. Did he have any idea the effect he had on her? And was it safe to continue to see him, considering the potential for misunderstanding and hurt if she became too attached?

*To hell with it. I like being with him. That's good enough.*

\* \* \*

STEVEN, 6:00PM

Steven searched Marilyn's face for a sign. Had she enjoyed dinner? She seemed distracted, but that was almost her normal state. Although he had finally dumped his guilt about Tanya's murder, she was finding it harder to move on due to Ted's ongoing harassment. He squelched irritation at the man, as it would do no good. He was powerless to get Ted out of her life, so it never seemed the right time to press his suit, and sometimes he wondered if he was just too afraid to try. Whatever the reason, it didn't feel the right time to declare his interest in a more personal relationship.

Sighing inwardly, he pushed his worries aside. "Was dinner OK? You seem to be miles away." He smiled warmly, hoping to encourage her to confide in him, and he wasn't disappointed.

"I'm sorry, Steven. It was lovely, as always. You're so kind to get me out of the house...out of myself. Such a good friend." He cringed inwardly at being stuck in that category. "And I can't thank you enough for welcoming Tammi. She needs the socialization, and she likes you."

"Is she enjoying obedience class?"

Marilyn sighed gustily. "I don't think so. She's incredibly smart. She learns everything the first time, but then doesn't want to be asked to repeat things. Like it bores her. And she is awful at walking on a leash. I never had the heart to do what they told me and yank her off her feet when she was little, and now she's too big to reprimand. The teacher had me get a halter collar for her, and the first time I put it on and we tried to heel with the other dogs, Tammi started bucking straight up in the air like a bronco. She hates that thing."

The dog in question sat next to Marilyn, head almost even with the tabletop, dark brown eyes staring intelligently at Steven as if she understood every word they said. The animal was too big, too smart and too human for his comfort, but inviting the dog seemed to guarantee Marilyn's appearance, so he'd become a dog lover. He was convinced the dog saw through his making nice.

"Let's leave the dishes. I'll do them later. I want to ask your advice on a project."

Marilyn's blue eyes lit up with curiosity. "Really? What project?"

"Don't get too excited. I mentioned before that I wanted to redecorate. I haven't a clue what to do. I only know I can't leave it like this." His hands pointed toward the living room, and Marilyn looked at him sympathetically. She knew it reminded him of Tanya.

"Steven, I have no experience in decorating. I'm not sure how I could help."

He couldn't let her get out of it that easily. "It doesn't matter. You have to be better than I am."

"Are you implying something sexist?" Her left eyebrow cocked up in what he fervently hoped was mock offense. It could be so hard to tell with women.

"Of course not. I just need a second opinion, and I trust your judgment. Will you help me?"

She sighed as if he'd asked too much of her, and his heart plunged. "OK." She wasn't enthusiastic, but at least she'd said yes.

"Could we walk through the house and discuss options?"

"I guess so. Where shall we start?"

"The living room." It was the worst place for him. Well, in daytime, the bedroom was the worst, but at night the lights were out, so he didn't have to see it. Every time he walked through the living room, he remembered the fights he'd had with Tanya, the last one so like others where she'd hurled venom at his retreating back as he escaped to the golf course to avoid her alcoholic needling. He was certain she'd embarked on her affair with the serial killer shortly after that last fight, because her attention mercifully shifted away from him, as it always had when she cheated on him. He'd been grateful for the respite until she'd crashed the car and ended up in rehab. Funny how he'd always fantasized about being divorced, having some peace, but he'd never really expected it to happen. And then when it did, peace had been stolen from him when she was murdered by her lover.

Marilyn stood quietly, watching him reminisce, and he shook his head. "This is why I want to redecorate. It will help stop the memories this garish decor triggers. I really do want to move on."

"Of course," she said, sounding unconvinced. Well, he was determined.

He opened the drapes in the living room, something he rarely did, because it only made the sight more repugnant. But they needed the light to fully evaluate the situation. She stood beside him, surveying the room as the golden evening light fell across the animal-skin themed couch, a print of a cheetah hanging on the wall above it. Tammi sat at Marilyn's side, a quizzical look on her furry face. As if telepathic, Marilyn reached down and petted the big black head. "We're just looking around, Tammi. Not going home yet." Marilyn nibbled on her lower lip, eyes narrowed. She was taking this seriously. "You want my honest opinion?" she challenged after a moment of silence.

Gulping, he nodded. "Hit me."

She grimaced, then grinned. "I don't know your budget, but I'll try to prioritize. The color scheme isn't bad. Using red as an accent to the black and white is good, but there's too much red. In my opinion. The blood red shag rug bothers me the most. The overabundance of animal skin in the furniture is the next thing I'd change. Maybe if you replace the carpet with something neutral and get a new couch with a couple other chairs or recliners, it would be fine. The art would probably look OK then. But at least replace the carpet and couch."

He tried unsuccessfully to visualize the change. "What color carpet is neutral?"

"Any light color. Not white, though. Beige or oatmeal or cream. And Berber is nice, but expensive. Just don't get shag. And not red."

He nodded, attempting to picture the room with a lighter carpet and almost got a sense of it seeming larger and less angry. Yes, that would help a lot. "What color or design for the furniture?"

"Leather is nice, if you can afford it. You don't have pets to worry about." He was momentarily speechless. That statement bothered him. She obviously had no dreams of living here, but then, why should she? He'd never broached the subject. "I think you could go with black, but brown would work fine, too."

She regarded him apologetically. "Don't put much into what I say. I have no experience with interior design. Maybe you should hire a professional." She hadn't understood his crestfallen look. He needed to police his reactions better.

"Nonsense. I like your ideas. Let's go to the next hot spot." She didn't say no, so he led her down the hallway to the master bedroom. She'd seen it during the home tour some time ago, but he still cringed at the thought of her critiquing it. He hadn't decorated, but still, didn't it say something about him that he lived here?

They stopped just inside the bedroom, and he put a hand up and went over to open the drapes. Wincing, he looked at the room through her eyes. It looked like a bordello, and not an expensive one. "Go ahead, tell me the truth."

She eyed him as if she felt his pain. "What can I say? I think your wife had a love affair with red. Was she a very angry person who was blatantly sexual?…Don't answer that, you've shared enough in the support group to confirm that. This room definitely is her, not you."

She'd said that with such certainty, but although he liked the idea of not being mistaken for an angry man, he wasn't sure it was a compliment that he wasn't blatantly sexual. He was beginning to think of himself as asexual anyway, and he wasn't eager for her to agree. He held his breath so that she could continue.

"Too much red, again. How can you sleep in a room this red? It practically vibrates." She blushed, having caught the unintentional word choice. "The nice thing about the bedroom is by changing your linens and bedspread, you will change the whole tone of the room. The carpet needs to go, of course. A more masculine, intellectual color scheme would be good. Maybe navy and brown or maroon and black. But a neutral, lighter color rug. I'd avoid very dark or very light colors for the carpeting."

Still unable to really picture the transformation, he was encouraged by what she said. "Would you help me choose the particulars when the time comes? I have such a problem visualizing what will work and what won't. I'd hate to invest in another disaster."

"Sure. What are friends for?"

There was that word again. Well, friends was better than nothing. Maybe this project would draw them closer together. "Thanks. I really appreciate it."

They wandered back to the dining room, where Steven pulled a dessert wine out of the hutch that held his meager booze collection. "How about a small glass of wine before you go home?"

"Sure. How about we sit in the African room for that?" Her eyes glinted with humor.

"Yeah, it'll be like waiting at the water hole for the lions to make a kill."

"Let's go in and imagine what atmosphere you want to create instead."

"Sure thing." The rest of the evening was golden. He looked forward to more times like this with her. At some point, he'd get up nerve enough to declare his intentions.

* * *

SAMANTHA, 2:10AM WEDNESDAY

The gentle knock on the bedroom door yanked Samantha out of a troubled dream. *Oh, God!*

The door cracked open, revealing Mary Beth holding a phone. "Samantha, it's for you. Hospice calling."

Samantha hadn't even heard it ring. She leaped off the bed, instantly wide awake, and took the phone. "Thanks." She put it to her ear and sat down on the bed, stomach in knots.

"Ms. Taylor, it's about your Mom. She won't be with us much longer. I thought you might want to come in."

Just for a second, Samantha considered declining. Mom hadn't been aware of her the last few days, and it tore her up to watch her suffer, but that excuse wasn't enough to release her from this task. "I'll be right there. Thanks for calling."

She stood by the bed, temporarily lost, then set about dressing. It didn't really matter what she wore, so she put on the same clothes she'd worn that day. A soft knock preceded Mary Beth sticking her head around the door. "Samantha?"

"It's Mom. She's going. They wanted to give me a chance to say goodbye." Or at least be there.

"Would you like me to go with you?"

Samantha almost said yes, but it was too selfish. "Nah. She probably won't even know I'm there. No need for us both to go." She sat on the bed heavily and slipped on her sandals, velcroing the straps.

As she exited the bedroom, Mary Beth gave her a hug. "Would you like some coffee when you get back?"

She hated to keep Mary Beth up for an undetermined period of time, but it sounded like rescue from falling into a dark pit. "That would be great. I don't know how long I'll be, though."

"No worries. It will stay warm."

As she drove through the moonlit streets, Samantha noted the resemblance between Palm Lakes and a graveyard. Not a sign or sound of life but her making her way spectrally to her mother's deathbed. Hummingbird Haven Hospice was only a mile from the entrance to Palm Lakes, and she arrived before she was ready to face the inevitable. Not for the first time, Samantha wondered how calculated the location of the hospice was, just minutes from Palm Lakes, but she was too tired and too stressed to pursue that line of thought.

There was a motherly quality to the night attendant who stepped forward and offered to shake hands. "Ms. Taylor? I'm Julianne. You got here fast." Dark curls surrounded a plump face with brown eyes that seemed to have seen everything, but managed to retain humor and humanity.

Samantha immediately felt more at ease. "Yes, I came as fast as I could."

"Go on back. Sandra is with her."

Nodding her gratitude, Samantha made her way quickly through the hushed corridors that led around the darkened, silent hummingbird courtyard which was closed off to the night's chill. A portly, middle-aged woman with gray hair in an 80s perm sat at Mom's beside, holding her hand and whispering softly. She stood when Samantha entered.

"Thanks for staying with my Mom."

"It's a privilege, dear. Thanks for coming. I'll leave you with her if you wish?"

"That will be fine, thanks."

Samantha sank into the chair that was steeped with the warmth from its former occupant. Mom's eyes were shut, and Samantha felt her heart jump as she worried she had arrived too late, but then a ragged inhale assured her that Mom still clung precariously to life.

Part of Samantha knew Mom already had one foot in the next world, and yet, she stubbornly believed she was aware of her daughter, even if unwilling or unable to acknowledge her presence. Samantha decided the best tack was to just be there, so she began to chat the way she always did these last few days, a one-sided conversation she hoped got through to Mom on some level. "Remember I told you that they had a fire at Jack's business last week? I was given time off, which was good, so I could be with you more."

She squeezed Mom's cool hand, still wondering at how fragile it was. Mom had loved to do her own gardening, was never afraid of physical labor, but the osteoporosis had leached the strength from her bones, robbing her of the joy of puttering in her yard. The jewelry hobby had consumed all her time and focus after that, and these hands had crafted beautiful objects that would live on for years. A tear slipped from Samantha's eye.

"Jack told me to say hello. He's busy with the insurance company and repairs. He wanted to come see you, but I said no. I was sure you'd prefer that. I hope I was right. He really cares about you.

"Mary Beth offered to come with me tonight, but I wanted you to myself. Was that selfish?" The infrequent inhalation and exhalation were alarming, and Samantha knew it was a signal of the approaching transition. "The realtor on your house, Shari, called this afternoon. The house sold. I had to lower the price, but the buyer has cash and was eager to make a deal. Shari said it's a widow who was effusive about your yard and the way you'd made the laundry room into an office with built-in oak shelving. She was amazed to hear you'd done that yourself. The fenced yard was also a factor, because she has a dog. It sounds like she'll love the place for you." Samantha wiped tears from her face. "I'm sorry it didn't sell earlier. I know there were things you wanted to do. I wish..." She didn't know what to say. She had done all she could, but couldn't help feeling responsible for Mom's unfulfilled dreams.

"I love you, Mom. I appreciate everything you did for me. You gave me permission to choose happiness, and I'll never be able to repay you." She swallowed a lump. What if Jack was having second thoughts? He'd been distant since her last day at work. No matter how often she told herself he had a lot on his mind, she wondered if he'd had enough of secrecy, drama and waiting. Embarrassed that her thoughts had diverted to her own problems, she focused on Mom. There was no returned squeeze or any awareness from her. "Mom, I'll miss you."

She sat silent vigil until Mom's last exhale, surprised at how peaceful the actual transition was. After lingering a few minutes, she collected herself and released Mom's hand. She stood and leaned over and kissed the paper-thin skin of her mother's wrinkled face, still trying to process that she was gone. Reluctant to leave, as if walking out would make it true, she stood staring at Mom for minutes. Then she trudged out to the reception area to Julianne, who gave her a hug and assured her everything would be taken care of as they had planned.

As she retraced her route home, she mentally prepared for the funeral at the nearby cemetery. Mom and Dad had plots next to each other in the military section. Dad hadn't served, but Mom had been in the Navy in WWII, so she would be buried with honors. She needed to contact those she wanted to attend. Mom had few real friends. She hoped Jack would come. She'd call him tomorrow. No, today. It was nearly dawn.

Using the spare garage door opener Mary Beth had given her, she pulled into the garage and steeled herself for the coming day. She was surprised she didn't feel exhausted, but then, she didn't feel much of anything. Mary Beth met her at the door to the garage and hustled her into the kitchen, placing a warm mug of coffee in her hands. They sat at the table, saying very little at first, then sharing stories about Mom that eventually led to laughter as the sky lightened in anticipation of the new day.

## 11

# FRIDAY, NOVEMBER 8, 1996

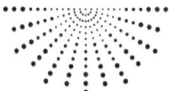

SAMANTHA, 8:00PM

*S*amantha sat on her bed, a pillow between her back and the headboard, sharing with Mary Beth about her day. Mary Beth occupied the sole chair in the guest room at Samantha's insistence. It was her house, after all. While it was a bit strange to hide out in the bedroom, chatting in here afforded privacy for Samantha's coming revelation. Ethan was watching TV in the living room.

"You're sure Ethan doesn't mind you disappearing like this?" Samantha knew she was wound too tight, but couldn't help it. Mary Beth was like her anchor in the hurricane her life had become, and she didn't want to offend her or Ethan.

Mary Beth pushed thick, wavy hair back off her face, tucking it absentmindedly behind her ear. "Of course, not. Don't be silly. Tell me the news."

"You can share any of this with Ethan. I just feel funny saying it in front of him." She wasn't sure why that was so, since Ethan had been supportive and kind. "The divorce came through. I got the paperwork in the mail today."

Mary Beth whooped and punched her fist in the air, prompting a smile from Samantha. "Finally! I thought that envelope looked promising."

"Well, the property agreement was so hard to finalize. Arthur found out Mom's house sold, and he wanted half the proceeds since it sold while we were technically married. I waffled about it. But I decided I just want it over. And he's right. He gave me half the value of our house. It just pissed me off that he acted deserving in spite of his lack of love for Mom. But in the end, I agreed, just to get it done."

Mary Beth's penetrating brown stare made her flinch. She probably thought Samantha was a coward, and she'd be right. When Mary Beth said nothing, Samantha continued, "I saw him drive by the house today."

"Who? Whose house?" Mary Beth looked alarmed and confused.

"Arthur. By your house. He drove by slowly. It creeped me out. The divorce is final. I gave him half of the proceeds from Mom's house. Why is he stalking me?" She was not only indignant. She was scared.

"Do you think he's mentally unbalanced?"

Samantha had asked herself that same question after seeing him drive by. "I don't know. I gave in on the big things he asked for, but I did demand a fair share of our assets. It's put him in a bind. He probably can't continue to live as we did on his retirement alone. No doubt he sees this change in lifestyle as my fault." She let out a big sigh. When would it ever be over? Tension tightened her muscles, and her head began to throb.

"You should stay here for a while."

Samantha struggled to resolve conflicting compulsions. One was to run from Palm Lakes screaming and get as far away as possible from Arthur. The other was to hunker down with her friends. "I've been imposing on you for too long as it is."

"Samantha, you don't want to invest in a lease on a place if things work out with you and Jack, and I'm sure they will. Plus, I don't want you living in some dump all by yourself if Arthur turns into a stalker. Take a few weeks. See how things go with Jack now that you're free. You're welcome to stay as long as you like. I know the commute is long, but you'll save in other ways." With that, Mary Beth rose. "Don't decide now. Sleep on it. Talk with Jack." She walked out of the room, leaving Samantha to navigate the torrential currents of her emotions.

Talk to Jack. Right. He'd been different since the fire, and she wasn't sure why. Too much had been happening for her to open another can of worms, but she couldn't wait any longer. She hadn't called him about the divorce, because she'd only found out after returning from work. She wanted to share the good news, but what if he'd changed his mind? He hadn't so much as patted her arm since the fire. Surely that meant something bad.

A phone call would be unsatisfactory. She wanted to see his face when she told him. Then she'd know. But telling him at work didn't feel right. They both had tried so hard to keep things professional during working hours. She didn't want to wait to tell him, anyway. God, it was Friday. She couldn't wait until Monday. She needed to know now if her decision to divorce Arthur was going to lead to the beginning of a better life or simply turn her into a lonely divorcee. It hit her then how Arthur must feel. At least she could start over somewhere new. He had to weather gossip, judgment and prying questions, none of which were his strengths. She'd felt sorry for the financial hardship the divorce was causing him, but this was the first time she'd regarded the social fallout from his perspective.

She hadn't divorced Arthur to punish him for his failings, but she couldn't pretend with him anymore. For that reason alone, she knew she was right to leave him. But that didn't calm her need to know the direction of her own future. She should go see Jack and tell him the news. So much depended on him now.

It seemed so logical, she wondered why she'd waited so late. She slipped her shoes on and went into the bathroom to check how she looked. A shower would take too long, so she splashed her face with cool water, tasting the salt that it rinsed off. Mom had always warned her how bad it was for the skin to leave the salt from sweat on it.

Thinking of Mom caused her eyes to fill with tears. If only Mom had lived to see this. She had encouraged Samantha to grab happiness, probably because she'd never had much of her own. "Mom, I did like you said. I hope it turns out."

She dried her face, blotting the tears, and looked in the mirror. Were those frown lines around her eyes new? She patted flyaway hair back with damp fingers. There wasn't time to redo the braid; it was too hard to do when her hair was dry, anyway. What did it matter how she looked? Jack had seen her at work today. Suddenly she was gripped with indecision. It would be late by the time she got to his house. What if he didn't want to see her?

That was ridiculous. Of course he'd want to know. But she could call him and tell him. She didn't need to drive over there. No, she had to see his face. Her mind was all knotted up. She couldn't feel her way to the right choice.

*To hell with it. I'm going.*

She grabbed a light jacket against the night chill and snagged her fanny pack off the dresser. As she passed through the living room, she told Mary Beth and Ethan she was going to tell Jack the news. She didn't linger to see their reactions. She was too afraid they'd try to change her mind, and it was made up.

During the drive, which was only 30 minutes due to the lack of traffic, she rehearsed what she wanted to say, but she couldn't come up with anything that felt right after the part about the divorce being final. Oh well, she'd play it by ear. Not her normal way, but she was too frazzled to care.

Jack's neighborhood was nearly as quiet as Palm Lakes, the main difference being the signs of children in residence. The occasional bike laying on its side in a driveway, a basketball hoop near a garage door, swing sets visible in back yards. This was an older neighborhood, but well cared for. It had a vitality Palm Lakes lacked, in spite of its pristine newness, or maybe because of it. Houses here varied widely in design and colors, but she found that appealing and more spontaneous than the sameness of the homes in Palm Lakes.

Second thoughts stole into her mind as she pulled into Jack's driveway, but she had no time to act on them, because Beau began barking, having recognized the sound of her truck. The outside light flicked on, and she marched up the walk to the front door, which flew open to show Jack in black gym shorts and a scruffy t-shirt. Nothing had ever looked better to her.

He opened the screen door, a question in his eyes. She stepped inside and said, "The divorce is final."

* * *

## OLIVIA, 8:30PM

Sharing a post-prandial drink, Olivia regarded Nick with a mixture of curiosity and concern. He'd brushed off her question about how he was feeling, as if she were imagining the slight limp, the occasional grimace of pain and the way he moved more carefully than normal. He was hurting, and she knew it, but he was a grown man, and if he didn't want to tell her, it was none of her say-so. She was more stung than she wanted to admit by his unwillingness to share, but didn't want to dwell on that.

She covered her hurt by playing hostess. "Can I refresh your drink?" She knew he wasn't ready yet, besides never having more than one bourbon after or before dinner, but that was a more neutral topic than what she was thinking.

"No, thanks. This will do me." He wasn't a big drinker, and she was glad of that.

"How's the silversmithing class?" she ventured onto another bland subject.

His blue eyes sparkled, and whatever was bothering him vanished as he embarked on an unusually detailed response. It was obvious he loved the class. She felt a pang of envy. What could she find to do that would inspire her enthusiasm? That's one reason she loved being with Nick; he was living life to the fullest. But she didn't want to live vicariously. She wanted to live.

She snapped out of her musing. *Listen to the man. Enjoy this rare garrulous moment.* He finally paused in his story, and she asked, "Are you making something special, like a belt buckle?"

A shadow flicked through his eyes, and she knew his answer would be a lie. *God, why can't I find a good topic of conversation?*

"I'm not sure yet." So they were back to short answers. Oh, well.

Why would he not say? He was being so mysterious tonight. "I'd love to see whatever you make. I'm so impressed with your creativity and willingness to try new things. I wish I were like that."

The hooded eyes turned to cold blue flames. "How can you say that, you who foiled the rapist no one else could be bothered to catch? What I do can't compare to that."

She felt a warm buzz from the compliment, but wouldn't relent. "I

187

mean, I don't do much of anything now. Maddie made beautiful jewelry. Mary Beth is a gourmet cook. Helen is writing a novel. You ride a horse and make silver jewelry. What do I do?"

His quizzical look irritated her, as if he had no idea where she was coming from. "Never mind. I just need to find myself. Moving here, then losing Sophie and Maddie…" The tears threatened, but she blinked them back angrily. She wasn't going to cry in front of him.

Nick stared, but his eyes had warmed with sympathy. "There are lots of clubs here. You're very active. You walk and do that exercise class. It's not like you're watching TV all day. Why don't you join a club if you have time on your hands?"

She sighed. "I just can't think of what to do. The things I used to love, like gardening, seem to be beyond my physical abilities. I hate feeling old." *Where had that come from?*

Nick regarded her with something akin to surprise. "You always seem so competent and full of life to me. You don't seem old."

She could tell he was serious. "Thanks. But I guess what matters most is not how we appear to others, but how we see ourselves. Breaking my hip made me look at my age and limitations, but I've fought every step of the way. Lately, though, I'm tired of the fight." She hadn't meant to be this candid or depressing.

"How old *are* you, Livvie?"

Her eyes popped open in shock. "What a question!" she huffed. She paused, then thought, what the hell. "I turned 85 in August."

"That's not old. I turned 84 this past January, and I'm damned if I'm old, but some days it's harder to believe than others." He chuckled, then looked tentative. "I fell off Rudi today."

"You what? Is that why you're acting sore? Did you break anything?" She panicked at the thought of Nick being seriously injured.

"Calm down. I'm just banged up." He paused as if gathering his thoughts. "It's not like it was my first time being bucked off a horse, but it was the first time in years. He's young. The wind spooked him. I didn't react fast enough. Getting old stinks."

She smiled in sympathy. "You can say that again." What could she do to help him feel better? She didn't want him riding if this is what it led to. "What are you going to do?"

"Do?" He looked bemused. "What do you mean?"

She shoved the annoyance she felt to the side. "Are you going to keep riding? Don't you think this is a wakeup call? You were lucky this time. What about next time? Was there even anyone around to help?" She held back her exasperation; she knew fear was fueling it.

"Next time?"

Why was he acting so dense? Did he really think it couldn't happen again? "You could have been killed today. How can you be sure there won't be a next time? Besides, you don't even wear a helmet, and you go out in the desert all alone. That can't be safe." She couldn't believe she was dressing him down. He had a right to make his own choices, but she didn't want him to kill himself by being so macho.

His confusion morphed into a lopsided grin. "Thanks for caring so much." Then he became serious. "I don't know what to do. I'm not ready to give up riding, but Rudi lost it today, and I wasn't able to control him."

"Maybe you need a horse more like you. Older and wiser instead of young and foolish."

He frowned. "I love training horses, but it could be you're right. I didn't want to admit my reaction time has slowed that much. A bombproof horse could be the answer. I'd hate to give up Rudi, though." He seemed so sad, she couldn't bear it. Being physically active was important to him, but she hoped he'd see reason.

"Promise me you'll think about it."

"OK. I'll think about it." He didn't look convinced.

"If you don't, I may have to turn you over my knee." She broke into a smile at his shocked reaction. "Just so we understand each other. No going out and breaking your neck."

"Yes, ma'am. I'll see what I can do about it." He went back to sipping his bourbon in silence, but it was a companionable one.

\* \* \*

JACK, 8:45PM

Had she said the divorce was final? Jack reached for Sam and drew her far enough inside to close the front door. Her hair was disheveled, and her eyes were bloodshot, as if she'd been crying. Why would she be upset about the divorce being final?

"Did you say what I thought you said?" He could hardly believe the waiting was over.

Then, the realization triggered the fears he hadn't been able to resolve, and it must have reflected in his face, because her eyes became hooded and she spoke with hesitation. "I'm sorry to barge in without warning you. I wanted to tell you in private." Her eyes searched his, looking for something, then she looked down, as if embarrassed. "I shouldn't have been so impulsive. It's just that it's been so long, and I didn't want to wait to tell you, and I needed to see your reaction."

She obviously thought his concerns had to do with how he felt about her. Well, that was one thing he had no doubts about. He reached out and pulled her into his arms, hungrily seeking her lips, feeling so free that it was as if he were flying through the air.

She relaxed into his arms and kissed him back just as eagerly. He paused long enough to growl, "Don't even think about going home tonight." She glanced at him with surprise, and he put a finger on her lips. "Don't you dare. I'm not waiting another day." And he went back to kissing and nuzzling her face and neck as he pulled her back towards the bedroom, Beau trailing along, bouncing with happiness that Samantha had come to visit.

She came along with only token resistance. "I didn't intend…"

"I know you didn't plan to seduce me, but too bad. You're staying, and that's that. Just try to get away from me now that I know you're a free woman." Love chased the worries from her blue-green eyes, and for the first time, she smiled shyly. "That's more like it. I know we have a lot to talk about, and I'm sorry I've been putting it off, but now isn't the time for talk." He backed her up until her legs hit the bed and gently pushed her. She fell across the bed and didn't try to get back up.

"I've been waiting for this for a long time and so have you." He crawled onto the bed and began to undress her slowly, fighting the desire to tear off her clothes.

He'd gotten her shoes, jacket, shirt and shorts off before she looked meaningfully at the bulge in his gym shorts and hesitated. "I'm not prepared. I didn't bring anything. I just meant to tell you the news." Sam tried to sit back up, scooting back towards the head of the bed, still in bra and panties.

"Well, I've been prepared for a long time." He gently pushed her back down and reached over to the drawer in the nightstand and pulled out a box of condoms. Her eyes widened.

"OK," was all she said.

He lay across her, supporting his weight on his arms. "Last chance. If you don't want to, you have to tell me now." He tensed, waiting for her answer, not sure she wouldn't slip away, wishing he hadn't felt obliged to give her an out, but her vacillation concerned him. He couldn't bear for her to have regrets tomorrow.

"It's not that," she said vaguely, not really boosting his confidence.

"Show me what you want, Sam."

She sighed deeply and tears filled her eyes. "All I want is you, and I feel like I've been waiting forever. Are you sure you want me?"

How could she doubt? "Do I want you? Are you nuts? I want you so bad, I'm going to go off like a rocket, as least the first time. I hope you won't judge me by that." He pressed his erection against her and watched as her eyes widened further.

Suddenly, he knew her reaction meant she had no more doubts about them than he did. Well, he wasn't interested in talking about his wretched business or her complicated finances right now. All he wanted was to make her his. Sam was going to know how much he loved her, because he was going to love her every way imaginable, even if it took all night. He hoped it would.

As he tamped back his ardor and began to kiss every bit of skin he revealed as he removed her underwear, he fed off her sighs and moans, feeling himself turn to steel. Finally, he had her unwrapped like a Christmas present. She was gorgeous, skin soft and smooth, just slightly freckled where the sun had kissed it. He pulled the elastic from her braid and ran his fingers through her thick, long hair, letting it spread on the pillow in a halo. He ran his fingers teasingly from her hair down her front, brushing her nipples, which were already taut. He caressed her inner thigh, reveling in her hitched breath.

"When do you get naked?" Her hand reached for the waistband of his shorts and tugged gently. He grinned in response and shucked them off so fast, she looked startled. Then he pulled his t-shirt off and tossed it on the floor. "How's that?" Her eyes scanned him up and down, lingering on his erection with what appeared to be approval. He rubbed against her skin, nearly fracturing from the exquisite contact. "I won't be able to hold out for long this time."

She stared at him directly. "Then put it in, for heaven's sake."

He grabbed a condom and sheathed himself and paused only long enough to assure that she was ready for him. She was so ready, his face cracked with a wide smile. He kissed her deeply and plunged into her. He stroked hard and deep, but tried to hold back the finish as he felt her climb higher and higher. Then everything exploded into the most powerful orgasm he'd ever experienced. Shuddering with wave after wave of pleasure, he felt her climax as if it were his own. He thrilled at watching her eyes as she experienced ecstasy he'd given her and then kissed her deeply, their tongues entwining with passion as they slowly descended from the heights.

His arm muscles began to quiver, and he lay down on her body. "Am I too heavy?"

"Never." She wrapped arms tightly around him, holding him as if fearful he might disappear. As if. He felt himself respond to her entwined limbs and welcoming body with a speed that surprised him. Satisfaction flowed through him. It was going to be a good, long night.

## 12
# SATURDAY, NOVEMBER 9, 1996

OLIVIA, 1:45PM

𝓜ary Beth sat on the sofa at Olivia's apartment sipping iced tea, waiting to hear the tale, so Olivia plunged in. "Diana called this morning about Thanksgiving. That's what has me disturbed." Or was it upset? She inexplicably felt as if she wanted to cry. "My three girls and their families are coming down for Thanksgiving and want to take me out to dinner. At least I won't have to cook."

"That sounds nice," said Mary Beth cautiously.

Olivia snorted. "What it means is that one or all of them aren't planning on coming for Christmas. They almost never come for both holidays." She waved away Mary Beth's compassionate look. "They have in-laws and other people. I can't hog them, but I notice they tend to do Christmas elsewhere. Even when I had the house, they only showed up one out of every three or so Christmases. But that's not what's bothering me. I told them I wanted Nick to go with us."

Mary Beth smiled. "Of course. He doesn't have anyone coming for the holiday?"

"No, but that isn't the only reason. Part of me wants my girls to meet

Nick, but part of me is scared. We're just friends, but we've grown close, and he matters to me. I chickened out at the last minute and didn't tell Diana everything. I just told her he was a widower I knew who was spending the holiday alone, and I felt sorry for him. I made him sound like some kind of sad sack, which is so untrue, but in some way, I wanted them to think that's how I saw him, so they wouldn't suspect anything else." She wrung her hands. "I was so foolish. He could let anything drop during the meal that would show we're spending a lot of time together, then they'll really be on me for details."

"So what? It's none of their beeswax. I'm glad you invited Nick. I know you care about him, and he seems so nice. Just don't borrow trouble."

It sounded so reasonable, but felt impossible. "I suppose my conflict is more to do with what is going on between us than what my daughters might think."

Mary Beth raised an eyebrow, and her cat-green eyes twinkled. "And what is going on? Care to share?"

Olivia huffed. "Nothing, is what. Nothing at all. But we do eat dinner together most of the time. He isn't much of a talker; he's more of a doer. And yet, he hasn't said or done anything to indicate any real interest in me. I've grown attached to him, and I shouldn't. After what happened with Sophie and Maddie, I don't know what I'd do if he died." Olivia paused and rubbed her eyes. "What a stupid thing to say. Of course, he's going to die sometime. We all do. I just can't face it."

Mary Beth reached over and touched her arm in reassurance. "It's a risk to care about someone, but the alternative is awful lonely. I know you've had a hard year, but if you're enjoying your time with Nick, squeeze every drop of happiness out of it. With Ethan being significantly older than me, I've had to adopt that attitude. I can't spend time worrying if he's going to die on me."

"You're right, of course. It's more than that. If this relationship turned into anything, my daughters would go nuts. I hate to say it, but they seem to be counting down to getting their inheritance, and my having a serious relationship would muddy the waters. I have a good bit in the bank thanks to the house sale, and if I were to marry, it would no longer go straight to them. Already, they've been pushing me to put one or all of their names on my bank accounts. I've declined, but there is a certain logic to it. If something happened to me and I were out of commission, they could pay my bills. But I can't get over the feeling that they want to get their hands on my assets. Well, some of them do. I'm not sure they're all greedy."

Mary Beth formed an O with her mouth. "I guess that's the down side of having anything. My Mom had very little, and Maddie had nothing except her house. People get funny about money."

"I never worried much about it in the past. I figured I wouldn't be here to see. But if I remarry, what happens if I predecease my husband? Does he get it all? He has a son he doesn't see often, and I guess we could write wills to make it fair, but no matter how you look at it, they're going to see it as a delay and a smaller piece of the pie for each of them."

"Maybe you ought to tell them you're leaving everything you have to charity." There was a mischievous glint in Mary Beth's green eyes.

"I like how you think, but I can't do that. I'd like to help my girls and their children. I just wish they cared more about me and my happiness than they do about my money."

"I say screw 'em," said Mary Beth dismissively. "Do you think they worry about how you think of them? Are they constantly doing nice things for you? From what you say, they can't be bothered to give you the time of day. Susanna sounds pretty good, but the other two, not so much." A speculative look lit her up. "Hey, that's it! This would be a great test. Go ahead and let them think something is going on between you and Nick. That will tell you for sure where you stand."

"Mary Beth, you are such a caution." It actually sounded like a reasonable plan, but she wasn't sure she'd have the nerve to follow through. "I'll play it by ear."

"Just quit worrying yourself to death. You can bet Nick and the girls aren't losing any sleep over this. It will all work out."

She hoped Mary Beth was right.

## 13
# THANKSGIVING, THURSDAY, NOVEMBER 28, 1996

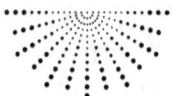

SAMANTHA, 4:00PM

*S*amantha wrapped honeydew melon balls in pieces of prosciutto, the tip of her tongue poking out of her compressed lips in concentration. "There, that's the last." She rotated the platter, gazing at it in satisfaction. Finally, she looked up at Mary Beth, who was checking the homemade cannelloni in the oven. "Our family always did turkey on both Thanksgiving and Christmas, but I kind of like breaking tradition. God, that does smell heavenly!" The herb and garlic infused aroma of the cannelloni had finally reached Samantha. "You are such a great cook!"

Mary Beth smiled at the compliment, but then brushed it aside. "I'm glad you and Jack don't mind eating Italian for Thanksgiving. Ethan and I aren't keen on turkey."

"I never complain when someone makes me a gourmet meal."

Mary Beth shrugged. "It's no big deal."

"My Mom sure thought it was. You gave her joy by cooking her favorite foods. She hated to cook. Olivia seems quite grateful, too."

Mary Beth shrugged. "It's easy to make big batches and share. My mother filled her freezer, because she never seemed to get it through her head that she didn't have a traditional, big Italian family. I inherited the tendency to cook in large amounts. I enjoy sharing it."

Jack's head popped around the door frame. "Boy, something smells great! I'm grabbing a brew for me and Ethan. Do you ladies want anything?"

Mary Beth nodded. "I'm ready to open a bottle of wine. What about you, Samantha?"

"Wine for me, too, thanks. Shall I bring the appetizers out?"

A grin displayed even, white teeth in Jack's tanned face. "I was hoping for something to eat. It's hard work watching football."

Mary Beth waved him away dismissively. "I'll bring our wine, Samantha. Go feed the boys."

Jack walked past Mary Beth and reached into the refrigerator for two bottles of Stella, then left with a smile on his face.

Samantha picked up the platter and followed Jack into the great room, where Ethan was engrossed in the football game on the TV. She placed her offering on the coffee table in front of the men after stepping over the recumbent large yellow dog. Beau, aware she was carrying food, snapped to attention, dark eyes pinning her with hope. "No, Beau. Not for you. We'll share the main course later."

He huffed a grumble and lay his head down between his paws. She decided to help Mary Beth with the wine and walked towards the kitchen, passing the picture window that overlooked the street. A blue-gray car was trolling slowly past, and she stepped back from the window in shock. It was Arthur's Honda Accord. She had seen him clearly. Had he seen her? Jack's truck was parked outside at the curb, magnetic sign proclaiming it belonged to Temple Landscaping.

She practically ran the remaining steps to the kitchen and sat at the breakfast bar, her heart beating wildly, as if she were running from a tiger.

"What happened? You look like you just saw a ghost." Mary Beth handed her a glass of red wine and sat next to her.

Samantha sighed, shrugging off a shiver. "I just saw Arthur cruise by, and your house is on the way to nowhere, so he's stalking me. And Jack's truck is sitting outside." She felt a tear trickle down her cheek. "Why is he doing this? I gave him what he wanted. I just want to start over. Maybe I need to get out of Palm Lakes now."

"What? And leave before dinner? Relax. He's alone today and wondered if you were still here. I agree that it's a shame Jack's truck is there. It's an admission that the two of you are together. But your divorce is final and has been for a while. Do you think Arthur's the type who might snap or go beyond checking out where you are?"

Samantha paused. "I never would have thought he would be a stalker, so this has me rattled. I wouldn't have thought him capable of violence, either, but I was wrong about the stalking, so I don't think I can trust my judgment."

Mary Beth reached over and patted Samantha's hand. "Don't borrow trouble. He's lonely because it's a holiday, and obviously, no one took pity on him and asked him over for dinner. He'll get over it."

"I sure hope so. Do you think I ought to leave Palm Lakes? I agree with what you said about getting a lease on an apartment if I'm going to move in with Jack eventually, but maybe it would be better if I weren't so close by."

"Are you ready to move in with Jack? I think you should stay here until you decide one way or the other."

Samantha pushed another sigh out. "The fire at his business has thrown things off. We haven't really been able to thrash out how our relationship is going to work. I need to do that tonight."

"That sounds like a good idea. See if you're both thinking the same way. If so, and it feels right, move in. But you have a place here until you're sure. Don't leave just to put distance between you and Arthur."

"Thanks. I don't know what I'd do without you. I think Jack and I belong together, but I haven't wanted to rush things."

"I think that's smart coming off a divorce. Now let's join the guys. Dinner will be ready soon."

They rose, linked arms and sauntered out to the living room. Samantha felt her heart ease as she looked at the peaceful picture of two men and a dog snacking and watching football. She decided not to spoil Thanksgiving worrying about what Arthur was up to.

* * *

HELEN, 4:30PM

Helen and Alexander moved around the kitchen in a graceful dance born from creating many memorable gourmet meals together. Cooking was how she'd met Alexander, and she felt blessed to have this shared passion with her husband. This *other* shared passion. She smiled at her husband's "Kiss the Cook" apron. He wore the silly thing only because she'd given it to him. Or maybe because it did indeed get him more kisses when in the kitchen. Which led Helen to leave the salad and drift over to him while he checked on the duck roasting in one oven and the potatoes roasting in the other.

He didn't flinch in surprise as she stroked his back. He gently closed the oven door and turned around and gathered her into his arms. "Time to 'Kiss the Cook' again?" he asked playfully.

She kissed him, then placed a hand on his cheek. God, he was so handsome, it was hard to breathe. "I'm actually glad we aren't entertaining. I wouldn't get to do this if we were."

He hugged her tightly. "I agree, though Mary Beth was kind to invite us. But still, you're a little put out with Warren and Lena, and with Sally for waiting until the last minute to inform you she wasn't coming."

Helen sighed and pressed her face into his chest. He smelled of sandalwood. "You know me too well. I *am* glad to have you to myself, but I confess I'm a bit hurt. I understand Warren and Lena not coming for Thanksgiving, but I can tell they aren't coming for Christmas either, even though we went to them last year."

Alexander leaned back, regarding her with emerald concern. "What about Sally? You can't use distance as her excuse for declining our invitation, and I know she's your favorite, so she has the power to hurt you worse than the others."

"Right. I'm surprised she didn't jump at the chance for a free gourmet meal, but she doesn't give much away. I don't even know if she's with the same boyfriend. She put me off the last few times I tried to call and visit. I worry about Camille. Sally loves her in a negligent way, but she's too engrossed in herself to give a child proper attention. I must have been a bad mother, or at least one of my kids would have turned out well." She blinked back unexpected tears.

"That's enough. You did the best you could, and the rest is up to them. Let's put that subject aside for now and enjoy our meal. It's ready." He gave her one last encouraging look, then began to serve up dinner. She contented herself with taking the shredded brussels sprouts Asian slaw to the dining room, then retrieved their half-full wine glasses from the kitchen. When all the food was laid out on the table, she laughed heartily. "We sure got carried away, didn't we?"

He looked at the feast in amusement. "At least we didn't make a turkey. But we'll still be eating leftovers for a few days."

Helen looked around the dining room. "I know I said let's eat inside, but it feels so formal, just the two of us. Why don't we load our plates and eat out on the patio? It's gorgeous."

"Sold."

They piled their plates up and trooped out to the patio, where the sun was sliding towards the horizon, but still pumping out enough warmth to make it pleasant.

"Need a sweater?" he asked.

"No, this is great."

They dug in and ate in peaceable silence, then went inside for cleanup. Helen breathed in the rich aroma of roast duck as she looked at the mess in the kitchen and the serving plates still loaded with food. "It never takes as long to clean up as I think it will, but it sure looks like a disaster."

Alexander chuckled and began to collect and package leftovers in plastic containers. When he was done, he reached into the wine chiller and pulled out a bottle. "I saved a little surprise for last. I think we ought to celebrate your finding an agent."

Helen clapped her hands together. "Champagne? Oh, wonderful! Though I'm not sure hiring an agent is such a milestone, but still, it's one step closer to publication." She couldn't resist the compulsion to minimize the importance of this event.

They took their glasses and the bottle into the living room to capture the sunset. He handed her a glass of bubbly. "Congratulations on your accomplishment, my little author. You are getting closer to publication every day, and I demand that you acknowledge your success. Many people think about writing a book; you've actually written one, and now it's got representation."

She looked down and twisted a handful of her slacks as she always did when she was nervous. Alexander kept trying to get her to have more self-confidence, but it just wasn't something you can flick a switch on. She felt she was letting him down, so she put on a brave smile. "I *am* excited about having an agent. I'm not as sure as you are about me finding a publisher. Maybe if I find one, I'll get cocky like someone I know."

"Cocky? We need to discuss who you are describing and how you define terms." He put his glass down and hauled her onto his lap, kissing her neck and nuzzling her. "Now that I have you softened up, I wanted to ask what you are thinking about our move." His green eyes pierced her. She was surprised, but not. She'd been dodging the subject for a while.

"I'm sorry I've been waffling so much. I *do* want to move to St. Croix. I love the idea of living near the sea. It's not that I don't love the desert, but it feels like it's time to live somewhere else. I'll miss our friends, but the pull of the sea is strong. I still feel kind of funny about seeing how poor some island people are. I know it's hypocritical, but I'm leaning towards living in a gated community like this. I've been spoiled and sheltered, and I'm not sure I want too big a dose of reality. Is that cowardly of me?"

He reached for his glass and held it up in salute. "No, it's not. I was hoping you still wanted to move. I do, too. We can take it slowly. Maybe we should plan a trip back this winter and check out options. Are you up for that?"

"Sure." She smiled in relief. "This has been a lot nicer day than if my kids had come."

There was a glint in his eye. "We'll get to dessert a lot faster, too."

"Dessert? What dessert? We decided we'd be too full."

He grinned slyly. "Dessert is just a sweet course served after a meal."

It finally hit her. "Oh. When you put it that way, I'm *really* glad we don't have company."

\* \* \*

OLIVIA, 6:10PM

Olivia dragged her feet as she crossed the restaurant's parking lot with her extended family. The Thanksgiving meal had been exhausting, mainly because of the obvious curiosity her girls had about Nick, who appeared to thankfully be unaware of their interest.

"Mom," hissed Diana secretively as she wound her arm through Olivia's as if to share gossip. "Why does he call you Livvie? He's kind of hot for an old guy. What are you two up to?"

Leave it to her youngest to ask so blatantly. Youngest. My God, Diana was pushing 50, but Olivia still saw her as a kid. Diana didn't look a day over 35, if that. The fashionably ragged bleached blonde hair, toned body and youthful clothes helped sustain the illusion, but then, she'd always looked young for her age.

Annoyed, Olivia answered louder than she meant to. "Really, Diana, the poor man is on his own today. What do you expect me to do? Quit trying to make something of it."

Nick's voice boomed in her right ear. "That's right, Diana. I'm just a lonely old fart. Thanks for having me join you for dinner. No need to make something out of it."

She was shook up for not realizing he was right behind them. His jaw was clenched, and his lips thinned. Anger, and possibly hurt, simmered in his blue eyes. She hadn't meant for him to hear that. It wasn't even true. She just wanted to shut Diana up. Now she'd offended him.

Diana had the good grace to be quiet, and they moved en masse to gather around the various vehicles. "I can take three in mine," announced Diana, who had no husband or children to pack into her compact car.

Susanna and her brood stepped up to a mini-van nearby. "We have room for a few in our car, too." Joanna's family split up between the two cars, and Olivia made a snap decision. "Nick will take me home, so you can all go back home and to your hotels. I'll see you tomorrow?"

Diana lifted an eyebrow, but said nothing.

"Sure, Mom. We'll see you tomorrow," said Joanna. Susanna smiled knowingly and waved. She seemed to think there was a romance brewing. Olivia was too flustered to react. Nick opened the passenger door for her, and she slid in. She was holding her breath when he buckled up and started the engine, waiting for him to light into her, but he said nothing. His jaw remained clamped shut, and he drove carefully, arriving at the parking lot of Desert Breezes twenty minutes later, not having spoken a single word. Olivia was sweating in spite of the mild temperature. She didn't know where to begin.

So she said nothing, which she instinctively felt was a mistake, but still. They arrived in front of her door before she could pull herself together and get a plan. "Thanks for letting me come with your family to Thanksgiving dinner." He wasn't smiling. He turned to leave, and she reached out to his retreating back, but he was already halfway down the corridor.

She went inside and practically fell onto the couch. Her legs were wobbly, and she had to wipe tears from her eyes. Why did she have to say something so untrue, so insulting about Nick? Why was she afraid of telling her daughters the truth? She wished for the hundredth time that she'd taken Mary Beth's advice and gone the other way, letting them think whatever they wanted. The fact was, she didn't have any idea what their relationship really was, and maybe she was afraid to put a name on it. They'd been living in an enchantment, everything going so well, that she didn't want to break the spell. Well, the spell was broken, and he wouldn't want anything more to do with her. Worse yet, he'd think she meant what she'd said, and it was all lies.

If she didn't do something, it would be over. Even if she did something, it might be too late to salvage much. He was so quiet, he seemed like the unforgiving type, and she wondered if she were simply rationalizing her fear. If he was going to be done with her, it should be for the truth, not for a lie.

Without thinking further, she picked up the phone and dialed Nick's room, wondering if he'd ignore her call. He seemed angry, but not having ever seen him angry, she wasn't sure how upset he was.

"What?" he barked. OK, so he was mad.

"It's me. I owe you an apology. Would you please come over and let me fix you a drink and apologize? And maybe explain?" She held her breath.

"What's the point? What's to explain? You taking pity on me again?"

She was so disturbed, she almost giggled from fear. Stomping it, she did her best to sound calm. "I was lying to them. If you come over, I'll try to explain. But please, I want to apologize. I didn't mean to be hurtful."

He heaved a sigh. "OK." He hung up without further words. She hoped he wasn't going to be too angry. He was so imposing physically, anger would be frightening on him. If he raised his voice to her, she was sure she'd pee her pants.

She knew he'd be there quickly, so she stiffened her spine and opened the door before he had a chance to knock. They walked into the living area, shying away from each other. He had an injured look in his blue eyes, and she hated herself for putting it there.

"Have a seat. Your usual?" she asked as she lifted the bourbon bottle.

He nodded curtly. She poured two fingers of neat bourbon in, then thought, what the heck, and poured another finger. She handed it to him. He barely acknowledged her. She poured herself a glass of wine and went back to the couch, sitting down more than an arm's length away. She sipped her wine, collecting her thoughts. "I'm so sorry, Nick," she began. "I didn't even mean what I said to Diana. I was defensive all evening. My girls and I don't always see eye to eye." She put her glass down. "I was afraid they'd read something into our relationship that wasn't there, and after doing so, would jump to conclusions and start in on me."

The sharpness in his eyes softened. "What do you mean?"

"I'm not sure what I mean, but Diana and Joanna are always trying to run my life. They act like I'm senile."

"Senile? The woman who caught the Desert Breezes rapist?"

She shook off the compliment. "They don't know about that."

Now he looked incredulous. "You never told them? Why not?"

"It didn't seem important. They don't think of me the way you do; I'm not sure they would even have believed me. I'm telling you, they think I'm barely all there. They pushed me to sell my home and quit driving and give up my dog, and they want me to put them on my bank accounts so they can 'manage' my assets. As if I can't do it myself. I often wonder if they're wishing I'd save them a lot of trouble by dropping dead."

He polished off his bourbon and put the glass on the coaster. "What does this have to do with you and me?"

Why were men so dense? She couldn't bear to put ideas in his head, but there was no alternative. "If I'd told them the truth, they'd be afraid you and I were an item, and before you knew it, they'd be giving me trouble about it."

She could see awareness dawn slowly in his eyes. "Ahhh," was all he said.

She squirmed on her seat and picked up her glass, not sure what to say next, if anything. She certainly didn't want him to suspect she had designs on him.

Finally he broke the uncomfortable silence. "Why is it women always dream romance up where there is none?"

She was mildly annoyed at the suggestion that such things couldn't happen between them, though she was glad he wasn't focusing on her anymore. "How should I know? I think they're worried about protecting their inheritance. I got a lot of money from selling the house, even after taxes."

She hadn't meant to make it sound like she was rich. Maybe that would put him off. Men could be so funny about money. "Can I get you a refill?"

He shrugged a shoulder and handed her the empty glass. "Yeah, why not?"

He never had more than one drink. Maybe she had shocked him. Olivia refreshed their drinks and returned and sat a bit closer, still leaving reasonable space, but no longer an obvious neutral zone. He sipped his drink, then said, "What business is it of anyone's what you and I do?"

"It's nobody's business. I was taking the coward's way out. I promise to tell them the whole truth tomorrow."

"They're your kids. You decide what to say or not. But it probably is best to be honest. It's not like we have anything to hide."

"Indeed." And why should that thought irritate her so much?

\* \* \*

## MARILYN, 5:30PM

"This wine is delicious. Thanks for bringing it." Marilyn raised her glass in salute to Steven, who sat on the other side of the remains of Thanksgiving dinner looking pleasantly sated. Tammi sat beside her, alert to her every move. She reached over and petted her furry head and then sipped the wine.

"It's the least I can do for such a feast."

"I insist you take some home for later." She eyed the turkey, which was still largely intact.

"I love turkey, and you did great on this one. Tender and juicy. I'll be happy to take some off your hands. Saves me cooking for myself."

The ringing of the phone interrupted the comfortable atmosphere and set Marilyn's heart racing. Steven picked up on her alarm. "Expecting a call?"

"No." The phone rang again.

"Want to answer it?"

"Not really." But she rose and slowly went to the phone, handling it like a live grenade. "Hello?"

"So how's my ex-wifey on Thanksgiving?" slurred Ted's voice arrogantly.

She punched the button to end the call.

"Wrong number?" asked Steven.

There was no use lying. It must be written all over her face. "No. It was my ex. He sounded drunk." The phone rang again, and she fumbled it in surprise.

"Don't answer!' ordered Steven. She'd never heard him so sharp and take-charge.

"I had no intention to." She put the phone down. "But the ringing is annoying and hard to ignore."

"Unplug the phone."

Why hadn't she thought of that? The ringing stopped when she pulled the plug out of the socket. "There!"

Feeling a little shaky, she returned to the table and took a gulp of wine, not tasting it.

"Has he called before?"

She shook her head negatively. "I think he got drunk and got bold. I hope he's at home. Maybe I should have tried to find out where he is." She shivered at the thought of him being nearby.

"Nonsense. You did the right thing. You don't want to reward that kind of behavior. What did the PI say?"

She heaved a sigh. "In the Thanksgiving excitement, I forgot to tell you. I got his report. I don't know what I was expecting or hoping for, but it wasn't that helpful. Ted got fired. I told you that. He's taken to drinking and getting rowdy, but the cops are cutting him slack because he's one of theirs. No sign of his taking another job. His credit is OK for the time being. Our house was paid for, and I left without saying anything, so he didn't have to pay me for half of it. Not that I care. I had kept my money separate, and I had my pension and a good buyout package. It appears there's nothing really to keep him there if he gets it into his head he wants to take a trip."

The silence stretched uncomfortably. Tammi stared intently at her, as if trying to understand the cause for Marilyn's upset. She stroked the big black furry head, grateful once again to have a good watchdog.

Finally, Steven spoke. "You could get an alarm system installed."

"I have one." She pointed at Tammi.

"Yeah, well, I suppose that's true. You got the Posse and the cops on speed dial?"

"Yes to both."

"You got me on speed dial?" His look said he was going to be disturbed if she said no.

"Look, Steven, I don't want to involve you in this mess. But yes, I do have you on speed dial. We talk often. But I'm not calling you if he shows up. He's unpredictable and capable of violence."

"I'm already involved. You're my friend. And my decorating consultant. I need to protect my interests."

They both laughed, even though it was forced, and the atmosphere lightened.

"I'm OK, Steven. I sleep with a .38 under my pillow."

His eyes widened. "I'm not a gun person."

"Just being careful. I keep hoping enough time will pass that Ted will move on, but if he turns into an alcoholic and has no job and little money, I know who he's going to blame, and it won't be himself."

Steven shook his head. "Don't do anything rash."

"I'm going to get an unlisted phone number. I've been thinking about it, and now I'm sure. I don't know if that will help or push him to come out here, though."

"I think you should do it."

She drank a bit of wine, wishing they could recapture the holiday feeling. Fat chance of that. Her mind raced after possible futures involving Ted, and they ranged from distasteful to downright frightening. Why was she so sure he wasn't going to leave her alone?

"Not to change the subject," Steven said sardonically, "but I heard today that my new living room furniture is scheduled for delivery December 2nd. I hope it looks good when it's done." An uncertain note had crept into his voice.

"Of course, it will be wonderful. The carpets are superb. They've changed the place dramatically. It looks more like you now."

"I'm not sure that's a good thing," he muttered.

She was surprised how quickly his mood had deteriorated. His self-esteem was so fragile. "I meant it in a good way. It's going to look classy and more masculine."

He grinned sheepishly. "Huh."

"I'll look forward to seeing it when it's done."

"I'll make dinner to celebrate. I never could have redecorated without your help."

"I didn't do much, but I'll appreciate dinner." She reached over and stroked Tammi's head. It soothed her somehow.

Steven watched her pet Tammi. Marilyn got the impression that he was a little afraid of the big dog, but didn't want her to know. Well, most people were afraid of Tammi. That's the main reason she'd gotten her.

Steven appeared to divine her thoughts. "I'm glad you have her. It's safer than being alone. And having her might scare him off if he showed up, which I doubt he'd do."

It made her squirm, talking about Ted; time to shift to another topic. "Barbara mentioned that you and Ben are playing more golf."

He smiled warmly. "I used to golf as an escape. It got me out of the house and away from Tanya's sharp tongue. Now I play golf because it's fun and I enjoy spending time with Ben. It's amazing how different the same activity can feel. It's like I'm emerging from my cave."

"Funny how things turn out. Kind of like you and me both showing up at that support group."

Steven refilled his wine glass, a pensive look on his face. "I only went to placate Barbara. She'd made so many meals for me, it would have been churlish to say no. You being there was why I kept going."

She wondered what, if anything, he was implying. No, she was just being silly; they were just good friends. "You being there helped me, too. I wish I could say I've made as much progress as you. I can't seem to shake loose of Ted. You've begun a new life, and I'm still grappling with the old." Saying it out loud made it depressingly real. And they had somehow gotten back to the subject of Ted. She ground her teeth in annoyance.

"Tanya being gone was a two-edged sword for me, but it has allowed me to move on, once I got over my guilt. Maybe we should take out a contract on Ted." His tone was serious enough that she knew he was angry for what she was going through, and that made her feel oddly better.

"Very funny. Talk about guilt. I can't even honestly say I wish he was dead. I just wish he'd leave me the hell alone." She was surprised at the anger fueling those words.

"You *have* started a new life. Ted's thousands of miles away. Don't let him spoil Thanksgiving."

She put on her brave face. "Let's clear the table and pack up the leftovers. Then we can vegetate with a movie on TV."

"That sounds like a plan to me." Steven rose and started gathering empty plates and silverware.

Marilyn reached for the platter with the turkey. "If you load the dishwasher, I'll put the food away. I'll pack some for you to take home."She took the turkey into the kitchen, followed by a hopeful dog. In fact, Tammi stuck to her like a burr as she brought the leftovers into the kitchen and packed them into plastic containers. Marilyn relented towards the end and put a saucer down for Tammi that held bits of turkey and stuffing. She found herself able at last to stop thinking about Ted and the future as she lost herself in the homey activities of the rest of the evening.

By the time Steven departed with his goodies, she was even feeling optimistic. When she went to bed, she didn't put her gun under the pillow for a change. In the nightstand, it was still close enough to reassure her, and doing that seemed to release her from the grip of fear. It really would be stupid for Ted to invest in a trip out here. What could he possibly gain by doing that? She needed to stop being ruled by fearful imaginings. She slipped into a dreamless sleep for the first night in ages.

\* \* \*

SAMANTHA, 8:30PM

As she pulled her truck into the driveway behind Jack's pickup, Samantha promised herself she wasn't going to be distracted from what she needed to say tonight. Every time she tried to broach the subject of their future, Jack managed to lure her into bed, and that was the end of the discussion. Tonight, she was not going to be derailed. She smiled to herself; that was easier said than done.

She grabbed her bag and the plastic container of leftovers and slid out, wordlessly accepted Jack's outstretched hand and walked to the front door, Beau barreling ahead of them both as if they were racing. Once inside, she put the big Tupperware container in the refrigerator. That was dinner tomorrow taken care of.

Jack reached past her and pulled two Heinekens out. "Let's have a beer while we talk."

She shut the refrigerator door, shocked that he was initiating the discussion. "Oh, so you're willing to talk now?" she asked with irony.

"I know you, Sam. You're going to burst if we don't at least get some kind of a plan. I want you to move in with me. What will it take to make that happen?" He dropped lazily onto the sofa and stretched his long, jean-clad legs out to rest on the coffee table and patted the spot next to him. He always seemed so confident, while she was juggling all kinds of difficult questions and scenarios of the future. Probably that was one attraction he held for her. He was her anchor in a shifting world. She sank next to him, taking a pull on the beer. She wanted things to work out with Jack so much, but she had to be honest. "You know I love you. I want to live together, but I need certain things settled, and I need to understand my place in this relationship before committing."

He frowned at her. "You think all I want is a bedmate?"

"Let's face it. The physical attraction between us is powerful. But I want more. Much more. I want to improve on what I had with Arthur. I was young when I fell for him, and I assumed a lot of things that later turned out to be false. I can't blame him; he didn't hide anything, but we never really compared our viewpoints, what we wanted, and once we got to living together, I could see we were not a good match. I don't intend to repeat that mistake." She reached over and held his hand, their fingers intertwining. "If I move in, it will be because I intend to stay." She looked into dark eyes filled with love.

"I agree. Where do you see our relationship going?"

This was the question she'd been waiting for. It didn't matter that she'd rehearsed an answer many times; she was still scared how he would react, because what she wanted would be a huge change for him. But if it was going to work, it had to be based on truth. "I know you've worked really hard to build your business, and I love your values and the quality of work you offer. I'm not trying to insert myself where I don't belong, but I can't be just a housewife to you, and I want to be more than an employee. I believe we make a good team. Your business is desperate for an injection of cash because of the fire. I have enough to rebuild Temple Landscaping even better. I want us to join all our resources and be full partners in life, in love and in business, but what do you want?"

She held her breath, her heart pounding. This was the moment that would determine her future. Would she be able to back off if he didn't want what she wanted? She was terrified of losing him, but she couldn't stay with him if he wanted less than a full partnership.

He drank his beer, appearing to consider what she'd said. Then he cracked a crooked smile. "Like I don't want the babe, the money *and* the successful business? How dumb do I look? I admit I've struggled, knowing you wanted to help. My pride has always been a problem. But I can't do this without you. Yes, I want us to be equal partners. We'll share everything. So now it comes to the big question? When are we going to make it legal, so I can change the title on the house and we can sort out the business details?"

"You really don't mind accepting my money?" Her stomach quit flipping. "Did you just ask me to marry you?"

"Marriage is just a formality to me. You're the woman I want to spend the rest of my life with. Your Mom liked me. I know she wanted this. I'm sorry she isn't here to see it happen."

Tears filled Samantha's eyes. "Wherever she is, Mom is seeing it, and she's happy." She leaned over and kissed him on the mouth, then clinked their bottles in celebration. Her dream life was coming true. She couldn't wait to tell Mary Beth.

# 14

# SATURDAY, DECEMBER 14TH

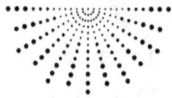

SAMANTHA, 1:25PM

*D*eeply engaged in designing the Fallons' landscaping, Samantha
didn't notice the ruckus out front until the volume ratcheted up
enough that the familiar voice registered with her. Arthur was here.
Caught by conflicting emotions, she stood up, went to the doorway and
listened, heart racing.

"Where is Samantha Taylor? Where is my wife?"

*Oh, God, he's making a scene.* What had gotten into him? She'd never
seen him like this. She overcame a strong desire to run away and fortified
herself for the confrontation. Poor Suzie needed assistance, and perhaps
the news would help Arthur to let go.

As she headed for the receptionist's desk, though, panic set in when she
saw Jack stride in from outside, oblivious to what he was walking into. She
rushed to be there and head off trouble.

Just as she arrived at Suzie's desk, Arthur turned and challenged Jack,
"You motherfucker! You stole my wife!" He lunged at Jack, hands
outstretched as if to grab a fistful of shirt, but Jack stepped back and
Arthur lost his balance and fell in Jack's direction.

Samantha hurried around the desk, uncertain how to stop what seemed to be an inevitable fight, as Jack caught Arthur and steadied him. She arrived behind Arthur. Did she smell alcohol? Arthur rarely drank to excess. This was unbelievable.

Annoyance bubbled to the surface. "Arthur!" she yelled louder than she intended. All eyes turned to her. It was encouraging to note a guilty shadow cross Arthur's face. "What do you mean by creating a scene where I work? The divorce was final several weeks ago. I am *not* your wife."

Arthur shifted on his feet and glanced floorward, but said nothing in his own defense. It was time to play her trump card and end this nonsense. "As a matter of fact, I'm *his* wife." She raised her left hand, displaying a gold ring, then pointed at Jack. She was grateful Jack didn't smirk. He merely nodded affirmatively.

Arthur's shoulders dropped as if in defeat, and he appeared to shrink, though he was never going to look imposing while standing next to Jack. She felt a flash of pity mixed with guilt as she thought of how strong and young Jack looked next to her ex-husband. She hadn't married Jack for his looks, but he was a prime specimen of manhood, and he was certainly behaving better than Arthur.

Eager to resolve this confrontation, she maintained momentum. "You need to go home, but you've been drinking and can't drive." Samantha looked at Jack. They needed to take two cars, but who would drive Arthur? Samantha wasn't intimidated, but she didn't want to give Arthur further chance to vent, and leaving Jack and Arthur alone together seemed a prescription for disaster, especially with Arthur liquored up.

Suzie spoke up. "I'll get Juan to drive this man home. Jack can follow and bring Juan back." Suzie left to find Juan, not expecting any arguments. Samantha stared in shock at the young woman's ability to take charge in such an emotionally charged situation.

Pulling herself together, Samantha glared at Arthur. "Can you behave if Juan drives you home?"

Like a castigated schoolboy, he nodded affirmatively.

Jack turned towards the door. "Let's go." He stalked out, followed by Arthur, then Samantha. Arthur climbed into the passenger seat of his Honda, and Jack grabbed the door before he could close it. "I'll be following and give Juan a ride back. If you do so much as a say a harsh word, I'm going to press charges."

Samantha wasn't sure what kind of charges Jack could press, but Arthur nodded wordlessly. Juan came rushing out the door. "You need me to drive?"

Jack pointed at the Honda. "You're going to drive Mr. Taylor back to his home in Palm Lakes, and when you get there, he's going to give you a generous tip, and I'll bring you back." He looked sharply at Arthur, who shook his head in agreement.

Tuned in to the undercurrents, Juan calmly got into the driver's seat. While Arthur handed over the keys, Jack turned to Samantha. "Why don't you stay here?" Then he slammed Arthur's car door.

She didn't want to, as she'd worry until he returned, but she knew her presence would be an irritant. "OK."

"See you soon, Mrs. Temple." Jack leaned over and kissed her on the mouth.

She smiled shyly, aware that Arthur was looking at them, but couldn't hear through the closed window. "OK, husband. Drive carefully."

"Piece of cake." He was in his truck and out on the street behind Juan as she wondered. Arthur seemed properly chastised and sobered up, but would the knowledge she was remarried put an end to this? Was her remarrying so soon inappropriate? And why did she always see things from other people's point of view? She hadn't cheated on Arthur; he'd done this to himself.

It was time she quit blaming herself for his emotions. He'd never be happy she remarried, and it was none of his business. End of story. Still, she felt niggling guilt, probably because that's what he would have wanted. It wouldn't occur to her until much later to ask how Arthur was able to identify Jack, when to her knowledge, he'd never met the man.

* * *

OLIVIA, 4:40PM

Nick parked near the entrance to the stable, waiting for the disturbed dust from the dirt road to settle before getting out. There wasn't another car in sight, in spite of it being Saturday. The boarding facility was out in the desert about twenty minutes from Palm Lakes in a small development of mostly modular homes on ten-acre parcels. Everyone seemed to have horses, and this property was very nicely appointed with multiple spacious turnouts and a substantial barn to accommodate the equine residents.

Olivia waited for Nick to get her door. He gave her a hand out, and as always, she marveled at his bearlike strength and big hands. Surely he could pick her up like a rag doll if he chose. The twinkle was back in his brilliant blue eyes, but there was something new as well. She couldn't put her finger on it, but there was a change, and not the awful one she'd feared after the Thanksgiving debacle.

"We won't be long," he said gruffly. "Just want to see Rocky and give him a treat." He pulled an apple out of his jacket pocket and headed into the stable.

She followed, drinking in the smell of hay, horse sweat and manure. They arrived at Rocky's stall, and Olivia watched as Nick cut the apple with a pocket knife and fed the big white horse a piece at a time.

"Want to feed him?" Nick turned and offered her a slice of apple.

"I'd love to." She took the fruit and reached out, palm flat, so Rocky could take it without nipping her. She stroked the velvety white nose. "He's a beauty. Rudi was a lovely boy, but Rocky is even more handsome."

"To be honest, I hadn't wanted a white horse. Too flashy. And he's a Lipizzan, one of those snooty dressage breeds. But he's retired—25 years old—and they were practically giving him away, because the owner died. He's got papers and some fancy Italian-sounding name, but what I like is he's steady and smart. I was riding him down the road to the trailhead last week, and some moron came by on a Harley, making a big racket. Rocky completely ignored it."

"I'm relieved he's so steady. Do you miss Rudi?"

"He's got a good home with a young man near here who will care for him properly. You were right. I need a more mature mount. Rudi was a good horse, but too green for me. Rocky's great, and we're going to do fine together." He wiped his knife on the leg of his jeans, folded it and slipped it into his pocket. "Shall we go to dinner?"

"If you're ready."

"I'll be back tomorrow for a ride, boy." He gave Rocky a final pat, got a nicker in return, and they walked back to the car. The sun was low in the sky, and a chill breeze reminded Olivia it was December. "It always takes me by surprise," she sighed.

"What?"

"Winter. I can't believe it's already December. Sure, we had Thanksgiving, but it was delightfully warm. It's like you don't get fall here. You go from horrible summer heat to pleasant warm weather—what I remember as summer—then, bang, winter's here."

"I know what you mean. We seem to have only a week or two of spring and fall. I shouldn't complain. It's so much milder than New York, but I miss having four seasons."

Olivia reached to open the car door, but he took her by the shoulder and moved her so he could do it. "Allow me."

As he handed her into the car, his jacket fell open, revealing the handgun in his shoulder holster. It didn't bother her, but she wondered why he wore it. Every time they came out here, he was carrying a gun.

When he slipped into the driver's seat, she decided to ask. "Why are you packing?"

He grinned at the wording. "It's pretty isolated out here. I always have a gun with me. I might need to shoot a rattler."

"Is that an ex-cop thing?"

The brilliant blue eyes had a haunted look in them this time. "Maybe. I was the second responder on the scene when Owen Schmidt killed Tanya Cooper. It was a bloodbath. My friend Eric Johnson, who was also on the Posse at the time, was the first responder. He lived next door to Mrs. Cooper, but he was too late to save her. When I got there, Eric was bleeding bad, surrounded by a lake of blood. Owen had stabbed him in the back just before Eric shot him dead. Lydia was doing her best to staunch the flow of blood. Eric quit the Posse over it, and I left a bit later. I couldn't bear the thought of another call like that." He put the car in drive and ambled slowly down the rugged dirt road to the highway, his lips clamped together grimly.

Olivia quietly digested all he had said. She'd known the basic facts, but he'd never said how hard it hit him. "I have always admired the volunteers on the Posse. They shouldn't have to deal with things like that, but I'm so grateful people like you and Eric look out for the rest of us. And I agree that at some point, you need to retire from it. That was a really bad situation, and I'm sorry you and he got involved in it."

"I'm not anticipating problems, and I don't want to have any, but I intend to be prepared. That's why I have a concealed carry permit."

Nick hadn't talked deeply about emotions with her in the past, so she appreciated this insight into his motivations. It was a fifteen minute drive to their favorite Mexican restaurant, and the remainder of the trip passed in silence, but to Olivia, it wasn't a hungry silence that begged for words; it was a peaceful quiet that spoke of a harmony between the two of them. Or that's how she saw it. She wondered how he saw it. At least he didn't seem to hold a grudge about Thanksgiving.

Carmen's Casita was a hole-in-the-wall establishment huddled between a pawn shop and a dry cleaner in a dusty strip mall out on the edge of development. As they entered, Olivia could see that the tables were occupied mostly by Hispanic families. The takeout counter had a line, and when she spotted a small empty table in the corner, she tugged on Nick's sleeve. "There's a table."

They navigated their way through the crowded room, finally arriving at the two-person table. They seated themselves and began to peruse the menus that were stashed in the slot behind the condiments. The fragrances from the kitchen were beginning to work on Olivia. "I'm hungry."

Nick smiled. "Me, too."

The meal was exceptional, as it always was, and the price was ridiculously low. Olivia couldn't understand why Carmen's hadn't been discovered by Palm Lakes residents, but she wasn't going to complain. It was busy enough. As was often the case, they talked very little during the meal, other than to comment on how good it was. Nick picked up the tab, and Olivia let him, because she knew she would make it up to him by giving him a home-cooked meal (or a reheated Mary Beth meal). Since her daughters had commented on their relationship, Olivia was more aware than ever how comfortable she was with Nick, how natural it felt doing things together, how much they enjoyed similar things, and most of all, how attached she was becoming to him.

When they got back to Desert Breezes, Olivia invited Nick in for his usual after dinner drink, and he said he needed to get something from his room, so she left the door open and poured him a bourbon and herself a glass of white wine while waiting for his return. When he came back, he'd shed his jacket and his gun, but he had a small box in his hand. She felt a flutter in her heart when she saw it, because it was obvious he was going to give it to her. Her first thought was that she hadn't gotten him a Christmas present. Not for lack of wanting to, but because she couldn't imagine what to get him. He seemed to have few material wants.

He walked over to the couch and sat down next to her and handed her the box. "This isn't a Christmas present. You don't have to give me anything. But I made this for you. I hope you like it."

She put her wineglass down and took the box, which was gold foil-surfaced, so it didn't need wrapping, and when she opened it, she saw a beautiful silver horse on a thick sterling silver chain. She lifted it out of the box and turned it in the light, admiring the detail. "You made this?"

"In silversmith class. It's not all that hard once you learn the basics. Would you like to put it on?" He reached over and took it, unclipping the clasp, and then draped it over her chest and fastened it.

She turned towards him, and he smiled. "That looks nice on the black blouse."

Jumping up, she said, "I need to see it in the mirror. I'll be right back." She went into the bathroom and switched on the light. The necklace was stunning. It was just about the prettiest thing anyone had ever given her, and it was especially precious because he'd made it. Her late husband wasn't one to buy her jewelry, and she didn't mind that much, but it was so romantic to have a man give you a pretty like this. It almost made her wonder if he felt more for her than he had said. Maybe this was meant to say something. The problem was, messages like this were so easy to misinterpret. She cared more about him than she should already; she couldn't bear the thought of losing anyone else after losing Sophie and Maddie this year. Admitting she cared seemed dangerous somehow.

*Enough of being maudlin. He doesn't have anyone else to make stuff for. That's all it means.* She was still filled with gratitude. She walked back into the living room, where Nick was sipping on his drink. "So, you like it?"

"Like is too weak a word. This is the most beautiful thing I think anyone has ever given me."

He frowned. "You must be kidding. Surely your husband bought you nice things."

"He wasn't much for buying baubles, as he called jewelry. Accountants are pretty practical."

He beamed, his blue eyes sparkling. "I'm glad it's special to you. I enjoyed making it."

"Maddie made jewelry, and she made me a lovely turquoise necklace just before she died. I cherish it, but somehow this feels different." Maybe she shouldn't have said that out loud. "Probably because you're a man."

"Glad you noticed," he drawled, a grin on his face.

She went over and sat next to him, then impulsively leaned over and kissed him on the mouth. Just a tender, closed-mouth kiss, then she turned and picked up her glass to cover her embarrassment and held it up for a toast. "Thank you for being such a good friend to me."

"It's my pleasure, but I think we're beyond friends at this point. Don't you? Or am I making more of it than I should?"

Her heart nearly stopped. Seconds dragged by, and she panicked. If she didn't say something fast, he'd feel rejected, and she certainly didn't want that. It was time to make a choice. She knew she wanted him in her life, and to heck with worrying about the future.

He was looking at her intently, though patiently, as if he knew she was battling conflicting thoughts. When had she fallen in love with him? She'd been trying to avoid admitting it for a while now.

"You're right. I haven't wanted to say out loud what I feel. I didn't want to pressure you, and even if you feel the same, I'm scared about the future. I've lost people I loved this year, and it hurts."

"It only hurts because you loved them and had good times with them. We have that. I think it's time to act on it."

What was he talking about? Weren't they way beyond that sort of thing? Or was he suggesting marriage? Or moving in together? Swamped by confusing thoughts, she sat there with her mouth open slightly.

He reached over and took her hand in his big paw. He was like a sturdy old oak, so solid and full of life and history. She felt so safe and grounded when she was with him. "Livvie, I'll let you decide, but I'd like to suggest something. I want to spend the night with you. If it's all right."

Her blood pressure spiked as she wondered what exactly that meant to him. She and Leroy hadn't had sex for the last several years of her marriage. She wasn't sure she knew how anymore. "Just to be together?"

"Just to be together. One of the hardest things for me has been the nights. They seem long and empty, like lying in a coffin. I'd like to feel your warm body next to mine, to wake up next to someone and face the day together. What do you say?"

"Tonight?" She wasn't sure if the shiver was anticipation or fear. Maybe both.

"No time like the present."

She gazed into his eyes, trying to read his thoughts, but couldn't. "Go get your toothbrush and pajamas."

"I don't usually wear pajamas, but I'll make an exception for you." He grinned at her shocked reaction. His chuckles told her he was pulling her leg.

She pushed his upper arm gently, noting how solid it was. "Go on and get your stuff. We'll have a drink, watch some TV, then go to bed." She hadn't said anything that racy in years. He got up and left her to drink her wine, wondering if she'd made a mistake, but tingling with expectation and thrilled at being chosen by such a handsome man. Maybe her life wasn't over after all.

* * *

BARBARA, 6:30PM

Barbara glanced around the great room, checking for late arrivals to greet, but saw no new faces in the crowd. And it was a crowd. The night was chilly for the low desert; none of the guests had opted to sit on the patio in spite of the cheery fire in the fire pit.

The many platters on the counter were still loaded with goodies, but predictably, her hot crab dip was already gone, though she had made a double batch. It was the most popular item at her parties, and she suspected there'd be a riot if she ever forgot to serve it.

Ben waved at her from the bar, his Santa's helper cap perched crookedly on his head as he doled out drinks with an eye towards cutting off revelers' alcohol as appropriate to assure no one drove home drunk, or staggered home drunk, since many of the guests lived on this street and had simply walked to the party.

Regarding overindulging, she scanned the room for Bernie. Poor Bernie. He meant well, but last year Ben had to drive him home and put him to bed, because he'd brought a flask with him, so Ben hadn't realized how much he'd imbibed. There Bernie was, talking to Marilyn, who was putting as much distance between them as possible in the crush as Steven stood by bemused. Steven's ex-wife Tanya hadn't needed or wanted protection, and Steven seemed to be out of his depth with Bernie, who was socially inept to the point of being a nuisance. In addition to standing too close to Marilyn, the bearlike man was a shambles, dressed in wrinkled old clothes, but everyone overlooked his faults, since he was so adrift without his wife, whom he had lost to cancer. Bernie didn't appear drunk yet, but she'd consult Lydia, who could tell just by reading his aura.

Satisfied that all was well, Barbara decided to visit with her special friends from yoga class, who with their spouses formed a contingent in one corner of the room. As she approached them, she noticed that Ian and Jean, who were in conversation with Emma and Julio, appeared subdued. Both of them held drinks and watched attentively as Julio gesticulated with his hands, but their smiles seemed forced. The contrast between the brightness and laughter around them was striking. What was that about?

Slipping between people, smiling and touching shoulders and patting arms, she finally arrived at her destination. Alexander fixed her with an emerald gleam. "Great party, Barbara." He lifted his glass in salute, his smile devastatingly disarming as always.

"Thanks, Alexander. We love throwing a party, so it's our pleasure."

Helen beamed at her, a vision of youthful beauty in a cream silk blouse and black slacks and flats, wearing the turquoise and silver necklace and earrings Maddie had made each of them as a final gift. Mary Beth also wore hers, but with a white dress that set off her thick, dark hair. Funny how all three of them had independently chosen to wear Maddie's jewelry to the party. Maddie and her husband Stanley had never attended any of Barbara's parties in spite of being asked, so this was almost like having Maddie here. She pushed aside the sadness of losing a kind and generous neighbor and smiled back at Helen. "So where are you jet-setters traveling to next?"

"We're gong back to St. Croix soon," replied Helen. "We've decided to move there," she added shyly.

Another loss. Living in Palm Lakes had many things to recommend it, but the high turnover in residents wasn't one of them. Oh, well, at least they were leaving for a positive reason. "I'm sorry to hear that. I'm going to miss you. When do you think you'll be moving?"

"We're not sure yet. There's no big hurry," answered Alexander.

Mary Beth interjected, "I can't allow that to happen. I just moved next door to my dear friend and can't bear to lose her." But there was merriment in her green eyes and warmth in her voice, and Helen smiled.

Ethan put his arm around Mary Beth. "Maybe we should move to St. Croix, too."

Mary Beth cast a surprised look at him. "Don't tempt me."

Oh dear, was she going to lose two friends? Barbara spied Lydia staring at her and shrugged off the worry, though she knew it was impossible to hide anything from Lydia's x-ray vision. "How's the house hunt going, Lydia? You and Eric aren't defecting, too, are you?"

Lydia was short, but her presence was larger than life. In her customary garb—peasant blouse and long, colorful skirt, dark hair cascading to her shoulders, she radiated energy. Her brown eyes flashed at Barbara. "No freakin' way. We've found a house we like in Palm Lakes. We just prefer to sell our condos first, so it's a matter of choices, like how low to set the asking prices. The place we like isn't far from here, on Saguaro Lane. I'll let you know how it goes."

Barbara was relieved by the news. "I'm glad you're staying in Palm Lakes. I meant to ask you…have you seen Bernie tonight?"

Lydia raised a dark eyebrow. "Of course. He makes sure to greet all the female guests in his own unique way."

"Is he OK?"

"Are you asking if he's over his limit or still being obnoxious even when relatively sober?"

"Either. Both." Any information would be useful for heading off trouble.

Lydia grinned. "Bernie actually has done some work with us these past months, and I believe he's made a lot of progress. He isn't drinking nearly as much. He's a bit lit up tonight, but should be OK to drive if he doesn't drink a lot more. As to how he's behaving, I haven't seen him put hands on or near any of the women, so I think that's progress."

Progress, indeed. Hopefully, Ben wouldn't be chauffeuring him tonight. "That's good to hear." She turned to include Eric in the conversation. "Not to change the subject, but what are you two planning for Christmas? Want to have dinner with us?"

Eric smiled at the invitation, but shook his head. "Thanks, but we're going to Helen and Alexander's."

Barbara nodded. "No problem. I just wanted to make sure you were covered. Ethan and Mary Beth have company coming, and Emma and Julio have family for dinner. Jean and Ian told me they're going to Helen's, and Marilyn and Steven are planning a quiet dinner together. Looks like it will be just Ben and me and the kids and grandkids."

"That's not exactly a small group," said Lydia.

"To me, it is. I'm so used to massive numbers of people at Christmas. But I won't complain. Less work for me, I guess." She couldn't wring the sadness from her voice.

Lydia touched Barbara's hand. "It's sad that Helen and Mary Beth are talking about moving, even if it doesn't happen. You rarely find a group of friends like ours. It will be hard if they go. But we'll still have Jean and Emma and Marilyn. I don't think any of them are planning on moving, and they're all pretty healthy."

"Thanks, Lydia. I was feeling a little down thinking about Maddie being gone and all the changes on our street this year following Tanya's murder…I shouldn't complain. Eric went through hell after that. How insensitive of me. I think the brain tumor scare threw me off balance, and I'm still trying to settle down and feel safe."

"Why don't you come by our office and do a session with Ian and Jean? No charge. It's good practice for us."

Barbara shied away from taking any more free services, but they certainly had helped her. A lot. "Maybe I will." She put on her bravest smile. "I'm going to talk a bit with Jean and Emma before going back to check on the food situation."

She migrated through the din to where Jean, Ian, Emma and Julio were chatting. Jean and Ian still looked pale and pinched around the eyes. Emma was laughing at something Julio said, her crystal blue eyes flashing, touching him lovingly. The younger man's chocolate eyes returned the volley of love as he continued to expound. "Our business is finally taking off. We are getting more design jobs, and we have a good number of yard watching contracts for the winter. Emma is so good with the customers." He put an arm around her waist and tugged her closer. Both Jean and Ian listened with brittle smiles. Emma and Julio appeared not to notice. Barbara wondered how business was going for Jean and Ian. She made a mental note to call Jean tomorrow.

"This is good news, you two," said Barbara. "Can I interest anyone in something more to eat or drink? I'm out of hot crab dip, but still have lots of other goodies." Jean and Ian declined, while Emma and Julio said yes, and Ian and Jean retired to a love seat across the room and sat down. Surely something was wrong there, and she couldn't believe there were marital problems. She trailed Emma and Julio across the room and paused by the bar. Ben was pouring a glass of red wine for Steven. When he finished, he turned to her. "Have you been naughty or nice this year, little girl? As Santa's helper, I need to know." He leered at her with glistening blue eyes, and she nearly cracked up.

"You can wait until after the party to ask me that."

He straightened to his full height, looked around to make sure no one was nearby and in a sober voice said, "After the party, I'm going to have more than asking to do."

She grinned. "Promises, promises. Just like last year. By the time you got home from Bernie's it was almost 2am and you were exhausted from practically carrying him inside and putting him to bed."

"Well, he is a rather big dude. But this year I am being more vigilant and won't be required to see anyone home. I'll be putting someone prettier to bed."

"Like I said. I'll believe it when I see it," she said good-naturedly. She leaned forward and kissed him, then headed to the counter to check on the food levels.

\* \* \*

## TED, 11:15PM

There were still a smattering of cars parked along both sides of the street thanks to the party going on at the house next to Marilyn's, so Ted's vehicle blended in. The rest of the streets in this burg were as deserted as after the apocalypse. Ted shrugged deeper into his light jacket, shivering from the cold, and took a long pull on his flask. Thank God he had whiskey. The fuckin' desert was supposed to be warm, but he was freezing his nuts off. Should have checked, but the trip was an impulse. He'd just gotten into the car with a small duffle holding a change of clothes and some accessories and headed West. The only thing in his mind was to teach that bitch ex-wife of his a lesson. The packages he'd sent her and the phone call she'd hung up on left him hungry for vengeance. He needed to see and smell her fear; this long distance shit didn't cut it.

He turned on the car and ran the heater for a bit, but didn't want to draw attention to himself, so turned the car off after it warmed a bit. When would that fucking party ever end? He knew Marilyn was there, because he'd seen her walk over hours ago as he was making a sweep of the area. In fact, he'd nearly been spotted by her, and that wouldn't have been good.

His mouse of a wife wasn't that social. What the hell was she doing all this time? Could she have a lover? His chest ached and his hands clenched at the thought. She'd robbed him of everything, and now she lived in a nice new house in a fancy retirement community while he was unemployed, living in their old dump, a social pariah. She fucking deserved to suffer for what she'd done to him. He didn't like to face it, but she was still under his skin like a damn chigger. The only way to dig her out was to show her who was boss, ex or not.

She looked pretty good for her age as she sashayed down the sidewalk to the party. She'd always kept herself fit. But he didn't care for the gray hair. She could look ten years younger if she'd dye it, but she had always blown off his suggestions. Never mind, he had plenty of opportunity for younger trim as a job perk. He had a right to step out on her if she disregarded what he wanted. She'd never defied him in big things, but she got stubborn about little ones. She knew he fancied a young look. It got him hot.

In spite of that preference, right now thinking about teaching Marilyn a lesson got him hot. Nothing got him harder than roughing her up and smelling the fear on her. She wasn't good at sex, but her fear was an aphrodisiac he couldn't resist, and it had been too long. Slapping her around a little, getting his hands on her neck and squeezing just a bit. Oh, that would be so good. He felt himself hardening just thinking about it.

He was so caught up in his fantasy that he almost didn't see Marilyn ambling down the street towards her house, escorted by a man. He wasn't touching her, but his posture was protective, maybe even proprietary. Ted's member shrank instantly, and his stomach began to ache like an animal was gnawing on it. Too much whiskey and too little food. He rubbed his stomach, teeth clenched. If that shithead went inside with her or even kissed her, he was going to kick his ass from here to the ocean and back. Then he'd deal with the bitch. The adrenaline was running so high that he was almost disappointed when Dudley Do-Right left her unkissed at her door and sauntered back down the block in the other direction. He entered the house on the corner. Maybe he was just a do-gooder after all.

Shedding thoughts of the white knight, Ted reviewed his plan. There was a fence around her back yard, but it wasn't impregnable. It made sense to go around back to avoid attracting attention.

He had skills with unlocking locked doors. Maybe he could get inside before she even knew he was there. But did she still have that dog? Was it even hers? He'd only seen it once back in Virginia from a distance. Maybe she'd been petsitting for a friend. And though she'd always been careless about security, he wondered if she kept a gun nearby. She was a fair shot.

With courage boosted by whiskey, he pushed aside his concerns. He had fifty pounds and five inches on her. If he took her by surprise, nothing could stop him. But should he go now or wait until she was asleep or wait until the whole block was in bed?

Nah, now was the time. His car didn't stand out, and the noise of the party would cover anything he did. He reached under his jacket and fingered the piece in his shoulder holster. He didn't intend to shoot her, but he was definitely going to knock her around some. And what else? What would be punishment enough? Maybe a fuck for old times' sake? She'd fight him; he was sure of that. And he liked it rough, even if she never had. He'd always had to pay for it the way he wanted, even when they were married, because she wasn't a good sport. Maybe it was time for her to put out once for her husband the way he liked it. Yeah. But then, his DNA would be all over, and that wouldn't be good. Maybe he'd just have to snuff her after. If he used gloves and a condom, he could get away with it, and he'd brought both. After all, he lived 2000 miles away, and while he didn't have an alibi, no one knew he was here. If he got in and out clean and left no physical evidence, they couldn't pin it on him. He'd have his fun and head home. He'd have to drive straight through to get there before they started sniffing around, but it would be worth it.

The more he thought, the more solid his plan felt. Finally, he could get some satisfaction. Her leaving him flat in the middle of the night had been a shock and an insult to boot. He needed to make things right.

He watched other partygoers get in their cars and drive away. It wouldn't do to be the only car on the street. Someone might remember, and this was his personal car. He couldn't afford to have it recognized. Maybe he should move to the next street over. But on any other street, his would be the only car. His whiskey-marinated brain struggled to figure out the best move, but it eluded him. He took another long pull on his flask. What he needed was action; that was his strong suit, being the 'force' in enforcement. He grinned and pulled surgical gloves out of his jacket pocket and slipped them on. Then he got out of the car and headed towards Marilyn's house, a predator on the hunt.

* * *

MARILYN, 11:20PM

Marilyn had forgotten to leave a light on, and Tammi rushed up to her, woo-wooing in protest at being left so long in the dark. Marilyn leaned over and hugged her dog. "I'm so sorry. I forgot to leave a light on. I know you don't like that."

Tammi accepted the apology, and Marilyn walked down the hall, the dog clinging like her shadow, and flicked on the bedroom light. She was tired and buzzed from the wine she'd had at the party. Steven was acting funny, but she didn't know why. He seemed to hesitate at the front door, the look in his eyes almost pleading. She kept wondering if he had ideas about their relationship, but she was too distracted to give it her full attention. The last thing she needed was more man problems.

She began to undress. It would be good to fall into bed and sleep. She slipped on her nightgown and threw her clothes into the hamper. She washed off her makeup and sat on the edge of the bed. There was something she'd forgotten to do. As she pondered what, Tammi erupted into fierce barking and ran to the living room and blasted through the dog door. That was it. She hadn't locked the dog door. She froze briefly, then reached for her pistol and headed numbly for the living room.

* * *

TED, 11:20PM

The fence had presented a minor obstacle. If he'd been more sober, it would have been no problem at all, but he found himself caught on a pointy wrought iron cap and had to carefully extricate himself so as to avoid injury to the family jewels. The gravel was noisy as hell, so he tiptoed as quietly and slowly as possible towards the back door, sticking to the shadows near the house. Thank heaven there was no moon to speak of. Once on the small patio, he was out of sight, and he sighed in relief. Now, all he needed to do was to pick the lock and get inside. As he examined the arcadia door and contemplated his next move, what sounded like a lion roaring was followed by a large bang, nearly causing him to fall over in surprise.

A huge, bearlike black and white animal attacked him, teeth flashing in the dim light from the neighbor's house. It was the dog he'd seen in Virginia, but way bigger than he remembered. He was knocked over by its weight and put his arm up to fend it off. It was the biggest dog he'd ever seen, and it was barking rabidly. He pushed himself up against the patio door and found he was in the unpleasant position of being between the dog and its pet door. The terrifying growls and feints from the beast had him wishing he'd never made the trip west. If only he could get out of here, he'd never come back. He didn't think it could get any worse, and then the dog leaped at him and sank its teeth into his arm with an iron grip. The terror caused his bladder to cut loose as he yelped in agony.

Urine trickled down his leg. It was the first truly warm feeling he'd had all night.

A light went on in the house and he heard Marilyn shout. "Tammi, what are you doing?" The beast was female? Shit. He couldn't escape, and the bitch had his arm so he couldn't reach his gun.

The patio door slid open a few inches, and Marilyn's voice said shakily, "I've called the police. You stay put until they arrive."

The dog hadn't let go, hadn't even moved, and the thought of enduring this pain and humiliation for even another minute was too much. "Call your damn dog off, bitch."

"I don't think so. I've got a gun pointed at you; don't make me use it. I suggest you just sit still until the police get here." Her voice was still quavering, but he was enough of a cop to know that mixing fear and guns was a bad combination. He didn't think she'd shoot him in these circumstances, but he wouldn't take any bets.

Ted slid to the ground in defeat. His wet pants were turning cold and clammy. The fucking dog still had his arm in her mouth, but wasn't doing anything but growling and gripping more tightly every time he moved. There was no way he was going to get out of this. The damn bitch had screwed him again. This could mean jail time.

Within minutes, two rent-a-cops were bundling him into a cruiser labeled "Posse." He felt nothing but relief, getting away from that furry monster. His arm hurt like hell and probably needed stitches, but it didn't feel broken. His brain was too fuzzy to contemplate his situation. He lay down on the seat and everything began to spin. The car seemed to whirl in a circle, and he felt his gorge rise. Mercifully, he passed into blackness.

* * *

STEVEN, 11:30PM

Steven raced out of the house without a jacket, heedless of the cold. His heart was pounding in his throat when he arrived at Marilyn's door, which was open behind the wrought iron security door.

A couple of Posse cruisers were parked at the curb in front of her house. He thought he saw a man lying across the back seat of one, but he couldn't be sure. One officer stood watching the two cars, probably waiting for the local cops to arrive.

He knocked on the door, desperate to see Marilyn. She had sounded shook up on the phone, even though she promised she was unharmed. She appeared at the door and let him step inside, turning to the uniformed officer behind her. "This is the friend who lives nearby, the one I told you I called?"

The Posse guy was maybe late sixties, carrying a sizable beer belly and sporting a balding head with a fringe of gray hair. "Come on in. I'm just taking a statement while we wait for the cops."

A local black-and-white picked that moment to pull up the driveway, lights flashing, but no siren. All three of them stood there watching while two officers emerged and strode up the walk. When they got to the front door, the Posse guy pointed at his cruiser. "Perp's passed out in my car. He needs medical attention."

An eyebrow raised, the older officer, a dark-skinned man in his thirties, asked, "What kind of medical attention?"

"Dog bite," answered the Posse guy laconically.

Both cops grinned. The older one said, "Dogs. Don't you love 'em? OK, we'll transfer him to our ride and get him looked after. Can you stay here until the other guys come to take the statement?"

"No problem," the Posse guy assured them.

Minutes later, Ted was in the back seat of the cop car and speeding off to incarceration and medical help, probably in that order, considering the way the officers had smiled. The second Posse guy came to the front door. "Mind if I go now, Fred?"

"Sure, go ahead. I'll be along soon."

Before long, the street was deserted, the remaining partygoers having gone home after gawking a bit at the brouhaha. Lights were on at Barbara's, but she'd be cleaning up, not watching at windows. Steven followed Posse guy and Marilyn back to the living room, where Tammi lay locked in her crate. She looked troubled, as if she wasn't sure she'd done well. Marilyn barely glanced at the dog, which was not like her at all.

"Marilyn, can we let Tammi out now?" Steven inquired.

Her eyes like mirrors, Marilyn paused. She might be in shock. "OK. I think. Do you mind, Officer?"

"I love dogs," said Posse guy.

Steven went over and released Tammi, who accepted his praise and petting, even fell on the ground and turned on her back. Marilyn didn't appear to notice her dog being so submissive. He stood up. "Marilyn, you need something. How about a cup of tea or a glass of wine? Or maybe a shot of whiskey?"

"That might be a good idea, ma'am," said Posse guy. "You look a bit shocky."

Marilyn nodded, her face pale and eyes empty. Steven noticed the revolver sitting on the coffee table. He'd find out about that later. He got her a shot of whiskey and handed it to her. "Drink this."

She held the glass cupped in her palms for a little while, then began to sip it. Tammi had positioned herself up against Marilyn's leg, as if giving her support. "I think I need to sit down," she finally whispered and sank onto the couch. Tammi lay across her feet.

A knock on the door announced the next set of cops. Posse guy let them in and went on his way. Steven sat next to Marilyn as she described, as best she could, what had happened. It appeared that Ted had staked out her house and tried to enter it after she returned from the party. Fortunately, she'd forgotten to lock the dog door, and Tammi accosted him, pinning him on the patio and biting his arm to keep him in place. She hadn't let him go until the Posse arrived and Marilyn ordered her to. The cops had found a lock pit set and a loaded 9mm handgun on him, plus a nearly empty flask that had whiskey in it. He was obviously inebriated and had peed himself when Tammi attacked him. Marilyn had arrived at the back door, her .38 in hand, and told Ted to sit tight. He had expressed displeasure, to say the least, but he was terrified of the dog. The Posse had arrived several minutes later.

Steven was both horrified and thrilled at the story. Tammi had saved Marilyn, of that he was certain. His estimation of the dog went up a notch. He'd always known she was smart, but she was amazing. Ted obviously had planned to break in. The gun indicated ill intent, and the surgical gloves were creepy. He shivered to think what might have happened if Tammi hadn't been here. He reached down to pet the big black head.

The cop left after telling Marilyn they'd be in touch tomorrow. She sat on the couch, limp and lifeless. Steven felt helpless. She needed strength, but he wasn't sure she wanted him around. Well, she'd just have to accept him, since he was all she had. "I'm staying tonight on your couch or in your guest room. You say which. I'm not leaving you alone after this."

She turned to him, and her eyes filled with tears. "Thank you, Steven. I know it's silly, but I am afraid to stay alone tonight. The guest room is made up. I think I'll go to bed. I feel really tired." She stood up, put the glass on the table and trudged down the hall, Tammi behind her. Steven sat on the couch for a while, then checked the front door and locked the dog door and waited until Marilyn's bedroom light was off and picked up the revolver and walked down the hall to the guest bedroom and turned on the light. He didn't have anything to sleep in, but that was no biggie. And he had his own en suite bathroom. He closed the door, put the gun on the dresser and stripped down to his skivvies. A few minutes in the bathroom, and he slipped beneath the covers. He was thrumming with adrenaline so much, he wasn't at all tired. What he felt like doing was beating the shit out of Ted, but Tammi had done pretty well at that. He hoped she wouldn't get in trouble for attacking an intruder. You never knew these days.

If punching Ted wasn't an option, his next preference would be to hold Marilyn and soothe her until she felt back to normal, but she was still acting skittish about him, and when she was vulnerable was not the time to press his suit with her. It never seemed to be the right time, damn it. This was killing him, being with her and never being able to show how he felt.

## 15

# CHRISTMAS, DECEMBER 25, 1996

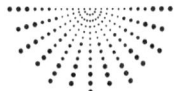

NICK, 10:30AM

*N*ick paused before exiting Livvie's apartment, his belly replete with a breakfast of homemade Eggs Benedict and two cups of freshly ground Costa Rican coffee. He was in heaven. "I need a crane or something to carry me back to my place."

Livvie laughed softly. "Don't be silly. You didn't eat that much."

"I beg to differ." He pulled her into a hug and kissed the top of her head, smoothing her white hair and letting his fingers brush the length of her neck. The feeling was positively electric. "You have the softest skin."

He felt her shiver, then she looked up, her brown eyes warm. "Flatterer."

"A meal like that deserves better compliments than I could ever think of. Thank you. I shudder to think of the alternative."

"Bite your tongue," she said into his chest. "The dining room must not be spoken of on Christmas." Livvie didn't stir in his embrace, which surprised and pleased him. They'd spent every night together for nearly two weeks, and he was slipping into a comfortable routine of sleeping, getting up, eating breakfast with her and then going back to his place, almost as if he were heading out to work. Then he returned for dinner. They were like an old married couple, almost. It was the almost that was bugging him. He had recently admitted to himself that he wanted more than the platonic relationship, but wasn't sure what to do. Besides, he wasn't even sure he could handle sex at his age. The spirit was sure willing, but the flesh might be past it.

She interrupted his reverie. "It was fun making a special breakfast. I would never have done it just for me. And maybe now we can both hold out until Mary Beth's for more food. I'm going to get fat if I keep eating like this."

He couldn't believe she was serious. He stepped back, still holding her shoulders, and looked at her carefully from head to toe. She hadn't bothered to dress before making breakfast, and the pink silk wrap she wore over her nightgown had curves in all the right places. Generous breasts. A nice waist for a woman her age who had born three children. Hips that flared out just right in slacks or dress. "You've gained maybe two pounds since we met."

She widened her eyes in shock. "How can you tell?"

"Just can." He had no idea how he knew; her shape was simply imprinted on his eyes, and he could see even slight changes. "Looks good on you." Without thinking, he ran his hands down the silk from shoulders to hips in admiration, then kissed her head again. "I'm out of here. Have to call Joe and wish him a Merry Christmas, even though he probably doesn't want to hear from his old man. See you later."

He turned and fled, aware that she was scandalized by his taking liberties. He'd shocked even himself, but he hadn't felt this alive in years. Back in his room, he saw that Joe hadn't called, or at least, hadn't left a message. He picked up the phone and dialed, but got no answer, and he was averse to talking to a stupid machine, so he left no message. He hung up, his good mood squelched. He hated that he let the boy annoy him so. It didn't occur to him that maybe, like his father, Joe hated talking to answering machines.

It was only 10:50. How was he going to fill the hours until he was due back at Livvie's? He needed a shower and a shave, but the day stretched before him in shades of boredom. Maybe he'd go ride Rocky. The chilly air would help clear his head. Rocky was a great mount, which turned his thoughts back to Livvie. It was her doing that he'd exchanged Rudi for a more steady ride, and she had been right. It was a pleasure to ride Rocky, not a training chore. Livvie had a subtle way of adding quality to his life.

He didn't want to say it, didn't even want to think it, but it felt like when he was apart from Livvie, he wasn't really living. It seemed like all the joy in his life was connected somehow to her.

He grunted at the epiphany and changed into his riding clothes, donned his shoulder holster, slipped the gun into it and braved the winter chill. Something about being on a horse always made him feel better about life. And his life was getting better day by day.

\* \* \*

SAMANTHA, 4:00PM

Samantha dropped the fresh pasta into the boiling water and stirred it a few times. The garlic bread was warming in the oven, sending out a savory fragrance that blended beautifully with the herbal aroma of the homemade pasta sauce that had been simmering in the dutch oven for hours.

Jack slipped up behind her and gently wrapped his arms around her waist. "Isn't it time to eat yet, Sam?" he whined playfully, kissing her on the neck.

"Are you referring to our unconventional Christmas dinner or something else," she quipped.

He growled in response and nuzzled her neck, giving her a play bite. "Sadly, dinner," he finally replied. "Breakfast was a long time ago, you know."

"For heaven's sake," she pretended to complain, "you ate enough at breakfast to feed a bear all winter."

"But I'm not a bear," he pointed out helpfully.

Samantha grinned, enjoying the repartee. "I will serve up in about two minutes." As good as her word, she piled food on the plates two minutes later, watched intently by two sets of dark, hungry eyes. She placed the basket with the bread on the center of the dining table next to the freshly grated Parmesan, and then put both plates on the festive mats she'd gotten for the holiday. Satisfied, she announced, "You may sit down and eat."

Beau cocked his head at her in question. "You get yours after we eat. I'm not feeding you at the table like Mom did. Sorry."

He huffed at her insincere apology and sank to the floor, still attentive. Maybe he was hoping for someone to drop some food.

They sat down and dug in, tasting the pasta sauce and munching bites of crunchy garlic bread.

"Mary Beth's recipe is a keeper," said Jack through a mouthful.

"She's given me a couple of family recipes—just the easier ones. Real Italian cooking seems to be an all-day affair involving many women. Not to be sexist. You were a big help, doing all that chopping."

He smiled at her lovingly. "My pleasure, especially if it turns out this good."

She could hardly believe she was eating Christmas dinner with her husband, Jack. Husband. She regarded him frankly as he chowed down, unaware of her scrutiny. His raven dark hair was tied in a neat ponytail that hung down between his shoulders against the Western style shirt in shades of red that highlighted his dark skin and hawklike face. He wasn't classically handsome, but he oozed masculinity in a cross between a cowboy and an Indian, exotic, strong and very grounded. "My Mom really liked you," she blurted.

He looked up, still chewing, his eyes alight. "I believe she did. I'm sorry she wasn't able to see us marry."

Samantha's eyes filled, but there was gladness as well as loss in her heart. "She would have loved this Christmas dinner, especially if she didn't have to cook it. My Dad would never have allowed it; he was so traditional." She brushed her eyes and went back to eating.

Jack raised his wine glass. "May I propose a toast?"

She nodded and reached for her glass.

"To Maddie O'Neill, wherever she is. Thank you for giving me your blessing. I promise to do my best to make Sam happy."

Samantha clinked glasses and sipped her wine. "I love you, Jack."

He grinned in response. "I love you, too, partner. This coming year we rebuild Temple Landscaping into the premier landscaping company in the area. Together."

She sighed at the vision. "I never could have predicted a year ago what I'd be doing today. I feel so good about our future." She went back to eating. Later, as she cleaned her plate, she said, "I'm glad we stayed home. Mary Beth has a full house. She was kind to invite us, but I have to think she's glad to have me gone. And I'm liking our alone time."

He raised an eyebrow. "There's plenty more of that left in the day." There was a lustful glint in his dark eyes. The future just kept looking better.

* * *

MARY BETH, 4:45PM

Mary Beth savored the fragrances of roasting meat and herbs as she and Olivia enjoyed a glass of wine in her kitchen. "I'm so glad you're here. I told you to come early, so I'd have nice company before Ethan's kids arrive," she whispered conspiratorially. "Winnie's a dear, but William and Ethan do not get along, and William barely tolerates me."

Olivia raised her glass. "Thank you for inviting us. Old folks like us get overlooked by their families at holidays sometimes." She paused, a frown lining her face. "I shouldn't complain. My daughters have family besides me. Anyway, you're like a daughter to me, and I couldn't be happier than to spend Christmas with you. You've done most of the work, too."

Mary Beth chuckled. "I love to cook, though turkey isn't my favorite. The kids and grandkids wanted it, so I gave in. I only had to put up a tiny ceramic tree, and Ethan helped with the cleaning. He's on edge about William. It's such a blessing that you and Nick are here. William won't act up in front of you." Her heart skipped a beat. "But that's not why I invited you." Mary Beth loved Olivia and wouldn't want her to misunderstand her motives.

Olivia smiled gently. "Of course not. It's good to feel needed, though."

"Speaking of Nick, how's that going?" ventured Mary Beth, wanting to change the subject.

237

Olivia blushed.

"You two aren't…" Lost for words, Mary Beth faltered.

Olivia seemed to regain her composure. "Yes and no."

What a cryptic answer. Yes *and* no? Mary Beth was curious as hell, but refrained from digging deeper.

"We're sleeping together," admitted Olivia, "but not for sex," she added emphatically.

"That's nice," said Mary Beth lamely.

"I guess you young people might say we're shacked up." Olivia cast a glance towards the doorway to the living room, where Nick and Ethan were watching a football game on the big TV. "We're not yet living in sin."

"Do you want to?" blurted Mary Beth.

Olivia seemed to consider the question. "I'd prefer marriage for any number of reasons, but I don't know how he feels. He's not much for talking about feelings." To Mary Beth, she sounded disappointed and a little confused.

"Wow, that's pretty progressive of you, sleeping with a man who hasn't said the words."

Olivia waved her off and spoke with confidence, "Better than sleeping with one who said the words but didn't mean them."

Mary Beth heard the history in that statement, but didn't push for details. "I like Nick. He seems so genuine and solid."

"Exactly," agreed Olivia. "I'm thinking of seducing him tonight," she added in a matter-of-fact tone.

Mary Beth nearly spit out a mouthful of wine. "Did I hear you right?"

"It's not like either of us is getting any younger. Why waste time? I think he cares for me. My daughters will raise cain, but so what? I almost lost him over that mess at Thanksgiving, all because I didn't have the courage to be honest with them. I'm not going to make that mistake again."

"Well said. I wish you two all the best. If you need any moral support, I'm here for you, just like you've been for me. You know, I faced some challenges with Ethan, and I sympathize. Do what makes you happy and to hell with the naysayers."

"My thoughts exactly, dear."

Mary Beth was reminded suddenly of her friend Catherine, who had been so supportive of her marrying Ethan before she passed away. Sometimes your biggest support comes from outside the family. She loved Olivia and intended to be there for her.

Winnie arrived with her brood, and soon after, William and his family joined them, and the big house became crowded and a bit crazy, the children running around with their new toys and showing them off. Ethan, Nick and William attempted to watch the game while the ladies set the table. Mary Beth thought she spotted a Honda Accord drive slowly by as she passed the living room window. Could it be Arthur looking for Samantha? She and Jack were enjoying a peaceful holiday at Jack's place, and Mary Beth was grateful for that. Samantha had told her about Arthur showing up at Temple Landscaping drunk and disorderly. She made a mental note to tell Samantha that maybe Arthur was still carrying a grudge.

Her concerns were soon forgotten in the swirl of activity surrounding Christmas dinner and TV watching afterwards. She was relieved when Ethan's kids finally left to go to their motels, and pleased that Olivia and Nick delayed and left last. She didn't know if Nick was aware he and Olivia were a buffer, but she was eternally grateful. The day had gone very well, all things considered.

As Nick and Olivia drove off, she went into the kitchen to begin cleaning up the mess, and Ethan joined her and put his arms around her. "I can't thank you enough for being such a gracious hostess."

"It was nothing. Winnie is a charm. The kids are all cute. William behaved himself. And Olivia and Nick are great. It's been a good day."

Ethan hugged her more tightly. "It's been better than good. I am so glad I have you. Somehow, it makes it easier for me to let go of what William does. I'm sorry he isn't warm with you, but it appears we have a truce of sorts. He didn't say or do anything to you?"

"He was just fine, Ethan. I know how to take care of myself. I suspect he senses that and won't step over a line that would cause me to smack him down. You know how I am."

He grinned. "My passionate Italian beauty. Show me how you are. I'll do dishes in the morning."

Why the hell not? "Whatever you say, Lord and master."

239

* * *

## HELEN, 6:15PM

Helen occupied a tiny oasis of calm in a sea of voices as she surveyed their dinner guests, arrayed on either side of the dining table with Alexander at the head, on her left. They had pulled out all the stops for tonight's dinner, and as she watched the reactions to the dessert of New Orleans bread pudding with brandy sauce, she was pleased. Even Eliot, at the end of the table on her side, attired in a too-small t-shirt celebrating a rock concert from several years ago, was gushing. All she heard of his exclamation was "so delicious," but his dreadlocks were swaying in time with his enthusiasm as he crammed another spoonful into his already full mouth.

Helen's 9-month-old granddaughter Camille sat in a booster chair between Helen and Sally, her focus on her mother, who tempted her with a spoonful of pudding. After the first bite, Camille signaled her approval with waving hands and babbling that seemed to be a demand for more.

In spite of the diverse guests, the day was going well. Jean and Ian had arrived looking strained, but now both were glowing and laughing. Ian and Alexander were talking about sports, of all things. The fine wines were certainly lubricating any points of friction between generations. On the opposite side from Helen at the far end of the table, Lydia was engaging Eliot in lively conversation. Since she read auras, she must have decided he was OK, which was reassuring. Helen had spent so little time in Eliot's company, she wasn't sure what to make of him. She couldn't wait to talk to Lydia for feedback later on. Lydia's husband Eric made eye contact and raised a spoon in salute, making her grin.

Alexander reached over and squeezed her hand, a question in his emerald eyes. Just looking at his chiseled features and swept-back silver mane made her melt. She still wondered how she'd gotten so lucky to have him in her life. She squeezed his hand in return, a promise in it for after their guests left. He raised an eyebrow and smiled in acknowledgement.

Spot, who had been sitting patiently beside Helen's chair, barked once. Her dark eyes pierced Helen with a demand. "OK, here's your dessert." Helen extracted her hand from Alexander's and put a spoonful of pudding on the saucer she'd been feeding Spot from during dinner. "Just one bite.

Sugar isn't good for you." The little butterscotch fluffball expressed her dissenting opinion in one sharp bark.

Helen laughed at the sass and put the saucer on the floor between her chair and Alexander's. Camille watched the entire interaction with interest, as Spot was a favorite of hers. Sally had gotten distracted in conversation with Eliot, and Camille, impatient for Sally to feed her, had dived into the small bowl of pudding with her fingers. Before Helen could react, Camille took a tiny handful of bread pudding and threw it onto the floor. Spot appeared immediately to vacuum it up, and Camille giggled and clapped her hands. Helen grabbed the dish from Camille's tray to head off further dog feeding, and Camille objected by shrieking loudly. Silence descended on the room at that, causing Camille to pause as all heads turned her way. Then she burst into tears.

Helen waved a hand. "Don't worry. My fault. I had to stop a bread pudding avalanche. Camille caught me feeding Spot and wanted to participate." She picked up the new rattle from the table and shook it, distracting Camille, who turned her attention to the shiny new toy, Spot and tears forgotten. Conversations started up again as everyone finished dessert. Alexander offered seconds on the dessert wine, but everyone declined. A short while later, Sally and Eliot took Camille home, as she was falling asleep. Ian and Jean thanked them and left after offering to help with the cleanup and being refused. Lydia lingered briefly to share with Helen, then she and Eric left Helen and Alexander to survey the extent of cleanup.

Alexander poured them both a small glass of dessert wine and led Helen to the living room, the least messed up room of the party. "So tell me what you learned from Lydia," he asked.

She smiled at him. "You don't miss much. She had a conversation with Eliot, and she said he seems like a decent guy. He got an IT job where Sally works—apparently he's given up trying to make a living as a musician—and she says he has a kindness about him. He probably smokes too much weed, and he isn't terribly adept socially, but he's a nice guy. I feel relieved. I don't have any issues with him being black; I just want her with a gentle guy who pulls his own weight."

"Do you think maybe you've adjusted your standards downward?"

Helen laughed out loud. "I am certain I have. You always want the best for your kids, but then reality sets in as you see the choices they make, and you just hope they won't make any drastic mistakes. Sally has been with a lot of losers—excluding Eric, of course, but he was a rebound relationship —and I'm hoping this guy has the right combination of traits to make it in the long haul with her. It's too soon to tell, but I'm hopeful."

Alexander sipped his wine. "I'm glad to hear you're feeling better. You won't mind leaving Arizona?"

Helen sighed gustily. "I vacillate. Most of the time I'm OK with it. I have no illusions about what I mean to Sally. I have been thinking—maybe I'm just rationalizing—that if we lived farther away and they only saw us once a year, it would be better. But maybe I'm kidding myself. I know I don't want to be drawn into any drama, but I do want to be a part of her and Camille's life." She shrugged and drank some wine.

"I know it's hard for you. There have been so many changes in your life this past year. But for me, too. And mostly, they've been good." He smiled at her tentatively.

"Good? That's too weak a word. I was lost before you came into my life. I agree it's been tough trying to sort my kids out since I've remarried, but I'm happy for the first time in my life, and they should be happy for me. Warren and Lena will probably never come around, but Sally has enough self-interest, I think she may make an effort. However, I am under no illusions about them loving me. And that's OK. I do think in their own ways, they love me, but without you, my life would be empty." She put her glass down and took his hand. "Thank you so much for loving me."

He beamed his movie star smile at her. "I'm lucky, too."

"It was a wonderful, if crazy, day. I guess we ought to do dishes."

He rose and held out his hand. "It never takes that long. It looks bad, but we'll have it done in no time."

He was right. In less than 20 minutes, the dishes were in the dishwasher and all the surfaces cleaned. He turned and hugged Helen, and she reveled in the warmth and tightness of the embrace.

Stroking her back, he said, "We're on a grand adventure, and I expect it is going to be more than good."

She stood on tiptoe and kissed him. "You know what I expect will be good?"

A glint in his eyes, he replied, "Our post-dessert dessert?"

"Exactly."

* * *

STEVEN, 6:45PM

Steven pushed back from the dining table, projecting enthusiasm he didn't feel. The dinner had been flat, and Marilyn's distraction worried him. "Let's retire to the living room with an after-dinner drink."

Marilyn replied quickly, "Not for me. I've drunk more than enough."

Deflated, he rejoined, "Then let's go in there anyway and enjoy my new furniture."

Tammi stood at the same time as Marilyn, and they silently trooped into the living room. He suppressed irritation at the funereal atmosphere. That bastard Ted was ruining everything. He couldn't allow Ted to win. He simply didn't have a clue what to do. Tanya had always jeered at his people skills; maybe she was right.

He sank onto one end of the leather sofa and glanced around. "I really like how it turned out," he ventured. "Thanks for helping."

Marilyn pulled herself out of a fog and scanned the room with little interest. "It is a lot better."

Unsure what to say, Steven offered, "We could watch TV."

She grimaced. "Steven, I am so sorry I'm such bad company. My mind is elsewhere." As if she needed to say.

"I know. You have a lot on your mind. How can I help?"

Marilyn shook her head and frowned. "I don't think there's anything either of us can do."

"Do you mind telling me what the lawyer said? I'm not a criminal attorney, and I'm not current with Arizona statutes and procedures, but maybe I can help."

Her pale blue eyes pleaded with him. "I'd rather not talk about it now. I don't want to ruin Christmas."

"Ted's already done that," he muttered bitterly, immediately regretting it. "I shouldn't have said that."

"No, you have every right. You cooked a magnificent meal, but I pushed the food around on my plate, because I have no appetite. This is so unfair to you." She rose as if to leave, and he panicked.

"No. Please. Sit down." His mind raced in different directions, trying to salvage the holiday. It seemed there was never going to be a good time to say how he felt. Frustrated as hell, he decided to open up. "I've been thinking, and maybe I have a solution."

She gazed at him with guarded curiosity. "Really?"

Encouraged, he plunged forward. "I've been wanting to say this, but it never seems to be a good time." A look of fear flitted across her freckled face, but he wouldn't be deterred now. "I know you have a lot on you now, but I'd like to help. I want to be more than friends. I think we're compatible. We like each other and have similar interests. We enjoy being together. If you lived here with me, you wouldn't be alone. We could face the Ted thing together. He'd think twice about coming after you if you were with someone." He faltered, worried by the shock on her face. "Oh, I know I'm no physical threat to him, but he's a predator. He won't like the odds of taking on both of us."

Marilyn stared at him, mouth slightly open. Then she sighed and shook her head. After a silence that stretched too long, she spoke. "I am so sorry, Steven. I never meant to encourage you to think I had romance in mind. I'm still a mess from Ted. I'm not ready for what you're offering. It would be dishonest and selfish if I accepted your suggestion, because I don't think of you that way. I won't deny your logic—I would feel safer—but I can't." She wrung her hands and tears filled her eyes.

Now he'd done it. He'd managed to make her feel worse. "I'm sorry. I didn't mean to upset you." He was so crushed by her rejection, he felt ready to weep himself. He should never have sprung it on her now. He didn't know what he'd do if he lost her. "Please forget it. Any time you want, you can stay in my guest room. As a guest. No strings attached." It cost a lot of emotional currency to make that offer. What if she never got past seeing him as a friend? Now wasn't the time to ponder that. She needed him. He loved her and would do anything for her, but he didn't dare to say that. Yet. "I'm going to make coffee. How about a cup?"

She smiled wanly. "Yes, thanks. For everything," she said with feeling.

Warmed by her gratitude, he prepared coffee and came back with two mugs and proceeded to chatter about inconsequential subjects. Anything to conceal his humiliation and pain. He could tell she wasn't fooled, but she pretended.

After a half hour of stilted conversation, she let him walk her and Tammi home. He didn't even get a hug. The easy warmth between them had been replaced by an uncomfortable distance.

When he returned home, he sank onto the couch, unable to face the remains of their Christmas dinner. He'd fucked up royally. That was all there was to it. He'd said too much, too soon, and now she was going to be guarded and distant. A curtain of sadness swept through him, plunging him into loneliness. The thought of losing Marilyn drained the joy out of his life. He rarely thought of Tanya anymore, except when he was in a self-deprecating mood, and he had found a woman he respected and valued—yes, loved—and wanted to be with. But did he have a chance with her after tonight? He groaned and inwardly kicked himself. What a dick he was.

Rising from the couch, he gathered dishes and went to the kitchen to clean up. The monotony of the job soothed his hurts, and by the time the kitchen was in order again, optimism had replaced depression. Marilyn needed him. She liked him. Maybe she wasn't in love with him, but how could he expect that with Ted harassing her? If he persisted, things could work out.

He walked back to the bedroom and surveyed the changes. The navy accents and cream rug were relaxing and attractive. She'd chosen well. He was determined that one day, she would live here with him. It might take time, but he was persistent.

Finally confident, he prepared for bed and contemplated a New Year's Eve celebration that would grant him progress. Too bad he couldn't take out a contract on Ted. Then it occurred to him. Even if she didn't accept Steven's suit, he could refocus Ted's attention away from Marilyn by confronting Ted and presenting himself as her protector. No, that wouldn't work. He didn't know one end of a gun from another, and he lacked a threatening physique, in spite of being in the best condition he'd been in for years. The only kind of fight he excelled at was with words, and that was weak ammunition against an animal like Ted.

Defeated, he shelved the topic. He wasn't going to solve this tonight. The important thing to remember is that there were options. And he was going to find a good one.

* * *

## MARILYN, 8:15PM

Marilyn leaned against the inside of the front door, knees weak. She staggered to her bedroom and flopped on the bed. Tammi padded after her, nails clicking on the tile in the hallway. Too much wine and not enough food. That had to be why she felt so wobbly. Tammi pushed a cold, wet nose under her hand. "I'm OK, sweetie."

But that wasn't really true. She was on the edge of a nervous breakdown. When Steven had asked, she wanted to spill the sordid details of Ted's incarceration, but she held back, knowing Steven would want to fix it.

Her attorney said that pressing charges was the right choice. If Ted came back at her and she hadn't pressed charges, it would weaken her case against him. Apparently being nice was an invitation to be attacked. The bad news was that Ted probably would be released soon, because although he had trespassed, he had done nothing else wrong, except maybe drive drunk. He had no record in Arizona and was a former cop, however tarnished his reputation. They wouldn't jail him for something that minor.

Marilyn had been livid at the injustice and terrified that Ted would come after her as soon as he was released, but the lawyer promised they would escort Ted to the state line. That was pretty far away. That's all they could do. The Posse promised to cruise by her house more often for the near future, but manpower issues prevented more help than that.

She couldn't admit to Steven she was frightened. She felt stupid thinking Ted had come to hurt or kill her, but she just knew it was true. You can't jail someone for bad intentions, though.

The big question was would he be mad enough to turn around at the state line and come back and finish what he started, knowing he'd be the prime suspect? She hoped he was sane enough to see he'd been lucky to get off, but she knew his pride was wounded when she pressed charges. He now had a record, however minor.

Tears spilled down her cheeks. She was consumed with self-pity and a sense of powerlessness and hated herself for it. She should feel more upbeat. She and Tammi had beaten Ted. He would think twice before returning. Wouldn't he?

Her stomach twisted in pain (and probably hunger). She had been eating barely enough to stay upright lately. She needed to take better care of herself.

Then she thought about Steven and the look on his face when he offered her love and sanctuary, and she refused. The poor man didn't argue, complain or threaten to hit her. He was everything Ted wasn't. Why couldn't she fall in love with him?

She lay her head other pillow, then shot upright. Had she locked the dog door? Yes, she did that before they left for dinner. She felt like her grip on sanity was slipping, as if she were sliding into a swamp of terror, out of control. She could feel the edge so close. This couldn't go on. She needed to reclaim her power, but how could she do that?

And why wasn't she attracted to Steven? He was a great guy. Too tired to analyze herself further, she lay back down, fully dressed, and slipped into a troubled sleep.

* * *

OLIVIA, 9:20PM

Olivia stood in the bathroom fidgeting, painfully aware that Nick was awaiting her in the bedroom. Should she or shouldn't she? Her bold words to Mary Beth about seducing Nick had been impulsive, but she wanted them to be true. Biting her lip, she took off her robe and hung it on the hook on the back of the closed door. The unflattering light—she hoped it was the light—caricatured her body, emphasizing lumps and bumps that didn't belong and mocking the effects of gravity on her breasts and skin. How could he possibly think she looked good? It made no sense. But she had to admit, his hands were expressive of his appreciation this morning. His touch electrified her, warming her in places she'd long forgotten about.

Leroy had been a good, steady husband, if not an accomplished lover. Just what she'd needed after that jerk Bob had romanced and dropped her like a piece of trash. She'd been so young and innocent, she'd believed every word Bob had said. Such an old story. So embarrassing. Tall, dark, handsome and a fine dancer, Bob—all the girls called him Bobbie—was such a dream, but he was a beautiful fruit with a rotten, wormy center. Too bad she found out too late.

Bob was 25 to her 18, and she had been such an inexperienced girl. He was the first man she'd fallen in love with, and she thought it would last forever. He'd had to work hard at it, but he finally got her to say yes to his desires with false promises and pretty words. Her first time had been unromantic. In the dark hayloft of her father's barn, it was hurried, painful and colored black with shame.

He dropped her immediately after and went on to his next conquest. And his next. Last she'd heard, he had gone into politics and become quite successful. But that was years ago. For all she knew, he was dead now. Was it awful of her to kind of hope so? His betrayal had shaped her lifelong mistrust of passion, propelling her into a marriage that was more about security and loyalty than desire. Was she getting ready to make another rash decision that would backfire?

She put the robe back on and brushed her teeth, then flossed them, pondering the potential side effects of a wrong decision, and all of them were ugly. She dropped the dental floss in the trash can. Enough worrying. Her heart told her this time, it was going to be all right.

So what was the best way to do it? Keep the room dark; the curtains were open to allow moonlight in. That would set the stage and minimize her embarrassment. Remove her robe and stand naked on her side of the bed long enough for him to notice. Then, get in and see what happened. She'd been his bedmate for a while now, and he'd never touched her, but after this morning, she was convinced he wanted to. And she wanted him to. She didn't think beyond being naked in bed together. Just cuddling would be enough for her. Maybe not for him, but did she really care which way it went as long as he didn't laugh or holler at her?

She sucked in a deep breath and reached for her robe. It would be anticlimactic if she went out there and he was snoring away, so she better get moving. He'd not drunk much at dinner; he rarely did. The three glasses of wine she'd had all day were just enough to give her Dutch courage, but not enough to make her doubt her rationality. She tied the wrap on her robe, turned off the bathroom light and went into the bedroom.

The light by her side of the bed was on, as usual. He let her control the lighting, almost as if he instinctively knew she was skittish. He sat at the foot of the bed in a plaid robe that somehow looked Christmas-y. He turned his head when she entered, smiling a welcome with perceptive blue eyes.

She walked over to her nightstand and switched off the light, standing in silence and letting her eyes adjust to the darkness. Before long, the moonlight seemed brighter, though it was only a faint glimmer shafting across the bed in her direction. Until this moment, she'd done nothing unusual, but still, he stared at her in question, as if anticipating a different outcome than each of the previous nights they had shared this bed. She tried to smile, but it turned into a grimace, and she felt her confidence eroding. If she didn't act now, she'd have to return to the bathroom for her nightgown, pretending some other mission.

She reached for her sash with trembling hands and undid the tie and slipped the robe off her body. She almost felt the cold moonlight dance across her naked skin, but on second thought, it was his gaze, riveted on her with what appeared to be hunger and longing. She blinked, unbelieving, and slipped under the bed covers. A moment later, he had stripped out of his clothes and crawled in next to her.

His voice rumbled under the blanket. "It surely must be Christmas, because Santa brought me what I wanted most." His big hands reached over, gently found and caressed her shoulders and arms, and then pulled her into an embrace.

His body was so warm, big and solid, she nearly shot out of her skin. As he wrapped her in his arms, her breasts touched his chest, and her thigh pressed against his, and she almost passed out from the strength of her response to the contact with his bare skin.

He stroked her neck and said, "You do know I love you."

His words coursed through her body like a current. "I love you, too."

He sighed and pulled her closer, murmuring into her neck. "It's been a long time for me, and I'm not sure I can love you the way you deserve."

It suddenly hit her that he was referring to sex, and she was surprised at her sharp reaction to his masculine pride. "Don't be an old fool. I only want to be close to you. Whatever happens, happens. Or doesn't." She could feel his smile against her skin. He pulled her even closer, and she wondered at the radiance, the incandescence, that flowed through her.

Errant thoughts battered her consciousness, but she firmly shut them out. Tomorrow she'd think about the future, but not now. She was madly in love for the second time in her life, and she intended to savor this unexpected gift. Merry Christmas, indeed.

# ABOUT THE AUTHOR

As a writer of contemporary boomer women's fiction, author Maggie McPhee based her *Autumn In The Desert* series on her experiences living in a retirement community in Arizona in the 1990s. She also writes nonfiction under her real name, Maggie Percy.

www.ingramcontent.com/pod-product-compliance
Lightning Source LLC
Chambersburg PA
CBHW070900250626
47159CB00003B/1139